51 Reasons
to Ask
51 Questions

Screenplay

by

Paul D Escudero

WORKBOOK PRESS LLC
187 E Warm Springs Rd,
Suite B285 Las Vegas NV 89119 USA

Website: https://workbookpress.com/
Hotline: 1-888-818-4856
Email: admin@workbookpress.com

Ordering Information:

Quantity sales. Special discounts are available on quantity purchases by corporations, associations, and others. For details, contact the publisher at the address above.

Library of Congress Control Number:

ISBN-13:   978-1-965732-21-2   Paperback Version

REV. DATE: 02/04/2025

51 Reasons to Ask 51 Questions

ARRIVAL

<u>FADE IN.</u>

<u>EXT.CGI. SPACE. FIERCE WARRIORS CLOUD PEOPLE ROYAL YACHT APPROACHING THE CAMERA. 60 SECONDS.</u>

Not far from the sun, almost the distance that Venus orbits, the 猛将云人 [Fierce Warriors Cloud People] (猛将云人 PINYIN: Měngjiàng Yún-Rén pronounced: Mung-jung yoon-ren) maneuvered into a hyperbolic orbit around the sun as the Royal Yacht slowed and slowly took on a more circular path allowing the mother ship to absorb a vast amount of energy directly from the sun.

> VANCE
> Why are we going to the planet in a shuttlecraft?

> *WÁNMĚI DE HUĀ* SHÈNGDÀ DÁ QIÈ SĪ
> (pronounced: Wan may da wa sheng da chia sue)
> [完美的花盛大达切斯]
> PERFECT FLOWER GRAND DUCHESS
> Normally we would simply use our transporter to deliver us to your planet's surface. But since your body may not withstand the transporter stresses involved; we'll take you to Earth in one of our shuttlecrafts.

> VANCE
> Why didn't we just take the Royal Yacht down to the planet's surface?

> *WÁNMĚI DE HUĀ*
> Drago advised me not to put the Royal Yacht at risk to make sure we have a way to get home.

Vance quickly responded as he felt slight invigoration of finally coming home for a while if not permanently.

> VANCE
> Is that typical?

> *WÁNMĚI DE HUĀ*
> We often use shuttlecraft for many aliens in similar circumstances.

VANCE
That's fine with me.

EXT. CGI. SPACE. SHUTTLECRAFT DEPARTING MĚNGJIÀNG YÚN-RÉN ROYAL YACHT 35 SECONDS DURING FOLLOWING VOICE OVER.

The brightness around the shuttlecraft quickly faded into darkness as it left the _Měngjiàng Yún-Rén Royal Yacht_ and maneuvered on a course to intercept the path of the Earth. The transit would require virtually only minutes, as the speed was incredible.

Looking out towards the vast expanse of space this shuttlecraft offered with its well-designed control room that allowed great visibility in the direction of travel, planets and stars appeared to move, just as if they were in time lapsed photography, as the shuttle's velocity made the relative motion appear magnified by the velocity of the craft.

Měngjiàng Yún-Rén Royal Yacht speeds were so excessive that red and blue shifts appeared depending on the direction Vance looked, looking at the rear view display all the stars appeared to have some sort of red hue to them while those directly ahead developed a blue hue as they ventured closer to earth.

EXT. CGI. SPACE. 猛将云人 FIERCE WARRIORS CLOUD PEOPLE SHUTTLE FLYING DOWN TO EARTH DURING THE FOLLOWING VOICE OVER. 15 SECONDS.

VOICE OVER
Wánměi De Huā Shèngdà Dá Qiè Sī [完美的花盛大达切斯] _Perfect Flower Grand Duchess, often referred to as Tang Grand Duchess_ [唐太宗夫人 _Táng Tàizōng Fūrén by the Royal Court] enjoyed sitting next Vance in the shuttlecraft._

The two now embarked towards what Vance thought might be his destination, planet Earth.

Note: here is one of my videos that could give guidance on how to film this scene including a style of music to use:

https://www.youtube.com/watch?v=5io-Cy9dPQU

Vance De Huā, experiencing the unexpected quark and fascinating discovery of Vance, had played with him merely as if he were her personal pet.

Being a million years more advanced than Vance, Wánměi De Huā experienced the novelty evolving into something quite extraordinary.

Vance experienced grief over the loss of his companion Doctor Kara which he learned via REN secret probes after he was rescued but presumed dead during galactic intervention on Jeeapa. With Kara's loss, Vance was quite emotionally vulnerable.

Wánměi De Huā's capability of changing forms into almost any type of physical appearance, would sometime humor Vance with appearances of individuals from his memories to help alter his mental disposition.

VOICE OVER
(During travel and landing at Area-51)

Vance's memories might have dulled over the years, but Wánměi De Huā's incredible capability of discovering and refreshing Vance's memories also allowed her to telepathically discover everything about Vance.

That deep penetration into Vance's primitive psyche developed a situation that Wánměi De Huā never would ever expect possible while her fondness gradually developed an uncharacteristic affectionate bond that was considered rare if not almost impossible.

Energy beings were never destined to mix with mineral eaters. Their physiology was so diametrically opposed and made no sense that any type of bond could ever exist.

But out of tragedy, suddenly this strange event thrust the Royal Mother Ship off into a far distance in the Galaxy seldom ever visited by the inter most galactic civilization.

Planet Earth, the Wogar Greys Aliens, the Tall Whites and others were a very long distance to the Měngjiàng Yún-Rén; hence, their paths seldom crossed.

In those few rare occurrences where Wogar Greys and Tall Whites did meet Měngjiàng Yún-Rén, any show of arrogance or misdirected assessment of capability quickly gave the Wogar Greys and Tall Whites reasons to further avoid exposure to the Měngjiàng Yún-Rén.

The Wogar Greys and Tall Whites also determined if they avoided the Měngjiàng Yún-Rén, they were usually not harassed or experienced any form of serious harm and were left alone.

Meanwhile, the galactic scale war on going at not-so-distant star systems led to the Tall Whites to come to Earth on their way to the intergalactic warzone.

It took the Tall Whites eight months to travel to Earth, their midpoint stop-over to the intergalactic war zone.

The Tall Whites' performance in the intergalactic war was not developing in the way they had anticipated. The fighting now took on a war of attrition and the Tall Whites slowly were losing ground.

The Wogar Greys were often accused of playing both sides, seemed to avoid that area and were not currently involved, though Tall Whites suspected the Wogar Greys were somehow connected as the Měngjiàng Yún-Rén spacecraft appeared suddenly.

The 猛将云人 *Fierce Warriors Cloud People Royal Yacht* was a very capable spacecraft was far more advanced than any spacecraft Vance experienced during his travels, including his vast experience with the Mergenky civilization.

Wánměi De Huā asked even though she didn't need to since she knew everything Vance was thinking with her vast mental telepathic probing of his thoughts.

WÁNMĚI DE HUĀ
Where do you wish to arrive on Earth?

Vance responded wondering how their reception might unfold.

VANCE
The only place I think we can safely go now is Area-51.

***

EXT.CGI.SPACE. *MĚNGJIÀNG YÚN-RÉN ROYAL YACHT SHUTTLECRAFT* APPROACHING EARTH 15 SECONDS.

The penetration of the ionosphere and radiation belt had hardly any noticeable effects. The *Měngjiàng Yún-Rén Royal Yacht Shuttlecraft* entered Earth's atmosphere and slowed down directly above Nevada where it made a vertical descent.

EXT.CGI.SPACE. *MĚNGJIÀNG YÚN-RÉN ROYAL YACHT SHUTTLECRAFT.* HOVERING A FEW FEET OFF THE RUNWAY ADJACENT TO BUILDING 27 AT GROOM LAKE. 15 SECONDS.

By the time Earth's Space Command, a secret international organization made up of all the major advanced countries such as America, Russia, China, and European Union discovered the traces of an inbound extraterrestrial ship, the *Měngjiàng Yún-Rén Royal Yacht Shuttlecraft* was already hovering a few feet above the runway adjacent to what appeared as hanger or on base facility maps, building 27 at Groom Lake.

Vance's arrival in the shuttle with *Wánměi De Huā* in broad daylight with a lot of "uncleared" people moving around the base in a downgraded posture, added to an immediate sequence of events.

BASE SECURITY OFFICER
(MAJOR BARNES)

General Brazile we have moved self-propelled tracked missile launchers now pointed directly at the alien spacecraft.

GENERAL BRAZILE

Major Barnes order your men to not arm those missile launchers unless I give permission.

BASE SECURITY OFFICER
(MAJOR BARNES)

General Brazile, understand do not arm the missile launchers without your permission.

<u>INT. DAY. *MĚNGJIÀNG YÚN-RÉN ROYAL YACHT SHUTTLECRAFT*</u>

VANCE

It looks like we have a welcoming party.

WÁNMĚI DE HUĀ

There are a few Earth people approaching.

Vance noted as he observed:

VANCE
There are quite a few military personnel behind the
self-propelled missile launchers and a couple of black
SUVs and HUMVs that looked well-armed.

Wánměi De Huā knew what Vance was thinking.

WÁNMĚI DE HUĀ
We might as well go down and greet them.

The *Měngjiàng Yún-Rén Royal Yacht* shuttlecraft deployed a ramp that appeared
to have a red carpet on it. That cover was anti-skid but served also as a royal
decoration with the various *Wánměi De Huā* Shèngdà Dá Qiè Sī insignias
integrated into the design.

Wánměi De Huā took on an image that would pass for a glamorous Movie
Star with a physical shape that would humble the most illuminated terrestrial
minds.

The black vehicles moved in front of the missile launchers and pulled up near
the shuttlecraft, doors opened and uniformed men as well as a few with suits
on got out and approached Vance and *Wánměi De Huā*.

One of the men in uniform, obviously an important figure seemed to take
command of the conversation and spoke first.

GENERAL BRAZILE
We were not expecting any visitors today, and whoever
you are, you have really caused me a lot of difficulties
since the base is not in a security profile or posture for
your visit.

Vance responded in such a manner he thought someone was putting thoughts into his
mind, which *Wánměi De Huā* was controlling as she telepathically modified Vance's
thought processes to say everything as she wanted.

VANCE
I apologize. We didn't think it would be safe to
arrive in any other fashion since Earth Defense Grids
didn't know what our intentions were. We know you
had recent issues that could have created a hostile
reception.

The high-ranking military person demanded:

GENERAL BRAZILE

Who the hell are you, and where did you come from?

VANCE

I'm an Earth person; my name is Vance, but I'm acting as a translator for this woman *Wánměi De Huā Shèngdà Dá Qiè Sī* who only communicates telepathically.

GENERAL BRAZILE

What star system did you come from?

VANCE

We came from the other side of the Milky Way, obscured from Earth's view by large hydrogen and helium clouds between here and there.

GENERAL BRAZILE

Vance, since we were not expecting you, a lot of personnel are not cleared to see you are now around the base doing their routine work.

VANCE

I apologize for our abrupt arrival, but we saw no other way to arrive safely.

GENERAL BRAZILE

I'm General Brazile by the way, director of research here. I suppose you know where you are at?

VANCE

Yes, Area 51.

GENERAL BRAZILE

Vance, you should understand we have problems with satellite reconnaissance of the base all the time, that's why we need to get your ship out of their view.

VANCE

What do you suggest?

GENERAL BRAZILE

We can hide your ship until you leave. Please move your ship into hanger 27 over there.

General Brazile pointed to the hanger that had a big number 27 painted on the large doors.

VANCE

That should not be a problem, we'll relocate the shuttle to inside the hanger.

GENERAL BRAZILE

We'll get the doors opened shortly and you can move your ship inside.

General Brazile turned to the civilian in suit and tie standing next to him.

GENERAL BRAZILE

Call over to building 27 and have them open the hanger doors, we are going to move a METSV (maneuverable extraterrestrial space vehicle) inside.

Over the walky-talky the civilian called:

AREA 51 CIVILIAN

Building 27, from General Brazile, open the access doors, we have an METSV we need to move inside.

The doors momentarily opened and briefly the alien ship retraced its stairway then slowly moved into the hanger with the group who had been talking, walking and following on foot a short distance away.

The group entered the large hanger. Suddenly the large doors slid shut behind them, obviously from remote control.

VANCE

It feels like the floor was moving.

GENERAL BRAZILE

The floor of the hanger deck is an elevator about four times larger than what is installed on American Aircraft Carriers.

General Brazile turned to his staff operations officer Colonel David Jones.

GENERAL BRAZILE

Colonel Jones, contact Grak and Struyograb and have them come here immediately.

General Brazile was thinking these two Aliens would help size up these new Alien arrivals he'd never seen or heard of before.

Grak, a Grey Alien approximately 450 years old, slightly over half his life span filled the role as the Grey Consulate for planet Earth. Grak was semi-restricted to Area 51 Base for his own protection but also the government was not in any sort of mood for Alien disclosure especially since he did not look humanoid.

Struyograb, one of the Tall Whites, considered young had recently enjoyed his 250th birthday also was a member of the Tall White Inter-Galactic Diplomatic Corp.

Grak and Struyograb never conversed with each other and General Brazile had been advised to keep them apart as much as possible for fear that one of them would end up dead because of their galactic histories.

Vance and *Wánměi De Huā* were suddenly aroused upon Grak and Struyograb entrance to the hanger after the huge elevator had gone down 4 levels and stopped at a large opening.

General Brazile stated in a very professional manner:

GENERAL BRAZILE
Will you please park your ship here while you visit.

Wánměi De Huā using mental telepathy, signaled to the crew members remaining aboard the shuttle to move it into the large parking area apparently reserved for them or other visiting dignitaries.

Grak and Struyograb were led up to Vance and *Wánměi De Huā* who observed the ship silently and slowly moving into position into the 4th floor underground hanger parking stall.

As Grak and Struyograb arrived within 10 feet of Vance and *Wánměi De Huā* they suddenly fell to their knees and bowed, which triggered a thought in Vance of his remembering Japanese he knew sincerely bowed in a similar manner during a most auspicious occasion.

General Brazile was suddenly surprised to see the two most arrogant aliens he ever met suddenly acting so humbled in their actions.

After mumbling some alien languages nobody but Vance understood, the aliens stood upright and glanced upon Vance and the other distinguished guest *Wánměi De Huā*.

General Brazile being somewhat sophisticated and well versed in dealing with 8 different alien races that secretly visited area 51, S-4 site, asked the obvious question:

GENERAL BRAZILE
Are you some kind of Royalty?

VANCE
General Brazile, you can kind of say that.

About that time Struyograb suddenly spoke.

STRUYOGRAB
General Brazile, the female is *Měngjiàng Yún-Rén.*

GENERAL BRAZILE
Do you know a lot about the *Měngjiàng Yún-Rén?*

STRUYOGRAB
Měngjiàng Yún-Rén. rarely make their presence.

GENERAL BRAZILE
I take it you have met them before.

STRUYOGRAB
We have encountered them less than a dozen times over the past 100,000 Earth years.

GENERAL BRAZILE
You are aware of *Měngjiàng Yún-Rén* existence?

STRUYOGRAB
Painfully so.

GENERAL BRAZILE
Are they of the Imperialistic type?

STRUYOGRAB
No, they avoid us to the maximum extent possible.

GENERAL BRAZILE
Do they cause you trouble?

STRUYOGRAB
They have intervened in some of our wars and slaughtered many of our military.

Grak suddenly spoke up

GRAK
Only because of the *Gāodà de Báisè* [Tall White] have
a habit of invading and plundering other worlds.

General Brazile suddenly fearful the Grey and the Tall White would be choking each other to death was caught off guard and suddenly fearful of the consequences. But his thoughts were suddenly interrupted with a very loud voice.

VANCE
Stop!

At that time the Alien and Vance held an arm out giving what might be construed as an intergalactic hand signal could sense in ways that General Brazile suddenly had thoughts.

VOICEOVER (GENERAL
BRAZILE) THOUGHT
Měngjiàng Yún-Rén does not appear pleased.

Once again Grak and Struyograb were on their knees in a Japanese style bow on all fours, like *Shogun Era* respectful pleas.

After Vance received his mental telepathic instructions he very loudly said:

VANCE
Please stand up.

Grak and Struyograb slowly rose both suddenly exposing a new demeanor. It's just as if something had suddenly modified their personality.

Having studied Grak and Struyograb for a half dozen years, General Brazile realized they were acting quite a bit differently than he had ever witnessed before.

Grak and Struyograb natural way of condescension towards the inferior Earth people had left raw marks on General Brazile's feelings towards them.

When General Brazile was first cleared and stationed at Area-51, Sector-4 as the deputy commander, he felt exhilaration unlike any time in his life. However, it only took about a year of dealing with these two Aliens before he dreaded every day in his life, and Grak and Struyograb added routinely to the stress.

When General Brazile's predecessor General Duncan was accidently killed by one of the Tall Whites (or reported as such), he was suddenly thrust into a role he greatly regretted being in.

Furthermore, General Brazile had no way to leave the project since the Joint Chiefs, who were now overly concerned about recent developments in nearby star systems that might affect earth, would not consider a transfer request considering that situation.

VOICEOVER (GENERAL
BRAZILE) THOUGHT
Is that why the Měngjiàng Yún-Rén came?

It was as if someone had given him a mental nudge; he somewhat involuntarily said

GENERALBRAZILE
Wánměi De Huā and Vance would you like to join
me for some refreshments, and we can discuss your
sudden appearance?

VANCE
We would be delighted.

GENERAL BRAZILE
Follow me.

The group walked about 50 feet and a door with an obvious sensor automatically opened to a room that was empty and after they all were in the room the door suddenly shut, and they could feel movement.

Having experienced anti-gravity and unusual gravity fields Vance knew instantly they were dropping. The apparent movement lasted about a minute then suddenly he could feel the pressure or sense of positive gravity forces.

The door then opened to a long well lighted passageway.

Armed guards were in body armor and appearing to be very serious at their jobs came to an attention as the General Brazile walked by then abruptly turned into a concave entrance to what appeared to be and executive office suite where it appeared clerks and analysts were working on various items. All were well dressed, wearing suits, ties, and women were in dresses or business suits, giving a most professional appearance.

One of the workers suddenly looked like he saw a ghost. Vance thought for some reason the person looked familiar, and indeed he did. It was Clark Douglas, a man from his past who worked for one of the major aerospace firms that developed and tested high performance aircraft that were probably tested at Area 51.

Wánmĕi De Huā quickly made the association and conversed with Vance in mental telepathy and quickly obtained all his memories of Clark from a bygone area.

CLARK DOUGLAS
Hello Vance.

VANCE
Fancy meeting you here, Clark.

General Brazile appeared amused.

GENERAL BRAZILE
You guys know each other?

CLARK DOUGLAS
It's been a long time General.

VANCE
Yes, it has, Clark.

Clark surmised that since Vance was with the group of aliens, including one he had never seen before, Vance had somehow got involved in the project.

CLARK DOUGLAS
Vance, are you working here now?

VANCE
No, we are just visiting.

CLARK DOUGLAS
I see.

Clark responded in a friendly manner but was interrupted by General Brazile.

GENERAL BRAZILE
This way please.

General Brazile led *Wánmĕi De Huā,* Vance, Grak, and Struyograb into his private office which had a conference table that ran perpendicular off his desk for what was probably required for routine meetings to deal with the extraordinary demands of the underground complex.

17

GENERAL BRAZILE
Please make yourselves comfortable.

General Brazile then pressed a button on his desk to summon one of his aids in who arrived very promptly, and well-manicured.

GENERAL BRAZILE
Please provide everyone here with some drinks and refreshments. We have probably everything you might want.

VANCE
General Brazile, that will not be necessary for Wánměi De Huā.

GENERAL BRAZILE
Your friend does not get thirsty?

VANCE
No, her physiology does not require food and water; *Měngjiàng Yún-Rén* internally synthesize their own with a physical condition that you would not understand.

GENERAL BRAZILE
What do they ingest then? Everyone requires some sort of nourishment.

VANCE
This might sound kind of strange, but the *Měngjiàng Yún-Rén* intake plasma balls for nourishment.

GENERAL BRAZILE
I've seen or heard a lot of strange things about aliens, but never anything like this!

VANCE
I've not had a soda in quite some time, I'll just have one of them please.

In due time the General's aide very efficiently delivered beverages for some of them. The Wogar Greys and the Tall Whites had slowly taken a liking to some of Earth's drinks, thus participated as a form of respect as well as for their own desires.

GENERAL BRAZILE

Ok let me ask you the $50 question, why did you come to Earth?

VANCE

I kind of felt sad because I missed Earth. *Wánměi De Huā Shèngdà Dá Qiè Sī,* who is *Měngjiàng Yún-Rén* treats me well, and suggested I come back to Earth for a visit.

GENERAL BRAZILE
Is that her official title?

VANCE

Wánměi De Huā Shèngdà Dá Qiè Sī, is the *Měngjiàng Yún-Rén* Tang Grand Duchess.

GENERAL BRAZILE
Is that how I address the Tang Grand Duchess?

VANCE

Wánměi De Huā is, referred to as *Tang Grand Duchess* [唐太宗夫人 Táng Tàizōng Fūrén] by the Royal Court. You can address her simply as *Wánměi De Huā.*

GENERAL BRAZILE
Vance, do you realize you put me in a serious position?

VANCE
No doubt.

GENERAL BRAZILE
Did you come with anything to offer us or is this just a social visit?

VANCE

For now, it's strictly social and I would like to spend some time here and show *Wánměi De Huā* around a bit.

GENERAL BRAZILE
What do you have in mind?

VANCE
A long road trip.

GENERAL BRAZILE
That might be kind of difficult for us to allow.

VANCE
Why is that?

GENERAL BRAZILE
Well for instance, we do have some protocols; you obviously do not have any medical clearances.

VANCE
I assure you, General, my health and any virus or bacteria I might be carrying is far less significant than anything you currently have, since the *Měngjiàng Yún-Rén* medical technology is about a million years more advanced than the Earth.

About that time the phone rang. It was Major Barnes from security.

GENERAL BRAZILE
Major Barnes, what can I help you with?

Major Barnes made an astonishing report about the alien spacecraft.

General Brazile screamed into the telephone receiver. Looking mildly pale, quickly recovered.

GENERAL BRAZILE
What!

MAJOR BARNES
General Brazile, we have a security video of the spacecraft I'll email you shortly.

GENERAL BRAZILE
Call me if any new developments occur.

Then General Brazile turned to Vance.

> GENERAL BRAZILE
> Vance, did you do some fancy trick with your
> spacecraft?

Vance was unaware of *Měngjiàng Yún-Rén* technology and was soon talking via mental telepathy from *Wánměi De Huā* as she explained things he never knew and would normally be beyond his grasp of understanding.

Then *Wánměi De Huā* planted the thoughts in Vance who then responded to General Brazile being the spokesperson as directed by *Wánměi De Huā*.

> VANCE
> General Brazile, the Měngjiàng Yún-Rén felt it would
> be an inconvenience for you to store their spacecraft in
> Hanger Bay four.

> GENERAL BRAZILE
> What exactly did they do?

> VANCE
> The *Měngjiàng Yún-Rén* miniaturized it then
> transported it back to their Royal Mother Ship; they
> can send it back to us when we need it.

> GENERAL BRAZILE
> It seems like an impossibility to miniaturize and
> teleport a shuttle. Why didn't you just teleport here in
> the first place?

> VANCE
> General Brazile, the only reason why they used
> the shuttle to bring me here was my body is not
> accustomed to their transportation device, and they
> feared it could possibly injure me, so they took the
> conservative approach and brought me back to Earth
> in the shuttlecraft to make sure I was not harmed in
> any way.

General Brazile had seen a lot of mysterious things in his lifetime but had never encountered anything like this before.

> GENERAL BRAZILE
> Vance, how did you get hooked up with the *Měngjiàng*
> *Yún-Rén?*

VANCE

A long while ago I was abducted by the Mergenky
who visited Earth after their Scout Class Spaceship
was accidentally exposed to me.

GENERAL BRAZILE
Why were you abducted?

VANCE

Because of Earth's Galactic Quarantine they could not
allow me to return to Earth. As part of their way of
compensating me for taking me away from my society
here on Earth they asked me what I wanted to do for
the rest of my life.

GENERAL BRAZILE
What did you want to do?

VANCE

I was interested in space travel because of my trip from
Earth to the Dome City Quom on their planet Gwaba.

GENERAL BRAZILE
What did you end up doing?

VANCE

Based on my interviews with Mergenky Space Force,
they assigned me to be a crew member on the Scout
Class Ship S1 that was involved in my abduction where
I served under their top commander in the Mergenky
Space Force, Commander Kwongab who trained me.

GENERAL BRAZILE
Is that how you got involved with the *Měngjiàng Yún-
Rén?*

VANCE

I was involved in space battles between the Anarchie
and the Mergenky Empires in two wars. During the
second war I was promoted to be the Navigator on a
Mergenky Battlecruiser.

GENERAL BRAZILE

I'm sure how you became the Navigator on an Alien
Spaceship is a story all to itself.

VANCE

During a major Anarchie attack, that Battle Cruiser
suffered severe damage from laser attacks resulting in
internal explosions.

No sooner than a few survivors and I made it to the escape pod the antimatter magnetic
resonator transformers blew and we were flung out into space at a great distance. Most
of the other crew members immediately perished as their bodies could not withstand
the incredible G forces.

GENERAL BRAZILE

I would be happy to hear more about this battle.

VANCE

I would be happy to discuss that with you later when
you are not terribly busy.

GENERAL BRAZILE

I'll set some time aside, I'm interested in how all that
came about.

GENERAL BRAZILE

It sounds like you were very lucky.

VANCE

Yes, I know that. I somehow survived and was clinging
to life and when a *Měngjiàng Yún-Rén* spaceship
found me a few days later I was still unconscious,
almost expiring.

Wánměi De Huā manipulated General Brazile's thoughts that led General Brazile to
make his next statement.

GENERAL BRAZILE

This part of your story is just as amazing as the fact
you were a Navigator on the Mergenky Battle Cruiser.

VANCE

I suppose had they found me a few hours later I would
have died. I woke sometime later feeling remarkably

refreshed after they revived me with very advanced technology.

GENERAL BRAZILE
That begs the question why the Měngjiàng Yún-Rén took such interest in you.

Wánměi De Huā manipulated Vance's thoughts telepathically for a sharper discussion.

VANCE
The *Měngjiàng Yún-Rén* were kind of curious where I came from and after DNA tests revealed I was an Earth person they were even more curious because I was a very long distance away from Earth and it seemed almost impossible to discover an Earth person near the other side of the Galaxy.

GENERAL BRAZILE
How did you become involved with Wánměi De Huā?

VANCE
The *Měngjiàng Yún-Rén* eventually took me to their planet where I was asked a lot of questions and as I explained my experiences of the past years living with the Mergenky, they became more interested in my story.

GENERAL BRAZILE
I have to say this is an interesting story.

VANCE
There are no secrets in the Měngjiàng Yún-Rén worlds.

GENERAL BRAZILE
Why is that?

VANCE
Due to mental telepathy, everyone knows everything about each other.

GENERAL BRAZILE
How did you meet *Wánměi De Huā?*

VANCE
In due time *Wánměi De Huā Shèngdà* summoned
me to her Gōngdiàn Tǎ Emerald Palace and took
quite an interest in me and became my benefactor.

General Brazile, now fully engaged in this curious person's story, knew that he obviously was in the company of some extraordinary individual and based on the way that Grak and Struyograb suddenly changed in their presence was a meaningful event.

General Brazile also pondered the Wogar Greys, and the Tall Whites just might not be the big kids on the block, which made this quite a bit more amusing.

GENERAL BRAZILE
Vance, what are the *Měngjiàng Yún-Rén* people and
their cities like?

VANCE
General Brazile, as you can probably imagine, a very
advanced civilization has evolved to where quality is
more important than quantity.

GENERAL BRAZILE
Vance, that was my foregone conclusion.

VANCE
Pollution is rare, moral and ethical behavior is strictly
followed as a way of life. Crime doesn't exist, and
they avoid interfering in other worlds' events, and
keep their distance.

GENERAL BRAZILE
How do the *Měngjiàng Yún-Rén* avoid interacting
with other alien civilizations?

VANCE
As an example, when Anarchie arrived in a distant
star system close enough for possible discovery, they
evacuated their entire civilization to another star
system far away from the Anarchie to avoid contact
and any type of interactions.

GENERAL BRAZILE
Are the *Měngjiàng Yún-Rén* space nomads, so to
speak?

VANCE

If there is anything such as space nomads, the *Měngjiàng Yún-Rén* come as close as you get.

GENERAL BRAZILE

Do the Měngjiàng Yún-rén live in homes or in a beehive-like environment?

VANCE

I suppose you could call it a beehive-like existence, but up in the clouds."

GENERAL BRAZILE

What does that mean?"

VANCE

All their homes are in the clouds, they float around the planets they inhabit.

GENERAL BRAZILE

Why do they not live on the surface of the planet in houses and buildings?

The Měngjiàng Yún-Rén evolution took them to the clouds, they do not desire to live amongst all the terrestrial slime that exists throughout the Universe.

GENERAL BRAZILE

Are their homes nice?

VANCE

To put it simply, if you had a chance to live there, you probably would not want to come back to Earth.

GENERAL BRAZILE

Well then, why did you come back?

VANCE

General Brazile, in my travels I've experienced Alien civilizations and experienced much that you will never understand, but even so I do have fond memories of Earth and view it as my natural home.

GENERAL BRAZILE

You had nostalgia for planet Earth?

VANCE

I wanted to return to experience it at least one more time. The fact the Tall Whites are getting their butts beat in the intergalactic war presented an opportunity for me to come back.

GENERAL BRAZILE

What does that intergalactic war have to do with planet Earth?

VANCE

The Tall Whites are fighting some extremely vicious and poisonous entities that would plunder earth and most likely utilize the population as slaves and a food supply.

GENERAL BRAZILE

Is that one of the reasons why you arrived here?

VANCE

I came here partly as an assessment of the galactic circumstances we now find Earth in.

During Vance's statement, General Brazile looked over at Struyograb and observed some behavior he had not seen before.

GENERAL BRAZILE

Struyograb, what do you have to say about the intergalactic situation out there?

STRUYOGRAB
(Tall White)
General Brazile, as Earthman Vance has elucidated, it's a tough battle, very tough indeed.

GENERAL BRAZILE

Is there a possibility you may lose the war?

STRUYOGRAB

General Brazile, we've been fighting for 500 earth years. Win or lose I think will take at least another 500 years for the outcome.

GENERAL BRAZILE

Grak, what do you think about that?

GRAK

General Brazile, as Struyograb has said it will probably take another 500 years.

GENERAL BRAZILE

500 years gives us time to plan for it and deal with it if we must.

GRAK

The risk is high and if there were some sudden technological advancements the enemy could overcome the Tall Whites sooner.

GENERAL BRAZILE
How would that affect Earth, Grak?

GRAK

General Brazile, the Tall Whites enemies would most likely follow the Tall Whites Fleet back to Earth and plunder this planet as they head for the Tall Whites capitol Grantis to annihilate it.

General Brazile suddenly had a sickening feeling in his gut. And it may be this earth person with these strange aliens may be the final straw as far as Earth defenses were concerned.

Ok Vance, I'm sure we can accommodate you in some way; however, as you should be aware, I have some staff members that would like to debrief you and get a feel for the situation you came from; so, as part of your visit, we would like to use some of your time.

VANCE

Not a problem, General Brazile, I would like to make a proposal.

GENERAL BRAZILE
Sure, what do you have in mind?

VANCE

You know those beautiful SUVs that came up to meet our ship?

GENERAL BRAZILE
Yea, what about them?

VANCE
How about giving me a set of keys to one of them,
and you can have your secret agents go with us as we
travel around and while we are sightseeing, they can
ask all the questions they want?

GENERAL BRAZILE
That may not be possible, those are special cars
and ...”

Vance interrupted General Brazile via *Wánměi De Huā* telepathic manipulation.

VANCE
Come on General, you know that if you have Grak
and Struyograb hanging out here, it would be easy to
provide an SUV.

The General grumbled and gave some wishy-washy statements before Vance
interjected.

VANCE
(via *Wánměi De Huā* telepathic manipulation)
Also, General Brazile, you and I both know those
Cash in Advance boys were in the SUVs.

GENERAL BRAZILE
And how do you know that?

VANCE
The Měngjiàng Yún-Rén know everything that goes
on in Area 51.

Vance speaking from the mental telepathy that *Wánměi De Huā* inserting doing and
reacting with his sub-consciousness in a way he didn't realize he's not the person really
thinking, nor did General Brazile recognize *Wánměi De Huā* telepathic manipulations.

Vance was simply being used as a high-tech biological speaker output for *Wánměi De
Huā*.

Vance remained unaware that his fate had been sealed. Vance thought that since he had
been living among the Měngjiàng Yún-Rén he felt better than at any time in his life.
Soon he would discover why.

Even though Mergenky had extended Vance's life probably 50 to 100 years, *Wánměi*

De Huā directed her top medical specialists to extend Vance as long as possible, and they later informed her they believed he would live another 1000 years.

Vance would not know for probably another 100 years or so that his destiny had been re-charted. Of course, when that realization finally took hold, he would have some subtle sadness when he realized no trace of his friends or relatives would exist long afterwards while he continued to exist.

Finally, General Brazile had a spontaneous revelation, but he too didn't know he also was being manipulated by Wánměi De Huā while she wanted to make her Prince Vance happy and manipulated the General's thoughts.

GENERAL BRAZILE
Okay, Vance. We would probably need to send a couple
of agents along with you for your protection and if
you will answer their questions as you drive around
the countryside, we can probably work something out.

Having captured every memory Vance had including those that were buried deep into his sub-consciousness, *Wánměi De Huā* also knew some of the logistics that would be necessary for Vance to execute his plan, so she further helped him by inducing more thoughts and activated his speech without him realizing.

VANCE
General Brazile, I have one other request.

GENERAL BRAZILE
What is that?

VANCE
It's been many years since I've been here on Earth,
so I don't have any identification. You had to provide
Grak and Struyograb with identity when they leave
their compounds and visit places like Reno and Los
Vegas.

GENERAL BRAZILE
How do you know that?

VANCE
Like I said, General, the Měngjiàng Yún-Rén know
everything there is to know about Sector Four here in
Area 51.

GENERAL BRAZILE
Is that so?

VANCE
Yes, you had the Cash in Advance boys produced fake
Identification for Grak and Struyograb like they do for
most of their spies, so it should not be too difficult for
them to also provide me with an I.D.

GENERAL BRAZILE
I'll investigate it.

VANCE
General Brazile, I think that after you have some
more conversations with Grak and Struyograb,
you will quickly discover it's in Earth's best
interest to be on good terms with Měngjiàng Yún-
Rén especially if the Tall Whites were to suffer a
serious military setback.

One day soon, Struyograb may explain to you how they plan on using Earth
as a military base if the war zone moves this way.

When General Brazile suddenly looked towards Struyograb he suddenly didn't
like the look on Struyograb's face. Grak and Struyograb's behavior shifts upon
the Měngjiàng Yún-Rén sudden unexpected arrival troubled General Brazile,
and he suddenly realized the Wogar Greys, and the Tall White Aliens may not
be such a powerful enough force to protect Earth.

Vance, thinking back on his past experiences including the Anarchieborgs
thought:

VOICEOVER (VANCE) THOUGHT
*These people really have no idea how bad it could get
if Anarchie were to show up.*

GENERAL BRAZILE
Ok give me some time; I'll see what I can do.

VANCE
Thank you General Brazile.

GENERAL BRAZILE
In the meantime, let me show you around, I'm
interested in what you might have to say about some
of the things we show you.

The group then followed General Brazile out of his office, then down the hallway and
back into a large elevator.

Wánměi De Huā surprised General Brazile when she asked using Vance telepathically.

VANCE
General, why is this chamber a mile underground?

VOICEOVER (GENERAL
BRAZILE) THOUGHT
Seems like Vance knows a lot about this facility

GENERAL BRAZILE
We have some very dangerous equipment down here
including alien power plants. We put it down deep in
case something goes wrong.

VANCE
You mean about your reverse engineering program?

GENERAL BRAZILE
How do you know about that?

VANCE
Well, Měngjiàng Yún-Rén knows a lot more about
Area-51 you can imagine.

GENERAL BRAZILE
So, it seems.

After a brief period, the lift came to an abrupt halt and the door opened and they exited.
Somehow Vance knew they were now only ½ mile below the surface, as they walked
into a large open bay, full of people wearing white lab coats and a few with face shields
and protective gloves.

Numerous strange devices were laid out around the area. Grak and Struyograb had
never been in this compartment and were surprised what they were seeing. It was all
advanced alien technology, some of which they recognized.

As they walked along, General Brazile asked:

GENERAL BRAZILE
Vance, does any of the equipment look familiar?

General Brazile didn't know *Wánměi De Huā* could read all his thoughts, and as they walked by certain equipment as General Brazile who knew a lot about the alien equipment, his mind was read, which Vance was fed from the strange mind link that existed between him and *Wánměi De Huā*.

Vance identified a few devices and which alien race had built them. Since there had only been 15 people in this room that saw these objects, his clarification of the various devices left an impression in General Brazile that Vance's knowledge was genuine and vast. Grak and Struyograb were also taken in by the ruse.

VANCE
General Brazile, I have another question: Do we need
to send our ship to come pick us up for the night, or
can you provide us with a place to stay until we are
ready to drive out of here?

GENERAL BRAZILE
Since there are only the two of you, we have a few
extra *Officer's Quarters* available you can stay in. I'll
make all the arrangements.

Vance and *Wánměi De Huā* were soon escorted to the elevator, then up to the surface where they were ushered out into a waiting black SUV that suddenly drove them a couple miles away from the underground complex to a series of buildings that looked drab on the outside, but quite different on the inside.

Like most of what went on in Area 51, every aspect of the base was under some sort of disguise. And were quickly escorted to a room provided and gave them privacy.

<u>INT. EVENING. AREA-51 *BACHELOR OFFICER'S QUARTERS* ROOM.</u>

After *Wánměi De Huā* and Vance were left alone, Vance kicked off his shoes and laid back on a nice large king size bed.

VANCE
I assumed the room was probably bugged but I do not
care.

Wánměi De Huā, under tight surveillance being monitored by the Royal Yacht scanned everywhere she went including monitoring her conversations with Vance. In doing so Měngjiàng Yún-Rén informed her:

MĚNGJIÀNG YÚN-RÉN
SURVEILLANCE OBSERVER

Wánměi De Huā Shèngdà Dá Qiè Sī, we detected numerous acoustic and video sensors hidden in your temporary quarters.

WÁNMĚI DE HUĀ
(Telepathically)

Vance, If the Area-51 staff monitoring us is going to spy on us, we might as well give them a good show.

VANCE
What do you have in mind?

Wánměi De Huā smiled then started undressing. The body she had created was stunningly beautiful and provocative. The CIA (Cash in Advance) boys observing the video from the command center had a few cat calls until a female agent sitting not far from them asked:

FEMALE CIA AGENT
Do you guys really mind? I hope you don't act that way around your wives.

VOICE OVER
(During the Alien Style Love Making)

Wánměi De Huā walked over to Vance, bent down and kissed him on the forehead then did something that put the CIA observers into a state of shock.

Wánměi De Huā dematerialized into a new form that best could be described as a small green fairy probably two feet tall at most, with wings flapping, flying above Vance. She then dropped down upon him and her body dissolved into his!

The Měngjiàng Yún-rén created a splendid euphoria by a total body emersion. Once the two bodies were completely turned into one, their souls touched. However, a total fusion of the souls was not permissible because one of the 2 would die and cease to exist.

From observation, all the CIA technicians could see was Vance remained, who now appeared to be in a trance. He didn't move for several hours.

*Then suddenly, Wánměi De Huā, suddenly exited
Vance's body and then flew with her flapping green
wings until she was in the center of the room and
then reformed into the human form she previously
exhibited.*

Within an hour after the body fusion process, General Brazile watched the video several repeats in time lapsed photography.

General Brazile had a strange expression on his face when he suddenly felt as if his whole human psyche was being tested and his faiths and beliefs challenged like never before.

GENERAL BRAZILE
Is she some kind of God or something?

General Brazile's assistant quickly had chills running up his spine watching that strange body fusion process replayed several times at high-speed playback.

GENERAL BRAZILE'S ASSISTANT
(Colonel Jones)
Now you know why we like hiring atheists.

GENERAL BRAZILE
I'm going back to my office, if anything else interesting
happens let me know right away.

General Brazile felt dismay as he knew his report to the Joint Chiefs was not going to make them happy on many levels. The first thing General Brazile now realized is all the wealth they had expended in buying protection from the Tall Whites and the Wogar Greys, was apparently not a wise investment.

The Wogar Greys exacted a heavy price in that the Pentagon had to agree to allow them to abduct citizens from time to time. And since none of them were ever returned, the horrors they experienced would never be known.

VOICE OVER (GENERAL
BRAZILE) THOUGHT
Perhaps the Měngjiàng Yún-rén could tell us what the
Wogar Greys do with the abductees?

The mere thought of cannibalism or organ harvesting did not set well with General Brazile as he was coming more and more devoted to his religion to cope with all these unpleasant discoveries that seem to come more and more often with eight alien civilizations now infiltrating earth.

The Tall Whites seemed like genuine friends. But General Brazile summed up the obvious:

VOICE OVER (GENERAL
BRAZILE) THOUGHT
Tall Whites might also be unreliable defenders.

*Vance's sudden presence seems to have uncovered Tall
Whites vulnerability by exposing the true nature of the
Tall Whites battlefield posture, where the Tall Whites
enemies might be getting the upper hand.*

Wánměi De Huā, now fully in human-like form settled in next to Vance where she kept her ever vigil, to her soul mate Vance.

Little did Earth know one of the most powerful men in the galaxy now was Vance as the royal court followed any of *Wánměi De Huā's* orders that would be heavily influenced by Vance from now on.

The strange affection *Wánměi De Huā* had for Vance was unprecedented because civilizations a million years more advanced would normally never acquire any sort of emotions towards such primitive entities.

But Vance was quite unusual and as Wánměi De Huā fully infused her body into his, and their souls touched, the lack of millions of years of development was quickly erased by the *Universal Mystery of Souls* that are timeless.

Through these body fusion experiences, and Wánměi De Huā's psychological analysis of Vance's memories, gave her new interest in his spiritual development.

Měngjiàng Yún-Rén accepted an intelligent design and superior being just like Earthlings; however, they were never close enough to God to receive direct messages, though mysterious circumstances often left them wondering and soul searching.

The *Měngjiàng Yún-Rén* never experienced the miracles that Vance had learned about in his religious upbringing, but they had previously discovered such miracles were noted on numerous worlds and civilizations in the galaxy.

Some of the mysteries of humans increased *Wánměi De Huā's* interest in Vance, which now magnified over a million times every time their souls touched in this very strange body fusion that did not exist anywhere else in the galaxy.

The millions of years of advancement eventually developed energy-based beings like *Wánměi De Huā,* with such extraordinary features, now had a quite a startling impact on the Cash in Advance people studying them.

Meanwhile, General Brazile was receiving numerous requests directly from the Joint Chiefs for more information concerning Vance and the *Měngjiàng Yún-Rén.*

The request to the DD/P (covert ops) for sets of identities, added to more confusion and interest that normally would be bound by the special compartmentalization created for black projects, especially those under the Majestic 12 preview.

Thanks to numerous surveillance videos, taken since their arrival, a series of identification forgeries were put together including an entire history in case for some unforeseen circumstance they were scrutinized by any entity not cleared in the program.

By the time Vance awoke the next morning, Cash in Advance personnel arrived at Vance's Area-51 BOQ temporary quarters, with manufactured I.D. and a briefing so they would know who to portray in case they were ever forced into any element of investigation or discovery.

Early in the morning, a specially modified Black SUV with California license plates backed out of a C17 transport plane, followed by another white backup SUV looking identical except for paint color. The second car, which had electronic links via satellite to the other car had secret video and communications surveillance capability installed. Every conversation that would occur over the next couple weeks would be recorded and played back and analyzed numerous times by CIA Agents assigned to the new case.

A knock on the door which Vance answered soon allowed him to meet two Cash in Advance Agents who would be their escort and data gatherers. The vehicles would no doubt record interesting conversations and events experienced in the next couple of weeks. There were also two other agents assigned to them who would be traveling with them in the second SUV.

After breakfast, they were escorted to the SUV by two of the CIA agents Gus and Roger assigned to accompany them on this trip.

ROGER
I will be doing the driving until we get down to
Interstate-15 on our way to Las Vegas, where we
intend to spend a couple days taking in the sights."
VANCE
May I make a recommendation?
ROGER
What's your recommendation?

VANCE
I do not think you guys need to be wearing suits with
us all the time. I think that will cause people to get
suspicious and draw undue interest in us. I suggest you
change into more tourist-looking clothes.

After some consternation and discussion, Gus and Roger shifted into Polo shirts and
shorts and tennis shoes, with Gus's grumbling.

GUS
We didn't bring along a wardrobe for tourism on this
trip. We were sent out of Washington DC last night
without any warning to bring your new identities.
We were not planning on going on this impromptu
vacation.

The two female CIA agents also assigned were well prepared for the trip but had been
local and did not have the same issue.

Vance understood these CIA agents' situations and felt sorry for these two guys who
probably got jerked around quite a bit, sent out on DD/P missions without much
warning making it hard to live a normal life with their families.

DD/P Agents' wives typically were carefully indoctrinated as they needed to be prepared
for the rigors of being part of the *company family* where they were indoctrinated,
they couldn't ask any questions and knew that in their husbands' roles they were not
entitled to know anything about it.

These CIA agents had high visibility and oversight from their supervisors in every
aspect of field operations. They were well respected by their peers in the DD/P.

The minute the CIA agents left D.C. they were on Company Time, salaried, and
scrutinized, quite often trailed by troubleshooters who acted as a rear guard, always in
position to call in the cavalry if necessary to help them out in a fix. The Russians do the
same thing but call them watchers or watcher watchers in some cases.

EXT/INT. DAY. AREA-51, S-4. GUS AND ROGER DEVELOPMENT. VIDEO
MONTAGE.

Gus and Roger were unique in the DD/P because they were handpicked to be liaison
to Area 51. Hence, they had all the briefings and were exposed to the freaks and lizard
people out at Area 51.

Like many DD/P personnel they were handpicked because they were atheists and had
no apparent vices such as drug abuse, adultery, alcoholism, or gambling addictions.

VOICEOVER

CIA agents Gus and Roger were not boring people,
simply they were the types that wanted adventure and
accepted great responsibility without fear for their
own lives, always willing to do the company's work.

Like many people working for the Deputy Director for Planning DD/P, they had other qualities that made them essential candidates.

First, they didn't volunteer for the job. They were discovered by routine penetration of schools and military and approached in a very private manner and recruited without them at first knowing they would be working for the Cash in Advance boys.

Roger, who was kind of unique, was recruited out of the Navy. As a submariner, he had already learned how to deal with stress and strange things.

Gus was recruited at Stanford University right out of the statistics department.

After spending some time at Langley Virginia, where they signed their lives away in triplicate, the fun began.

Gus and Roger's indoctrination became intense and when they were eventually selected to work under the DD/P, they were given several choices. But the most appealing option which the agency highly desired for both was in covert ops. DD/P was rebuilding a depleted organization that had disintegrated under a recent administration who was long on promises and short on effective leadership and lacked understanding of the critical nature of INTEL and covert ops.

The dirty little secret the former president couldn't cope with was that America was not alone in covert ops, torture, and activities the public did not enshrine because of the values we like to exhibit to the rest of the world which in turn goes about their business despite our best intentions and gullibility.

Even though the former president was popular with American voters, he was not respected by the DD/P who always vets Presidents so they can sugar coat the INTEL in the flavor the president desires.

The president thought he ended *extraordinary rendition* by executive order, but during the next president swearing in, a Secret Service agent whispered a few things into his ear that made him turn red. He had been misled about a lot of things and the CIA knew all his dirty laundry. [Extraordinary rendition - Wikipedia]

The DD/P had Gus and Roger trained in martial arts and meditation. Their physical well-being was slowly upgraded as they homed in their martial arts when suddenly they were given an assignment that neither man expected nor desired: Marine Corp Boot Camp.

Both men were in the same Marine Corps recruit company together throughout boot camp at MCRD San Diego and sworn to secrecy as to who they really were.

Gus and Roger's martial arts training and meditation came in real handy and allowed them to have a major jump on all the other recruits since they were already in very great physical shape, thanks to the training at Langley.

When Gus and Roger graduated from Marine Corp boot camp, they were viewed as some of the best Marine Corp recruits that ever came through there, and like all good DD/P projects, their instructors were fully interviewed getting all the information on their performance in the veil of a phony security clearance investigation. Their real identification was never revealed as these two spooks Gus and Roger attended the training under an alias.

One of the critical factors closely observed was how well Gus and Roger performed during their self-defense training by the Marine instructors. Almost every technique taught had already been mastered at Langley in the martial arts classes; hence, their drill instructor was quite impressed at how these two men excelled at the hand-to-hand combat training.

Roger and Gus's fitness reports and service records were comments of exemplary nature of the way they conducted themselves. Appearing a few years older than most of the recruits, it was obvious to the casual observer their maturity level was quite a bit higher than the typical high school graduate recruits they normally trained.

Roger and Gus's drill instructors had seen other *company men* come through similar training regiments, and even though they never knew for sure they were *company men* (CIA), the suspicions were there, and these men were never seen again after boot camp, and their identity seemed to disappear along with all their records.

Occasionally in a covert op, the military is integrated into a team where firepower is required. Navy Seals, Marine Corp Recon Rangers, Green Beret and other highly specialized individuals such as former 82nd Airborne parachute instructors.

Suddenly former drill instructors were matched up again with their former students that now somehow a different identity, and thus confirmed these men were spooks.

When such revelations occurred that military component was indoctrinated in the secrecy surrounding the mission, including signing non-disclosure forms which also stipulated he would never reveal the identity of the covert mission personnel assets. Plus, they really didn't know their true names anyway.

Since the Office of Naval Intelligence was officially in charge of security at Sector S4 and most of Area 51, a Marine Corps General such as General Brazile was usually put in command. Though he answered directly to the Joint Chiefs, he had mostly agency people on his staff including scientists and engineers involved in the numerous crashed alien spacecraft re-engineering efforts.

Vance stated the obvious after Gus and Roger returned now dressed in more tourist-appropriate clothes to blend in better.

VANCE

That looks better, now you're not such a dead giveaway
as *Gov-Guys*.

Gus replied in a slightly negative tone.

GUS

Last night as I was enjoying a nice baseball game and I
got a text message to report back to my office, I wasn't
informed I was going on a vacation.

VANCE

I'm sorry if I caused you any undue grief.

Gus responded to Vance.

GUS

Many agency personnel were jumping out their asses
last night preparing your new I.D.

VANCE

I imagine I probably caused a ruckus.

GUS

If you only knew how it was a late-night frenzy getting
counterfeiters and computer hackers lined up to build
your new identity along with Sandra's (new identity
given to *Wánměi De Huā*).

VANCE

I hope you had a smooth flight out here.

GUS

The only consolation was Roger and I, were alone on
the Gulf Stream 650 flight out to Area 51 which had

nice reclining seats that allowed a very restful 6-hour night flight out to the Nevada site, touching down at Groom Lake right around sunrise.

<u>EXT.DAY.AREA 51 INSIDE LEAD AUTOMOBILE.</u>

Roger did the driving as Gus sat in the back seat next to Sandra wearing his earbuds and hidden microphone in direct contact with the navigator in the second car also similarly equipped.

In case they were stopped by local law enforcement, they had U.S. Marshall Badges and with the cooperation agreement between the two agencies, their contact information was in the Marshalls' computer data bases in the event there was any inquiry. Traffic stops were not uncommon.

As the short caravan pulled out of the parking lot by the officer's quarters, Vance inquired:

VANCE
You mentioned going to Las Vegas first?

GUS
Yes, some in our group wanted to stop off there to see the sights and take in a couple shows before we hit the road.

VANCE
How are we getting to Las Vegas?

GUS
I was planning on taking highway 95 into Vegas.

VANCE
Would it be possible to take 93 instead?

GUS
Why is that?

VANCE
It's been a while, but years ago, when I drove up to Ely Nevada to look at their railroad museum, I drove up 93. I'm just curious as to how those small towns look now.

                    GUS
You mean like Crystal Springs, Ash Springs, and
Alamo

                   VANCE
                  Exactly.

                    GUS
They haven't changed a bit in 20 years. They only
exist because people stationed here at the base go there
for shopping and some recreation.

                   VANCE
         I could imagine that's a security nightmare.

                    GUS
It is. We routinely station agents in every bar in
those towns to make sure someone doesn't reveal
information they shouldn't.

                   VANCE
             How's that worked out?

                   ROGER
                Not too bad.

                    GUS
The permanently assigned people here know which
side their toast is buttered and are tight-lipped.

                   VANCE
        Sounds like you all have it under control.

                    GUS
Yes, and any information leaked out can easily be
traced to the source since Sector Four at Area 51 is
highly compartmentalized.

The two autos sped out to the northwest entrance of the base and turned north shortly and emerged from a wye in the road and then a dozen minutes later another junction before turning due east.

Vance, a former avid sightseer looking to the south, could observe the mountain ranges and hilltops, which made a wonderful natural barrier to Groom Lake making it almost impossible to film any activity. It seemed like it was only a brief period, and the cars suddenly came upon the town of Rachel.

                    GUS
The town of Rachel up ahead is located by Nevada Highway 375 we are traveling.

                    VANCE
What's Rachel like?

                    GUS
Rachel and is quickly turning into a ghost town.

                    VANCE
Anything special about Hiway 375?

                    GUS
Nevada Highway 375 is better known as *Extraterrestrial Highway.*

As they drove past the Little Alien Restaurant and bar, Roger commented.

                    ROGER
When you go inside that joint the ceiling is covered with dollar bills and currency from around the world. The owner one time told me he's had probably has $30,000 worth of money hanging on the ceiling people write their names on.

                    VANCE
Where do people buy gas from around here?

                    GUS
Unfortunately, since most of the population has left fearing the aliens, they mostly drive over to Ash Springs or if they have base access there's a gas station there where it's a lot cheaper.

                    VANCE
The U.S. Government claims aliens do not exist, so why should they be scared?

                    GUS
These people know better since some of them use to work on the base and a few of them have friends with big mouths.

VANCE
Not much of a town.

GUS
No there is not. Without the Little Alien Restaurant,
there probably wouldn't be much of a town Rachel
left.

Soon the town of Rachel was far back in the rear-view mirror as the two cars sped east
slightly above the speed limit. Soon they were going through Crystal Springs.

ROGER
Crystal Springs was another desolate little place.

Gus then drove by Crystal Springs and turned south on Highway U.S. 93.

GUS
Not much here to write home to Momma about.

A short while later the two cars drove through Ash Springs where the Shell Gas station
exists. Vance remembered from many years back, when he drove through there and
stopped for gas and snacks on his way back from the Ely Nevada when he visited
Nevada Northern Railroad Museum.

Then the two car CIA caravan drove on and in a short while was suddenly driving
through Alamo Nevada.

GUS
The population of Alamo Nevada is around 1100,
that is starting to grow again thanks to several area
entrepreneurs and people retiring at Nellis Air Force
Base, who want a country like community.

ROGER
Alamo is country looking.

Vance saw a hotel ahead that looked like a Bead and Breakfast.

VANCE
How's that Bead and Breakfast over there?

GUS
That's a Dude Ranch, but short on horses.

Gus chuckled.

ROGER

City Clowns wouldn't know the difference.

GUS

Yea, all the Indians have been crying in their beers for decades until they figured out how dumb the white man was for letting him set up all his gambling casinos.

VANCE

The Foxwood Casino in Connecticut was quite impressive when I saw it.

Gus remembered when he was there during the first month they opened.

GUS

Foxwood may have had a huge negative effect on Atlantic City.

ROGER

Why would anyone from New York want to go down to a crime ridden area like Atlantic City when they can drive up the scenic route to Mystic Sea Port in Connecticut, and take the shuttle over to the Foxwood Casino in Norwich?

VANCE

The Casino's down in San Diego County were also very impressive.

GUS

I didn't realize until I was just down there on assignment that Barona was as large as any of the Vegas Casinos.

VANCE

Those five lush golf courses at Barona really draw gamblers and vacationers in. The Chief empties their pockets in the casino then he sticks it to them again on green fees out on the golf course.

Roger turned toward Sandra (a.k.a. *Wánměi De Huā).*

ROGER
Sandra, you do not speak too often.

She then smiled at Roger as Vance responded with his mental telepathy induced comment.

VANCE
Wánměi De Huā rarely talks. The *Měngjiàng Yún-Rén*
usually only communicates with mental telepathy.

Suddenly Sandra (a.k.a. *Wánměi De Huā)* spoke, which surprised Vance since it was extremely rare.

SANDRA (A.K.A. *WÁNMĚI DE HUĀ)*
I will talk if I feel it's necessary to help Vance in
some way, but otherwise you will not know what
I'm thinking, because I don't find primitive people
communication methods appealing.

Vance knew the rest of the way down to Vegas would take a while and felt bored.

VANCE
If you guys don't mind, I'd like to put on some music.

Gus acting as man in charge responded.

GUS
Sure, go ahead, after all this is your government paid
vacation.

Vance turned on the FM radio and due to the distance out of Las Vegas was only able to pick up a PBS station which was playing classical music at the time which had high fidelity and sounded nice.

<u>C.U. SANDRA (a.k.a. *WÁNMĚI DE HUĀ)* AS SHE TELEPATHICALY COMMUNICATES TO VANCE.)</u>

Note to the director:

> *During the sequences where Wánměi de Huā speaks telepathically to Vance, and he responds with thoughts for telepathic communication. The sounds of their telepathic thoughts/communications are heard for the audience and to each other but nobody else. In each of these telepathic exchanges, a C.U. of the speaker is shown but no indication of lips moving or communication to any third party.*

> *Film it like a voice over.*

> *WÁNMĚI DE HUĀ*
> *(TELEPATHICALY)*
> That's lovely music, who created it?"

All Vance had to do is think:

<u>C.U. VANCE AS HE'S THINKING [TELEPATHIC THOUGHT].</u>

> *VANCE RESPONSE*
> *(TELEPATHICALY)*
> *Sibelius, Violin Concerto in D minor opus 47.*

Sandra immediately understood. Then she added in another telepathic communique:

<u>C.U. SANDRA (a.k.a. *WÁNMĚI DE HUĀ*) AS SHE TELEPATHICALY COMMUNICATES TO VANCE.)</u>

> *WÁNMĚI DE HUĀ*
> *(TELEPATHICALY)*
> Even though Earth people are so primitive, it's amazing that they created such lovely sounds.

<u>C.U. VANCE AS HE'S THINKING TELEPATHIC THOUGHT.</u>

Vance all too familiar with the *Měngjiàng Yún-Rén* romantic fusions thought:

> VOICEOVER (VANCE) THOUGHT
> *The exquisite sounds you make also have beauty endearing that no Earth person can possibly comprehend or imagine.*

<u>C.U. SANDRA (a.k.a. *WÁNMĚI DE HUĀ*) AS SHE TELEPATHICALY COMMUNICATES TO VANCE.)</u>

> VOICEOVR (*WÁNMĚI DE HUĀ*) THOUGHT
> *Sandra (a.k.a. Wánměi De Huā) felt a slight amount of tingling sensation as she deduced partial splendid euphoria that Vance felt thinking about their last romantic fusion which now had the Cash in Advance people back at area 51 replaying repeatedly, coming to grips with what they saw.*

Back at the Area 51 video lab one CIA agent commented:

CIA AGENT #1

There are no atheists in any foxholes in wars, but a Christian would have a hard time understanding all this.

CIA AGENT #2

Now you know why Majestic 12 still insists upon not disclosing Alien presence here. People cannot handle it.

CIA AGENT #1

I suppose so. Such disclosures would probably lead to chaos.

CIA AGENT #2

You know it would.

***

The small caravan continued South on U.S.93 heading towards Interstate-15 Northeast of Las Vegas.

VANCE

Where are we all going to stay in Vegas?

GUS

I thought we would check in at Caesar's Palace, I have friends there working in management.

VANCE

Why not 'Circus-Circus?

GUS

Why would you want to stay there, Circus-Circus has a longer walk to the center of the strip?

VANCE

Circus-Circus does remind me of my life many years ago, can't be all that bad?

GUS

Thanks to my connections with Ceasar Palace management we can stay in far more luxury without much difference in price.

VANCE
Alright, that sounds fine with me.

GUS
I have another reason for staying at the Caesar Palace.
My friend there in security will make sure our cars are
parked someplace safe and under constant supervision.

ROGER
Vance, we have some expensive electronics, in the
other car we can't afford to lose.

Vance started wondering what that was all about when Sandra *(a.k.a. Wánměi De Huā)* telepathically informed Vance since she had read Gus's mind.

SANDRA *(a.k.a. Wánměi De Huā)*
(TELEPATHICALLY)
The CIA installed secure communications devices in
the car behind us that have direct satellite links to be
able to communicate from anywhere in the world.

Vance suddenly realized the gravity of the situation they were in. The spooks at Area 51 were all over them all the time. Surveillance would be heavy duty from now on.

Spooks is often a term used for people in the Intel business since many of them in the past traveled on phony identity, hence earned the spooky name.

Once the CIA caravan took the onramp to Interstate-15 it did not take long to reach Las Vegas.

After Sibelius, then Prokofiev "Piano Concerto #2," Gustav Mahler "Symphony #3," Wagner's "Tristan und Isolde I," Beethoven "Moonlight Sonata" and some Chopin's Nocturnes, the SUV's turned off Interstate-15 and onto Los Vegas Blvd and quickly arrived at Caesar's Palace valet Parking.

Gus called his old friend Alex.

GUS
Alex, I have just been pulled up by your Valet Parking
attendant near the main entrance, could you please
meet me here.

ALEX
I'll be there shortly, Gus.

Within about a minute Alex was there with a couple of his assistants, former Navy Seals he hired on his security detail.

Alex, who was wise to the world and having cooperated with some black projects from time to time providing special services and untraceable means, helped Gus accomplish projects that would be considered by the Watergate attorneys as highly illegal.

But necessity ruled Gus and Roger's lives. Since most of the gullible American public were too dumb to come in out of the rain, when it came to intelligence gathering for national security.

Looking at the two SUVs and the sophisticated looking women dressed and probably packing some firepower, was obviously a Cash in Advance operation.

ALEX
You staying at Caesar's, Gus?

GUS
Yes, didn't know I would be coming this way until
about 9:00 p.m. last night, and only knew it would be
this morning; otherwise, I would have called ahead.

As Alex stood there thinking he thought:

VOICEOVER (ALEX) THOUGHT
These do not look like rental cars.

ALEX
Where did you come from?

GUS
You know I can't tell you that, but I'm sure you'll
figure it out somehow.

Alex winked at Gus knowing damn well if he didn't fly into McCarran then it was Groom Lake.

GUS
Can you keep your eye on these two cars for me, same
deal as before?

ALEX
Yea, I'll put it in a VIP stall where we have constant
physical security backed up with cameras and guns.

GUS
That works

Gus knew Alex would have his two Navy Seal buddies move the two CIA SUVs into a private parking area where only millionaires and billionaires who spent a lot of money at Caesar's were allowed to park.

A lot of times when they picked up their cars, they discovered they also had been washed and vacuumed out.

<u>INT. CEASARS PALACE LAS VEGAS.</u>

The group checked in and Gus immediately got a list of all the top shows going on and booked some reservations for a couple musical performances and a comedian show.

GUS
Vance, I noticed you and your friend Sandra are traveling kind of light, in your billfold we supplied you with a couple company credit cards, and you might want to get at least a change of clothes.

VANCE
You read my mind.

GUS
There are a lot of beautiful shops your friend can go shopping in.

VANCE
Thank you, we'll see to all that shortly.

SANDRA *(a.k.a. Wánměi De Huā)*
(TELEPATHICALLY)
Vance, do you enjoy gambling?

VANCE
(TELEPATHIC THOUGHT)
Not really, was never good at it, and always considered it a waste of my time.

Sandra said to Vance when they were finally alone in their room:

SANDRA *(a.k.a. Wánměi De Huā)*
(TELEPATHICALLY)

Vance, I read the thoughts of many of the gamblers
and some of the dealers we walked past, would you
like to go try your luck? I can help you win.

VANCE
(TELEPATHIC THOUGHT)

Sure, I can try but I'm not going to waste a lot of time
at it.

Sandra and Vance quickly headed back out of the hotel room downstairs to the Casino.

SANDRA *(a.k.a. Wánměi De Huā)*
(TELEPATHICALLY)

Vance, try your luck with Blackjack.

For some strange reason Vance stayed one step ahead of the Blackjack Dealer
Rodriguez who happened to be one of Vegas' best and not amused he was stuck
dealing for tourists because there was a lack of high rollers in town that weekend.
But he knew he would *make quick work of this chump sitting in front of him with his
good-looking dame.*

VOICEOVR (RODRIGUEZ) THOUGHT

*There is something strange about that dame, I can't
figure it out.*

Then in the span of twenty minutes Vance beat the Blackjack Dealer Rodriguez in
every single hand.

Rodriguez was not one to lose to a punk tourist and took it as a personal challenge and
decided he was going to do everything in his power to beat this chump.

Hand after hand Rodriguez kept losing the Casino's money and the Blackjack *pit boss*
watching from the video room realized something was up and mentioned to Carlos
standing next to him:

BLACKJACK PIT BOSS

I bet that son of a bitch is counting the cards, us throw
his ass out of the casino.

CARLOS

Not yet boss, we need to discover what trick he has
up his sleeve because NOBODY beat Rodriguez hand
after hand like that. They are cheating somehow, but
we must find out what it is that they're doing.

53

Shortly after getting Gus's cars parked and right under the surveillance cameras Alex stopped by the video room checking up on the affairs of the Casino when he started overhearing some of the conversation between Carlos and the pit boss.

Alex walked over and looked at the TV screen focused in on the Blackjack table of prime interest. The pit boss looked at Alex.

BLACKJACK PIT BOSS
We got some sort of cheat going on, that dude is kicking Rodriguez's ass on almost every hand. Rodriguez is our very best dealer and he's coming unglued.

Alex was suddenly stunned and blurted out:

ALEX
I know that guy!

BLACKJACK PIT BOSS
Oh yea, who is he?

ALEX
He came in with the group of CIA thugs; I just took care of their cars.

Sandra who had been making notes of Vance's earnings.

SANDRA *(a.k.a. Wánměi De Huā)*
(TELEPATHICALLY)
Vance, you're up $10,000; think it's time to quit and go do something fun?

VANCE
(TELEPATHIC THOUGHT)
I suppose, ok let's go.

Vance then grabbed up all the chips, left several for Rodriguez as a tip that amounted to $1000.00 and headed towards the cashier to cash out his chips. Moments later the pit boss Guido and Alex came up to Rodriguez with a new dealer following behind to relieve him.

BLACKJACK PIT BOSS
Where did the party go that was gambling here?

RODRIGUEZ
They just left, didn't see where they were going.

Guido then looked at Rodriguez and in a scornful look.

> BLACKJACK PIT BOSS
> I've never seen you lose so fast like that before, what happened?

> RODRIGUEZ
> It had to be pure beginner's luck.

> BLACKJACK PIT BOSS
> Why do you say that?

> RODRIGUEZ
> Well to start with he didn't know jack shit about blackjack, his lady friend seemed to nurse maid him along.

> BLACKJACK PIT BOSS
> Maybe she was counting cards or doing something like that?

> RODRIGUEZ
> No, it couldn't be, because I switched the decks on them 4 times!

> BLACKJACK PIT BOSS
> I saw that in the video and was surprised to see he still won.

> RODRIGUEZ
> There was something very uncanny going on, never seen anything or felt anything like it in my life.

Alex looked at Guido.

> ALEX
> Boss, I think I have some idea what might have happened, let's go back to the video room where we can talk.

Moments later.

> BLACKJACK PIT BOSS
> Ok Alex, what do you think happened?

ALEX

They were part of that CIA group that are Hotel Guests here. I'm not sure what the hell they do. I've never seen them before, but I've done some reading in the past concerning experimentation in mind control. Of course, the government denies it, but the Montauk project subjects are out talking about it now.

BLACKJACK PIT BOSS
That's how they beat Rodriguez?

ALEX

The video clearly shows Rodriguez was under some sort of mental distress. I think Rodriguez was being psychologically manipulated.

BLACKJACK PIT BOSS
What's this Montauk project?

ALEX

Conspiracy theorists claim experiments were carried out at Camp Hero, Montauk Air Force Base on Long Island for the purpose of developing psychological warfare techniques and research into time travel.

BLACKJACK PIT BOSS
Do you really believe that baloney?

ALEX

After reading a book on the matter, I was talking to several guys in my security detail, and there is this one fellow, Steven Burgess, a former member of the British Special Air Service, in covert ops. Steven claims the British Special Air Service were in on some of the Montauk experiments including the cover-up of the Apollo Lunar Landing?

BLACKJACK PIT BOSS
You mean the part where the government faked it and filmed it on a stage set out in the desert in California?

ALEX
No, the landing wasn't faked.

BLACKJACK PIT BOSS
Then what was?

ALEX
Apparently, according to Steven Burgess, Aliens came upon the lander and were not too pleased with our presence and made themselves known.

They had to cut that part out to eliminate the Alien disclosure as Majestic 12 ordered it.

BLACKJACK PIT BOSS
Did we really land men on the moon?

ALEX
Absolutely.

BLACKJACK PIT BOSS
And Aliens were there to meet us not in the friendliest way?

ALEX
Our astronauts were lucky to leave there alive.

BLACKJACK PIT BOSS
If true what kept the aliens from killing them and sending a message to Earth not to tamper with the moon?

ALEX
According to one of my sources the Greys and the Tall Whites do not get along too well and had the Greys killed our men, the Tall Whites were ready to attack.

BLACKJACK PIT BOSS
I get it. There were three alien groups up on the moon. What utter nonsense.

ALEX
So, it essentially became a three-way Mexican standoff as our Earth people slithered off the moon and went back to the orbiter and returned to earth.

BLACKJACK PIT BOSS
You believe that nonsense?

                    ALEX
                  Absolutely.

              BLACKJACK PIT BOSS
              Man, you are crazy.

                    ***

<u>INT.DAY.LAS VEGAS. CEASARS PALACE. HALLWAY PASSING BY NUMEROUS SHOPS AND STORES.</u>

                    VANCE
            These 1000-dollar bills are making my wallet feel kind
            of heavy.

Vance and Sandra walked back towards the hotel room waiting for Gus to call them to dinner. As they were passing a men's shop, Sandra suggested:

            SANDRA *(a.k.a. Wánměi De Huā)*
              (TELEPATHICALLY)
            Why don't you stop here and pick up a change of
            clothes.

                    VANCE
                  (THOUGHT)
              What about you?

            SANDRA *(a.k.a. Wánměi De Huā)*
              (TELEPATHICALLY)
            Vance, I looked at a lot of female apparel as we walked
            around, I did all my mental shopping. I don't need
            to buy the clothes since I can synthesize them with
            my mind and make those items part of my synthetic
            wardrobe.

Vance responded as they walked through Ceasars Palace.

                    VANCE
                  (THOUGHT)
            There are distinct benefits being a *Měngjiàng Yún-
            Rén.*

SANDRA *(a.k.a. Wánměi De Huā)*
(TELEPATHICALLY)
Not to mention our longevity.

Later after, and a hot shower and Vance put on his new polo shirt, slacks, and shoes, he felt good.

Soon afterwards, as Vance was relaxing in his hotel room channel surfing the TV, the phone rang.

GUS
Hello, this is Gus. Are you guys hungry? We are ready
to go get some dinner.

VANCE
I could probably use a bite to eat, but Sandra only eats
about once a month and she's not due to eat for about
another 25 days. Nevertheless, she will come with us.

GUS
Fine, meet us down in the lobby in about five minutes,
and we'll go out from there.

By the time they were leaving, Sandra had switched her attire to one she saw window shopping earlier with Vance. The sticker price of the actual *couture* garment was around $15,000 and it looked impressive.

With Vance, Sandra, Gus, Roger, and the two female agents Crystal and Beverly in tow, the group headed down a large corridor that had some male models posing as Roman Gladiators, all buff with six-pack abs. As soon as they were far enough away to avoid the models hearing the conversation Beverly asked Crystal:

BEVERLY
Crystal, do you think that blonde headed dude is a sex
goddess?

CRYSTAL
No, I think he's queerer than a three-dollar bill.

BEVERLY
Why do you say that?

CRYSTAL
As a trained observer, the way he smiled at that

businessman with the gray suit on telegraphed he was
gay and available. The man in the gray suit is queer
too, so it was a dead giveaway.

The women didn't really know for sure, but they chuckled anyway because of the sick joke.

Crystal and Beverly top notch CIA agents having executed serious missions of national security behind enemy lines were fully briefed they were in the company of an Alien who apparently had some kind of relationship with this Earth person Vance who came in from nowhere that had been missing for many years.

Out of curiosity Crystal asked:

CRYSTAL
SANDRA (a.k.a. Wánměi De Huā) , what did you
think of the Roman gladiator actor back there?

Without disclosing the fact, she had confirmed Crystals' suspicions with her special talents, she responded in one of her very rare audio responses using lingo, she had sensed Vance utilize in the past.

SANDRA (a.k.a. Wánměi De Huā)
Yes, the Roman Gladiator Actor is definitely a *switch-hitter*.

Not expecting any sense of humor from an Alien after dealing with the Wogar Greys, Tall Whites, and Larians, Crystal was flabbergasted and taken back by the not too subtle response from Sandra. Then she suddenly started thinking.

VOICEOVER (CRYSTAL)
THOUGHT
This might not be such a dull trip after all.

Alex spotted Vance's group on the video monitor as they met in the lobby and made their way to the restaurant.

VOICEOVER (ALEX)
THOUGHT
What are they really up to?

Alex knew the CIA didn't put agents up at Caesar's Palace for company paid vacations.

VOICEOVER (ALEX)
THOUGHT
This group is obviously working.

Alex started thinking about some of his personal gambling debt that had recently reached about $50,000.

VOICEOVER (ALEX)
THOUGHT
I should check in with my friend Boris Potemkin who
always pays good money for information about Nellis
Air Force Base or Area 51, especially if it dealt with
Aliens.

Though Alex felt bad that he would betray his friend Gus, because his gambling debts got out of control.

VOICEOVER (ALEX)
THOUGHT
I need to get cash any way I can, because people
like Guido are the reason why Southern Nevada has
America's largest number of unmarked graves out in
the nearby desert.

A lot of people went missing because there was no hope of them ever paying off their gambling debts and Guido and his friends didn't want them walking the streets proving they could skip out on their gambling debts.

In many cases their relatives suspected foul play was involved, but there were never any clues as to what happened to them since the penalty for getting yourself into debt with those kinds of people was a bigger price than what most people were willing to pay.

Alex had the distasteful task of cleaning up dead bodies from suicides in the hotel rooms before Guido had a chance to take them out in the desert to polish them off.

The hotel and casino operator never knew what was going on, nor would they ever.

Las Vegas police saw many people getting into trouble. That's why there were always more empty buses arriving in Las Vegas than leaving since so many cars were left behind as payment for their gambling debts.

Guido was a swell guy, he always made sure the *bums* had bus money to leave town if the car fetched enough money to pay for most of the debt. The car auctions in Las

Vegas are some of the biggest in America, and many of the automobile owners got free transportation from the auction to the bus station.

Vance and the group finally made their way into Wally's Steak House that also had Wally Burgers on the menu for kids.

The mahogany walls and chandeliers gave the room an ambience fitting for a high stake's winner.

The group looked like three couples. Nobody would ever suspect the complexities and machinations these six people have done in their lifetimes.

VOICEOVER

Even though *Wánměi De Huā* Shèngdà Dá Qiè Sī (Sandra as her new cover name) would appear to be a soft hearted and benevolent Monarch, she herself had given orders which laid waste to colonies of space migrants infringing upon *Měngjiàng Yún-R*én worlds.

Nobody at the table other than Vance ever participated directly in major space battles and understood how destructive those battles were.

One of the interests that *Wánměi De Huā* developed in Vance was his memories of those space battles.

Few men had ever seen their lover like Vance's a Mergenky MSF Ship Captain Vicki blown up into sparkling debris of a gigantic space battle Earth people could never comprehend the size and scope that such battles happen.

Vances memories of those space battles were vivid. *Wánměi De Huā* was able to recapitulate all those battles with the Anarchie by probing Vances memories.

Crystal and Beverly were good lookers. They had great taste in clothing and understood by their indoctrination they had to sometimes play on the weakness of men to exploit them for their covert ops.

Even though Crystal and Beverly were never explicitly directed to utilize every resource at their disposal, having been in the business a while, they knew vividly that some of their most powerful tools included seduction of men.

Looking at Sandra *(a.k.a. Wánměi De Huā)* who was impeccably dressed, perfumed with libido modifiers, and wearing the luster of the most beautiful made-up movie star, the CIA agents knew she must possess incredible power and talent.

When necessary, Sandra could speak and was fully fluent in Earth languages partly thanks to some of her implants that gave her intellect and memory that dwarfed any Earth Terrestrials.

In one of her rare statements, Sandra, looking and smiling at Beverly commented.

> SANDRA *(a.k.a. Wánměi De Huā)*
> Beverly, I love that necklace you are wearing, it looks
> so nice on you.

Beverly, somewhat awestruck by Sandra's comment, responded.

> BEVERLY
> Sandra, you look so gorgeous. Are all the women on
> your planet so beautiful like you?

> SANDRA *(a.k.a. Wánměi De Huā)*
> Yes, so many *Měngjiàng Yún-rén women* are beautiful
> in numerous ways as Vance will tell you.

Sandra looking at Crystal commented:

> SANDRA *(a.k.a. Wánměi De Huā)*
> Crystal, your hair looks very pretty.

> CRYSTAL
> My hair is sun bleached. My last assignment took me
> to Saudi Arabia where I got a lot of sunshine and more
> of a tan than what I wanted.

> SANDRA *(a.k.a. Wánměi De Huā)*
> Were you at Saudi Arabia a long time?

> CRYSTAL
> Far more than what I wanted.

> SANDRA *(a.k.a. Wánměi De Huā)*
> Why is that?

CRYSTAL
It's already hot enough at 102 degrees in the shade, but
as a woman we are required to wear a head scarf, and it
really adds to the heat and makes you uncomfortable.

VANCE
Didn't they have air conditioning?

CRYSTAL
No. I was mostly in remote areas where people were
lucky to have clean drinking water.

SANDRA *(a.k.a. Wánměi De Huā)*
How are the people that live there? Are they friendly?'

CRYSTAL
Women are treated differently. It's nothing like living
in America. The only time men are friendly towards
women over in that part of the world is when they are
trying to get in your pants.

Sandra *(a.k.a. Wánměi De Huā)* who had lived most her life in palatial settings had never experienced anything like these two female spies and she did not hesitate to probe deeper and learn more.

In doing so Sandra *(a.k.a. Wánměi De Huā)* would establish a far deeper understanding of Vance, whom she had already extended for at least another 1000 years to be her romantic partner. Her ability to examine these two female spy's memories unobtrusively gave her that powerful tool the DD/P would wish they could ever have.

It a short time Sandra *(a.k.a. Wánměi De Huā)* discovered the conditions that Crystal stated were not far from the memories she had experienced.

The Saudi's fighting terrorists from Yemen had some real bloody battles and the Cash in Advance boys (and girls) were in the thick of it.

Sent along as a technical advisor, and fully fluent in Arabic, Crystal was only alive today because she was an excellent shot and took out 24 of them before they could kill her.

When Crystal ran out of ammo, her 5th Dan black belt in Shitō-Ryu Karate put the finishing touches on the 3 or 4 remaining *rag hats* that had attempted to decimate their group and kidnap the King's favorite nephew who was then sobbing like a child having experienced the closest call he ever faced.

No doubt had the Yemen terrorist captured the King's favorite nephew; the young man's head would have been sent to the king in a plastic bag.

Sandra *(a.k.a. Wánměi De Huā)* turned towards Beverly and peered into her mind to discover what her life had been like working as a spy.

VOICEOVER

Beverly, the other CIA spy looked far too feminine to be a DD/P operative.

Nevertheless, Beverly enabled a task force in Moscow to escape while she gave the appearance their operation was still up and running.

This situation became one of the most dangerous periods in Beverly's life.

Finally, when the FSB (formerly KGB before the reorganization) senior officer ran out of patience, they stormed the apartment to capture the individuals as well as their equipment.

Beverly had since rendered all that equipment useless by slicking the solid-state drives with an emergency erase procedure designed for just an occasion. All members of the task force except for Beverly were crossing border into Finland during the time of the FSB Agents raid.

Beverly knew it was coming and predicted the timing quite well. Beverly survived by quickly killing three FSB agents and wounding two others.

Beverly escaped down the fire escape and with bullets flying towards her slid down the final 30 feet of the apartment building on a drainpipe where she hopped on an emergency get away mountain bike just barely parked there by a Russian national.

This man had who delivered the motorcycle had been on the CIA's payroll and had quickly disappeared into a crowd and made his way to a subway train.

Inside the train station the Russian operative went into

a bathroom, pulled off his face mask which had been provided by the Americans days before. This well-paid Russian traitor had on the disguise so that he could deliver Beverly's getaway bike without giving up his identity to the numerous face recognition software driven machines.

The DD/P assumed Russians scanned this apartment building which they knew was compromised only a month after the American Secretary of State mishandled intelligence information.

Beverly had one chance to make it, and this mountain bike which she rode had to make it to the outskirts of the city to a predefined exit point.

There she would dump the bike off the side of the road out of sight under a bridge, walk up a creek bed to an obscure road and wait for a taxi preplanned to pick her up at a home. Beverly knew in advance would not be occupied since the family living there was currently being entertained at the U.S. Embassy.

The parents of the family that lived in that house were also FSB operatives and would live in horror if they ever knew their own home was a designated pickup location for the American spy.

Beverly was an illegal, meaning she did not have diplomatic immunity. Had she been captured, she either would be waiting for a spy swap or tortured to the point of near death.

Capture was not an option for Beverly. Because of her excellent riding, poor weather overcast precluding helicopters following her, she found the bridge and creek and followed it up to her exit point.

The Russian raid on the apartment only advanced the timeline by a few minutes. The street was semi-empty, nobody appeared to be around as she made her way into the backyard, slipped out of her cover clothes now appearing in a dress, wig gone, mask as well, all fit snugly into a bag that she could not leave behind but had to risk having it on her until it could be properly disposed of.

Since Beverly would be traveling in the opposite direction of what the Russians were searching it was unlikely they would be stopped and searched.

The Russians had set up a roadblock 15 miles further down the road expecting her motorcycle there at any time as it appeared it was the direction she was attempting to make her escape in the same direction the other American spies fled.

The taxicab was nice and warm and because the clothes she was wearing were not good for Moscow winters as they had to be lighter since she previously had another layer of clothes covering them for a fast change like she had just accomplished.

Note to cinematographer:

In the next section Beverly converses with the Russian Taxi Driver in Russian language. English subtitles are displayed at the bottom of the page.

The taxi driver asked Beverly in Russian:

TAXI DRIVER
Where do you want to go?
Куда вы хотите пойти?
Kuda vy khotite poyti?

BEVERLY
Presnensky District, please.
Пресненский район, пожалуйста.
Presnenskiy rayon, pozhaluysta.

The cab driver smiled as he knew this would be a good fee.

As they moved closer to the City Center, the traffic was jammed badly and all the official vehicles traveling in the opposite direction made it worse for those heading towards Northwest Moscow.

The radio channel the Taxi driver monitored described a shootout with authorities, leaving 3 dead and 2 wounded and a manhunt in progress stating they were closing in on the criminals.

As the taxi got near where Beverly wanted to go, the driver asked:

TAXI DRIVER
Where to stop?
Где остановиться?
Gde ostanovit'sya?

BEVERLY
Bolshoy Deviatinsky Pereulok.
Большой Девятинский переулок.
Bol'shoy Devyatinskiy Pereulok.

Beverly didn't want to give the actual embassy address which might later be relayed by the cabbie to authorities.

Based on prearranged directions she was to meet Jack Pepperman, an embassy employee a block east of the Embassy and he would walk her through the entrance in case there were any problems with the Russian guards outside standing next to the U.S. Marines who were not armed.

Looking ahead she could see what appeared to be Pepperman waiting on the street and told the taxi driver to pull over half a block away.

Beverly asked the taxi driver:

BEVERLY
How much?
Сколько?
Skol'ko?

Looking like a frail undistinguished woman, but someone who appeared to have some amount of wealth, the cabbie responded:

TAXI DRIVER
Seventy-five rubles.
Семьдесят пять рублей.
Sem'desyat pyat' rubley.

Beverly knew she was being ripped off and should only be paying around 30 rubles, handed the TAXI driver 100 rubles telling him:

BEVERLY
Go have a drink for me.
Выпей за мой счет.
Vypey za moy schet.

A telltale scent of vodka in this taxi existed so Beverly knew the driver would hightail it to his favorite watering hole and be recovering from a hangover long after Beverly was out of the country.

Beverly then walked down the sidewalk half a block and met her contact.

BEVERLY
Hello Jack, I'm sure glad to see you.

JACK PEPPERMAN
Likewise, we don't have much time; your departure
flight is in 45 minutes.

The two walked another block to the American Embassy where Jack Pepperman always polished looking was with the frail looking woman the Russian soldiers would least suspect was up to anything.

Jack Pepperman with his embassy I.D. escorted Beverly through the entrance down a hallway where they entered an obscure office which was staffed with DD/P personnel the Ambassador thought were dumb passport clerks that seemed to not get much done ever.

The door to the office shut behind them which was on a cypher lock and temporarily disabled so nobody could interfere with what happened next. An artificial bookshelf slid out of the way revealing a door that accessed a diplomatic pouch area which had a small wood crate prearranged.

Beverly was instructed that after the plane reached the Gulf of Finland, someone would open the box for her and let her out where she would suddenly come up the service elevator on the wide body jet in a flight attendant's uniform.

Since Beverly only weighed around 125 pounds, two men could easily handle the box. Once she was inside and the screws on the top all drilled down with an electric screwdriver, the roll up door was raised, and the box was loaded into the American diplomatic pouch truck which promptly left for the airport.

The Russians suspected this was a French operation at the apartment building where Beverly was operating because as part of the ruse, the Americans all were required to speak only French throughout the entire operation and continued to do so when they were tipped off the FSB were on to them.

The Russians didn't know Beverly and her group were Americans, but they knew something was going on because the comings and goings and a serviceman sent out to read the power meters confirmed the power drain from the apartment was 3 or 4 times more than normal. The apartment was in direct view of Russian military headquarters located at Chaadayevka near Penza, Vagonov in Moscow.

Using special probes and sensors the American task force was able to intercept nearly all the Russian headquarters microwave and other communications that went throughout the Moscow Military district during the most important period leading up to January of 2011 when the command and control was being reorganized.

Hence USA got the entire order of battle and vast knowledge of its leadership and plans at this critical juncture when the Russian President Medvedev was reorganizing it to be poised to respond to American Exceptionalism around the world, including air defense networks being set up in Eastern Europe which infuriated Medvedev and Putin.

The situation was tense; the Russians didn't know to go after the French or the Americans. All they knew was three of their best agents were killed, and two more critically wounded in the hospital.

The FSB Colonel who overstepped his authority and did the poorly planned raid because he knew he was going to capture a hotbed of spies and become a national hero was one of the three deceased agents.

When confronted, the French Embassy vigorously denied it and flatly said:

FRENCH EMBASSY
SPOKESMAN
We don't have the balls to try something like that.

That seemed to satisfy the Russians who didn't have much respect for French Intelligence they routinely penetrated almost as easy as they did the British using homosexual operatives like in the case of the Cambridge Five led by the Queen's cousin Sir Blount and used the British super spy and British Diplomat Donald Duart Maclean.

Maclean gave the Soviets a lot of America's nuclear secrets and was eventually identified in the Venona Transcripts investigation. Maclean's actions also had a lot of detrimental effects to America in the Korean War and had a role in forcing Truman to assure the British Prime Minister Clement Attlee, a liberal we would not nuke or attack China when they entered the Korean war.

The Russians then knew all too well the only other possible perpetrators had to be Americans.

But using Chinese Hardware with French language sure made it tough to pin it on Americans, as whoever did it left without a trace.

When it all became too clear it was probably an American operation, Alexander Bortnikov in the FSB (KGB) became personally involved in the investigation asked his advisor:

ALEXANDER BORTNIKOV
Are there any American planes leaving today?

GENERAL ALEXI SHOYGU
No, all that was leaving had just left before the raid.

ALEXANDER BORTNIKOV

Any other Western Country flights leaving this evening?

GENERAL ALEXI SHOYGU

No. They're all long gone, only a Swiss Air passenger aircraft left about a half hour ago could possibly have taken them.

ALEXANDER BORTNIKOV

Any chances any American perpetrators got aboard that plane?

GENERAL ALEXI SHOYGU

No, there were no American Passengers, only Europeans and some cargo.

ALEXANDER BORTNIKOV
That could be it!

GENERAL ALEXI SHOYGU
How so?

ALEXANDER BORTNIKOV

They snuck them aboard that plane in Cargo holds. This would not be the first time. Send one of our jets after it and force it to land in Russia so we can inspect it.

***

Russian Pilot Dmitri Popov was virtually wasting another hapless day as an alert pilot set in his temporary quarters, watching crappy Russian TV bored to tears almost, resentful, and wanting to be home with his wife and drinking vodka.

Tonight, Dmitri Popov was struck on duty when suddenly he got called on the alert phone and was directed:

ALERT OFFICER
Scramble your jet, air traffic controllers will vector
you onto the target and give you instructions in route.

DMITRI POPOV
Yes Sir

Dmitri Popov grabbed his parachute harness and helmet and walked out to the flight line where his trusty SU27 set parked, fully loaded with fuel, missiles, bullets and everything else except enthusiasm.

VOICEOVER (DMITRI
POPOV) THOUGHT
Another stupid drill.

Dmitri Popov started walking around the plane doing some preflight checks to make sure the plane was ready to go when suddenly, a messenger sent from the tower ran up almost out of breath.

RUSSIAN AIR FORCE
MESSENGER
Sir, you are ordered to get airborne immediately!

VOICEOVER (DMITRI
POPOV) THOUGHT
*I hope the ejector seat was working since I cannot
preflight his aircraft. I do not like this situation one bit.*

Dmitri Popov nodded and responded:

<u>SHOW ENGLISH SUBTITLE ON THE SCREEN. Actor speaks Russian</u>

ДМИТРИЙ ПОПОВ [Russian]
[DMITRIY POPOV Russian IPA]
DMITRI POPOV

Я поднимусь в воздух, как только смогу привести
самолет в рабочее состояние.

[YA podnimus' v vozdukh, kak tol'ko smogu
privesti samolet v rabocheye sostoyaniye.]

I'll get airborne as soon as I can get the plane
operational.

Dmitri Popov put on his helmet, climbed up into the cockpit and started flipping switches which powered up and activated all his electronics, radar, etc.

Russian Air Force plane number 31 with its light blue, white, and gray camouflage scheme looked good from a distance, but when a person walked up to it closely, the cutbacks in Russian military spending were starting to show the fractures.

VOICEOVER (DMITRI
POPOV) THOUGHT
*This plane is not kept up to standards like they were
just a couple years ago.*

When the SU27's main computer stalled booting up, Dmitri Popov really got pissed, and yelled:

ДМИТРИЙ ПОПОВ [Russian]
[DMITRIY POPOV Russian IPA]
DMITRI POPOV
Черт возьми!
Chert voz'mi!
God damn it!

Dmitriy Popov hit the console sharply with his hand and knowing it's not going to do anything but relieve stress. Dmitriy Popov had no choice turn off the electronics and power-on-reset the electronics suite to reboot the computer.

VOICEOVER (DMITRI
POPOV) THOUGHT
Надеюсь, на этот раз хлам загрузится.
Nadeyus', na etot raz khlam zagruzitsya.
I hope this time the junk boots up.

On the third attempt the computer finally booted up all the way but had no flight plan to load since he didn't know where he was going yet.

After all the indications were green indicating satisfactory, the two jet engines were brought online and Dmitriy Popov quickly tested his wing surfaces, gave the signal to the ground crew to unhook the umbilical cord to the power generator since he was now on his own built-in generator and removed the wheel chalks.

Before Dmitriy Popov could even begin to think what, his next move was, he started receiving screams from the control tower:

КОНТРОЛЬНАЯ ВЫШКА
KONTROL'NAYA VYSHKA
CONTROL TOWER
(VOICE & English subtitles)

Рейс 31, вам необходимо немедленно подняться в воздух.

Reys 31, vam neobkhodimo nemedlenno podnyat'sya v vozdukh.

Flight 31, you are to get airborne immediately.

Dmitriy Popov then taxied down to the end of the runway in a safe manner and wasn't going to risk his life just because some idiot up in the control tower was getting impatient.

***

The Swiss Air Jet was nearing the Gulf of Finland, and the pilots were starting to feel better knowing they would soon be out of Russian airspace and possible abuse.

ДМИТРИЙ ПОПОВ [Russian]
[DMITRIY POPOV Russian IPA]
DMITRI POPOV

Рейс 31 — Вышке, прошу разрешения на взлет.

Reys 31 — Vyshke, proshu razresheniya na vzlet.

Flight 31 to Tower, request permission to take off.

КОНТРОЛЬНАЯ ВЫШКА
KONTROL'NAYA VYSHKA
CONTROL TOWER

Рейс 31, вам немедленно взлететь, повернуть на курс 330 и двигаться на боевой скорости.

Reys 31, vam nemedlenno vzletet', povernut' na kurs 330 i dvigat'sya na boyevoy skorosti.

74

Flight 31, you are to take off immediately and turn to a
course of 330 and go at combat speed.

Very soon the Russian Fighter Pilot Dmitriy Popov felt the SU-27 jet leap into the air.
Then as he pondered this stupid training-drill they were doing, banked his SU-27 jet
and was soon on a course of 330 and enjoying the fact he was being encouraged to
burn up fuel fast which had become kind of rare lately.

Right about the time the Swiss Air Jet hit the Gulf of Finland and was legally out of
Russian Airspace, the Russian air traffic controller barked over the radio:

ST. PETERSBURG CONTROL
Swiss Air 1110, this is St. Petersburg control; you are
ordered to turn your plane around and follow flight
instructions.

SWISS AIR 1110 HEAVY
St. Petersburg Control this is Swiss Air 1110 heavy.
We are now in international air space and behind
schedule due to lengthy delays on the ground, we can't
turn around.

Flight 1110 was quickly leaving the opportunity for Russia to force Swiss Air 1110
back.

<u>INT. EVENING. LUBYANKA BUILDING. MOSCOW. RUSSIA. FSB (KGB)
HEADQUARTERS</u>

ALEXANDER BORTNIKOV
General Alexi Shoygu, how much time before that
Swiss Air jet crosses over into Sweden?

After confirming with the control tower:

GENERAL ALEXI SHOYGU
Alexander, in about 10 minutes.

ALEXANDER BORTNIKOV
How far is our SU-27 fighter jet from intercept?

GENERAL ALEXI SHOYGU

In 10 minutes if we allow it enough fuel to make it back to Russia.

ALEXANDER BORTNIKOV

Tell the control tower to inform the pilot he must be ready to shoot down that plane and to use all the extra fuel necessary to get there right away and then if he must crash land in the ocean, we'll send out craft to rescue him.

<u>EXT. IN FLIGHT. EVENING. SU-27 COCKPIT.</u>

<u>SOUNDTRACK DURING THIS SCENE: SCHOSTAKOVITSCH SYMPHONY SEVEN. IV MOVEMENT. ALLEGRO NON TROPPO.</u>

Out of the pant legs pocket of his flight suit Dmitriy Popov pulled out a little picture of his wife and son and placed it on the aircraft's control console dashboard. He also knew there were probably Russian women and children on that airliner.

Dmitriy Popov looked at his fuel tank levels on the digital readouts and realized he barely had enough fuel to make it back to Russia. Dmitriy Popov now overheard the communications between Swissair 1110 and St. Petersburg control and understood the gravity of the situation.

Some criminal was getting away and the Russian government was pissed this airline was not cooperating.

Shooting Swissair 1110 down over a criminal didn't make sense and Dmitriy Popov also knew vividly, if he had to crash-land in the Baltic this time of year, his survival would be about 3 minutes before he died from hypothermia.

If Dmitriy Popov landed his SU27 in Sweden or Finland after shooting down Swissair 1110 airliner, the Russian Government would simply disavow him, and he would most likely rot the rest of his life away in a prison.

NATO was on alert now being fed real time data by the CIA, who wanted to get their spy back alive. NATO sent up four F16s out of Germany.

<u>SPLIT SCREEN</u>

<u>EXT. CGI. EVENING. FOUR NATO F16'S APPROACHING. LEFT SIDE. RUSSIAN IRBIS-E RADAR IMAGRY ON RIGHT SIDE. 30 SECONDS.</u>

The four NATO F16s were converging on the SU27, and Swissair 1110 and it wasn't too long before Dmitriy Popov, having been sent on a suicide mission, suddenly detected the NATO F16 radars on his radar intercept alert receiver on his heads-up display. Convergence would be quick, and he was quickly running out of options.

Sukhoi Su-27 Flanker

And soon Dmitriy Popov could see on his *Russian Irbis-E Radar* at least 4 NATO jets coming his way and would very soon be within weapons range. Four to one, he knew he was outgunned and the F16's had more than enough heat seeking missiles to shoot him down.

The odds were now impossible, and Dmitriy Popov had just enough fuel to make it back to base if he turned now and cut back on the throttle. Dmitriy Popov looked at his family picture once more, then pulled back on the throttle and began a slow sweeping turn back towards Russian Airspace.

<u>EXT. CGI EVENING. BALTIC SEA AREA NEAR SWEDEN. RUSSIAN SU-27 BANKING AWAY FROM SWISS AIR 1110.</u>

ДМИТРИЙ ПОПОВ [Russian]
[DMITRIY POPOV Russian IPA]
DMITRI POPOV

Диспетчер, это рейс 31. Меня перехватили четыре самолета НАТО, теперь они между мной и целью; возможности вступления в бой нет, разворачиваюсь и возвращаюсь на базу.

Dispetcher, eto reys 31. Menya perekhvatili chetyre samoleta NATO, teper' oni mezhdu mnoy i tsel'yu; vozmozhnosti vstupleniya v boy net, razvorachivayus' i vozvrashchayus' na bazu.

Control, this is Flight 31. I've been intercepted by four NATO jets, now between me and the target; there is no possibility of engagement, turning to return to base.

English subtitle printed on bottom of screen for the duration of DMITRI POPOV's statement plus five additional seconds to allow sufficient time for the audience read it.

As soon as the report made it back to Bortnikov, FSB/KGB official cussed then buried his face in his hands as this will be a tough one to explain to Medvedev who was about five times a bigger of a pain in the ass than Putin ever was.

Swissair 1110 landed in Stockholm Sweden, where the plane was to be refueled and continue to JFK airport in NYC. Since this was a fueling stop to take on extra fuel needed to cross the Atlantic, the crew had the opportunity to get off the plane and go out into the terminal where they could either get a good meal or buy some tax-free gifts while the cleaning crew cleaned the passenger cabin.

Only one flight attendant on 1110 knew about Beverly since she was a paid CIA operative and the rest of the flight attendants and crew didn't pay much attention when they simply walked off the plane, past customs officials since they had no baggage to claim and where airline employees were waved by without delay.

Out in the terminal a man in a suit who had recently looked at his briefing pictures, identified Beverly, then approached the two flight attendants.

DENNIS JOHNSON

Hi Beverly, I'm Dennis Johnson, and I've arranged transportation for you.

Dennis Johnson matched the description Beverly had received in her tactical evacuation plan and followed him out the terminal to a waiting car with a driver.

Dennis Johnson and Beverly got into the car which then drove a short distance and turned on an air freight service road and came up to a FEDEX building and stopped the car.

DENNIS JOHNSON

Your ride home is here.

Dennis walked Beverly through the front of the almost abandoned building because it was late in the day, and out parked behind it was a Gulf Stream 650 which Beverly immediately boarded which took her back to Dulles International. Beverly was met by company employees she knew by sight and whisked away without ever been identified in the tragic event back in Moscow.

Sandra *(a.k.a. Wánměi De Huā)*, looking at Beverly had sensed most of the story as she pierced her memory with her vast mental telepathic ability and put together many of the important pieces.

Even though Sandra *(a.k.a. Wánměi De Huā)* was an Empress to a very powerful advanced civilization, she recognized the extraordinary heroic actions Beverly had experienced, which is quite uncommon in many civilizations spread across the galaxy. Sandra *(a.k.a. Wánměi De Huā)* also recognized that these two female CIA agents Beverly and Crystal may be pretty, but they are also deadly agents.

Gus and Roger were no doubt proven soldiers, some of their experiences were not too different than what these women faced, and they too were living on borrowed time.

***

The waitress took the group's food orders and drinks. Vance ordered for Sandra *(a.k.a. Wánměi De Huā)* who did not eat food, but to make it look good. She did, however, consume part of the steak which she did for politeness.

Sandra *(a.k.a. Wánměi De Huā)*'s steak was quickly destroyed in her energy converter and added no nutrition to her body. Soon the waitress cleared off their table and brought the check and since Vance was sitting close to the tab, he grabbed it. The meal with all the trimmings for the six cost less than $800.

Vance grabbed one of those fresh $1,000 bills out of his billfold, put it in the pouch and when the waitress came back momentarily with coffee which Gus, Beverly and Roger all were drinking, Vance handed the tab to the waitress.

VANCE
Keep the change.

As the waitress went back to the cashier, she was overjoyed to see she had just earned a $200 tip for 40 minutes' worth of work. That happens in Vegas, but not all that often recently with a recent slack in tourism.

Gus was suddenly aware Vance had somehow come into a mysterious pile of cash.

GUS
Where did you get all that cash, Vance?

VANCE
I won $10,000 on the blackjack table.

GUS
No shit!

VANCE
Yep. Seemed like I couldn't lose.

VOICEOVER (GUS) THOUGHT
I wonder if the alien Sandra (a.k.a. Wánměi De Huā)
somehow intervened for the benefit of Vance and if she
did, then how did she do it?

The group then got up and as they were leaving the restaurant, Roger announced:

ROGER
Our entertainment is in this hotel; so, we do not need
to go anywhere.

<u>INT. EVENING. CASARS PALACE PERFORMANCE THEATER.</u>

Roger led the group as they made their way to a line that was forming for the performance of the music group *Chicago*.

It appeared that Alex came through for them and got them good seats for the show where they were not too close but close enough to get a good look at the band.

In due course, the band *Chicago* played many of their iconic songs. Vance grew up listening to the *Chicago* music performers group.

Not all the original band members were left. The band had evolved over the years and sadly some members had departed the group when they should have stayed. Others left due to age, taking a grip on their lives.

CHICAGO MUSIC CLIPS DURING THE VOICEOVER:

Chicago Greatest Hits Full Album 2024 - The Best Of Chicago Playlist Of All Time

Chicago - Live '93 Greek Theatre Concert

VOICEOVER

The brass section of the band gave it a dimension that added transcendental reality and had a surreal effect on Sandra (a.k.a. Wánměi De Huā).

Sandra (a.k.a. Wánměi De Huā) now analyzed these Earth people and determined they were far more special than she previously considered. Suddenly this trip Sandra made to Earth for Vance so he could reconnect with his native culture, became more meaningful to her as well.

Song after song, the band Chicago's acoustics resonated Sandra's psyche.

Sandra realized that even though Měngjiàng Yún-Rén worlds had a million years of more development beyond these Earth musicians, the fundamental fabric of their complex society created a sense of mystery.

The lyrics of one of the songs struck **Sandra** *(a.k.a. Wánměi De Huā) as they struck her when some of them encapsulated how Vance had traveled and experienced events in his life.*

The CIA people would one day get to view amazing moments in Vance's life thanks to Sandra's special capability as she had the means to pull out Vances vivid memories and transfer them via her telepathic

*transceivers and put the imagery up on a holograph
they could view.*

<u>EXT. CGI. SPACE. VIKI'S SCOUT CLASS SPACECRAFT BLOWING UP. 20
SECONDS, INCLUDING HUNDREDS OF LASERS STRIKING THE SCOUT
JUST BEFORE IT BLEW UP.</u>

VOICEOVER (continued.)
*One image that gripped the CIA viewers was Viki, a
captain of a Scout Class Spaceship blowing up from
savage hits by Anarchie lasers.*

<u>EXT. CGI. SPACE. VANCES BATTLE CRUIESR SPACECRAFT BLOWING UP.
20 SECONDS, INCLUDING HUNDREDS OF LASERS STRIKING THE BATTLE
CRUIESR JUST BEFORE IT BLEW UP.</u>

VOICEOVER (continued.)
*Sandra also pulled out the destruction of the Mergenky
Battle Cruiser Vance almost perished on. It was mildly
unnerving to the CIA viewers who got a taste of the
future they might experience themselves.*

*Vance knew something these CIA people failed to
recognize: Earth could be the next Jeeapa if powerful
Aliens showed up.*

*Those special presentations were for the future, for
now they would just enjoy the music.*

Earth people caused **Sandra** *(a.k.a. Wánměi De Huā)
a compelling curiosity with an alluring quality making
her presence even more dynamic as it all unfolded.*

When **Sandra** *(a.k.a. Wánměi De Huā) ordered her
security detail back to the Měngjiàng Yún-Rén Royal
Yacht soon after they arrived at Area 51, the crew was
not overly concerned.*

*Unlike Vance they did not require a shuttle craft to
retrieve Sandra's (a.k.a. Wánměi De Huā) from the
planet or send down extra bodyguards.*

*Měngjiàng Yún-rén bodies were developed perfectly for
a transporter. Hence, they could instantly materialize*

next to her to intervene in any circumstance that presents itself.

Just like all Měngjiàng Yún-Rén, Sandra (a.k.a. Wánměi De Huā) had implants. Sandra's well-being was being tracked closely on the mother ship with several hundred shock troops instantly ready to deploy via transporters if she was threatened in any way.

The elders did not approve of Sandra's adventure on Earth, but they could not overcome her strong will and mastership of manipulating the Royal Court and always getting her way.

Sandra's (a.k.a. Wánměi De Huā) implanted sensors and transmitters in her body were constantly sending signals to the Měngjiàng Yún-Rén Royal Yacht which had no issues detecting and processing.

Aside from being able to receive danger reports, the *Měngjiàng Yún-Rén Royal Yacht* also received good reports.

When Sandra's (a.k.a. *Wánměi De Huā*) psychology was performing at its maximum potential, experiencing splendid euphoria like she now exhibited, those positive impulses received on the mother ship added great happiness to *Wánměi De Huā's* chamberlain *Drago*.

Drago, who was Wánměi De Huā's most trusted associate, was, nevertheless, the source of constant agony because *Drago* was always counseling *Wánměi De Huā Shèngdà Dá Qiè Sī* on her duties and responsibilities.

***

FLASHBACK:

When tough decisions such as the time *Drago* informed *Wánměi De Huā* actions she just take concerning the *Lout*, the emotions became intense.

DRAGO

Wánměi De Huā you must wipe out these three
planets of *Lout* migrants who are encroaching upon
the Empire.

WÁNMĚI DE HUĀ
Mass slaughter is illogical to me

DRAGO
Migrants from the *Lout* civilization act like locusts and
if not checked now, in a few more centuries they will
expand to the point that removal might no longer be
an option.

EXPLANATION OF HOW THE LOUT IMPACTED *WÁNMĚI DE HUĀ'S* COSMIC
DEVELOPMENT.

The Lout civilization was not too different than Earth carbon-based beings and
technologically was several thousand years more advanced than Earth. If you traveled
to Lout overpopulated cities, you would think you were in Calcutta, Guangzhou,
Karachi, London, Paris, New York, or other densely populated cities on Earth.

Over thousands of years Měngjiàng Yún-Rén ambassadors calmly pleaded with the
Lout to enact population control and to stop expanding closer to their Empire.

But due to Lout internal pressures, greed, avarice, and imperialist objectives, and in the
face of Lout expansion, they posed a threat by more modern and capable interstellar
ships, it was only a matter of time for the big showdown.

The Lout offspring were not welcomed in the star system they came from. Their raw
presence wore thin any interstellar cooperation and patience as they were viewed by
competing entities as an unwelcome party since they never fulfilled or carried out any
agreement ever negotiated.

Lout stubbornness and transcendence towards appearing as nothing more than
interstellar locusts plundering and leaving to waste formerly pristine planets in the
process was legendary, and due time wore out their welcome wherever they relocated.

During their mass migration of 54 centuries the Lout moved into a direction that
seemingly was void of life, mainly because the Měngjiàng Yún-Rén did not like to
telegraph their presence or deal with the complications of interstellar relationships and
agreements that often failed and led to galactic-scale conflicts.

*Wánměi De Huā went through a period of great sorrow after she watched from the
Měngjiàng Yún-Rén command ship the numerous sorties of assault craft systematically
bomb the semi-defenseless Lout.*

*Such conflicts were not too different than what happened on Mars two hundred
and fifty million years ago when the Martians were wiped out by 2 huge Hydrogen
Bombs fried the planet and all its inhabitants as well as ripping off its atmosphere,
leaving behind vast destruction that had since then weathered to the point of not being
recognized by space probes.*

The few Martians that managed to make it to Earth which at the time was a wild semi-uninhabited galactic zoological reserve landed in what is now central China and spread out from there. Several other primitive races of people existed around that same time, and they eventually discovered each other, some of which wiped out the others or interbred, creating new species.

The North American extinction event took care of most of the tall red headed giants living there, but the mass migration over the Bering Straits, which was a dry lakebed during an Ice Age, brought in the former Martian hoards that eventually wiped out any last trace of the North American red head giants.

Advanced beings also visited Earth from time to time and enslaved some of the native population so they could use them in mineral extraction which had a focus on gold, platinum, and other precious or rare materials.

From those extraterrestrial visits, spawned Jews, Germans, and Japanese because of interbreeding and DNA modifications to produce a more advanced workforce to make a more highly efficient mineral extraction operations. Evolution took care of the rest.

The extermination of the Lout was complete. Post-extinction protocol visits surveyed the wasted planets with great precision to ensure the complete eradication. However, the psychological wounds Wánměi De Huā and many Měngjiàng Yún-Rén developed as they analyzed their handiwork would most likely preclude any similar future operation.

It was not long afterwards that Vance's Mergenky Battle Cruiser spaceship was blown apart and Vance was miraculously rescued. Soon after Vance arrived at Měngjiàng Yún-Rén Empire, Wánměi De Huā became aware, and curiosity peaked.

Drago introduced Vance to Wánměi De Huā and when that curiosity expanded into more interest, Drago used that new experience to help shift Wánměi De Huā's dire psychological condition from Lout remorse into a new invigorated interest and subsequent bonding.

As her role as the chamberlain, Drago shielded Wánměi De Huā from the royal court's politics and possible intrigues by those members who were not receptive towards a Měngjiàng Yún-Rén experiencing extraterrestrial interrelationships.

Drago just needed Vance for a while to make sure Wánměi De Huā did not end up doing something foolish because of her great Lout remorse.

Drago realized Vance had a rather limited lifespan, and would be gone in due time, hence was just another pawn in the game of highly evolved Royal politics and the Měngjiàng Yún-Rén were not immune from intrigue or palace upheaval like Earth had also experienced in its history.

Drago observed Wánměi De Huā slowly accumulated the sophistication and great understanding that would one day allow her to evolve into the Měngjiàng Yún-Rén leader that could sustain any attempted royal court's conspiracies that usually happened at least once or twice during their reign.

Drago was also mindful that Wánměi De Huā's lifespan was only half over, but Drago would expire in a few more centuries and time was critical that she prepared the young Měngjiàng Yún-Rén Empress to manage palace affairs on her own after Drago's natural exit.

During the most critical moment, simply by the act of this unexpected encounter in deep space with the dying Earth man Vance, the Empire was spared from a potential crisis had such a catalyst not suddenly presented itself.

Drago felt it was kind of ironic that Vance, a man from an inferior alien civilization, came to the rescue after they had wiped out the Lout.

***

<u>INT. EVENING. CASARS PALACE PERFORMANCE THEATER.</u>

As the band Chicago played more songs, Sandra (a.k.a. *Wánměi De Huā*), probing Vance's psyche, felt his invigoration and the subtle effects the music had on him.

The modulation of trombones and trumpets backed up by the perfect choreography of the saxophone advanced Vance's emotional personification by the impact the melody, also influenced emotions exploding inside Sandra.

The complicated feedback mechanism and spontaneous evocation soon intensified those emotions which resulted in a sense of splendid euphoria atypical of anything Sandra felt, including their period of body fusion which she thought up till now was the ultimate experience.

Each time the band hit a crescendo, Sandra exhibited those similar reactions enhanced by the vibrations of the unique brass instruments. The orchestra backup and the several pianos and electric organs added to the sound in a very unusual manner that brought forth the sizzle to the entertainment that now provided quintessential effects.

When it all ended, the crowd responded most favorably enticing several curtain calls and more applause, then the crowd started slowly exiting the show room and dispersed into the lobby and throughout the casino located adjacent to the performance.

Roger looked towards Beverly walking by his side.

ROGER
Wasn't that concert great?

BEVERLY
Yes, it was such a fantastic performance.

VANCE
What's next?

GUS
We got tickets to a comedy show which is right around the corner.

VOICE OVER
Soon the group sitting together was busting a gut in laughter as the jokes poured on.

Sandra had never experienced anything like comedy before, and since her experience with humans was highly limited, she didn't have the psychological profile and experiences in life to equate to what the human's thought were funny, and considered it mildly as mass hysteria.

What do you call a pig that does karate? A pork chop.

Nevertheless, she took quite an interest in how this performance affected everyone, usually in a similar way. She wasn't laughing but she smiled out of politeness and situational awareness to blend in as much as possible.

What do you call a musician with problems? A trebled man.

***

After the comedy show, the group hit one of the numerous bars in Caesars, and had a few drinks and conversations, then called it a night.

Gus, Roger, Beverly, and Crystal all went to their separate rooms where they did their own thing, mainly emailing and calling on friends and relatives, reading books, watching TV, taking Hollywood showers (15 minutes' worth or longer), and slowly wound down.

Meanwhile, as Vance was also winding down in his hotel room. Sandra suddenly dematerialized back into her Native fairy like green body flapping her wings.

Sandra (a.k.a. *Wánměi De Huā*)
Vance, what would you like to do next?

Vance was flipping through TV channels and paused momentarily on one that had porn video going on, and then he suddenly felt self-aware with Sandra's presence and flipped to another channel.

Sandra (a.k.a. *Wánměi De Huā*)
Why did you stop watching, the woman looked beautiful and passionate?

Vance lied:

VANCE
I'm not sure.

Sandra (a.k.a. *Wánměi De Huā*) immediately developed a sudden idea to please Vance and because of her vast memory, she suddenly rematerialized into a beautiful young Asian lady appearing identical to the one Vance had just monitored in the porn video, and then approached him.

Sandra's (a.k.a. *Wánměi De Huā*) curiosity to establish a thorough understanding of human females, as she passed by multitudes of women passing by in the hallways and throughout her travels in Las Vegas, Sandra probed their minds and obtained their most deep thoughts and secrets and explored the complicated social structures and how women reacted and were affected.

Sandra's (a.k.a. *Wánměi De Huā*) obtain the psychophysical and motor functions that were associated with the female's human experience. That critical knowledge and the combination of sensing all of Vance's thoughts enabled Sandra (a.k.a. *Wánměi De Huā*) to create an artificial lover that Vance would not know wasn't 100% real.

In this finely tuned composition and choreography of artificial reality Sandra (a.k.a. Wánměi De Huā) created, Vance's senses and psychological reactions were as if was copulating with a living Earth person.

The impact exemplified by Sandra's surreal manifestation providing Vance love making with a beautiful Asian lady soon caused Vance to capitulate and transcend to the most expansive splendid euphoric orgasm his primitive brain was able to accomplish as his brain produced increased levels of oxytocin, dopamine, and serotonin.

On this night as the *Měngjiàng Yún-rén* fusion process began, Sandra's emotions were engulfed in a sea of tranquility and her bio sensors reported this condition to Drago.

Those members of Sandra's (a.k.a. *Wánměi De Huā)* court that were also present, suddenly took a significant interest in this Earth person Vance who had spontaneously galvanized a surreal fusion, like none of them had ever experienced before.

As the fusion reached that critical state where the two souls were touching, the distinctive *memories* of the brass section crescendos of the band *Chicago* created that biofeedback that eclipsed all else and enamored Sandra's soul where that criticality held them in an almost plasma like state for several hours.

The visual perception if someone was watching almost appeared like a mini black hole right in the center of the room with a miniature replica of a Magellanic Stream that evaporated slowly into light blue cylinders of light that slowly twisted around and radiated outwards as the two lay in the fusion state in an almost catatonic state. [Magellanic Stream - Wikipedia]

Finally, Sandra knew it was time to exit this fusion state so as to not risk damage to Vance's soul. Sandra (a.k.a. *Wánměi De Huā)* then exited Vance's body and rematerialized as that young beautiful Asian lady that resembled the lady on the TV a few hours before.

Vance slowly succumbed to a restful sleep. His physiology had hit the perfect quiescence that placed him in almost a coma state he would slowly come out of and into human awareness after a good number of peaceful sleeps.

Wánměi De Huā) only slept once a month during her energy recharging that took place for a few hours.

While Sandra (a.k.a. *Wánměi De Huā)* was in this precarious state, only the Chamberlain was allowed alone with her. But as Sandra (a.k.a. *Wánměi De Huā)* requested Drago, she ushered Vance to her private chamber to allow him to watch the process.

No other being was ever permitted to watch this process. It was essential for Sandra's (a.k.a. *Wánměi De Huā)* long reign and the process must be kept quite secret for the maintenance of society.

Since Vance had been chosen to be her most important person, the exception was not only given to him, but Sandra knew that once Drago was gone, she would be on her own and rely on Vance until she was able to accept a new chamberlain that only Drago could determine worthy and acceptable to the young Empress.

Under normal circumstances, when a fusion and later official unification took place with a *Měngjiàng Yún-Rén Empress*, the chamberlain was not required to perform this function since *Wánměi De Huā's* father the emperor was available to handle those matters.

***

Alex wasted little time in contacting Boris Potemkin. Alex had a hunch and thought now would be the time to earn some extra cash to pay down his gambling debt which was starting to cause a negative drain on his day-to-day life as it became increasingly a burden.

The number was readily available on his smart phone as he called while making some rounds to show his presence to the casino employees who always provided a subtle reminder their performance was always being watched and it would not be in their best interest to work with a guest in beating the system in any way.

Sudden departures had sometimes been the subject of discussions as rumors spread after an employee came up missing, they might have made the fatal blunder of getting caught greasing their own palms or assisting someone for a reasonable kickback.

VOICEOVER

The recent case of Rodriguez, though difficult to explain at first, was an easy one to solve for Alex as he knew he was somehow being taken by individuals hanging out with people he knew to be CIA agents.

The women were somewhat new to him, and he had no doubt they knew their business and had a role to play.

As Alex watched the videos of them, the woman who had been at the blackjack table seemed out of place and he just couldn't figure it out.

The dude she hung around with at the blackjack table, and appeared to take great interest in, was not the CIA type he was accustomed to meeting, as he looked far too timid and not physically up to the challenge.

Alex spoke after hearing Boris answer the call.

ALEX
Hello Boris.

Boris, looking down at the caller I.D. showing up on his I-phone, answered.

BORIS
Yes Alex, what do you want?

ALEX
I think I got something you want.

BORIS
Oh really?

ALEX
Yep, straight out of Area-51.

The mere mention of Area-51 instantly caused a sudden jerk in Boris who responded.

BORIS
When can we meet?

ALEX
Any time, I'm working today.

BORIS
How about my favorite slot machine?

ALEX
Sure, I'll see you there.

BORIS
I'll be over there in a while, need to take care of a little
matter first, should not take long.

ALEX
Ok, bye.

The conversation ended then Boris set his I-phone down on his bed stand next to him then looked over at the attractive 22-year-old who was all smiles and ready to continue.

BORIS
Now where were we?

The young lady smiled and dipped below the covers and commenced to *soft off* Boris in ways he was willing to pay nicely.

***

Gus and his associates on the other hand exhibited the essence of an undercover type of agent prepared for multiple tasks with the tools and means to carry it out.

Alex had seen Gus working out in the hotel gym a few times and saw he was extraordinarily fit with strength and endurance necessary to achieve personal defense when the time came, since not all violence perpetrated included firearms.

In some cases, it was not permissible to have a firearm due to the location and the circumstance they were in that might be life threatening.

Gus in his vast training knew that just about anything could be a weapon in one form or another. He also knew that he had to gravely injure his opponent in a very efficient and timely manner because adversaries often did not travel alone, and one of the possible many had to be dispatched in time to receive the next attacker which often materialized in the line of business he was in.

The scenarios Gus sometimes experienced were far different than most of his colleagues who worked for DD/P. They were usually engaged with Russian, Chinese, Eastern European, Arab, and sometimes Japanese or Korean organized crime figures that required great skill and tenacity to overcome when the situations presented themselves.

Due to Gus and Roger's unique assignments out in Area 51, from time to time they had the experience none of the other agents except a few like Beverly and Crystal would experience, when they were brought in to deal with an Alien event.

Great care and patience were required especially since at any moment the Aliens like Grak and Struyograb could be at each other's throats in the process of killing one another.

It was not entirely unusual for Gus or Roger to have to step between two Aliens to prevent a situation from getting out of hand.

But also, a lot of the scientists and engineers working on the reverse engineering of wrecked alien spacecraft were nerds who didn't have the means nor the appetite to attempt to defend themselves from some of the Aliens.

Even though the Grey Aliens rarely stood more than 4 feet tall, they almost terrorized these physically and emotionally weak scientists merely by their presence.

Several of the scientists involved in Area 51 *Crashed Alien Spacecraft Reverse Engineering Program* were handpicked and recruited out of Cal Tech or Princeton and sometimes MIT where the best and brightest educated.

Cal Tech provided the majority since it was well known to be a feeder school for NASA.

A number of these *Nerds* started out as engineers and scientists who thought they were going to help design America's future spaceships. After the nerds were hired and cleared in the program for a while, were sent incrementally to Area 51.

At Area 51 the nerds often discovered the unfortunate nature of their career choice.

Since disclosure would inflict a great deal of punishment, leaving many in fear, but also fear itself from being around Aliens whom anyone would be ridiculed in public for suggesting Aliens existed.

VOICEOVER

Dealing with Alien technology and sometimes Alien interface was a thankless job, and any new technology derived from reverse engineering went straight to Majestic 12 committee who decided what corporation was going to get it.

Majestic 12 initially created by Edward Teller under presidential executive order by President Truman, had the highest levels of security clearance and the heaviest penalties to anyone who violated the committee's determination and viewed as acting outside of discretion given them.

Even though Edward Teller was long gone and no longer had a presence in Majestic 12, only one person remained that had been part of the committee back then, David Rockefeller also recently passed away.

The guidance and intent of the program set down by Majestic 12 remained constant without any deviation because that committee would not back down in its recommendations.

People such as Henry Kissinger and much later Richard Nixon also kept the same standards and discipline and every president since Truman followed the Majestic 12 recommendations with executive orders except one, President John F. Kennedy.

Kennedy was rumored to have received the ultimate consequences when he angered Majestic 12 by the proclamation, he would start the process of disclosure including disclosing Project Serpo, the personnel exchange with an Alien civilization from planet Serpo that existed on a planet approximately ten light years away.

People that Gus knew long retired had been sent out to Area 51 to get a complete briefing package to bring back to Kennedy who had planned to use it during a televised presidential address to the nation that was going to disclose the exchange of scientists that was planned to live on this alien world Serpo for a dozen years to learn from them advanced concepts including interstellar travel capability.

Since the head of the CIA had always been a member of the Majestic 12, Allen Dulles, had reacted very negatively and during a shouting match with Kennedy and was summarily fired, leaving Kennedy with no other option other than using the Bay of Pigs scandal as the chief reason for the termination.

Recent conspiracy theory indicates that Bissell, Angleton, Tracy Barnes and others supported Allen Dulles in his view that disclosure would cause major upheaval in society.

Apparently, Dulles reacted positively when a group of retired military officers in New Orleans and as indicated by various writers and researchers stated in their books that rich oil men in Texas approached people closely associated with Majestic 12 with the idea to eliminate Kennedy for a variety of reasons. Chief among the reasons Majestic 12 considered was the planned Project Serpo Alien disclosure.

Majestic 12 then had all the cover it needed. With retired military and rich oil men in position to be the fall guys in case anything went wrong, the plan to remove Kennedy advanced swiftly.

The first attempt in Miami was thwarted by secret service personnel who were not only patriotic but were also very professional and took their presidential escort assignment very seriously.

The next attempt also failed as the presidential driver was temporarily lost and turned a block too early which was just one block from the kill zone in Chicago.

By the time Kennedy went to Dallas, a different driver and another quite different secret service detachment was assigned to make sure things did not get screwed up because Lyndon Johnson was due in Federal Court the following week on major corruption scandals with Bobby Baker and Billy Sol Estes. Hence time was running out.

The planning to remove Kennedy needed Johnson who conspiracy theorists claim was a willing participant to foster the cover-up and protection necessary after the fact.

Ostensibly since Nixon had been a member of Majestic 12 and a longtime associate of the CIA and good friends with the principal Texas oilmen contributors for the $2 million necessary to pay Sam Giancana for the hit.

Nixon was chosen to be the courier of the money from Texas to his designated CIA interface who was waiting for him out in California the day before the assassination. The agent then flew the Cash in Advance money directly to Chicago in an unmarked private Jet the company often used for clandestine operations.

Chicago mobster Sam Giancana's brother Chuck, has written extensively on his brother's involvement in the assassination in the book Double Cross. *The 15-minute missing section of the Watergate tapes had barely been erased before the congressional hearing representatives along with Justice Department employees took possession of the Nixon tapes.*

Majestic 12 had ordered that section of the tapes erased since in it Nixon was having a discussion with E. Howard Hunt who was blackmailing him at the time to get a presidential pardon for his involvement in the Watergate building break in.

The most damaging information erased on the tape included Hunt telling Nixon that he "knew Giancana and the New Orleans mobster Marcello had hired Lucien Sarti and 2 other Corsican accomplices to do the hit and that he knew Nixon personally hand carried the money from Clint M. to his CIA contact out in CA the day before the assassination to make the payment.

Alien disclosure was not going to happen any time soon.

Later it was alleged by some conspiracy theorists that when President Bill Clinton shared ideas about disclosure and his wife Hillary blabbed the intent to a CIA mole that worked in the White House and close to the Clintons and had been involved in the drug running out in Mena, Arkansas, the mole tipped off the CIA which Majestic 12 was duly informed.

Word was sent back with a warning that Clinton could have some serious issues if he attempted to do Alien disclosure. Naturally Bill Clinton clammed up and his Monica Lewinsky and Paula Jones sexcapades quickly obscured any desires to bring Aliens to the forefront.

***

Boris, a middle aged, slightly overweight bald FSB (KGB) agent had been assigned to Las Vegas for some time. He had proven his dedication and kept a low profile and seldom participated in gambling so over the years his supervisor and later director, Alexander Bortnikov, developed great confidence in him and his reports.

The little extra funds Boris used for his call girls was well worth the quality as well as the quantity of information Boris extracted from people, he met that worked at Nellis or Area 51.

The few times Boris met someone from Area-51 S-4, including Naval Intelligence Engineer Robert Lazar who discussed things with him, he became quite fascinated.

The old guard KGB back in Moscow kept telling Boris repeatedly the Alien business at Area 51 was just disinformation to hide the fact other activities had gone on such as A12, SR71, SR-72, TR-3B, Have Blue, and the other Have programs. [Lockheed Have Blue - Wikipedia]

Information for Boris giant rabbit hole: [The Area 51 File: Secret Aircraft and Soviet MiGs | National Security Archive]

When Boris eventually was able to provide photographs of the D21 (drone) mounted on the back of the M21 (A12 spy plane), taking off from the runway at Groom Lake, the KGB no longer criticized his interests if it continued to provide such tantalizing INTEL.

That program which was used to design and test scram jets and high-speed drones for Intelligence gathering behind enemy lines, and for future military applications, was canceled after the 2nd crash killing all onboard the M21, which was a modified A-12, the forerunner of SR-71. [Lockheed D-21 - Wikipedia]

D21

Later that day, Boris' dream come true encounter happened most unexpectedly. An older gentleman who seemed to have a disposition of a "bent trash can" was sitting at Boris' favorite slot machine, which he had picked out that had great observation of all the approaches to it and nothing behind him so that he could always fully maintain situational awareness.

Being somewhat anxious because he was expecting Alex at any time with another hot lead, he politely approached the gentleman.

BORIS
Sir, if you don't mind, would it be possible for me
to use this slot machine, because I always meet my
girlfriend here, and it's kind of like my favorite.

Boyd Bushman looked up at Boris with a *you got to be kidding me* look and responded.

BOYD BUSHMAN
There must be a half dozen empty slots right over
there, why not just go there?

Boris, being a skillful manipulator and recruiter, spotted a Lockheed tie-clasp the gentleman in a suit was wearing and suddenly viewed the situation slightly differently.

<u>CEASAR'S PALACE CASINO SLOT MACHINE AREA.</u>

NOTE: during the voice over Borris is watching Boyd Bushman playing the slot machine.

VOICEOVER (BORIS) THOUGHT
*Obviously, this man is dressed up as if he were going
somewhere important. Alex will probably come along
shortly with some more stale piss, but this situation
presents an unexpected opportunity.*

Boris an INTEL gatherer and a recruiter for the KGB and later FSB which replaced the KGB when the Russian government combined the KGB with the Border Guards, Boris just could not go do cold calls.

Otherwise, it would quite possibly expose him and make him subject to possible negative consequences.

On the other hand, when a target of opportunity suddenly manifested out of thin air, such as Boyd Bushman wearing a Lockheed tie clasp, Boris knew it was like a gift from heaven.

Aside from this man possibly a person of interest the mere fact he was in Las Vegas not far from Nellis or Area 51 suggested there might be some worthwhile information that could be obtained in this unexpected encounter.

The other unique aspect of this encounter was the location of that very slot machine allowed the surveillance necessary to ensure nobody would be listening in, possibly compromising what might occur during the spy recruitment and interview process.

BORIS
I see you got a Lockheed emblem on your tie clasp.

BOYD BUSHMAN
Yea that's right?

BORIS
Do you know Kelly Johnson?

Boyd Bushman
Who doesn't?

BORIS
Ever work with Ben Rich?

BOYD BUSHMAN
Hell, I taught him everything he ever knew about propulsion.

BORIS
No kidding, are you some sort of engineer?

BOYD BUSHMAN
You might say that.

BORIS
Wow that's fantastic, I love airplanes.

Boyd then looked at Boris in a very condescending manner and asked:

BOYD BUSHMAN
Are you a tourist or do you live here?

BORIS
Oh, I live here, been here ever since the 1970s.

BOYD BUSHMAN
Really, what do you do?

BORIS
I own a liquor store in downtown Vegas.

BOYD BUSHMAN
That's probably a good business to be in for this Town.

BORIS
I make a good consistent income, enough money to come here and play the slots every week.

BOYD BUSHMAN
Do you ever make any money playing the slots?

BORIS
No, I usually lose my ass, but I think the casino lets me win now and then just to keep me coming back!

Boyd chuckled about that.

BORIS
You're all dressed up; don't see too many people wearing suits in here unless they just came from a wedding or a funeral.

Boyd responded with a hint of Texas drawl in some of his words.

BOYD BUSHMAN
Well, I just came from a conference a bit ago.

BORIS
Some sort of professional seminar?

BOYD BUSHMAN
Oh no, nothing like that, in fact Lockheed looks down upon my recent activities.

BORIS
Why is that?

BOYD BUSHMAN
Well, I've decided to come clean on a few matters.

BORIS
Such as?

BOYD BUSHMAN
Aliens.

Suddenly Boris felt an exhilaration like few would know. He realized the public would consider Boyd a freaky character, but the aggressive, old fashion type personality told Boris something different.

Boris also knew this man didn't get his Lockheed tie clasp being some doofus, that this was a genuine target, and he just said the magic word, *Alien.*

VOICEOVER (BORIS) THOUGHT
You cannot simply imagine a total stranger like this
suddenly sitting in the interview chair; this is far too
good to be true.

Suddenly Alex descended upon them and Boris gave him a friendly welcome and under his breath quietly said in a way that Boyd could not hear with the music and slot machine noise going on in the background.

BORIS
I'm with a prospective client, could you come back in
about 15 minutes?

Alex nodded then walked away, noticing the man with the suit and that most likely with Boris' background something not good would come of all that.

Boris then stepped back over next to Boyd

BORIS
Sir, do you believe in Aliens?"

BOYD BUSHMAN
Absolutely, in fact I've seen them.

BORIS
Is that so?

Those words dug deeply into Boris's psyche as he had felt that since his interview with Robert Lazar a few years back, the American government was covering up far more than the public was aware.

In his heart, Boris also felt that the Russian Government and people such as Alexander Bortnikov and General Alexi Shoygu knew far more about extraterrestrial activity than what they were willing to reveal.

BORIS
What do they look like?

BOYD BUSHMAN
The ones I've seen are about 3 to 4 feet tall, have a large head, small torso and small arms and legs and stink like hell. You almost want to throw up the first time you smell them."

BORIS
Did you discuss these Aliens at the conference?

BOYD BUSHMAN
A little, but I was not able to present much of my materials since there is evidently a group there that purposely does not want this to get out, cutting my time short.

BORIS
That's too bad. Do you have any evidence of what you are claiming?

Boyd smiled then grabbed his pouch next to him that was jammed full of items and pulled out a photograph.

BOYD BUSHMAN
Here's one of them?

Boris was stunned and a chill went up his spine as the photograph was taken in a lab and the detail and realism in it surely could not have been faked.

BORIS
Where did you take this photograph?

BOYD BUSHMAN
I didn't, one of my associates at Area 51 took it and passed it on to me.

BORIS
I see.

Then Boris doing some fast thinking pulled out a business card to his legitimate liquor store which provided him with a needed great cover and alias to shield him from possible government investigators, since he was an "illegal" not here under diplomatic protection.

Boris handed his business card to Boyd Bushman.

BORIS

Here's my card, anytime you want a free bottle of liquor stop by my shop and I'd love to talk to you about these aliens.

BOYD BUSHMAN

Sounds good, but I will not be in Las Vegas for very long.

BORIS

I think this is an incredible story, and I think the public has the right to know, but we know how secret the government is and want to keep all of us dumb.

BOYD BUSHMAN
You got that right.

Then Boyd gave Boris another gift that was keenly not anticipated. He handed Boris a 3 by 5 card that had the name Michael and his contact information including phone number and email address

BOYD BUSHMAN

Call this guy and have him tell you about the CIA guy he interviewed who was sent out to Area 51 by President Eisenhower to find out what was really going on at area 51.

Boris took the card then asked:

BORIS

Are you going to be in Vegas a while in case I want to get in touch with you?

BOYD BUSHMAN

No, I'm leaving in a couple days heading back to Fort Worth.

BORIS

That's too bad, I would really love to discuss this with you further, but I need to get back to my liquor store before the employee there goes home for the day so I can close out the books.

Boris held out his hand to shake Boyd's.

BORIS
It's truly been a pleasure meeting you. By the way,
what did you say your name was again?

BOYD BUSHMAN
Boyd Bushman.

BORIS
Ok Boyd, I'm Jack, it was nice meeting you. Are you
staying in the hotel here?

BOYD BUSHMAN
Certainly.

BORIS
Great hotel to stay in, I hope you get lucky and have a
good trip home.

BOYD BUSHMAN
Thanks, will do.

Boris then turned and then started walking through the Casino to the far side and out
of the shadows, Alex approached him.

Alex gave Boris a serious look.

ALEX
We need to talk about a few things.

BORIS
I'm available now; what's up?

ALEX
No not here, meet me across the street at the Flamingo
Casino Bar in 15 minutes, we'll talk there.

It was around Alex's break time, so he went up to the Video room and approached
Guido.

ALEX
I'm taking off for some lunch, and I'll be back in a half
hour or so.

GUIDO

See you when you get back, we need to talk about a
few things then.

ALEX
Sure.

Alex turned around and left.

Boris made his way across the pedestrian bridge going over Las Vegas Blvd, and the stairs down, where he came upon the two Flamingo girls that were often out there.

Boris took out a $20 and stuffed it down the blonde's top and, in the process, was able to see a little more than just cleavage. The girl didn't mind, she enjoyed getting those $20 bills from that dirty old man several times a week, which always paid for her lunch money.

The Casino was half empty and most of the bar seats were available, so Boris picked one at the end where he had good observation and some seclusion. He quickly could sense the bartender, his acquaintance Phil, whom he saw often was perturbed; he sat all the way at the end of the bar forcing him to walk down to the end to serve him.

PHIL
Want the usual Jack?

BORIS
Sure.

Jack was Boris' nickname and preferred name used on the strip, given to him by some of his buddies. Since he was in the liquor business Mr. Jack Daniels was given to him as kind of a joke at first, but it stuck.

About the time Phil served Jack's drink, Alex showed up and sat down beside him. Phil also knew Alex from many trips to this bar where he boozed up women and lubricated them for future events later in the evening.

Phil asked as he also knew Alex's favorite.

Phil
Miller Light?

Alex
Yes please

PHIL
You got it.

Phil always knew Jack and Alex were up to some shady business so he moved down to the other end of the bar; so, he could avoid hearing what the two were discussing. He began routine house cleaning since there was no crowd to serve and it was early in the day.

Now that the two had an element of privacy, Boris asked:

BORIS
So, what was so urgent about the phone call earlier?

ALEX
I got some information you might want to hear about."

BORIS
Oh yea, what is it.

ALEX
Not so fast, this is valuable stuff.

BORIS
You know I'm a generous man.

ALEX
Ok, but you should know I could use the cash and I'm
not feeling good about telling you what I'm about to.

BORIS
How much are we talking?

ALEX
I think this is worth at least $20 Grand.

BORIS
Ok tell me what you have to say, and I'll let you know
if it's worth $20 grand.

ALEX
Yesterday, a couple of CIA guys checked into the hotel
with a group.

BORIS
So? Everyone needs a little vacation now and then.

ALEX
There was a total of 6 of them and I know for a fact
they are here for business of some sort.

Boris started wondering if they were here to eavesdrop on that UFO conference Boyd
was telling him about.

BORIS
Go on.

ALEX
I've done favors for these guys before.

BORIS
Oh yea?

ALEX
In fact, I have their 2 vehicles in our VIP guarded
parking area right now.

BORIS
Is that so?

ALEX
They are concerned about someone tampering with
the vehicles, while they are enjoying Vegas; they knew
where to come to.

BORIS
Just because they're a couple CIA people here having
a good time doesn't mean much.

ALEX
They just came from area 51.

That bit of information suddenly hit Boris real hard as now he realized this truly might
be something significant. Then he said,

BORIS
Do you know what they are doing there?

ALEX

They would never reveal what their work is, but I bet the fact they're nervous about their cars has something to do with it.

BORIS

They are probably fearful someone might put a bug in it.

Boris smiled as new ideas suddenly crept up in his thinking.

ALEX

Must be. But it could be more; they might have some fancy equipment in it.

BORIS

If there is, it's probably well disguised.

ALEX

`So, what do you think?

BORIS

Well, it's probably worth $20 grand but I might need your help in another matter.

ALEX

Such as?

BORIS

Help accessing the cars with all the security you guys have there.

ALEX

I do go out there at a designated time and then to give the guards breaks, we could arrange for you to slip in plumbers while I relieve the guards for an extended break such as lunch or dinner.

BORIS

How long will these CIA people be staying?

ALEX

According to their reservations which I checked on when I printed them out their parking ticket, 2 more days including today.

BORIS

We'll have to act fast, and I'll need to bring in experts. Might be tough to arrange it so quickly, but if I can swing it, do you think you can make certain arrangements for around dinner time tomorrow evening?

ALEX

Sure, how about around 7:00 p.m. tomorrow which is when I often give them breaks, just before I finish work in the evening?

BORIS

I'll call you a little later after I have time to decide what I want to do.

ALEX
Okay.

BORIS

How would you like to double the $20,000?

Alex was suddenly elevated in his attention and quickly responded in a very enthusiastic manner.

ALEX
Of course, what do you have in mind?

BORIS
You have a hotel guest by the name of Boyd Bushman.

ALEX
Okay.

BORIS

He was just at that freaky UFO conference they're having nearby. He has a satchel with him loaded with photographs of aliens and stuff.

ALEX
That's probably all make-believe shit.

BORIS
Maybe, maybe not.

ALEX
So, what are you asking?

BORIS
I've done some good photographing lately with my
I-phone."

ALEX
Me too, I pay all my bills that way.

BORIS
Ok this is what I want you to do, I want you to go in
his room when he's out and photograph all his pictures
with your cell phone and email them too me.

ALEX
That shouldn't be a problem.

BORIS
Remember that old guy with the suit and tie who I was
talking with a while ago, at my favorite slot machine?

ALEX
Yea what about him?

BORIS
That's Boyd Bushman.

ALEX
I see.

***

When Vance woke up in the morning, he almost jumped out of his bed seeing the naked
young Asian lady lying next to him, but his stirring immediately caused Sandra to open
her eyes and look at Vance and talk in that soothing voice Vance was accustomed to.

Sandra (a.k.a. *Wánměi De Huā)*
Did you rest well?

Vance quickly responded as he suddenly remembered how *Wánměi De Huā* seduced
him the night before.

VANCE
I had the most surreal dream, but I never felt better.

Sandra's (a.k.a. *Wánměi De Huā)*
I'm so glad.

Vance then got up and did his normal morning routines that included showering and shaving, then called Gus.

VANCE
Good morning, GUS, I'm getting kind of hungry.

GUS
Why don't we drive over to Boulder City, I know this nice restaurant over there that has excellent food and brew.

VANCE
Sure.

GUS
Ok, I'll get the crew together; leave here in say half an hour?

VANCE
That would be fine.

Vance got dressed, watched some news, made a cup of coffee and looked at the paper the hotel had delivered early this morning.

Meanwhile. Sandra (a.k.a. *Wánměi De Huā)* continued her meditation that she had been doing just before Vance awakened.

Drago was remotely monitoring *Wánměi De Huā* via her telepahtyic transceivers from the *Měngjiàng Yún-Rén Royal Yacht*.

Drago had been Sandra's (a.k.a. *Wánměi De Huā)* chamberlain for over a thousand years, was also her emotional and structural prime assistant.

Drago was almost a surrogate mother to Sandra (a.k.a. *Wánměi De Huā)*, remained pleased at the routine sensor reports, but was becoming alarmed at intelligence reports she also received concerning the eight alien races now secretly inhabiting a bigger portion of earth than the humans were aware of.

Because of the extremely sensitive and powerful *Měngjiàng Yún-Rén* sensors it was impossible for these other aliens to hide from them as well as disguise any of their communications.

Any attempt at encrypting their communications would be extraordinarily ineffective to prevent *Měngjiàng Yún-Rén intercepts and decryptng*.

As more and more of these reports surfaced, Drago decided to send a protection force to Earth to keep a closer eye on Wánměi De Huā and more so for Vance, since he was considerably more fragile.

The secret protection force's spontaneous arrival in the sprawling hotel casino mecca in Las Vegas went by largely unnoticed. With their adaptability and mind probing ability they were very easy to blend in.

Within a few minutes of arrival, the security force reported back via telepathic transceivers surgically installed in their brain a status report.

SECURITY FORCE
COMMANDER.
*In just the span of a few hours we discovered Tall White
and Grey Alien Spies roaming around monitoring
Vance and his group.*

Drago quickly became alarmed.

DRAGO
*You need to establish whether the Tall White or Grey
Aliens plan to try to kidnap Vance or Wánměi De Huā.*

SECURITY FORCE
COMMANDER.
We are attempting to make that determination.

DRAGO
Of the two, only Vance will be a problem due to his
vulnerability and fragileness.

SECURITY FORCE
COMMANDER.
As far as *Wánměi De Huā* was concerned she could
be instantly teleported back to the Royal Yacht along
with any perpetrators that might want to attempt such
foolishness.

***

By the time Gus gathered the group together in the Lobby to head out to Boulder City, the *Měngjiàng Yún-Rén* spies were in place also monitoring telemetry sent by *Wánměi De Huā* monitoring pulses sent from her implants.

Wánměi De Huā monitoring pulses biophysical telemetry data including all her vital signs, also provided real time location in the event they had to do an emergency extraction that would be the case if an enemy Armada suddenly came in from space unexpectedly.

Returning Vance would be problematic because they would have to send the shuttlecraft for him; hence, the need for the *Měngjiàng Yún-Rén* spies to be on hand to manifest that quick recovery.

Within an hour after the *Měngjiàng Yún-Rén* spies' arrival they had obtained all necessary terrestrial support, including transportation allowing them to follow Vance and Wánměi De Huā necessarily at a distance but be close enough to intervene in just about any possible type of crisis that might occur.

Gus led the group to the Valet parking attendant who oversaw the whole operation and didn't have to ask any questions. The facial recognition software had identified all six guests and their two vehicles in the VIP parking, and he simply stated

VALET PARKING
ATTENDANT
Mr. Vandyke, your cars will be here momentarily.

Alex, who was now back in the video monitor room, got the security request immediately from the parking attendant to allow the guests to receive the cars. Such protocols made car theft there virtually impossible.

This did however present a form of logistics problem for Alex who wanted to earn his extra $20,000 that afternoon, so he immediately picked up the telephone receiver and clicked the icon on his computer display that ran the parking lot attendant.

The head valet parking attendant knew that phone call was coming from the control room based on the warning he now saw on his computer screen of an important incoming call and from who it was.

VALET PARKING
ATTENDANT
Yes Alex, what do you need?

ALEX
Ask Mr. Vandyke when he expects to return so I can
make sure I have 2 good spots reserved for his cars.

VALET PARKING
ATTENDANT
Sure, one moment please.

Alex could hear over the phone the attendant asks Gus:

VALET PARKING
ATTENDANT
Excuse me, Mr. Vandyke, my boss Alex wants to know
when you plan on returning, so he can make sure he
has two good spots reserved for your cars when you
get back?

Gus just guessing announced:

GUS
We might be taking a helicopter tour as part of this
sojourn to Boulder City. I think we should be back
by 6:00 p.m. because we reserved a couple shows
reserved and will want to get some dinner beforehand.

Alex, who had heard it all, cut off the attendant when he started to repeat it back.

ALEX
I heard him say around 6:00, tell him thank you and
send them on their way.

As the two CIA SUVs turned right onto Las Vegas Boulevard the *Měngjiàng Yún-Rén Spies* who now kept the group under constant surveillance, had the advantage of communicating either telepathically or via the telepathic converter implanted in their brains which went a long distance.

Since *Měngjiàng Yún-Rén Spies* had direct links via the Royal Yacht that was also configured as a Command Ship, the Since *Měngjiàng Yún-Rén Spies* also received all communications and if they were within approximately 100 miles or so, got direct broadcast from *Wánměi De Huā* communications implants.

As such, the *Měngjiàng Yún-Rén Spies* were able to hear on a real time basis everything she heard as well, which means they already knew where the group was heading.

A short distance and moments later the car swung right as it passed the MGM Hotel and Casino, and before long had eased onto the interstate 15 freeway heading south. Gus in the lead car, exited on the Henderson Turnoff and before long was bearing down on Henderson which they passed through.

Eventually the 515-freeway ended, and Gus drove the SUV east on 93 until he got downtown Boulder City.

Highway 93 eventually comes to a point where it makes a 90-degree left turn but if you drive straight ahead, the road becomes Nevada Way, which the 2-car caravan traveled.

A half dozen blocks later, they turned into Arizona Street and shortly into the diagonal parking in front of the Dillinger restaurant where they were going to eat.

Vance, being mindful of today's events, thought it was prudent before he left the hotel, broke a couple of his $1000 bills into $100s and a few $20s to make it easy to do business.

Vance, Sandra (a.k.a. *Wánměi De Huā)*, and the four CIA agents were soon seated and enjoying some fresh brewed coffee, though Roger, knowing this place also had craft beer, decided to sample a *Brew Dog Hazy Jane* since he wasn't doing any driving. Today Crystal was driving the other SUV, so Beverly followed Roger's lead and ordered a *Craft Haus Czech Pilsner* craft beer.

A couple carloads of *Měngjiàng Yún-Rén Spies* drove past the restaurant and prepositioned themselves for when the group was to leave again; they would be in position to follow right away. Both were Uber driven.

The *Měngjiàng Yún-Rén Spies* wisely picked Uber and since the reservation was via credit cards the *Měngjiàng Yún-Rén Spies* could simply create by surveillance and counterfeit techniques; the drivers were very happy to earn vast amounts by a continued fare. It didn't take long, however, for the Uber drivers to figure out they were hauling around some sort of spooks who didn't say much but tended to follow the black and the white SUVs.

Vance ordered crab cakes for both him and Sandra (a.k.a. *Wánměi De Huā)*, but the rest ordered a variety of sandwiches. When the food was finally served, Vance was starving. Vance wolfed down his crab cakes before the rest had a chance to even get a couple bites into their sandwiches.

SANDRA (A.K.A. *WÁNMĚI DE HUĀ)*
Vance, you look so hungry, why don't you have my
crab cakes, I don't feel like eating now.

After their meals were complete, ladies using the bathroom, and a few other minor events, the group hopped back in their cars, retracing their path back to 93 where they followed it towards the Boulder Dam and soon came upon a helicopter tour office where they stopped and got out.

Gus knowing Las Vegas well hooked up with these guys who said they could arrange for two helicopters to carry all six passengers on about a two-hour tour which included the lake and a nearby Native American Indian Reservation by air.

Once the *Měngjiàng Yún-Rén Spies* figured out what was going on, they too made quick arrangements with another firm and were shortly airborne themselves giving the chopper pilot distinct instructions to trail the other two helicopters at a safe distance.

It was during this phase of the operation that *Měngjiàng Yún-Rén Spies* discovered the Wogar Greys were putting themselves in place to kidnap the Royal couple when the helicopters were to return to the origination point.

Gus was not yet aware that his mission had long been compromised by the Wogar Greys and each time he sent his secret reports back to Area-51, Sector-4, the Wogar Greys were immediately informed of what he sent by their mole they had in the communications center.

The Tall Whites expected the Wogar Greys to be up to something, but never quite connected the dots; otherwise, they might have taken the opportunity to intervene.

The Wogar Greys had developed Hybrids over the years. The latest generation had been developed so well using human DNA and stem cells, were almost impossible to detect. The Wogar Grey Hybrids didn't carry with them the pungent smell, nor did they seem to exhibit any trait that would give them away.

Conceived in a test tube and incubated in abductees who sometimes were simply disposed of in space, the children were born, raised, and educated with great care.

Wogar Grey's meager life aboard their giant monster size *Colony Class Planetary Conquest Vessel* (mother ship), often maneuvering outside solar systems in deep space, and was designed primarily for insertion into planets they planned to acquire through conquest, surreptitiously if necessary.

In 1958, the Wogar Greys signed a secret treaty with President Eisenhower allowing them to abduct a few people a year promising to treat them well to use them as a factoid to learn about humanity.

The Pentagon had special MJ-12 office that was notified upon an abduction which they did not react to, but after a period made inquiries to their disposition. The Wogar

Greys, being both lazy at times and brutal most often would never return an abductee especially if they had to get vicious with him.

In some cases, it was due to stubbornness on the part of the abductee but other times their procedures and methods drove the person to insanity, so it was more convenient to simply lie to the Eisenhower and later administrations' Reps at MJ-12:

MJ-12 OFFICIAL
We are inquiring what happened to John Doe #26?

GREY DIPLOMAT

The abductee agreed to travel back to our (Wogar Grey's) home planet and had no desire to return to Earth.

The stories of some of the survivors who made it back were often horrific, especially the women who were impregnated and used as an embryonic containment fixture.

In the 1960s the hybrid offspring did not appear all that beneficial, but as the Wogar Greys discovered in due time, they made better and better hybrids to the point they gave exact resemblance to humans with one minor exception, their DNA was different, but compatible in most respects.

Whereas humans have 23 pairs or 46 total chromosomes, the Grey Hybrid has 30 pairs or a total of 60. The extra chromosomes enabled them to have a human form yet live and exist in either Gray or Earth environments. If they were ever detected and checked the DNA would give them away.

The Tall Whites had discovered this, and pleaded with the humans to accept the reality but were never acknowledged since the Pentagon foolishly thought the gifts the Wogar Greys gave them were evidence they had more of a paternal interest in Earth's advancement.

Whereas the Tall Whites knew firsthand this was one of the planetary conquest methods the Wogar Greys had always used in early phases of their reach in and consequent grab of the planet and its resources.

The Wogar Greys have 400 billion people living in crowded civilizations at solar systems almost 80 light years away. They could only expand in the direction of earth now, because any other direction took them towards intergalactic warfare and strife the Tall Whites were currently engaged in.

Eight of the best trained *Wogar Grey Hybrid Spies* were traveling around Boulder City getting in position to perform the snatch and grab.

These *Wogar Greys* were almost impossible to pick out of the crowds because *Wogar Greys* paid attention to everything and the massive surveillance they did on earth thanks to the 30 years of successful *Wogar Greys hybrid* penetrations.

Constant surveillance provided the *Wogar Greys* with the latest information which was constantly transmitted to their mother ship stationed not too far from Pluto which then used that information to better train a subsequent new generation of moles they planned to continue inserting as the preliminary phase of the eventual invasion.

Wogar Grey Hybrids would be inserted into key infrastructure and command and control where they would facilitate taking down any defensive grids at the critical moment to allow the invasion to occur with minimal number of casualties on the part of the *Wogar Greys*. Any collateral damage to humans was not a consideration since they would most likely have to wipe them out to eliminate any resistance to their plunder.

The *Wogar Grey Hybrids* parked their cars a block or so away from where they followed Vance and the group, thanks to the locator beacon, they inserted into the SUVs before they left area 51.

Měngjiàng Yún-Rén Spies in due time located and identified the *Wogar Grey Hybrids* and each of the *Měngjiàng Yún-Rén Spies* received mental images through their telepathic transceivers so they could instantly identify the Greys, who now approached the helicopter tour parking lot. No sooner than the two helicopters landed than the Greys made their move.

Standing at the ready, the *Měngjiàng Yún-Rén Spies* initiated teleportation of 50 *Měngjiàng Yún-Rén Battlebots* to that location. The *Měngjiàng Yún-Rén Battlebots* were a strange looking, heavily armed, highly capable strike force just arrived behind the building and out of most public view.

Just as Gus activated the remote control that unlocked the SUV, the first of the *Wogar Grey Hybrids* appeared and pulled out a weapon, but to his surprise out of nowhere appeared a stranger who happened to be a *Měngjiàng Yún-Rén Battlebots* also with some strange weapon in hand.

All the *Wogar Grey Hybrids* had been committed and were in position to do a successful abduction or to their chagrin were suddenly the ones seized.

Gus looked extremely concerned and thought this was probably going to end up as the worst day in his life when suddenly the voice of the second man holding his gun pointed at the *Wogar Grey Hybrid* using the same exact voice the parking lot attendant used:

Mr. Vandyke, please get in your car and leave now. I recommend you go back to your hotel at once where you will be safe.

Gus then turned toward Roger and handed him the car keys.

GUS

Roger, I need you to do the driving. I think I'll be on
the phone most of the way back to Vegas.

ROGER
Sure.

Roger then took the car keys, and Gus then walked around to the passenger side and hopped in as well as Vance and Sandra (a.k.a. *Wánměi De Huā)*.

With the 50 *Měngjiàng Yún-rén Battlebots* pointing futuristic large blaster looking device at all the *Wogar Grey Hybrids, they* quickly lowered their arms and followed the instructions given them by the *Měngjiàng Yún-Rén Battlebots* who ordered them back behind the building just as a small crowd started forming.

As soon as all the *Grey Hybrids* and *Měngjiàng Yún-Rén Battlebots* were behind the air tour building they simply vanished as they were teleported to the Royal Mother Ship.

Moments later, Boulder City Police pulled into the deserted parking lot and started asking the few onlookers what they saw and received astonishing stories so they got in their cars and left thinking these nut jobs called 911 over fantasy.

As soon as the Caravan moved away heading back down 93 on its way back to I-515 with Gus looking in the rear side mirror where he could see the white SUV was close behind and safely out of harm's way; he called Beverly because he knew Crystal was driving.

GUS
You ladies, ok?

BEVERLY
Yes, but what the hell was that all about?

GUS

I'm not sure, but I think we may have just stumbled in
the middle of some intergalactic intrigue.

119

BEVERLY
It was scary for a while.

GUS
Beverly, I want you to be our rear lookout, keep your
eyes peeled and advise right away if it appears anyone
is following us.

The Uber drivers were both taking naps when there was a sudden knock at one car window a block or so away missing all the action. He spotted his customer, rolled down the window and asked:

UBER DRIVER
Are you ready to go?

MĚNGJIÀNG YÚN-RÉN SPY
Yes.

Only one *Měngjiàng Yún-Rén Spy* returned.

UBER DRIVER
Where are your friends?

MĚNGJIÀNG YÚN-RÉN SPY
They will not be coming. We can leave now; take me
back to the hotel.

The *Měngjiàng Yún-Rén Spy's* did not need to follow the SUV caravan too close because he knew where they were always. The Uber car never got within range of Beverly detecting them following them back to the hotel, as they retraced their path back to the VIP valet parking.

Gus and the two cars were slightly early, but Alex was anxiously waiting for them, so he could contact Boris and report the status of those two cars.

The white SUV had a satellite transmitter in it. They didn't have to worry about being outside cell phone towers or service. Gus put together a detailed report using his I-phone that had a special APP built for it exclusively by a major computer company that encrypted it. Due to the short distance to the other car, was able to easily send it to that device where it automatically uploaded it to a satellite.

Gus's reports immediately went to the DD/P's office at Langley where the duty officer received the alert and notified the department they had incoming traffic.

Within 15 minutes the DD/P was recalled back to Langley from his comfortable Georgetown home to handle the immediate crisis that may involve notifying the President that an unprecedented situation just occurred.

There would be the sticky little annoying detail of briefing the president on a matter he never heard about before which included an element he supposedly disbelieved existed, concerning Aliens.

No sooner than Roger turned off Las Vegas Blvd into Ceasars Palace, Alex arrived at the VIP valet parking attendants' stand with the attendant to welcome them back and get their cars parked back under the secure area again.

Just like clockwork the well-trained team in the white SUV pulled a strange looking device out of the car's dashboard that looked like an FM/AM radio, then put it in Beverly's purse and pulled a real FM/AM radio out of the glove box and installed it in the empty slot.

Both devices worked as the car's radio, but the one now carried in Beverly's purse was the brains to the networked device that made the car a traveling communications hub that could be used in a variety of situations.

However, without the plugin module, the network was utterly useless. The transmitter that was hidden inside the spare tire and battery powered only got activated when the plugin turned it on via remote control that ran off a trickle current that was in essence a watchdog timer that energized sections of the electronics as soon as it was powered up. A pre-encrypted message could be usually sent within 15 seconds of the power up sequence.

ALEX
Enjoy your day?

GUS
Yes, quite the day, nice helicopter tour of the Hoover
Dam and Grand Canyon.

ALEX
What do you have planned for tonight?

GUS
After we get freshened up a bit, we are heading out to
a concert.

ALEX
Oh yea. Which show?

GUS
The Moody Blues, one of my favorites.

ALEX
Enjoy the show.

The group split and went to their separate hotel rooms that were located adjacent to each other so they could provide some security for each other. Vance's room was in the middle.

No sooner than Gus got back to his hotel room, his cell phone rang.

General Brazile
Gus?

GUS
Yes.

GENERAL BRAZILE
General Brazile calling. Is it ok to talk now?

Gus knew his voice and the caller's I.D. showed it was General Brazile calling.

GUS
Yes, I'm alone.

GENERAL BRAZILE
Gus, there will be a car in front of your hotel in 15 minutes to take you to McCarran where we have a jet waiting for you to fly you up here where we are scheduled to have a Teleconference with the President as soon as you get here.

GUS
What about Beverly, Crystal, and Roger?

GENERAL BRAZILE
Leave them there in Los Vegas, to keep an eye on our guests, come alone. I'll call Roger in a minute and let him know you are departing momentarily. Be out front in 15 minutes.

Click, the receiver at the other end just then went offline and the dial tone was suddenly heard.

VOICEOVER (GUS)
THOUGHT

I wish I had time to take a quick shower before I leave.

Gus grabbed his pouch that looked like a laptop bag and walked out his hotel room on his way to the front of the hotel. He made a mental note of the time, realizing his pickup would suddenly appear in 14 minutes. He probably would not recognize them, but they would know who he is.

Roger received his phone call and General Brazile requested:

GENERAL BRAZILE

Please inform Beverly and Crystal that Gus has been recalled but will be back no later than in the morning.

Roger, now taking command of the mission, contacted Crystal first.

ROGER

Crystal, hey, Gus is going back up to Groom Lake and will be back probably by the morning.

CRYSTAL

I wondered how soon Gus would get the call after the excitement today.

ROGER

We need to escort our guests out for dinner. After dinner we got tickets to the concert.

CRYSTAL

Understand all. I can be ready in 15 minutes; want me to call Beverly?

ROGER

Sure, also call Vance's room and make sure they will be ready.

CRYSTAL
Will do.

ROGER
Thanks.

Vance had little to do to get ready. Sandra (a.k.a. *Wánměi De Huā)* required even less time, and just as before she scanned all the beautiful fashion shops

123

as they walked back to the rooms and picked out one of the stunning garments that was one of those $20,000 couture garments.

The store owner who spent $14,000 purchasing the designer dress would be horrified if she saw Sandra (a.k.a. *Wánměi De Huā*) now, meaning someone else had copied the design and it no longer retained its value.

The only reason why a lot of wealthy women purchased the couture dresses is they are certified by the designer to be one of a kind.

Sandra's (a.k.a. *Wánměi De Huā*) white garment showed plenty of cleavage. The image she portrayed left no doubt in people's minds she was well proportioned.

Sandra's couture clothing exemplified her hips and legs of perfect dimension that one would conclude like a world class ice skater performer. Her height was a couple inches shorter than Vance, so they looked like the perfect couple.

Department stores sometimes approached the wealthy women and purchased the couture dresses 2nd hand, then shipped them to Asia to be copied.

VOICEOVER (VANCE)
THOUGHT
How can Wánměi De Huā be able to do this transformation? Energy body species must have extraordinary ability to change their appearance.

Wánměi De Huā has the mental ability integrated with their energy converter that essentially was a very advanced form of 3D printing which Earth people had a long way to learn about, if ever.

Twenty minutes later the group met in the hotel lobby and left from there. None of the CIA agents realized they were being watched by several Alien entities at the same time.

In one part of the lobby was a *Grey Hybrid Spy*, and across from him a *Měngjiàng Yún-Rén Spy*. Both spies were reading newspapers and trying to be obscure.

The telepathic converter allowed the *Měngjiàng Yún-Rén Spy* to communicate remotely without making noise thanks to an elaborate implant.

All the *Měngjiàng Yún-Rén Spy's* had to do is think what they wanted to report and the brain to implant interface created those neuron pathway transmissions. The neuron pathway converter then transmitted the report in microvolts.

Due to the processing power of the *Měngjiàng Yún-Rén Spy's Proton Receiver Correlators*, the signals had a range of sometimes up to 100 earth miles. But as far as space communication if the location on Earth was pointed in the direction of the receiver those small signals were easily received and if necessary relayed to other *Měngjiàng Yún-Rén Agents*.

For the current mission underway it would not be possible for the Earth area where Las Vegas exists to point towards the *Měngjiàng Yún-Rén Royal Yacht*. Therefore, the *Měngjiàng Yún-Rén* sent out a dozen orbs to orbit the planet and relay the signals if necessary to make sure they never lost contact with *Wánměi De Huā* as the earth spun on its axis.

Alex anxiously watched the group fearing they might be there to observe the scheduled break in on their vehicles scheduled to occur at any moment, was relieved to see the taxi coordinator hail them a taxi which they all hopped into since there were now only 5 of them, which then drove off down to Las Vegas Blvd as they were heading off to dinner and see the *Moody Blues* concert.

Alex had become aware Gus left a while ago in a Limo, probably on a company operation or taking care of a personal matter.

About the same time the taxi taking the three remaining CIA Agents, and their two guests pulled out, Gus was walking out on the tarmac to board a Gulf Stream 650 sitting there waiting for him.

In 45 more minutes, GUS would be sitting in the conference room with General Brazile and a half dozen other military and CIA officials waiting for the President to come online.

Alex's phone rang, it was Boris.

ALEX
Hello.

BORIS
Are the cars ready?

ALEX
Yes, all the guests have left the hotel casino dressed up
in a taxi. And their leader left in a limo. I don't expect
any of them back anytime soon.

BORIS
When can my plumbers get access?

ALEX
I'm going over to relieve the VIP Valet attendant now;
he'll be gone for an hour.

In ten minutes the two *Plumbers* showed up wearing uniforms identifying them as locksmiths.

Alex handed the lead *Plumber* two sets of car keys.

ALEX
This is for the black SUV.

LOCKSMITH (PLUMBER)
Thanks.

Then Alex handed the *Plumber* the second set of keys for the white SUV.

Alex then looked out towards Las Vegas Blvd as the men went to the parking spots to begin their examination.

The black car was totally clean, nothing was installed which the burglars noted. They then went to the white SUV and looked around inside it. Finally, one of the plumbers said:

LOCKSMITH (PLUMBER)
I see some unusual wiring, but nothing here to explain
any of it.

The ingenious design of the spare tire totally threw the Plumbers off, they walked away semi-disgusted that those cars had nothing juicy in them to report back to Boris.

But now Boris' next project was underway. Alex called Borris. The conversation was all about Boyd Bushman since the Plumbers would give Boris their results.

ALEX
Boris, I have one of my former Navy Seal buddies
helping me do surveillance on Boyd Bushman. He
will let me know when Boyd Bushman's room is
temporarily vacant, so that I can go into it and do the
photographing of all his alien pictures.

BORIS
How's that working out?

ALEX
The biggest challenge is to get Boyd Bushman out
of his room long enough for me to get in there and
photograph the contents of his satchel.

Boris suddenly came up with an idea to help Alex.

BORIS
I'll invite Boyd Bushman out to dinner and be a
friendly UFO enthusiast and spend the time asking
questions and finding out more about what he knew.

ALEX
Since Boyd Bushman is staying at Caesars, it should
be easy for you to get ahold of him.

BORIS
I'm going to try to reach him, I'll let you know soon.

Boris did a google search for Caesars, and then clicked on the *contact us* icon which
in turn brought up street address and phone number to the hotel operator. Boris then
highlighted the number, clicked his "dial it" icon APP, which automatically called the
hotel.

After a few rings the hotel operator answered.

CAESARS PALACE HOTEL OPERATOR
Good afternoon, this is Caesars Palace, how may we
help you?

BORIS
I would like to speak to one of your hotel Guests
named Boyd Bushman.

CAESARS PALACE
HOTEL OPERATOR
One moment please.

Suddenly, the phone to Boyd Bushman's room started ringing. After about the 5th ring
Boyd answered the phone.

BOYD BUSHMAN
Hello.

BORIS (a.k.a. Jack)
Mr. Bushman?

BOYD BUSHMAN
Yes, this is Boyd.

BORIS (a.k.a. Jack)
Hello Boyd, this is Jack, we met yesterday at the casino and talked a little about aliens and I gave you my business card for my liquor store.

BOYD BUSHMAN
Oh yea, I remember you.

BORIS (a.k.a. Jack)
Say, Boyd, I was thinking about our conversation, and I really enjoyed talking with you, and decided, if possible, would like to get together and continue our discussion; so, I'd like to invite you out to dinner.

BOYD BUSHMAN
I was just thinking about going out to dinner myself here for a while.

BORIS (a.k.a. Jack)
I have a favorite restaurant just a little off the strip, where we can go and get some fantastic food.

BOYD BUSHMAN
I hope it's not a noisy place.

BORIS (a.k.a. Jack)
It's quiet enough where people can have a decent conversation

BOYD BUSHMAN
Is the restaurant here on the strip?

BORIS (a.k.a. Jack)
Yes, and I know the management well since I sell them all the liquor they use at their bar.

BOYD BUSHMAN
Well, I suppose I could go.

BORIS (a.k.a. Jack)
Fine, I can pick you up at any time; how soon would
you like to go?

BOYD BUSHMAN
I'll tell you what, how about 30 minutes from now?

BORIS (a.k.a. Jack)
Sure, I'll pick you up in front of your hotel at the main
entrance.

BOYD BUSHMAN
Sounds great.

BORIS (a.k.a. Jack)
Ok, Boyd see you then.

They simultaneously end the phone conversation.

***

Boris then pulled up his quick dialer APP and scrolled down to Alex's name on the
roster and selected it. The phone immediately dialed it.

ALEX
Hello.

BORIS (a.k.a. Jack)
Alex, this is Jack.

ALEX
I was just about getting ready to call you.

BORIS (a.k.a. Jack)
Fine. Hey, I've arranged to take Boyd Bushman out
to dinner. I'll be pulling up in my Limo in about 30
minutes; how about going down to the front and
inform your goons to let my car park at the entrance
while I wait for Boyd?

ALEX
Sure, no problem.

BORIS (a.k.a. Jack)
As soon as he's out of the room you can go to work. I should have him away from his room for a couple hours, which should give you enough time to photograph all those alien pictures he has.

ALEX
Why are you so interested in that Alien UFO Bull Shit? You know it must be fake crap that all these freaks bring to these UFO conferences we have in Vegas.

BORIS (a.k.a. Jack)
Alex, I do not know if it's fake and I want to see it.

Alex started thinking there must be more to it than what Jack was letting on.

ALEX
Ok since you are paying me the big bucks, I'll get you the pictures.

BORIS (a.k.a. Jack)
It will be money well worth spending.

ALEX
Great.

BORIS (a.k.a. Jack)
By the way, thanks for the help on the SUVs.

ALEX
No problem. How did that work out?

BORIS (a.k.a. Jack)
Unfortunately, my boys came back empty handed. The cars were clean.

ALEX
They're probably just on vacation.

BORIS (a.k.a. Jack)
Do you believe that crap? I got a Brooklyn Bridge I'll sell you.

ALEX
OK, well sorry you didn't find what you were looking
for.

BORIS (a.k.a. Jack)
If you see or hear anything interesting about that
group, please call me, it might be worth some more
cash for you.

ALEX
Will do.

BORIS (a.k.a. Jack)
Bye.

Suddenly there was just the dial tone.

Boris then called his Limo driver.

BORIS (a.k.a. Jack)
Jimmy?

LIMO DRIVER JIMMY
Yea, Jack, what's up?

BORIS (a.k.a. Jack)
Bring the Limo up front; I want you to take me down
to Caesars.

LIMO DRIVER JIMMY
Right away, boss.

Jack was living in a luxury condominium right on the strip next to the Hilton Hotel that
Donald Trump's sister and Donald had built together. It really was total luxury, and it
was close to all the action. 15 minutes later, Jack's phone rang.

LIMO DRIVER JIMMY
I'm out in front of the building, boss.

BORIS (a.k.a. Jack)
I'll be right down.

Jack packed his gun in his concealed holster he wore on the side on the side of his
upper torso, put on his suit jacket, then left his condo and took the elevator down and

right out to the entrance where the Limo was waiting. Even with all the traffic, the Limo pulled off Las Vegas Blvd into Caesars with about two minutes to spare.

Alex, true to his word, was standing with an attendant in an open spot directly in front of the entrance. Just as soon as Alex recognized Jimmy, Jack's driver inside the Limo, he stepped out into the road and pointed to the spot which the Limo pulled into.

Alex then went over to the Caesars attendant, and then said to him:

ALEX

Make sure none of the goofballs gives this driver any
shit. This is a VIP.

CAESARS ATTENDANT
Will do, Alex.

Alex then turned toward the limo which he could not see inside of because of the smoked glass windows, nodded, knowing Jack would see him, turned and walked back into the entrance of the hotel.

Going through the swivel door he spotted Boyd Bushman who was coming and had a small bag with him heading out. As soon as he was suddenly standing in the front entrance of the hotel, the window of the Limo rolled down and Boris yelled over at Boyd Bushman.

BORIS (a.k.a. Jack)
Hey Boyd, over here.

Boyd nodded and headed towards the Limo.

Jimmy got out of the Limo, walked around to the passenger side, opened the door, and then angled his arm towards the car in a gesture to Boyd Bushman *hop in*.

BOYD BUSHMAN
I wasn't expecting anything fancy.

Boyd took a little effort to crawl in the Limo despite the fact the door was 30% longer and had no seats in the way.

As soon as the car pulled away, Alex smiled from the Lobby, then rotated 180 degrees and promptly walked down the hallway that would eventually lead to the elevators.

Right as Alex was passing the Roman Gladiators in their costumes the strangest of the bunch gave one of those switch hitter smiles and said:

ROMAN GLADIATOR
ACTOR
Helloooo Alex.

Alex assumed the Roman Gladiator Actor said it in a way as to convey either a tantalizing hit or an outright taunt. Alex didn't know which it was but considered the guy a freak and paid no attention as he hustled to the elevator which he took up to the 17th floor.

Room service was at the other end of the hallway, preoccupied and didn't observe Alex pull out his credit card type door key and insert it in the slot which had a microchip reader. Being one of the top security guys he had a room key to get him into any guest room in the building in case he needed to let police in or assist authorities in some manner.

Alex had already logged into a workstation previously and put out the notification, he would be entering the room to do an inspection, which is often requested by Las Vegas police that want to know if they need to intervene and didn't have a court order.

Doing such favors for the Las Vegas Police cleared a legal hurdle that gave investigators a back door into the case before they had sufficient time to get a judge's warrant and permission. This procedure happened quite often in major drug trafficking cases where the evidence could quickly be lost or flushed.

Boyd Bushman, being a practical engineer, and somewhat of a messy one too, had left his satchel sitting up on the table that sat between the bed and the sliding glass window. Shades were open and there was ample light streaming in.

Alex walked over and saw a bunch of pictures and a few posters and other things wound up and stuffed in the satchel. One by one he pulled the pictures out and photographed them.

VOICEOVER (ALEX)
THOUGHT
These are damn good-looking fakes or they're the real things.

Alex began photographing photographs one by one. As it turned out there were about five photographs taken for each shot. Once Alex figured that out, he would take them out and pile them up and only take one of the five pictures each that covered the image and angle.

VOICEOVER (ALEX)
THOUGHT

*These are sick looking creatures. Each one of them is
uglier than anyone on planet Earth.*

The photographing went on for a lot shorter time than Alex expected. The real gem was the poster-like sheets that were curled up and in a tube.

Alex pulled the posters out and laid them as flat as he could on the table, then went into the bathroom and grabbed several water glasses, an unopened bar of soap and a couple of Boyd's personal effects to anchor down the three feet by two feet poster display.

VOICEOVER (ALEX)

THOUGHT

*These look incredible. These pictures show a lot of
UFOs.*

Most of the pictures were taken with black and white film and had high resolution. What was strange about a couple of them appeared to be some range finder device, kind of like what he remembered seeing in a movie about submarines.

As Alex looked closer, there was reference on the photo to a U.S. Navy Nuclear Submarine *USS Trepang SSN 674*, stating the photo had been taken of this *Alien UFO flying over Arctic waters in March 1971*, during a voyage from Iceland *to Jan Mayen Island* near Greenland.

Later that day Alex who was curious Googled *Submarine UFO Pictures* and discovered a treasure trove of pictures that looked real and had the same periscope range finder markings on them that allegedly were taken from nuclear submarines near an *Alien UFO Base* in Antarctica. He also found a link to the *USS Trepang Incident* near *Jan Mayen Island* near Greenland.

The pictures on google are damn nearly identical to Boyd Bushman's! Coincidence?

VOICEOVER (ALEX)

THOUGHT

*If these are real, I wonder why the government hasn't
taken them down? The pictures on google are damn
nearly identical to Boyd Bushman's! Coincidence?*

Then as Alex pondered it a while longer it hit him:

VOICEOVER (ALEX)

THOUGHT

*Maybe these pictures are an intentional leak by some
government official who wanted to overcome some*

*artificial boundaries set in place by some incompetent
person who may have previously denied release to the
public.*

What really got to Alex is that over a dozen different very elaborate photographs showed there appeared to be numerous types of alien spacecraft.

Then the thought hit Alex.
VOICEOVER (ALEX)
THOUGHT
*So now I know why Jack was so interested. This could
be the real thing.*

Then to really get to the bottom of it, after seeing several Lockheed insignias on it and a quick check of Boyd Bushman's luggage which showed his name and address and phone numbers, work and business, he then decided to make a quick phone call to confirm that Boyd was genuine, so he called the work number listed.

The phone rang at least a dozen times before some disgruntled employee answered and said in an angry tone:

LOCKHEED EMPLOYEE
Hello, can I help you?

ALEX
I would like to talk to Boyd Bushman please.

LOCKHEED EMPLOYEE
That crazy old fart no longer works here.

ALEX
Oh really, what happened to him?

LOCKHEED EMPLOYEE
Well, since it's kind of public knowledge now I
suppose I can tell you, he went totally crazy on UFOs
and then suddenly he was gone and management came
down to clean out his desk; he either retired, or got
fired, or quit. Management has been tight lipped on it.

ALEX
Is that so?

LOCKHEED EMPLOYEE
Yes. Boyd Bushman must be crazier than hell spouting out all that Alien UFO crap.

ALEX
So, you do not think Alien UFO disclosures Boyd made are true?

LOCKHEED EMPLOYEE
Hell no, it's all make-believe, the guy's an idiot.

ALEX
I take it you didn't get along with Boyd Bushman.

LOCKHEED EMPLOYEE
I never personally worked with him, but because I sit a short distance away from his old desk in this engineering office, I heard it all.

ALEX
You never checked up on his story to really know for sure?

LOCKHEED EMPLOYEE
How could it be, you know all that alien stuff is pure BS.

ALEX
Okay. Thanks for letting me know.

LOCKHEED EMPLOYEE
Sure.

Recalling what he overheard Boyd telling Jack as he approached them back at the casino, he decided to ask the Lockheed employee.

ALEX
By the way sir, Boyd claims he taught Ben Rich everything he knew about propulsion, what's your take on that?

LOCKHEED EMPLOYEE
Well, based on some of the photographs and memorabilia he had hanging up in the office, it's

clear that he worked at *Skunkworks* for a while, but I sincerely doubt he taught Ben Rich all he knew about propulsion.

ALEX

But wasn't Boyd Bushman a great jet propulsion designer?

LOCKHEED EMPLOYEE

Sure, I'll give him credit for smarts with the power plant, but that's as far as I'll go.

ALEX

OK, well, how long ago did he leave Lockheed?

LOCKHEED EMPLOYEE

He's been gone a while, maybe a year or two.

ALEX

Did he work at Lockheed for very long?

LOCKHEED EMPLOYEE

Yea, Boyd Bushman worked well over 40 years here from what I understand.

ALEX

I bet he saw some extraordinary planes.

LOCKHEED EMPLOYEE

He worked at *Skunk Works* especially with Ben Rich, then you know he did.

Alex now had fully vetted Boyd and knew he was onto something. He also felt more assured that BORIS (a.k.a. Jack) would be soon handing him over the cash.

ALEX

Okay sir, thanks for the insights on Boyd Bushman. Nice talking with you. Goodbye.

LOCKHEED EMPLOYEE
Goodbye.

***

Vance and the group arrived at the concert hall and the line was already starting to get long.

                    VANCE
Good thing we arrived a little early, this is probably going to be a big crowd.

Sandra turned towards and looked at Vance.

          SANDRA (a.k.a. *WÁNMĚI DE HUĀ*)
Do you expect this concert to be as good as the one last night?

                    VANCE
Definitely. This band is outstanding. Plus, the information says they have a backup orchestra to add all the terrific sound effects that makes their classic sound.

          SANDRA (a.k.a. *WÁNMĚI DE HUĀ*)
I'm looking forward to hearing the concert.

Beverly, who was standing next to Sandra looked as if she was really looking forward to the performance.

                    BEVERLY
I'm sure the Moody Blues will sound terrific.

          SANDRA (a.k.a. *WÁNMĚI DE HUĀ*)
Beverly, did you listen to Moody Blues music in the past?

                    BEVERLY
Sandra, Moody Blues music came out quite a few years before my time; they were performing even before I was born.

          SANDRA (a.k.a. *WÁNMĚI DE HUĀ*)
But you are familiar with the music?

                    BEVERLY
My parents listened to the Moody Blues music quite a bit when I was a very small kid.

Chrystal didn't say anything, but she smiled with an inquisitive look that portrayed the kid that was still wrapped up inside her and evidently eager for the night's event.

ROGER
The best part of it is we are getting paid to enjoy this entertainment.

Vance sort of understanding what Roger meant went ahead and asked him.

VANCE
How does that work Roger?

ROGER
Well Vance, we get paid 25% more while we are in the field for hazardous duty.

Recalling just what happened a few hours ago it all seemed clear to Vance that Roger had a good point.

VANCE
I can see why after what happened today.

ROGER
Not to diminish what occurred today, because the average Joe would have been shitting bricks if someone put the cannon that dude had today in their face.

VANCE
Yea never saw anything like it before, would have been interesting to see how it performed.

Roger, like most of the CIA Agents had never seen these Grey Alien *particle weapons* fired. Essentially when fired at a target, *particle weapons* gave the same effect as a lightning strike, without the large thunder.

The brilliance in the light stream emitted was almost blinding to anyone that had ever seen it before. The Greys have large black eyes to be able to quickly see after firing such weapons, as their adaptive sight re-compensated and re-established normal viewing within a second after the bright flash.

Humans, especially under darkness, would be blinded for several minutes if they were up close and saw the weapon fired. The target was usually instantaneously fried; there were no survivors of Grey Blasters.

ROGER
But I've been in worse scrapes before.

VANCE
I can imagine.

ROGER
Nothing like holding your dying buddy in your arms at 30 degrees below zero knowing that within a few minutes the North Koreans would be marching you to an interrogation center where you end up wishing you were dead.

VANCE
How did you manage to escape?

Vance recalled reading about brutal actions North Koreans were doing years ago before he was abducted by the Mergenky.

ROGER
I didn't escape.

VANCE
Then how did you get back?

ROGER
I got lucky; the Japanese caught one of China's best spies. CIA found out about it right away with various means we have, and we cut a deal with the Japanese to give us the Chicom, whom the CIA traded for me after I was beaten and tortured for three days.

VANCE
I bet the Chinese were happy about that deal?

ROGER
No, the Chinese were pissed.

VANCE
Why is that?

ROGER
The North Koreans stipulated the United States would

hand over the Chicom at the DMZ where we were exchanged. They apparently wanted some leverage with the Chinese government.

VANCE

Since they're allies, it would seem the Chinese would be happy the North Koreans obtained the release of one of their top spies.

ROGER

If you ever had to negotiate with the North Koreans, you'd think otherwise. It probably took the Chicoms a couple years to get their agent back.

Soon people showing up were behind Vance and the others, so the conversation ended until they got inside the facilities a short while longer.

***

Boris' Limo turned North on Las Vegas Blvd. Boyd sitting next to the window asked:

BOYD BUSHMAN
What's up on that tower up ahead there?

Realizing Boyd Bushman was asking about the *Top of the World Restaurant*, Boris responded:

BORIS (a.k.a. Jack)

That's a restaurant up there, wasn't planning on going up there but if you would like to try it instead, we could go there.

BOYD BUSHMAN
Yes, I would like that.

Boris then thought Jimmy was looking forward to Lawry's Prime Rib. Boris had a working arrangement with Jimmy who would go to the bar at Lawry's and have his meal while Boris entertained his guests with some privacy.

They had so many meals there, the Bartender automatically put Jimmy's tab on Boris' bill, including the required tip. Jimmy who was well paid also kicked in a little of his own tip money, so the Bartender, Mr. Magic was always glad to see Jimmy.

Unfortunately, on this trip to the Top of the World Restaurant, Jimmy would not be coming up with them, as that circumstance didn't work out up there.

Boris pressed the message button on his right console which had a speaker and microphone so he could talk to Jimmy when required.

JIMMY
Yes Boss.

BORIS (a.k.a. Jack)
Change of plans Jimmy, we are going to the Top of the
World Restaurant instead.

JIMMY
Roger that.

Jimmy didn't really mind; Boris always took good care of him.

The Limo pulled up in front of the casino restaurant. Jimmy got out. walked around to the passenger side on the right and opened the door for Boris. Boris got out first then Boyd followed. Right after Jimmy shut the car door, Boris handed Jimmy a $100 bill.

BORIS (a.k.a. Jack)
Jimmy, how about do me a favor, drive down to
Lawry's, have a steak on me and give Mr. Magic my
regards. I'll call you when we are ready to leave here.

JIMMY
Will do Boss

Jimmy then got back in the limo and drove off.
Boris and Boyd walked into the restaurant and headed up the long elevator ride to the restaurant several hundred feet up in the air.

Since the two men looked distinguished both had suits on and ties, they were perfectly dressed for the clientele and employees up in that swank restaurant with one of the most incredible views.

With the sun nearly setting, the chromatic effect of the slight cirrus clouds and the desert pastel colors added greatly to the ambience.

Boris enjoyed every time he went up there but wished that it was some bimbo he was getting ready to enjoy instead of this new INTEL source.

Boris learned his tradecraft from the KGB well. Even if this old looking guy was not current in the latest gadgets Lockheed was putting out, he was a credible source of information to who really was working on projects, which in turn allowed their espionage teams to develop the target via traditional manners.

Boris and Boyd Bushman stepped out of the elevator and in a few steps in a small lobby walked up to the beautiful blonde *Maître d'* with a New Yorker accent then asked Boris:

MAÎTRE D'
Do you have reservations sir?

Boris reached in his left pocket where he had just placed a couple $100 bills earlier, then responded

BORIS (a.k.a. Jack)
Yes, I got it here somewhere.

Boris pulled out a couple wadded up $100 bills and put it in the receptionist's hand and winked at her.

The *Maître d'* briefly turned around and spotted a nice table with a good window view looking down the strip.

MAÎTRE D'
Follow me please.

The transaction happened so quickly that neither Boyd nor anyone else caught it.

The view set well with Boyd, who being a worldly traveler had seen a lot, but this was also an outstanding view made a comment.

BOYD BUSHMAN
I hope the food here is as good as the view.

BORIS (a.k.a. Jack)
It's even better.

Boris had great knowledge of the excellent menu which their chefs executed with absolute fabulous perfection.

***

Alex very efficiently put everything back to exactly the way he found them. Boyd would never know anyone was in his room while he was away.

Alex silently left the room, then followed a course across Las Vegas Blvd, over to the Flamingo and stepped down from the overpass just in time to catch the two beautiful

Flamingo girls just before they were leaving for the day, and did his ritual similar to what Jack always did; this time he was allowed to see a little more than normal as she was starting to really enjoy all the money he was giving her.

Alex retraced his steps to the bar stool where he had usually sat next to Boris and waited shortly before the bartender brought him his usual Miller Light beer.

After a couple sips of his drink, Alex realized he had an element of privacy and started going through the pictures one at a time. They were all good. Alex had the latest I-phone that with megapixels performed better than a 35-millimeter analog camera of just a generation ago.

Alex didn't know if the pictures were real, but many of the pictures he noticed had some identifiers on them that indicated they might be government property.

VOICEOVER (ALEX)
THOUGHT

*If these pictures are for real, Boris' bosses back in
Moscow, are going to shit themselves.*

Alex had no doubt where those pictures were going or where the cash was coming from.

***

FLASHBACK:

As the Mergenky once described the *Měngjiàng
Yún-Rén* to Vance, who never made the connection
to the story to the *Měngjiàng Yún-Rén* he was now
associated with until they rescued him at the
conclusion of the horrific space battle:

MERGENKY BRIEFER

The *Měngjiàng Yún-Rén* were thought to be
almost supermen that nobody in the galaxy ever
wanted to take on in a one-on-one fight.

***

<u>INT. SPACE. *MĚNGJIÀNG YÚN-RÉN ROYAL YACHT* CONTROL ROOM.</u>

The Měngjiàng *Yún-Rén* security detail was 100% business. Their lives were totally devoted to the Royal Court and would go to whatever extremes were necessary to carry out their mission.

Even though today's event put a damper on the enthusiasm Drago was starting to feel about this sojourn to the primitive planet Earth these most recent *Wánměi De Huā* telemetry indications gave a rather positive measure.

Drago grew more and more convinced each day, the *Empress Wánměi De Huā* was experiencing a very rare but fantastic transcendence to a cosmic plateau in her relationship with Vance.

These feelings Sandra (a.k.a. *Wánměi De Huā)* exhibited as reported in telemetry were rare and as unique as some of the gemstones in Empress' *Wánměi De Huā* jewelry.

The *Měngjiàng Yún-Rén Chief of Empire Security* hailed Drago just outside her personal quarters.

The *Měngjiàng Yún-Rén security chief* had been summoned to make a personal briefing to Drago on what transpired down on Earth and give the status of the *Grey Hybrid Spies* they had detained.

DRAGO
Have you completed the interrogations?

MĚNGJIÀNG YÚN-RÉN
SECURITY CHIEF
Yes.

DRAGO
Any explanation as to why they were attempting to
kidnap the Empress?

MĚNGJIÀNG YÚN-RÉN
SECURITY CHIEF
They're like programmed robots, trained killers and
agents for their special directive. They don't know
many details.

DRAGO
Did you try enhanced interrogation techniques?

MĚNGJIÀNG YÚN-RÉN
SECURITY CHIEF
I'm not sure we could ever torture it out of them even
if they did have information they wanted to withhold.

DRAGO
Did you get any useful information at all?

MĚNGJIÀNG YÚN-RÉN
SECURITY CHIEF

Hinokatori Mind Probes revealed a superior who sent them on the mission is a Grey Alien named *Grak* who is presently assigned as a diplomat and Wogar Grey Alien liaison officer with the Americans at Area-51.

DRAGO

Is that all you discovered?

MĚNGJIÀNG YÚN-RÉN
SECURITY CHIEF

We are having difficulty with Hinokatori Mind Probes fully accessing their thoughts, so any information is slow coming.

DRAGO

Did *Grak* execute this plan with Earthmen knowledge and involvement?

MĚNGJIÀNG YÚN-RÉN
SECURITY CHIEF

The Americans are unaware of *Grak's* treachery.

DRAGO

Why do you suppose Grak would attempt to do something as foolish as to attempt to kidnap our Empress knowing we can lay to waste their entire civilization?

MĚNGJIÀNG YÚN-RÉN
SECURITY CHIEF

I have reasons to believe Grak is not aware of our abilities just like the Mergenky and Anarchie and any other entities that crossed our paths. Grak probably operated out of ignorance.

DRAGO

What is Grak's motive?

MĚNGJIÀNG YÚN-RÉN
SECURITY CHIEF

We do not know for sure because we need more

information, but we now believe based on INTEL reports, the Greys are no doubt engaging into the preliminary stages of planetary conquest.

DRAGO

What possibly could be the benefits of attempting to kidnap *Wánměi De Huā (*a.k.a. Sandra*)* she can be instantly teleported which they could not stop.

MĚNGJIÀNG YÚN-RÉN
SECURITY CHIEF

I think that since they underestimate our military capability.

DRAGO
How so?

MĚNGJIÀNG YÚN-RÉN
SECURITY CHIEF

The Wogar Grey's probably assume our slight presence here is an indication we don't have that much firepower and that by having the Empress or Vance as a hostage, we would not interfere with their taking over Earth.

DRAGO

What precautions have you taken to secure the Empress?

MĚNGJIÀNG YÚN-RÉN
SECURITY CHIEF

We are always maintaining either eye or electromagnetic visibility on *Wánměi De Huā*, while affording her some privacy while she and Vance are alone and possibly engaging in fusion.

DRAGO
Do you have sufficient manpower?

MĚNGJIÀNG YÚN-RÉN
SECURITY CHIEF

I've deployed our best secret agents that always remain in proximity to *Wánměi De Huā*. We have one hundred

Battlebots ready to transport to provide immediate assistance if our secret agents request backup.

DRAGO
That sounds reassuring.

MĚNGJIÀNG YÚN-RÉN
SECURITY CHIEF
Madam Drago, may I ask a question?

DRAGO
Yes.

MĚNGJIÀNG YÚN-RÉN
SECURITY CHIEF
How much longer do you anticipate we remain here?

DRAGO
It's up to Vance.

MĚNGJIÀNG YÚN-RÉN
SECURITY CHIEF
Why is that?

DRAGO
He must make the decision.

MĚNGJIÀNG YÚN-RÉN SECURITY CHIEF
Which is?

DRAGO
When we leave here if he wants to remain with the Empress he probably will never come back.

***

<u>INT. EVENING. TOP OF THE WORLD RESTAURANT, LAS VEGAS.</u>

BORIS (a.k.a. JACK)
Boyd, how did you get involved in all this Alien UFO business?

BOYD BUSHMAN
To be honest Jack, I never believed in the Alien stuff until I was working on the A-12 program.

BORIS (a.k.a. JACK)
What's the A-12?

BOYD BUSHMAN
It's a super high-performance jet which was a single seat forerunner of the SR-71 which is considered the fastest jet that ever flew.

A12 SINGLE SEAT AIRCRAFT

BORIS (a.k.a. JACK)
Oh really? When was it flying?

BOYD BUSHMAN
The A-12 flew over Vietnam during the war providing most of the photo intelligence until the two seat SR-71 took over during the second half of the war.

BORIS (a.k.a. JACK)
Why wasn't the military using satellites then?

BOYD BUSHMAN
Satellite photo reconnaissance was just being developed and the assets were scarce, and all satellites were being used over China and Russia our main threats.

BORIS (a.k.a. JACK)
I would have thought with all the rocket launches we saw on TV there would be more satellites.

BOYD BUSHMAN
We had such limited assets few were available for Vietnam.

BORIS (a.k.a. JACK)
So, did the A-12 fill the gap?

BOYD BUSHMAN
Yes.

BORIS (a.k.a. JACK)
What was the difference between the A-12 and the SR71?

BOYD BUSHMAN
The pilots.

BORIS (a.k.a. JACK)
What do you mean by that?

BOYD BUSHMAN
All A-12 missions were flown by CIA personnel, and all SR-71 missions were flown by the Air Force pilots.

BORIS (a.k.a. JACK)
That's the main difference?

BOYD BUSHMAN
A-12s were single seaters and more automated whereas the SR-71 had a back seater mission operator.

BORIS (a.k.a. JACK)
Why was there such a difference in the plane designations?

BOYD BUSHMAN
The Airforce must paint their jets nice and pretty, based on committee recommendations.

BORIS (a.k.a. JACK)
You must be kidding? Why were the A12's painted differently?

BOYD BUSHMAN
CIA paints their planes with whatever the hell the
contractor specifies for functional reasons and stealth

BORIS (a.k.a. JACK)
You mean Lockheed?

BOYD BUSHMAN
Exactly. But eventually the A12's were painted black
and looked about the same as an SR-71, but you could
see A12's remained a single-seater with the exception
of a trainer that was two seater.

BORIS (a.k.a. JACK)
What was your role with the A-12?

BOYD BUSHMAN
I worked on the D21 propulsion system.

Lockheed M-21 (Blackbird) | The Museum of Flight
Note the M21 has the D21 mounted on top of it.

D21.
U.S. Air Force -nationalmuseum.af.mil, Public Domain

BORIS (a.k.a. JACK)
What's D21 (daughter)?

BOYD BUSHMAN
It's an experimental craft we mounted and carried on
the back of a modified A-12 designated M21 (mother)
to test the feasibility of scram jets.

BORIS (a.k.a. JACK)
How did that work out?

BOYD BUSHMAN
As far as I'm concerned it was highly successful, gave
us Mach-9 capability, but the program was canceled
after two crashes because a Senator who liked to
stick his nose in our business was getting close to
discovering some things the CIA didn't want him to
know about.

BORIS (a.k.a. JACK)
What could that be?

BOYD BUSHMAN
Aliens, in Area 51.

Chills went up Boris' spine as he had just heard it from the man himself. Boris silently reflected.

> VOICEOVER (BORIS (a.k.a. JACK))
> THOUGHT
> Being Gods' children, what more could we possibly
> expect?

The waitress came by and delivered drinks they had ordered and took their food orders. When she departed and privacy was restored, Boris asked:

> BORIS (a.k.a. JACK)
> Boyd, how did the A-12 get you interested in Aliens?

> BOYD BUSHMAN
> From what I understand, Aliens left us alone until we
> flew the D21.

> BORIS (a.k.a. JACK)
> What makes you think they got interested then?

> BOYD BUSHMAN
> That's when our A-12 pilots started reporting UFOs.

> BORIS (a.k.a. JACK)
> Routinely?

> BOYD BUSHMAN
> No, just D21 launches.

> BORIS (a.k.a. JACK)
> So how did you find out about it?

> BOYD BUSHMAN
> The two crashes in my opinion were caused by Aliens.

> BORIS (a.k.a. JACK)
> Why do you think that?

> BOYD BUSHMAN
> During the second mission, right about the time the
> D21 was launched the pilot reported he saw a UFO
> that appeared to be flying side by side with him.

BORIS (a.k.a. JACK)
I imagine the pilot reported that incident?

BOYD BUSHMAN
Whatever it was chased the D21 as it kicked into Mach-9 flight and was instantly neck and neck with it, then suddenly, the D21 became unstable and tumbled out of control.

BORIS (a.k.a. JACK)
Did that cause the A-12 to crash?

BOYD BUSHMAN
A-12 crashes didn't occur until subsequent flights.

BORIS (a.k.a. JACK)
How did the people at Area 51 respond to the pilot?

BOYD BUSHMAN
They brought in psychiatrists; thought he might be going crazy.

BORIS (a.k.a. JACK)
Do you agree with them?

BOYD BUSHMAN
No, the pilot simply reported the truth they were not willing to believe at the time."

BORIS (a.k.a. JACK)
So how did the planes crash?

BOYD BUSHMAN
One of them crashed upon takeoff.

BORIS (a.k.a. JACK)
That sounds like a mechanical failure.

BOYD BUSHMAN
It was right after the Alien Ship zapped the poor sucker.

BORIS (a.k.a. JACK)
Right in broad daylight?

BOYD BUSHMAN
No, these flights were conducted at night; allowing a cover story of launching rockets would sound plausible to the public.

BORIS (a.k.a. JACK)
What makes you think an alien ship caused that crash?

BOYD BUSHMAN
One of my sources said they had some visual evidence of the alien craft coming in and going side by side with the M21 for a few seconds before the thing tumbled out of control.

BORIS (a.k.a. JACK)
So how do you think they disabled the M21?

BOYD BUSHMAN
I think an alien zapped the pilot and the M21 which then nose-dived to the ground since the pilot was no longer controlling the plane.

BORIS (a.k.a. JACK)
Sounds like a simple mechanical failure to me.

BOYD BUSHMAN
The way the M21 Mother Jet was trimmed, it required the pilot to hold back on the stick until it got up near supersonic was to compensate for the payload.

BORIS (a.k.a. JACK)
What about the second crash?

BOYD BUSHMAN
We took a few D21s up without launching them afterwards to check out stability problems the A-12 might have had to detect and rectify them. We went through a dozen pilots and a dozen psychiatrists who all came to the same conclusion, UFO incursion into the flight path as the pilot reported in every event.

Boyd took a sip of his drink then continued.

BOYD BUSHMAN
The aliens were obviously trying to give us a message, what we were doing was not appreciated.

BORIS (a.k.a. JACK)
How did it all end?

BOYD BUSHMAN
Because of the atmosphere with the pilots who were all close and knew each other we just about didn't make that final mission, it almost got scrubbed.

BORIS (a.k.a. JACK)
What forced the issue?

BOYD BUSHMAN
The President pushed the issue and said the Alien reports was a bunch of hogwash and we needed to move ahead because the Soviets were breathing down our backs on innovation of their own.

BORIS (a.k.a. JACK)
Did that cause the decision to go ahead and fly the mission?

BOYD BUSHMAN
Yes, the following day the last mission occurred.

Boyd took another sip and with great remorse almost tearing up but continued.

BOYD BUSHMAN
We had several F104 chase planes in position flying as high as they could go.

Just as the M21 and the F104s were in the launch basket, out of nowhere came another one of those UFOs.

Just as the D21 left the back of the M21, one of the chase plane pilots radioed the alien just zapped the M21 with some kind of ray and it all blew up into a fiery mess.

BORIS (a.k.a. JACK)
Then what happened?

BOYD BUSHMAN
The program was canceled that day, orders from
somewhere, and rumors are Majestic 12, to 'CANEX'
the mission. We were then ordered to incinerate all the
plans, drawings and destroy any hardware associated
with the project.

A moment later, the waitress arrived.

WAITRESS
Excuse me gentlemen.

The waitress then began serving their meals.

***

INT. NIGHT. LAS VEGAS FLAMINGO HOTEL AND CASINO.

Alex thumbed through the pictures one at a time. After he thought it was a good
picture, he clicked on the send icon, and it was on its way to Boris.

One by one, Alex had a growing awareness and firm belief that this wasn't made up.
There was just too much credible information.

By the time Alex sent his last photo to Boris, he had a hidden anger and no longer felt
remorse for helping the KGB in the past. He was now convinced more than ever our
government lies to us on the most important information that can grip mankind.

***

The short hop on the Gulfstream 650 Jet to Groom Lake happened so fast that Gus had
little time to collect his thoughts before the jet bouncing on the runway and pulled up
to hanger 27 or what was referred to as the *evil building 27*.

People like Robert Lazar were rumored to have been ruined in the *evil building* 27.

It was also here in the *evil building* 27 that one fatal day when the President insisted the
D21 mission be flown right away that soon led to the decision to curtail the program.

Boyd Bushman never knew he was certainly a person of interest to Gus Vandyke and
was observed at the UFO conference by CIA plants at the conference Boyd attended in
Las Vegas. Gus was reading reports on Boyd just before the Gulfstream touched down.

The report was mildly disturbing, but it would get worse before it got better.

Boyd was already in a lot of hot water removing pictures of dead aliens recovered from the Roswell crash and CIA photographs his buddies slipped him for his going away present.

Damage control was already in the works.

This would not be the first or the last time the agency put out disinformation. Americans learned the propaganda business well in World War II and even started to outshine the masters of the Art, the British in the 1960s.

Gus had studied Stewart Menzies British SIS, Code name "C" and during some of Gus's activities at DD/P also read all the "Q" files concerning Colonel Donavan.

VOICEOVER (GUS) THOUGHT

Times have changed. We can't even waterboard spies anymore. Throwing Viet Cong tax collectors out of Helicopters at 5000 feet over Vietcong known occupied areas was the kind of business the DD/P boys liked to do back in the good ole 'cowboy' days.

Their man Paul Vann certainly was no saint. If his buddy Daniel Ellsberg knew all the dirty secrets of operation Phoenix which Vann personally designed and managed, he might not have been so motivated in releasing the Pentagon Papers when he became upset over Vann's death.

The Viet Cong who was targeting Paul Vann finally nailed him in 1972, and with that, the Americans in Vietnam rolled up like a cheap whore after some scumbag got their $20 worth.

***

<u>EXT. NIGHT. BUILDING 27 AREA 51</u>

The crew opened the door to the Gulfstream and Gus got out. An Airforce officer was waiting for him.

AIRFORCE OFFICER
COLONEL JONES
How was your flight, Mr. Vandyke?

GUS
Smooth as my girlfriend's rear.

AIRFORCE OFFICER
COLONEL JONES
Good to hear. How was your day?

GUS
I missed out on a good concert tonight for another useless meeting here.

AIRFORCE OFFICER
COLONEL JONES
Well with this slow president, we must explain everything 10 times.

GUS
Yea, not like the good ole days when good guys used to watch our backs for us and keep the politicians from meddling in our affairs

AIRFORCE OFFICER
COLONEL JONES
It's not the good ole Cowboy days anymore.

Gus responded not wanting to sound like a whiner:

GUS
Those days, my friend, are over. Better get your spit ball machine out and oil it up since the next thing after taking away our water boarding, they will give us rubber bullets.

AIRFORCE OFFICER
COLONEL JONES
Can you imagine the public outcry if they ever found out we water boarded Aliens?

Gus recalled injecting some real nasty stuff into an Alien who refused to explain how his ship communicated.

GUS
Waterboarding was not the worst we ever did to Aliens.

AIRFORCE OFFICER
COLONEL JONES
Well, I shot down one or two of them in my day.

GUS
They probably deserved it, the way they were harassing
our test flights.

Colonel Jones then escorted Gus into the side door of hanger Building 27 and they wound up going down the elevator, a mile underground, to General Brazile's conference room.

INT. DAY. CONFERENCE ROOM. AREA-51, SECTOR FOUR.

Gus looked around and saw a dozen familiar faces and nodded at General Brazile.

GUS
Looks like we have got a full house here.

GENERAL BRAZILE
Yea, I had to invite a few of the politicians in who want
to brown nose the President.

General Brazile then winked at Gus.

General Brazile then looked at Colonel Jones.

GENERAL BRAZILE
Colonel Jones, please call the White House and tell
them we are ready.

The large screen before the people in the conference room was split in two. The left side had a power point presentation; the right side had the video of the White House National Security Advisor and several other people in the White House situation room, several stories underground.

And just like at Wright Patterson Air Force Base, the tunneling operations under the White House were ongoing, with some special chambers now reaching ½ mile underground in pure bedrock that was getting increasingly very hard to get through.

But thanks to Joy Global, they had a tunneling machine just like the one that dug the 20-mile new railroad tunnel in Switzerland which allowed the Swiss to travel easily into Germany in half an hour on high-speed rail.

INT. DAY. CONFERENCE ROOM. AREA-51, SECTOR FOUR.

With all the surveillance equipment, the power point was filled with pictures of the arriving spacecraft and its subsequent miniaturization and departure out of the underground hanger at level four. Then came the most shocking part: with the Alien

*Wánměi De Huā (*a.k.a. Sandra*)* turning into a surreal character that entered the human Vance's body.

Vance had been identified, and his history was put up via projector screen where the conference attendees were briefed about him.

> PRESIDENT
> Mr. Vandyke, what's your take on those military assets
> that came out of nowhere?

> GUS
> The latest developing information of the two groups of
> Aliens having the confrontation at the helicopter tour
> building is they are of unknown origin, but we think
> one of the groups is associated with the new aliens that
> arrived two days ago.

> PRESIDENT
> What kind of information did you get on them?

> GUS
> We only had a few photos that our agent Beverly was
> able to get with her hidden surveillance camera, of
> what we have termed 'Battlebots' as you see on the
> screen.

Gus really got some interesting dialog going.

> PRESIDENT
> Any good analysis of what their capability might be?

> GUS
> Mr. President, they seemed to be something like I've
> never experienced before in dealing with diplomats
> from eight Alien civilizations.

General Brazile spotting a new face in the room sitting a few chairs down from the President on the video monitor suddenly asked:

> GENERAL BRAZILE
> Is everyone present MJ-12 cleared?

> PRESIDENT
> We have one new member to our crew here, Anthony,
> he is now MJ-12 cleared.

General Brazile was relieved because he would not be happy if an non-cleared person suddenly saw and heard what was just about to unfold.

GUS

I'd say those *battle-bots* were 8 to 9 feet tall, and with all their armor and hardware they were packing and the size of their feet, perhaps 2 feet long, they could easily be 800 pounds or more.

GENERAL BRAZILE

The high-resolution pictures agent Beverly managed to get shows remarkable detail on the large screen briefing display.

GUS

It was another one of those quirks where we happened to have the right equipment staged at the right time.

PRESIDENT

Any estimates on that gun barrel thing each one of those monsters were carrying?

GUS

Since they were not fired, we do not know if it's laser or projectile.

GENERAL BRAZILE
What's your guess?

GUS

Due to the extremely advanced nature and sophistication, they are showing, they may be laser cannons.

PRESIDENT
What if they shoot bullets?

GUS

If they shoot bullets, they could be as much as 35-millimeters in diameter.

GENERAL BRAZILE

The large feet support the theory on the 2nd speculation to provide stabilization when firing.

PRESIDENT
Those beings that first drew their weapons on you,
what were they like?"

GUS
They appeared as if they were humanoids.

GENERAL BRAZILE
Any way of identifying them?

GUS
No, but their voice is well developed.

GENERAL BRAZILE
We would not know if they were not humans.

President casually commented as his psyche totally elevated into an infinite flow of conjectures.

PRESIDENT
Fascinating.

GUS
As you can see Mr. President in the PowerPoint one
image we got of the *battle-bots* and the others. The
first group that approached us appeared humanoid.
You cannot tell the difference between this group and
a typical Earth person.

General Brazile then outlined their plan and schedule which the President appreciated and secured the meeting.

PRESIDENT
Thank you. This was very informative.

The briefing display suddenly went green meaning the White House had ended the video conference call and all cameras were off, with no data shown.

After the meeting, many of the staff members slowly filtered out of the conference room back into their offices, some went home and others back to their rooms in the Bachelor Officer Quarters (BOQ); those who had to stay overnight at area 51, which occurred quite often, had rooms available.

General Brazile then turned to Gus.

GENERAL BRAZILE

Gus, I have some other matters that we need to discuss before you leave.

GUS

What do you want to talk about?

GENERAL BRAZILE

This concerns the email I sent you that our agents reported concerning the UFO conference the crazies were having.

GUS

I quickly read through it.

GENERAL BRAZILE

Mr. Bushman was there shooting his mouth off again showing those pictures he should not be in possession of?

GUS

My question is why haven't you had the U.S. Marshalls haul his ass in? He clearly is breaking the law.

GENERAL BRAZILE

We were just about going to do that, then our surveillance guys suddenly discovered Mr. Bushman is meeting with a Russian Spy.

GUS

Do you think Boyd Bushman is selling the RUSSIAN FSB information?

GENERAL BRAZILE

Well as you know, Mr. Bushman has a chip on his shoulder, anything is possible.

GUS

So, why the delay in arresting him?

GENERAL BRAZILE

I was informed NSA is now monitoring Mr. Bushman

and the Russian agent. The CIA wants to know who Boris Potemkin reports to in Moscow.

GUS
Why is that?

GENERAL BRAZILE
Ever since the reorganization of the KGB into the FSB, our government has had a hard time figuring out the organization chart for the FSB.

GUS
Sounds like the CIA is playing Bushman as a double spy.

GENERAL BRAZILE
It certainly looks that way. The Cowboys in Action (CIA) has identified one of Mr. Bushman's sources at Lockheed and are now using him to plant disinformation.

GUS
How did you manage to find that person?

GENERAL BRAZILE
One of the guy's Bushman worked with hates his guts, overheard a conversation one time and witnessed Bushman's friend passing on some pictures that were ordered to be shredded along with all other case file materials.

GUS
Lucky break.

GENERAL BRAZILE
Yea, the guy snitched on Bushman's friend by calling the espionage hotline number, we give all the people with high security clearances in yearly training in case they want to report some unexplained behavior.

GUS
So, what do you have planned?

GENERAL BRAZILE

Bushman was followed this evening going out to dinner with Boris Potemkin, we think they are negotiating some sort of transfer of material Bushman may have in his possession.

GUS

Any idea what that material might be?

GENERAL BRAZILE

At the UFO conference, Mr. Bushman showed people such as a George Norblay our other pain in the ass some of those pictures.

GUS

Interesting.

Mr. Bushman was just about to hand over a few pictures when our agent at the time interrupted them before Mr. Bushman could do that.

GUS

I see, so what do you expect out of me?

GENERAL BRAZILE

Turns out Bushman is also staying at Caesars Palace. I want you to arrange through your *special operative* in the hotel you are staying in, to break into Mr. Bushman's room and steal all those pictures.

GUS

He probably has more pictures at home or elsewhere, what good will stealing those pictures do?

GENERAL BRAZILE

We just want to keep them out of Boris Potemkin's hands.

GUS

As you know General I kind of have my hands full right now.

GENERAL BRAZILE

We don't expect you to do much other than act as a liaison to that guy in security you've used on occasion in the past.

GUS

You realize this is not going to be cheap?

GENERAL BRAZILE

Once you make the deal, we'll have agents bring you
the cash.

GUS

Now you know why everyone calls us *Cash in
Advance.*

Gus then smiled a bit.

GENERAL BRAZILE

Greasing palms sure makes our business a heck of a
lot easier.

GUS

True, but we also buy a lot of tainted bull crap.

GENERAL BRAZILE

You win some, you lose some, and unfortunately you
can't win every time.

GUS

When can I get a lift back to Las Vegas?

In a few minutes, a plane will be waiting for your departure. We are sending a couple
of agents along with you to prevent Mr. Bushman handing over any documents to
Boris Potemkin.

***

<u>INT. NIGHT. LAS VEGAS. LAS VEGAS MOODY BLUES CONCERT.</u>

Again, Alex came through for them with great tickets sitting in the middle about
12 rows back from the front. The crowd was energized, far more than what Sandra
observed at the Chicago concert, and she wondered why.

Moments later as the Moody Blues were performing Knights in White Satin, Sandra
started to see why with a different type of music. The Chicago Band played spectacular
especial with the Brass section, but Moody Blues had an orchestra backup that made
its sounds different but also very delightful.

Note to Cinematorapher:

> *If possible, to get a license to put some Moody Blues Concert video in the movie would accelerate the audience psychoacoustics.*

Moody Blues began their first song that quickly transfixed the audience:

<u>Moody Blues - Nights in White Satin</u>

Sandra smiled at Vance feeling a surreal sense of satisfaction and transcendence out of the euphoric state that occupied her throughout most of the *Moody Blues Band* performance.

The *Moody Blues* soon finished a couple songs; Vance was very cheerful and quite absorbed in all of it. Without any suggestion, out of a natural feeling, Sandra (a.k.a. *Wánměi De Huā)* grabbed Vance's hand and started to hold it.

SANDRA (a.k.a. *WÁNMĚI DE HUĀ)*
(Telepathically)
This music is very inspirational.

Vance
(Telepathically)
I enjoyed this music when I was a younger man before
I left Earth with the Mergenky.

SANDRA (a.k.a. *WÁNMĚI DE HUĀ)*
(Telepathically)
Vance, as you know I can read your memories.

VANCE
(Telepathically)
Yes, I know.

SANDRA (a.k.a. *WÁNMĚI DE HUĀ)*
(Telepathically)
Vance, I'm also able to determine if you had mind
implants from another being.

VANCE
(Telepathically)
Interesting.

SANDRA (a.k.a. *WÁNMĚI DE HUĀ)*
(Telepathically*)*
Vance, Kwongab has telepathic ability. He manipulated you and most likely a lot of other people that charted your destiny when you lived in the Mergenky Civilization.

VANCE
(Telepathically*)*
I would not believe that coming from any other person.

SANDRA (a.k.a. *WÁNMĚI DE HUĀ)*
(Telepathically*)*
Kwongab was your benefactor. He looked out for you. I was sure he took it hard when your Battle Cruiser was destroyed.

VANCE
(Telepathically*)*
Maybe someday I should go visit Kwongab to let him know I'm still alive.

SANDRA (a.k.a. *WÁNMĚI DE HUĀ)*
(Telepathically*)*
I can arrange that for you, but there will be some things we would need to brief you about before you go there. But for now, I want you to know when I discovered how much Kwongab tampered with your thoughts to guide you into your future and all the vast experiences you had with Kwongab, I decided I must do something.

VOICEOVER (*WÁNMĚI DE HUĀ)*
THOUGHT
I will have to prepare Vance to learn about what happened to Doctor Kara.

VANCE
(Telepathically*)*
What did you do?

SANDRA (a.k.a. *WÁNMĚI DE HUĀ)*
(Telepathically*)*

I sent an envoy to the Mergenky who met with General Kahn and had a meeting arranged with General Kwongab to explain your status.

VANCE
(Telepathically)
Kwongab's a General now?

SANDRA (a.k.a. *WÁNMĔI DE HUÁ*)
(Telepathically)
Vance as you know, from the two Anarchie Wars, Kwongab did some spectacular missions that you were with him and the results of the 2nd Jeeapa War, the Mergenky prevailed thanks to much of Kwongab's personal efforts.

VANCE
(Telepathically)
I learned a lot from Kwongab. I never had a better friend.

SANDRA (a.k.a. *WÁNMĔI DE HUÁ*)
(Telepathically)
Vance, I was saving something for you to observe at a special happy time in your life. I can tell this music is making you very happy so I would like to give it to you now.

VANCE
(Telepathically)
What is it?

SANDRA (a.k.a. *WÁNMĔI DE HUÁ*)
(Telepathically)
My envoy brought back a holograph of Kwongab's personal message to you. I can blend that holograph into the music you are now hearing. Would you like to see Kwongab's message now?

VANCE
(Telepathically)
Sure.

Wánměi de Huā started the telepathic implant holograph in Vance's mind blended with the music. For Vance's perception the holograph appeared as if it were real. Vances consciousness transcended from his seat in the concert to General Kahn's office where Kwongab was standing next to General Kahn looking somber.

KWONGAB
(Via Subconscious Holograph)

Hello Vance. I just received the extraordinary information that you are alive and well and were rescued from the escape pod and now visiting Earth with the Empress Wánměi de Huā. I'm looking forward to the day when you can visit and bring you up to date on everything that has transpired.

Your children took it rather hard when they were informed you were lost in space. After discussions with Wánměi de Huā's envoy, the decision was made to disclose to your pertinent information concerning Kara and inform your children that you are alive and well and will visit in the future.

Your children are doing well in life, and each has graduated from the University of Quom with honors.

Live well and prosper.

Sandra (a.k.a. *Wánměi De Huā)* knew the holograph she planted in Vance's mind would cause a psychological transcendence and the tears now articulated her speculation coming true. But she had the remedy to help bolster Vance's psychological reserves so that he would not have an emotional breakdown in the concert.

Kwongab provided the *Měngjiàng Yún-Rén Evnoy*, holographs of Vance's children in various stages of their lives.

As the Moody Blues music played on, Vance started seeing the recorded imagery that was transmitted from the Royal Yacht to *Wánměi De Huā's telepathic transceiver* who now inserted it into the spatial holographic nucleus in the perceptual part of Vance's brain, giving him a music hallucination combined with Kwongab's holographic visual component. [Musical hallucinations - Wikipedia]

Thanks to the creative music provided by the Moody Blues Band integrated into all the imagery Vance now received, calmed him and turned an emotional roller coaster into a euphoric transcendence of peace and tranquility.

Moody Blues music during Vances telepathic transcendence:

<u>Tuesday Afternoon-The Moody Blues-(Long Extended Version)</u>

<u>Ride My See-Saw</u>

<u>Moody Blues: The Story In Your Eyes</u>

<u>Candle Of Life</u>

<u>The Moody Blues - Your Wildest Dreams</u>

<u>The Moody Blues - I Know You're Out There Somewhere</u>

<u>Moody Blues / Forever Autumn - YouTube</u>

<u>The Moody Blues Seventh Sojourn 01 Lost In A Lost World</u>

<u>Moody Blues: The Story In Your Eyes</u>

<u>Moody Blues "One More Time To Live"</u>

<u>Moody Blues - The Dreamer</u>

<u>The Moody Blues: Too Our Childrens Childrens Children: Side1 Picture Show</u>

Sandra (a.k.a. *Wánměi De Huā*) telemetry readings from her implants were now starting to get Drago's attention that left no doubt concerning the Empress safety. Because of today's events, security was stepped up a few notches.

A few rows behind them were unidentified individuals that would easily pass for the average concert goer, were Měngjiàng *Yún-Rén Secret Agents*, sworn to die if necessary to protect the Empress. There were no Secret Agents in the galaxy nearly as capable as these Měngjiàng *Yún-Rén Secret Agents*.

Besides Měngjiàng *Yún-Rén* micro blasters which would be virtually impossible to recognize by present day earth technology, their martial arts skills were unmatched. These *Měngjiàng Yún-Rén Secret Agents* of course had shape shifting features but other attributes such as the ability to breathe underwater or jump thirty-five feet into the air.

SANDRA (A.K.A. *WÁNMĚI DE HUĀ*)
The concert seemed like it didn't last very long.

VANCE
Yea, I'm sure most of the audience would be willing

to hang out for another couple hours listening to more,
but they got their money's worth.

The group headed out of the concert hall with the crowd, and all got in a Limo for a
short drive on Las Vegas Boulevard back to Caesars Palace Hotel and Casino.

BEVERLY
I'm going back to my room. I have a few items I must
do.

CRISTAL
I'll take the elevator with you; I'm heading back too.

Cristal dreaded the emails and administrative work she now had to do as well as take
care of some of her personal matters such as bill paying and checking up on her mother
who was often driving her nuts by complaining that she wasn't giving her a bushel
basket full of grand kids.

ROGER
What are you going to do now, Vance?

VANCE
I thought I would go back and try my luck at the
blackjack table.

ROGER
I'll go with you.

The three walked into the casino and stopped by the cashier. Vance purchased $1000
worth of chips and handed half of them to Roger.

VANCE
Here's some play money for you. I don't plan on
staying too long. Suggest you leave after you lose it
all.

Roger smiled.

ROGER
Heck no I might win but, I'll be honest. I don't have
the passion to gamble. The casino usually wins, the
odds are against us.

VANCE
You got that right. Almost as good of odd of betting
against the 800-pound gorilla Wall Street.

Vance spotted Rodriguez sitting at his table with no customer sulking and approached
and sat down at the stool next to the table. Roger and Sandra sat next to him.

As soon as Rodriguez spotted Vance, the desire to get even with this guy flourished
within him.

RODRIGUEZ
Hello folks, how are you doing tonight?

VANCE
Great, just came back from the Moody Blues concert.

RODRIGUEZ
How was it?

VANCE
Was fantastic.

Roger
Deal me.

Vance also wanted a card, after placing a chip down to bet.

VANCE
Me too.

RODRIGUEZ
You're not playing, Miss?

Sandra (a.k.a. *Wánměi De Huā)* smiled and shook her head implying *no.*

Guido did not take long to spot the Vance, Sandra, and Roger on the Video display and
watch intently. Guido said to one of the video operators standing next to him:

VOICEOVER (GUIDO)
THOUGHT
I'm going to discover their system tonight.

SANDRA (a.k.a. *Wánměi De Huā)*.
(TELEPATHICALLY)
Vance, take another card.

Vance thought back knowing Sandra would be reading his mind, responded in the thought he knew Sandra would read:

VANCE
(TELEPATHICALLY)
*No help tonight, I'm going to let this fella win back
some of his money.*

Rodriguez started feeling like a shark. In no time, he was making mincemeat out of the two *clowns*.

VOICEOVER (RODRIGUEZ)
THOUGHT
Armatures, just like I thought.

As Guido watched he quickly discovered Rodriguez was handling the two gamblers the way he expected.

VOICEOVER (GUIDO)
THOUGHT
Probably was beginners' luck after all.

Guido now had declining interest in this couple, watching Rodriguez smile as he emptied their pockets.

***

After the plates were cleared off the table and Boris Potemkin and Boyd Bush both turned down the free dessert that came with their meals, the conversation continued as they were finishing off their drinks.

BORIS (a.k.a. Jack)
What does one of these aliens look like?

Boyd reached down in his bag and pulled up what appeared to be a picture of a dead alien lying on an examination table.

BOYD BUSHMAN
Like one of these.

Boris holding the picture could tell it was very old, probably 50 years, fading and looking ancient with the paper yellowing, instantly knew this wasn't something Boyd just recently manufactured.

The sight of the alien was stunning! Boris felt shivers as his exposure to this surreal image completely encapsulated every thought he had.

> BORIS (a.k.a. Jack)
> I'll be damned!

Boris carefully examined the picture.

> VOICEOVER (BORIS)
> THOUGHT
> *Alexander Bortnikov is going to have to take a serious examination of the facts and not try to diminish the significance of this report. The Americans, whom we think are easily penetrable, obviously know how to keep the most important secrets from us. Without Boyd's help we would never have known.*

> BOYD BUSHMAN
> I'll trade this picture for that one.

Boyd handed Boris another picture and took back the previous one that had what appeared to be a dead alien lying on its side.

> BOYD BUSHMAN
> As you can see in this picture, whoever took it placed the alien on its side showing the side profile which conveyed a since of fragility of the alien.

> BORIS (a.k.a. Jack)
> It sure has a big head and a small body.

> BOYD BUSHMAN
> Yea it probably weighs 60 pounds.

Boyd handed BORIS (a.k.a. Jack)a picture of what appeared to be debris of a crashed UFO and the paper in the photograph was extremely yellow and very old looking.

> BOYD BUSHMAN
> Take a look at this.

BORIS (a.k.a. Jack)
Is this a Polaroid photograph?

VOICEOVER

Boris was quite familiar with the old-style photographic equipment which the KGB used quite a bit during the cold war.

Since the cameras and film were easily obtained internationally during the cold war, helped to eliminate their spies from having to carry photographic equipment across international boundaries with the potential for exposure.

The resulting pictures taken by KGB and pictures provided by useful idiots helped them take, often were diagrams, tech manuals, or pictures of government installations and personnel.

Information provided by useful idiots was handed off to a KGB handler stationed at the embassy with full diplomatic immunity.

During the height of the cold war several thousand pictures were sent back every month to The Lubyanka building at Lubyanka Square in the Meshchansky District of Moscow, Russia.

Boris Potemkin was part of the old school and knew the KGB's history such as a Time Magazine Article in 1983, that reported the KGB was the world's most effective information-gathering organization.

Did Cash in Advance feel a sting from that revelation?

BOYD BUSHMAN
Yes, it is from a Polaroid camera.

BORIS (a.k.a. Jack)
Amazing.

BOYD BUSHMAN
Look at the writing on the back of the picture.

The writing on the back of the picture stated: RAAF ser 00397/7JUL1947 (TS NOFORN) and a few other markings including: source: *Sheriff Wilcox, picture taken at a pasture on Foster's homestead.*

This picture really got to Boris. The incident at Roswell, New Mexico remained a highly controversial subject.

BOYD BUSHMAN

The government's coverup of the Roswell incident has so many holes in it, you might as well cause it Swiss Cheese.

BORIS (a.k.a. Jack)

Even an amateur could know this isn't some crashed weather balloon.

BOYD BUSHMAN
Sure isn't.

Then Boyd handed him the next picture which really hit Boris hard.

BORIS (a.k.a. Jack)
Are those dead aliens?

BOYD BUSHMAN

Yes, that's Sheriff *Wilcox* standing next to the bodies with William Brazel, Major Jesse Marcel and a man in plainclothes, probably an OSS/CIA agent."

BORIS (a.k.a. Jack)
Any idea who that agent was?

BOYD BUSHMAN

No, I was never able to get his identity, though one of my sources said, that man had worked for Colonel Donavan and was Henry Kissinger's boss while he was used as a German translator near the end of WW2.

BORIS (a.k.a. Jack)
He would probably be operating under an alias anyway.

BOYD BUSHMAN
Don't they all?

BORIS (a.k.a. Jack)
Yes, pretty much so in my opinion.

BOYD BUSHMAN
The beautiful thing about going to work for the CIA I hear, it's like joining the French Foreign Legion, you get to become a new person, and your old identity dies off, usually permanently.

BORIS (a.k.a. Jack)
So, what happened to the crashed flying Saucer?

BOYD BUSHMAN
The 509th Bomb group of the Eighth Air Force, Roswell Army Airfield, took possession of it and the dead bodies and flew them to Eighth Air Force in Fort Worth, Texas.

From there it was sent to Wright Patterson Air Force base for examination.

The bodies of the aliens remain in cold storage there at Building 18 at Wright Patterson Air Force Base, but the craft was eventually moved to building 27 at Groom Lake.

Boyd Bushman then pulled out several high-quality pictures of UFOs.

BOYD BUSHMAN
Several of these pictures were taken from aircraft chasing the UFOs. A few of them were also taken from the American Nuclear Submarine USS Trepang (SSN-674).

BORIS (a.k.a. Jack)
I can see that. The pictures were close and high up in the air with a mountain range showing in the background.

BOYD BUSHMAN
The others were taken on the ground, and one of them was parked right in front of Area-51, building 27, a hanger.

BORIS (a.k.a. Jack)
This one doesn't look crashed.

                    BOYD BUSHMAN
                    No, it landed there.

                    BORIS (a.k.a. Jack)
                    It did?

                    BOYD BUSHMAN
                    Sure did.

                    BORIS (a.k.a. Jack)
            Do you know why the Alien ship landed there?

                    BOYD BUSHMAN
        That was part of a technology exchange which
        President Kennedy was going to disclose to the public
        but didn't happen because of the assassination.

Boris couldn't help but throwing out the comment that resonated with the old KGB:

                    BORIS (a.k.a. Jack)
        Why is it everyone in the world except you Americans,
        know who killed Kennedy?

Boyd responded in a matter-of-fact manner.

                    BOYD BUSHMAN
                    Some of us know.
Boris then went on to say:

                    BORIS (a.k.a. Jack)
            You know this is what probably got Kennedy killed.

                    BOYD BUSHMAN
                    Exactly.

                    BORIS (a.k.a. Jack)
        Whatever happened to that spaceship? Did it return
        home?

                    BOYD BUSHMAN
        No, it's still at S4, area 51. In fact, that's the ship that
        got Robert Lazar in trouble?"

BORIS (a.k.a. Jack)
How did that happen?

BOYD BUSHMAN
Robert, a scientist with the Office of Naval Intelligence, who was assigned by Edward Teller, the father of the hydrogen bomb, was having marital problems.

BORIS (a.k.a. Jack)
I would think that is understandable under the circumstances.

BOYD BUSHMAN
The security detail that kept a close eye on all those directly involved in the reverse engineering discovered he was starting to have problems such as drinking and gambling, hauled him in for interrogation and to ensure he maintained his silence.

BORIS (a.k.a. Jack)
Sounds just like a Soviet KGB operation.

BOYD BUSHMAN
Yep. As the surveillance intensified, it also made his life unbearable. Instead of committing suicide, which he considered doing, Robert decided instead to leak it.

BORIS (a.k.a. Jack)
When did this happen?

BOYD BUSHMAN
He disclosed it to Las Vegas reporter George Knapp in 1989. Sometime later Art Bell interviewed Bob Lazar and talked about his story on a radio talk show COAST to COAST which has an average audience of about four million people per night.

BORIS (a.k.a. Jack)
Did they arrest Robert Lazar?

BOYD BUSHMAN
No, because if they tried to prosecute him, his attorneys could bring forward the evidence they knew

Robert had acquired which would have drawn undue visibility to the project.

BORIS (a.k.a. Jack)
Did they do a character assassination?

BOYD BUSHMAN
Correct. They did a huge propaganda campaign and with the help of CIA plants in most newspapers immediately spread lots of disinformation including blaming the disclosure as a stunt to embarrass the U.S. who had gone after him and his security clearance for marital problems, gambling and alcohol issues.

BORIS (a.k.a. Jack)
I bet this screwed up his life.

BOYD BUSHMAN
Sure did. Robert was unemployable from then on, but eventually started his own business which is now thriving.

BORIS (a.k.a. Jack)
So, the government is no longer messing with him?

BOYD BUSHMAN
I think they kissed and made up and a couple friends tell me Roberts Company now does contractor work at Area 51.

My friends say he's now part of the team again and tightlipped. Anything he says about the controversy appears to be staged and designed by the agency he works for.

VOICEOVER (BORIS)
THOUGHT
After looking at all these pictures that Alex probably had fruitless results obtaining the photographs I wanted to share with Alexander Bortnikov, it's time to start thinking about what to do for plan B.

I might just have to kidnap Boyd Bushman and take him and his pictures back to Russia with me.

Boris picked up his I-phone and was getting ready to call Jimmy to come pick them up when he noticed he had thirty-five incoming emails from Alex.

While Boyd was carefully placing his pictures back in his satchel, Boris took a quick look at one of Alex's emails, then instantly smiled when he discovered it was a good high-resolution picture of some of the same pictures he was just looking at.

BORIS (a.k.a. Jack) THOUGHT
Boyd probably left copies of his pictures back in his
hotel room

Boris suddenly realized and smiled, closed out the email and clicked on the speed dial for Jimmy.

Within 2 rings:

JIMMY
You ready to leave boss?

BORIS (a.k.a. Jack)
Yea all I got to do is get my dinner bill paid, and I'll be
right down in front.

JIMMY
I'll be there waiting for you.

<u>INT. NIGHT. LAS VEGAS. LAWRY'S RESTAURANT.</u>

Jimmy then shut off his phone.

JIMMY
Mr. Magic, I hate to leave now but the boss is ready
to roll.

MR. MAGIC
Tell Jack I said hello and sorry I didn't see him tonight.

Magic smiled remembering the time that his bartender friend Tio went after that crazy female private detective he thought was an easy lay because she had been seen leaving Boris' condo with her professional styled hair messed up early one morning hours after the bar closed.

Turns out Boris didn't touch her because he had immediately figured out there was something wrong upstairs with that woman.

183

Tio made the grave mistake of taking the private Detective Debbie home to his condo he shared with his mother. Debbie turned into a fatal attraction. Tio took a year and damn near a restraining order to get rid of Debbie.

The day after Tio made that fatal blunder, Magic and Boris laughed when "Jack" (a.k.a. Boris) set Tio straight.

> BORIS (a.k.a. Jack)
> Tio, I never touched that woman, she threw herself on me, and I thought she had some mental problem, so I avoided that stuff!

Jimmy threw down five $20 bills that more than covered his prime rib sandwich and his coffee he had while shooting the shit with Magic over the past hour or so. Magic, who often performed magic tricks at the bar for customers, always liked Jimmy, who tipped well considering his income was a Limo driver.

NOTE:

> During the following VOICEOVER the action shows Jimmy waving goodbye to Mr. Magic, the bartender, going out to the Limo and driving over to the Top of the World Restaurant to pick up Boris (a.k.a. Jack).

> VOICEOVER
> *Mr. Magic like most others didn't know Jimmy was a Russian Spy by the name of Mikhail Chizhevsky who had been assigned as a watcher to Boris Potemkin (a.k.a. Jack).*
>
> *Boris thought Jimmy was just an FSB grunt sent along to do all his dirty work and handle small chores and drive his limo around to give an appearance.*
>
> *In 30-years' time, instead of wasting his money gambling and on prostitutes, Boris bought the Liquor Store facilitated by his fake KGB manufactured I.D. that usually required nabbing and killing a loner and stealing his identification to create the new personification of the agent they wanted to run.*
>
> *Through their network of agents, it was a tough chore, but they always were able to come up with loners after a while, someone with no known relatives, and drifters. The social security number of a dead Connecticut man came in handy for such purposes.*

The role of a watcher was to report back to Moscow to authenticate any information their agents reported as well keep an eye on them, so they didn't get into trouble.

If it appeared an FSB Illegal like Boris Potemkin was getting into trouble, the watcher either calls in an extraction force or preventer.

Preventers usually took matters into hand that mitigated a disaster or embarrassment to their government. One such case would be an illegal FSB agent like Boris getting caught performing his trade craft.

Watchers put into roles like Jimmy were trained that it was highly critical that their contacts such as Boris never knew their real role and to always play dumb and humble.

If the FSB watcher ever violated that policy, or the FSB spy which the watchers monitored discovered a watcher, then one or both would be recalled to Moscow and given some shitty job.

If superiors felt punishment was in order they would end up as a border guard where living conditions were not too good, and the chances of promotion or relocation were highly remote.

Mikhail Chizhevsky (a.k.a. Jimmy) knew his worst days doing menial jobs that Boris sometimes had to give him, was still better than the best days he could ever expect to experience as a Russian Border Guard that was now part of the FSB.

On some of the borders with former Soviet States existed, Islamic fundamentalism existed. It was really easy for a Watcher to be sent to dicey places like Chechnya were life expectancy for KGB Agents in the past had been cut very short.

If a Russian Border Guard did not speak with the local dialect, then that Russian Guard was immediately

*suspected as being KGB/FSB and Chechnyan gangs
went out of their way to discover the truth.*

*Discovery of affiliation with the FSB/KGB, would
more than likely lead to some accidental death or
suicide such as jumping off tall buildings.*

When it was all said and done, Boris' main activity for the past 30 years involved installing bugs or facilitating recruitment. Mikhail Chizhevsky had been his watcher for at least half those years.

As in the case of Boyd Bushman, many of those used by Boris were recruited without ever knowing it.

***

When Boyd Bushman traveled back to Fort Worth the next morning with MJ-12 agents would be hot on his tracks, Boyd Bushman had no idea he had just been handled by one of the top FSB (KGB) operatives in North America.

Since Gus was not able to get CIA burglar contractors in time to steal the documents Boyd Bushman carried in his possession a new plan was put into action.

General Brazile, very well educated in spy craft because of his unique position of carrying out MJ-12 directives assumed that if Boyd Bushman was having dinner with Boris Potemkin , that meant Boyd Bushman was being recruited.

Boyd Bushman remained oblivious to the serious situation he was in until he had his little unexpected meeting several days later with the Air Force Colonel sent out by General Brazile to have a discussion with him and reason with him.

AIR FORCE OFFICER
COLONEL JONES
Boyd, you crossed the line when you sat in front of a
film documentary camera.

Boyd responded knowing that he had just recorded his death bed confession.

BOYD BUSHMAN
There's nothing you or anyone else can do to me now.

Boyd assumed he would soon die of natural causes within days after this meeting. Or so it seemed.

***

General Brazile and Gus having just left the meeting were on the elevator heading up to the surface and out of building 27. Gus was heading for the GS650 plane waiting for him and General Brazile was on his way back to his BOQ room.

General Brazile was soon walking out of building 27 with Gus.

GENERAL BRAZILE

I'll walk you to your plane.

GUS

If I get any information on Boyd Bushman, I'll let you know right away.

GENERAL BRAZILE

I appreciate that.

General Brazil added to his next dilemma

GENERAL BRAZILE

Years ago, the former director of Skunk Works, Ben Rich came out with a death bed confession. It was shown later by UFOlogists in precisely the same way at a UFO conference and all the UFO nuts went crazy.

VOICEOVER (GUS)
THOUGHT

Government cover-up and propaganda was starting to get far more difficult and complicated.

GUS

Preventing disclosure is going to be tougher moving forward.

The Gulfstream 650 was sitting idling with jet engines running low RPMs in expectation of immediate departure as Gus and General Brazile walked out of building 27 towards the plane with General Brazile a short distance.

GENERAL BRAZILE

Good luck with your assignment, we are all going to have some sleepless nights here soon.

GUS

Yea, it's going to be rough until we find out which Aliens are involved and the impact it may have on Earth's future.

GENERAL BRAZILE
You know it's very difficult to find out things when *Project Alpha* comes up empty handed.

GUS
Project Alpha Secret Space Force is well established, and knows of the presence of Aliens, but direct knowledge of intentions and capabilities are sadly lacking.

GENERAL BRAZILE
Project Alpha does not seem to live up to its means.

GUS
It probably never will while we are still alive.

With that last statement, Gus climbed aboard the waiting Gulfstream 650 and was back to Las Vegas a lot sooner than he planned.

***

By the time the *company* Limo pulled into Caesars front entrance area, Alex was long gone as it was past his work shift for the day and was not around to see Gus arrive.

INT. NIGHT. LAS VEGAS CAESARS PALLACE. BUFFALO BAR.

Gus, feeling a little hungry since he missed dinner and was thirsty, went to the *Buffalo Bar* he knew would serve drinks and something light to eat. He sat down and grabbed the short menu that was tucked in between a napkin holder and salt and pepper shaker.

Gus wasn't the only one there with the same idea. Having spent a lot of time in Las Vegas, this quaint little Caesars Palace *Buffalo Bar* was often the gamblers' destination that didn't feel like hitting a restaurant or a buffet and wanted to pack down a good drink at a reasonable price.

Another great restaurant attribute was the lack of loud music where someone could hold a decent conversation.

As Gus was sitting down in the Caesars Palace Buffalo Bar there were already several conversations going on about nonsensical things or sports.

BARTENDER
What can I get for you, sir?

GUS
Give me a steak sandwich and I would like a glass of
Cabernet?

BARTENDER
How do you want the steak cooked?

GUS
Make it medium rare, please.

BARTENDER
You got it.

The bar tender turned around and punched some buttons on a terminal which would
keep track of Gus' bar tab.

A cute lady wearing a pretty dress came in and sat down next to Gus. Her perfume was
not suffocating; therefore, Gus assumed she wasn't one of the numerous call girls and
hookers roaming Las Vegas.

Even though Las Vegas police made Herculean efforts to keep the prostitutes off the
strip, they, nevertheless, hung around like flies and just as they got rid of one swarm the
next would show up. There were also numerous dudes handing out call girl invitation
cards to pedestrians.

Prostitution is legal in Nevada, but none of the Casino owners wanted them around for
one good reason: money spent on a hooker was less money spent in the casino.

Consequently, the Casinos acted like team members with the police force, and it was a
daily routine task Alex had with his security detail in getting rid of all the hookers that
came in trying to solicit a little action. They had devious tricks such as joining dudes
at a blackjack table or bars such as this one.

Gus smiled at the woman sitting at Caesars Palace Buffalo Bar, and she smiled back.

Gus assumed the woman sitting next to him at the bar was a tourist.

GUS
Enjoying your vacation?

FEMALE CUSTOMER
(a.k.a. Susan Jonhson)
Oh yes, having a fabulous time.

The bartender came over to the lady.

BARTENDER
What can I get you?

FEMALE CUSTOMER
(a.k.a. Susan Jonhson)
A glass of white wine, please.

BARTENDER
Chardonnay, ok?

FEMALE CUSTOMER
(a.k.a. Susan Jonhson)
Sure, that will do.

Gus just coming directly from the meeting without a change, had on a suit and tie, and appeared like a businessman or a lawyer.

FEMALE CUSTOMER
(a.k.a. Susan Jonhson)
Did you just finish work?

GUS
Yes, and of course I felt a little hungry, that's why I came here.

The woman then grabbed the menu and started looking at it.

FEMALE CUSTOMER
(a.k.a. Susan Jonhson)
I was getting a little hungry myself.

When the Bartender came back with her drink, he saw her holding the menu.

BARTENDER
Madam, would you like to order something to eat?

FEMALE CUSTOMER
(a.k.a. Susan Jonhson)
Yes, I would like a Caesar Salad.

The bartender turned away and the woman took a long sip of her wine giving off a good smile.

FEMALE CUSTOMER
(a.k.a. Susan Jonhson)
This is a good tasting wine.

GUS
The food and drinks here are usually pretty good.

Women are generally nosey, and quite a few of them Gus met in Las Vegas were also gold diggers and looks were deceiving. Many women Gus met in Las Vegas didn't have much money and were often on four or five-day vacation packages hoping to strike it rich, or find Daddy Warbucks, and if not at least a good 5-day lover.

What happens in Vegas stays in Vegas, is a good description of the sin city.

FEMALE CUSTOMER
(a.k.a. Susan Jonhson)
What do you do for a living that gets you off work this
late at night?

GUS
Well, I'm sort of with a security firm and I had to go to
a meeting, I just got back from.

FEMALE CUSTOMER
(a.k.a. Susan Jonhson)
I see. You do security for the Casinos?

GUS
No. I work for other entities, and they don't like me to
disclose them in public

FEMALE CUSTOMER
(a.k.a. Susan Jonhson)
Alright.

GUS
How about yourself?

FEMALE CUSTOMER
(a.k.a. Susan Jonhson)
Well, I'm just a plane old schoolteacher from
Cincinnati Ohio.

GUS
This is a long way to come, any reason why you didn't
go to Foxwood or Atlantic City; they're a heck of a
lot closer?

FEMALE CUSTOMER
(a.k.a. Susan Jonhson)
Well, five other teacher friends and I come out here
about once a year to have a girl's vacation together.

GUS
I bet that's fun, traveling with your friends?

FEMALE CUSTOMER
(a.k.a. Susan Jonhson)
It is but I like to get away from those crazy cooks now
and then and catch my breath.

FEMALE CUSTOMER
(a.k.a. Susan Jonhson)
My name is Susan Johnson, what's your name?

GUS
I'm Gus.

Gus would never give his real name in public and the alias identification he carried
while on assignment wasn't his real name, nor was he legally allowed to identify
himself in case the government had to disavow him should he be captured behind
enemy lines.

SUSAN JONHSON
Are you married Gus?

Gus would never give out personal information for the same reasons.

GUS
No.

Gus's answer was technically correct since he was recently divorced and not about to
reveal that to anyone.

GUS
How about yourself?

Susan responded as she quickly thought about Roy the boring science teacher at her school, and Gary the dashing electronics engineer who worked for an electronics firm up in the Cleveland area.

SUSAN JOHNSON

No not yet, but I got a couple prospective candidates
back home.

The bartender delayed serving the salad but because of his astute observation and sense of etiquette, waited until the steak sandwich was ready to be served then approached them both at the same time and served them.

BARTENDER

Any steak sauce?

GUS

Yes, A1 please.

The steak sandwich was really a New York strip sliced into about 10 pieces on toast, not something a person could pick up with their hands and eat. A side of large helping of French fries was also on the large plate. Gus was long overdue for the meal and the cabernet washed the steak down just fine.

The teacher, Susan Johnson dug into her chicken on top of the salad about the time the bartender asked:

BARTENDAR

Would you like some fresh ground pepper on your
salad?

SUSAN JOHNSON

Sure.

As he was rotating the pepper grinder above her plate and delivering

BARTENDER

Let me know when enough is.

Susan Johnson responded a moment or so later after an amount of pepper was provided.

SUSAN JOHNSON

That's good.

BARTENDER

Would you like some fresh cheese?

SUSAN JOHNSON
Sure.

The bartender did a similar act on a cheese shredder that delivered nicely thin shreds of very tasteful cheese that added an incredible pleasant addition to the Caesar salad.

The two ate and drank for a few moments without saying much. Gus was enjoying the experience having a pleasant moment with a woman who was no doubt a very nice unassuming person displaying the live and let live attitude, though he also thought she could probably give a wild ride in the sack.

Right about the time Gus was finishing up on his steak sandwich, an older guy carrying a pouch or satchel sat down on the other side of Susan on a barstool that had just been recently made available with a departing customer. Gus judged the man to be in his 70s, Graying hair, glasses, appearing like an old doctor or engineer type.

BARTENDER
What can I get for you, sir?

BOYD BUSHMAN
How about a glass of red wine?

BARTENDER
Merlot, ok?

BOYD BUSHMAN
That would be fine.

Boyd Bushman then turned toward Susan and spoke with what appeared to be a hint of a Texas dialect.

BOYD BUSHMAN
Hello.

Boyd Bushman had just returned from dinner with Boris (a.k.a. Jack) and felt a little high strung and wanted a glass or two of wine to calm himself down a bit.

Boyd's medications he was taking for his medical condition also didn't help his disposition, nor was the prognosis, he might not have long to live. But sitting next to the attractive woman was improving his demeanor.

Susan looked at the grandfather figure just as she too had just put the finishing touches on her salad, the bartender was clearing away the dishes and silverware.

SUSAN JOHNSON
Good evening.

Susan took a sip of her wine about the same time the bartender served Boyd.

Boyd thought Susan looked very pretty and assumed she was a vacationer.

BOYD BUSHMAN
Enjoying your vacation?

SUSAN JOHNSON
Certainly. Are you having a good time?

BOYD BUSHMAN
Definitely. Did the casino make you go broke yet?

SUSAN JOHNSON
No. I teach math and statistics at a high school back in Cincinnati. I already know the odds are against me here in Vegas. I mainly take in the shows with my girlfriends and give a donation or two to the slot machines.

BOYD BUSHMAN
How did those donations work out for you?

SUSAN JOHNSON
I got lucky today, earned all my dining expenses with a $5 investment, so I'll stay ahead and not visit the slot machines again during this trip.

Boyd smiled.

BOYD BUSHMAN
Smart move.

SUSAN JOHNSON
How about yourself, do you live here?

BOYD BUSHMAN
No, I'm from Fort Worth, Texas.

SUSAN JOHNSON
Here on Vacation?

BOYD BUSHMAN
No, I came up for the UFO conference being held
down the block from here.

SUSAN JOHNSON
Do you believe in UFOs and aliens?

BOYD BUSHMAN
Absolutely. I have no doubt whatsoever.

SUSAN JOHNSON
Have you seen any UFOs?

BOYD BUSHMAN
That part I can't answer, but I will say this: some of my
friends have given me a lot of pictures. I'm convinced.

VOICEOVER (GUS)
THOUGHT
*This would be a strange coincidence if this was Boyd
Bushman.*

While Susan was turned away talking to Boyd, Gus turned away slightly then flipped
on an image of on his I-phone which came from an email he received from General
Brazile, concerning Boyd.

<u>C.U. GUS I-PHONE DISPLAY SHOWING BOYDS PICTURE.</u>

Gus instantly observed the image, and then quickly closed the image on his I-phone
before Susan turned around.

VOICEOVER (GUS)
THOUGHT
*It's confirmed. This is our person of interest, Boyd
Bushman.*

He then sent a text message to Roger who was up in his hotel room.

<u>C.U. GUS I-PHONE DISPLAY SHOWING TEXT MESSAGE BELOW.</u>

GUS (TEXT MESSAGE)
I'm down at the Ceasar Palaces' *Buffalo Bar*, there is a
woman sitting next to me and on the other side of her
is an older gentleman in a suit named Boyd Bushman.

Boyd Bushman is a person of interest to the DD/P. Get ahold of a security detail and watch every move he makes.

***

<u>INT. NIGHT. SWITZERLAND. ROBERT SIMMONS (A.K.A. ALEKSANDR ZUBKOV) HOME.</u>

Gus was too late to intervene, while he was eating his steak dinner, Boris was emailing the images to Alexander Bortnikov with a detailed report. The report went to a Robert Simmons in Switzerland, which was Alexander's mail drop for Boris.

<u>MONTAGE.</u>
VOICE OVER
(During Montage)

Robert Simmons was the alias for Russian Spy Aleksandr Zubkov living in Switzerland. Aleksandr was a deeply placed mole first finding work in the Texas Oil patch to learn the nuances of American society so that more important roles would be chosen for him.

Robert Simmons performed fifteen years of loyal service performing support missions in the Dallas/ Fort Worth area where considerable espionage went on around Lockheed and the aerospace industry there.

A hand in the oil patch presented Robert Simmons (a.k.a. Aleksandr Zubkov) a plausible cover story. The drifter Robert Simmons was killed and disposed of to utilize his identity provided a good initial entry point the KGB could build upon.

Aleksandr Zubkov was a KGB illegal, had no diplomatic protections and was highly trained in the consequences of what would happen to him if he ever got caught. Aleksandr Zubkov kept a low profile and gradually moved up in the oil business and 15 years later was now the assistant driller on an oil rig just promoted a few years before.

One of the oil company's geologists where he worked had inside information on oil deposits on land, they had not been able to convince farmers to lease.

These oil deposits were ripe for easy picking. The Geologist was also familiar with some of the negotiations going on and the amounts being offered for the leases that would not necessarily mean any holes drilled any time soon but would lock the land up in their portfolio and prevent competitors from leasing it.

In recent years the Geologist became friends with the quiet Robert Simmons (a.k.a. Aleksandr Zubkov) and in due time through a third friend set up a dummy company, then out bidding on the leases of the best prospects in the county that didn't have any oil wells anywhere near, got the lease for $200 an acre for 5 years with the option of 5 more years, and the land owner with the mineral rights would only get 20% royalties.

Before the ink was dry, an oil rig suddenly appeared out of nowhere. Money between the Geologist, Robert Simmons, and the third party could scrape together was enough to hire a wild cat driller and start the exploration hole.

The Geologist, who had control of the company's seismograph equipment, was encouraged by the company to go out and illegally seismograph land with no contracts to get a jump on their competition.

The company never thought their choir boy Geologist could ever be a crook like them. As a result, this geologist knew that even before they started drilling there was an oil pocket down a couple thousand feet with no saltwater deposits to mitigate.

The only reason why the Geologist let Robert Simmons (a.k.a. Aleksandr Zubkov) in on the deal was he needed help with the seismograph trucks and the need for some additional cash, that Robert Simmons (a.k.a. Aleksandr Zubkov) seemed to accumulate really well by keeping a low profile and constantly working except for a few times when he said he needed some time off for some personal matters (such as breaking into Lockheed facilities).

As expected, the three entrepreneurs hit a large oil pool, and the third party armed with the details of the first oil strike in the county, had no problems convincing local "banksters" to invest in their enterprise.

The oil company never did learn it was their own Geologist who manifested one of the more lucrative oil finds in recent years.

With all that bank money, growth in the company was astronomical. Within a year, Robert Simmons (a.k.a. Aleksandr Zubkov) was a multi-millionaire, but still loyal to the KGB.

Robert Simmons (a.k.a. Aleksandr Zubkov) also had a KGB watcher who reported back to Moscow about what was transacting in Texas, which led some of the wiser KGB planners to develop a new role for Robert.

Now with his perfect American identity, and wealth, Robert Simmons (a.k.a. Aleksandr Zubkov) would be sent to Switzerland, living off his riches as a lucky oil man, but put in various roles beneficial to the organization.

Robert Simmons rags to riches Texan oil story opened a lot of doors and allowed him to meet a lot of wealthy people in Switzerland from all over the world, the KGB would soon try to exploit one way or another.

Because of Robert Simmons extraordinary loyalty plus paying for his own expenses, one of the tasks eventually given him was to set up a dozen different email accounts with the help of the KGB (FSB) to act as a mailbox to provide a firewall between their spies and Alexander Bortnikov.

Aware of the use of double spies which was the trademark of the CIA, under no circumstances could there ever be a direct reporting mechanism that would tie the spy in the field to their leader Alexander Bortnikov.

What Robert Simmons (a.k.a. Aleksandr Zubkov)

did with emails coming in from 12 different spies to an anonymous account his KGB handlers provided, was to copy the file, encrypt it, transfer the file via a memory stick to a laptop provided by the KGB, then encrypt it and transmit it to Moscow to a communications technician who then provided those reports to Alexander Bortnikov twice a day unless directed otherwise.

<u>INT. DAY. MOSCOW RUSSIA LUBYANKA SQUARE, MESHCHANSKY DISTRICT. FSB (KGB) HEADQUARTERS. ALEXANDER BORTNIKOV'S OFFICE SPACES.</u>

The communications technician sworn to his life to secrecy spent half his life at Lubyanka Square in Meshchansky District of Moscow.

When the KGB and the border guards were integrated after the fall of the Soviet Union, to what it is now: *The Federal Security Service of the Russian Federation (FSB) or Федеральная служба безопасности Российской Федерации (ФСБ), Federal'naya sluzhba bezopasnosti Rossiyskoy Federation*, most of the employees merely changed uniforms, their roles remained identical.

<u>C.U. COMMUNICATIONS TECHNICIAN LAPTOP DISPLAY READING ROBERT SIMMONS REPORT.</u>

Today was a pain in the ass for the communications technician and for a while he thought Robert Simmons had simply gone mad.

Had it not been for the fact Robert said in his email:

ROBERT SIMMONS
(EMAIL)
I'm just the messenger, I have no opinion in this matter.

The communications technician might have turned the matter over to internal affairs without the disclaimer to evaluate the suitability of Robert remaining in his role.

Therefore, the communications technician simply copied the files and decrypted them and loaded them up on the briefing laptop he then carried down the hallway on the Red FSB (KGB) carpet into Alexander Bortnikov office after the secretary gave him permission to enter the office.

ALEXANDER BORTNIKOV
Any good juicy stuff for me today?

COMMUNICATIONS TECHNICIAN
Yes, got a lot of pictures from agent Boris Potemkin.
His PowerPoint is the first one for you to review.

Alexander Bortnikov acted surprised and amused and responded

ALEXANDER BORTNIKOV
I'll have my secretary call you when I'm finished
reviewing all these communications.

COMMUNICATIONS TECHNICIAN
I'll be standing by.

The communications technician then turned and left heading back to his office.

Alexander Bortnikov could not reveal to the technician he was fully briefed on the America's secret space program.

VOICEOVER (ALEXANDER
BORTNIKOV) THOUGHT
I wonder: how the hell this Mr. Boyd Bushman got
these photographs? Getting pictures out of S4 section
of Area 51 was almost impossible for the FSB.

Alexander Bortnikov was a handsome man, and in a business suit that he usually wore, had an appearance that one could easily mistake as American.

Alexander had spent time at Harvard and MIT as part of Russian American exchange student back in the late 1980s where he developed a Boston dialect and subsequently sent on missions in America perfectly blended in very well and was never suspected of being a foreigner.

When Alexander Bortnikov traveled through Silicon Valley, Norfolk Virginia, and Austin Texas, he fit right in and his New England accent automatically disarmed any suspicious people as he went about recruiting them, with or without their knowledge.

Alexander Bortnikov received his advance degree in international relations at the University of Oxford in England, where he wrote a very provocative thesis which almost turned out to be the road map for the disintegration of the Soviet Union and the subsequent reorganization.

Shortly afterward he got into the business when he was recruited by the KGB in 1994, Alexander Bortnikov's friendships and relationships established at Oxford and MIT led to some significant recruitment that turned out to be better than any moles Russia had previously developed and dwarfed the intelligence successes even from John Walker who betrayed his country for almost two decades.

In the *Director's-Eyes-Only* text accompanying the photographs which the communications technician had read and observed as he was required to do, by Alexander Bortnikov internal procedures, there was a request for guidance flagged. It was evident the spy Boris Potemkin was asking for some guidance and feedback that now Alexander Bortnikov must painfully respond.

The reply started immediately.

<u>C.U. ALEXANDER BORTNIKOV'S LAPTOP DURING REPLY.</u>

VOICEOVER
ALEXANDER BORTNIKOV
RESPONSE

Dear Boris.

Thank you for your report. I cannot tell you how or why I know some of your report is factual. The information you reported is the state's secrets, but you can be assured, I consider your report 100% correct.

Even though some of the information contained had been previously received by other sources, I did glean some new information out of what you provided.

We are aware of Mr. Bushman. Unfortunately, he is under intense scrutiny and any further contact by you with him is not authorized.

We shall be sending additional personnel to evaluate whether you have blown your cover.

Take care of personal matters and be prepared to evacuate upon immediate notice.

12 hours later when Boris received his reply, he knew his days in Las Vegas were now numbered.

It would not be possible for Boris Potemkin to dispose of all his real estate or for that matter move much of his wealth before he was escorted out of the country.

Borris Potemkin would have to learn how to live like peasant in Russia since all this extravaganza would soon be behind him forever. In years to come he would be crying in his Vodka if they didn't dispose of him right away.

***

<u>INT. NIGHT. LAS VEGAS. CAESAR'S PALACE. BUFFLAO BAR.</u>

Roger knew exactly where to find Gus. But since this was an operational situation, he knew not to approach Gus, and took a barstool down several seats past Boyd and could see Gus through the bar's mirror. When they made eye contact Roger nodded his head which meant arrangements had been made.

***

<u>INT. NIGHT. AREA 51 GENERAL BRAZIL'S OFFICE.</u>

When General Brazile read the latest situation report that Roger sent him about the surveillance they set up concerning Boyd Bushman, he turned toward the Air Force Colonel Jones he just summoned into his office after he was recalled from the BOQ for this priority message.

GENERAL BRAZILE
I want you to make necessary arrangements to go down to Fort Worth after Boyd Bushman returns home and put the fear of God into him. If he doesn't shut up and hand over those stolen alien pictures, he knows how the game is played.

AIR FORCE COLONEL JONES
Do I need to turn on X division?

GENERAL BRAZILE
Find out how he responds first.

AIR FORCE COLONEL JONES
He knows you could never prosecute him.

GENERAL BRAZILE
That's part of the problem, this case will never see the light of day in a court room, there would be too much exposure to his lawyers, if it came down to that.

AIR FORCE COLONEL JONES
It wouldn't be the first time we had to take care of lawyers.

GENERAL BRAZILE
Our budget is getting more scrutinized, so *Cash in Advance* may not be an option.

AIR FORCE COLONEL JONES
Then X division is the only solution.

GENERAL BRAZILE
If X division is turned on, I want to make sure, there is no traceability, and it all looks like natural causes.

AIR FORCE COLONEL
The Tring owe us a few favors.

GENERAL BRAZILE
They certainly do.

AIR FORCE COLONEL
And the chemicals they provide us with leave no evidence.

GENERAL BRAZILE
Perhaps it's time Boyd got his wish, and we let him meet a real Alien.

AIR FORCE COLONEL JONES
The Tring looked so much like a Human; he probably wouldn't believe it.

GENERAL BRAZILE
Forget the Tring, make the arrangements with X-division and if he doesn't cooperate, don't waste any time. We can't risk anymore disclosure, our disinformation campaign will only go so far, and he's already got too much exposure on those YouTube videos he put out on his death bed confession.

AIR FORCE COLONEL JONES
He's the one who told the world it's a death bed confession, so he helped us.

***

<u>INT. NIGHT. LAS VEGAS. CAESARS PALACE BUFFALO BAR.</u>

Boyd Bushman continued discussing aliens with Susan for about another twenty minutes, and then suddenly Susan announced:

SUSAN JOHNSON
I think I'm going back to my room and get some sleep.
My friends kept me up too late last night.

Susan Johnson grabbed her check the bartender had laid out for her as well as he had done for all the other customers, she opened her purse, pulled out a couple $20 bills, put in the pouch of the bill holder laid it down, smiled at the bartender.

SUSAN JOHNSON
It's been nice chatting, have a good night.

As Susan Johnson turned, she smiled at Gus and Boyd separately.

As soon as Susan left, Gus had a full view of Boyd and could see some of the UFO materials he had stuffed down in his satchel.

What Gus knew, which the public wasn't aware, was that Boyd Bushman had Top-Secret MJ-12 Q-level classified documents exposed out in broad daylight.

VOICEOVER (GUS) THOUGHT
Many people would do far less and end up in prison.
Sadly, the government had to walk a tight line because
it would be extremely difficult to prosecute the case
without undue disclosure.

Other techniques were then required, and Gus suspected *Cowboys in Action* would play heavily into the solution.

Based on past observations Boyd Bushman would not be paid for silence, instead someone else would be paid to convince him to maintain silence.

The X-division was set up for special projects to take care of situations when all hope was lost. X-division had a lot of job security keeping the secret space program hidden.

Boyd Bushman finished his wine and put some cash in his check bill holder and laid it back down and said good night to the Bartender who then pulled out his tip money and put the rest in the cash register.

The Bartender was all smiles because the tips had been good tonight. With Boyd Bushman out of the way, Gus could see Roger and they finished their drinks, paid their bills and left the bar at the same time. Their conversation did not occur until another 100 feet down the hallway on their way to their hotel rooms.

ROGER
What's scheduled for tomorrow?

GUS
We were planning on going to Los Angeles and San
Diego, but I think that trip is on hold until we are
relieved off this Boyd Bushman investigation.

ROGER
How soon will we know?

GUS
Most likely first thing in the morning. I suspect their
going to call in X-division or run it out of Groom Lake
since we already have other challenges on our hands.

Gus and Roger went their separate ways to their hotel room and eased in for the night with the goal of getting some sleep.

***

INT. SPACE. MĚNGJIÀNG YÚN-RÉN ROYAL YACHT.

Vance, meanwhile, was already in fusion with Sandra (a.k.a. *Wánměi De Huā*) and the telemetry now reaching Drago was building a case that if Vance did not leave Earth with *Wánměi De Huā*, and there could develop a Monarch crisis.

The fear in the Court the Empress might not be capable of managing affairs, because it was now becoming clear her fusions with Vance were now reaching very powerful levels. Such readings normally are a good indication of reaching a point of no return.

Another fear Drago had was that if Vance chose to remain on Earth, *Wánměi De Huā* might do what other *Měngjiàng Yún-Rén* have done and combined the souls which would allow one of them to live.

But the other being would cease to exist. Another peculiar aspect is that which person lived was unpredictable. However, it seemed to indicate the person who had the larger desire to live ended up with both souls combined into one and slowly evolved into a new personality unlike the previous couple exhibited.

Drago wished it didn't come to that and if Vance's answer was negative, as to prevent the potential loss and demise of the Empress, she had no other recourse but to order *one of her secret agents to kill Vance* before *Wánměi De Huā* had the opportunity to merge their souls. Each passing day slowly counted down to the day of reckoning.

***

<u>INT. DAY. LAS VEGAS CAESAR'S PALACE.</u>

In the morning, Gus called the group to establish a time of departure.

Gus had also just received an email from General Brazile sent during the night:

VOICEOVER
GENERAL BRAZILE
EMAIL
Gus, X-Division will relieve you of responsibilities for Boyd Bushman.

VOICEOVER (GUS)
THOUGHT
Only thought Gus could now think: They're going to kill him.

If that were the case, they didn't want Gus and his group to be anywhere around Boyd when the tragedy struck.

Because of the complications of operations at Caesars, X-division was directed to await further orders from General Brazile before they took any lethal actions, especially since he wanted to give Boyd one more chance to conform to the wishes of MJ-12.

Gus met the group at the Valet Parking attendant's booth at the front entrance of the Hotel and the attendant already had the facial recognition confirmation responded as soon as Gus stated:

GUS
We'd like our cars please.

VALET PARKING ATTENDANT
They are on the way Mr. Vandyke.

About that time, Susan and her teacher friends happened to walk by and noticed Gus with the 3 gorgeous ladies and a couple dudes waiting at the curb and approached Gus.

SUSAN JOHNSON
Good morning, Gus.

Susan wore shorts and a very revealing low cut tank top, sunglasses, and an Eddie Bauer Women's exploration wide brim hat, appeared far more appealing than in her dress she wore the night before.

GUS
Hello Susan, how are you doing?

SUSAN JOHNSON
Great. My friends and I are just going out to do some sightseeing and have brunch.

Beverly and Crystal knew of Gus' reputation as a lady's man assumed, she might have been his latest conquest based on her overly cheerfulness, smiled at Gus in an inquisitive manner.

SUSAN JOHNSON
Are you going somewhere?

GUS
Yes, on a little road trip.

SUSAN JOHNSON
Will you be back later?

GUS
No, we have some other destinations to reach today.

About then the strange looking SUVs with darkened windows pulled up. As prearranged, Roger hopped into the white SUV with Beverly.

Gus grabbed the key for the black SUV from the attendant when suddenly, Alex appeared wearing a nice-looking business suit.

ALEX
Good morning Mr. Vandyke.

GUS
Good morning, Alex.

ALEX
I see you are checking out of the hotel.

GUS
Yea, we have some places to go.

Alex asked then smiled over the inside joke.

ALEX
Up north?

GUS
No opposite direction.

Gus, realizing he owed Alex something for his special services while they stayed, reached into his pocket and pulled out a wad that was $1000.00 that he meant for Alex to throw into some slot machines as a gesture for their appreciation for the great support he provided protecting their cars, and very slyly handed it to Alex as part of a handshake clandestine exchange.

Alex quickly understood he had just received a little *Cash in Advance* from Gus during what the two exhibited as friendly handshake.

Susan Johnson was rather adept at her observations, caught a glimpse of the money transfer and realized it was some sort of bribe.

SUSAN JOHNSON
Goodbye Gus.

Gus responded and smiled affectionately at the teacher then thought:

VOICE OVER (GUS) THOUGHT
I wish I were one of her students.

GUS
Bye Susan.

After the group was all seated in the cars, they quickly drove to Las Vegas Boulevard and made a right turn and headed down a distance turned right again, then over the overpass then onto the freeway onramp and were suddenly heading south on Interstate 15.

Alex was slightly amused at the schoolteachers, all decent looking and Susan Johnson, somewhat exceptional looking, speculated she might have been one of Gus's one-night stands, stood there enjoying the sight. He overheard some chitchat between Susan and her friends.

SUSAN JOHNSON
He's the guy I met at *Caesars Buffalo Bar* last night.

TEACHER #2
He's kind of cute.

TEACHER #3
He looks well-built and in great condition.

TEACHER #2
What did you say he did?

SUSAN JOHNSON
He said he did some kind of security business.

Alex thinking he would have some fun with the women and possibly score some points for a possible future rendezvous spoke up.

ALEX
Yea he's in the security business all right.

SUSAN JOHNSON
What do you mean by that?

ALEX
You probably didn't know by the way he's dressed, but he's packing a weapon, he's deadly.

SUSAN JOHNSON
Is he a mobster or something?

Alex
No, he's one of the good guys.

SUSAN JOHNSON
That's good to know.

With that Alex decided he had wet the schoolteacher's appetites enough.

ALEX
Good day ladies.

Alex turned around and walked back into the hotel.

One of the wilder looking teachers then turned towards Susan and announced:

TEACHER #4
I bet he's a CIA guy or something.

SUSAN JOHNSON
That would not surprise me.

Susan and her schoolteacher friends then started to walk towards the sidewalk and then to the pedestrian overpass that would soon take them past the Flamingo, and the casino's restaurants and shopping they wanted to do.

TEACHER #2
He looks like some kind of hunk.

TEACHER #3
Susan, did you get lucky last night?

Susan started toying with the other teachers.

SUSAN JOHNSON
You ladies know the ground rules, what happens
in Las Vegas, stays in Las Vegas, plus Gus was the
perfect gentleman.

Susan was sure of Gus being a gentleman.

***

TANYA
Jimmy's phone rang. This time of the morning it could
only possibly be one person, Boris. When he looked
down at the number, he instantly saw it came from
Switzerland.

JIMMY
Hello, what can I do for you?

Then he heard the voice he instantly recognized as the messenger Robert Simmons. Like anyone else who didn't have the need to know, he had no idea that Robert Simmons was the alias for Aleksandr Zubkov.

ROBERT SIMMONS
There will be a private plane arriving at 3:00 p.m. You
are to transport Boris to the airport and make sure he
gets on.

Suddenly Jimmy heard a click and a dial tone, Robert Simmons had delivered the message and hung up.

Boris realized his time was just about up after his email from Alexander Bortnikov, had one of his favorite play toys with him getting in some last-minute recreation.

Tanya was a stunningly beautiful half American half Vietnamese who had come to America as a little girl in 1975 when she was only 8 years old. She was educated in America, had been a gifted student all straight As and lived a good life with her family.

Her Father whom everyone called Bob, worked for aerospace firms and always had big pay checks and spoiled Tanya to her demise, including doing something irrational such as buying her a new Corvette when she was only 16 years old.

Tanya lived near a Naval Air Station and as a 14-year-old who looked older managed to sneak into the officers' club on that base and was banging a pilot who almost had a nervous breakdown when he found out how old Tanya really was and fearful that if his wife hauled him into divorce court not only would he be financially ruined, but probably kicked out of the service for having sex with a minor.

Tanya finally got tied up with a couple dipshits over a several years period, who ruined her life, so when she was in despair after her father's death, she dumped her kids on her mother and moved to Las Vegas to start over working in one of the Casinos. Because she was uniquely attractive and very brilliant, she got a position as a blackjack dealer and did very well at it.

One day at the casino while Tanya was working and contemplating life waiting for her next victim to come up to her blackjack table, an older gentleman, well dressed, somewhat balding sat down at her table and laid some chips down

OLDER GENTLEMAN
Deal me.

The man was in no hurry, nor did he place any large bets, but at least he was friendly to talk to and seemed like a magnet to others that joined the table whom she made a killing off for the casino.

As the man left, he pretty much left all his earnings that were not all that great but still nothing to snub your nose at, for Tanya as a tip.

Tanya's boss who had been watching her from the video room and could hear the audio of their conversations, approached her and congratulated her.

TANYA'S BOSS
You did a great job of wiping out those four victims
and at the same time a heck of a job earning that tip
from Jack.

TANYA
You know that man?

TANYA'S BOSS
Yes, I've known Jack who's been around the strip for
several years now.

TANYA
Really?

TANYA'S BOSS
Jack makes it a point to get to know casino operators
to enhance his liquor business as well as future efforts
in the event he might want to use some of their special
services.

Jack never made much money off the casino; he was a willing contributor, but the
casino never caught on to his true purpose in life and the way he did it was so slick,
had no idea how many Air Force guys he had recruited over the years.

For all the money the Soviets supplied Jack to conduct his espionage, they got back
10,000-fold.

As an example, a couple days before the U.S. Bombed Iraq in Desert Storm, Jack had
learned they would probably use the F17A stealth aircraft. Hence, the Soviets were
able to attempt knocking a few of them down so that they could reverse engineer them.

Even though Jack's espionage put them in a position to exploit that information,
nothing came of Jacks INTEL. Had they had better weapons and sensors back then,
it would have been a different story. Now with their S500 surface to air missiles it's a
new ball game.

One night when Jack made one of his visits to Tanya's card table, and she was about
due to get off duty, Jack was getting kind of hungry. He then got the idea.

JACK (a.k.a. Boris Potemkin)
Tanya, what time are you leaving tonight?

TANYA
Oh, in about half an hour.

JACK (a.k.a. Boris Potemkin)
How about I take you to dinner? I'm getting hungry.

TANYA
What do you have in mind?

JACK (a.k.a. Boris Potemkin)
I was thinking about Lawry's; it's not far from here.

VOICEOVER (TANYA) THOUGHT
Tanya, who had been in Lawry's before also feeling some slight hunger pains since she missed lunch today, thought to herself Jack looks gentle enough, and my manager likes him, he's probably safe.

TANYA
Sure. I'll go.

Time passed quickly, and Tanya and Jack were heading out the door. Jack had called moments before, and Jimmy was in front of the Casino in the limo to pick them up.

As Jack approached the Limo, Jimmy, as customary, got out of the Limo's front driver side, walked over to the rear passenger side, opened the door and waited.

Tanya was suddenly delighted that she was going to dinner with some rich dude instead of some douchebag that you typically meet around Vegas.

It didn't take long for them to reach Lawry's restaurant.

Jimmy got out of the Limo, opened the door for Jack who got out first with Tanya following.

Jimmy had a problem finding a parking spot; so, by the time he got the limo parked he had wasted twenty minutes, and when he walked in Lawry's he could see Jack sitting at the bar with Tanya and Mr. Magic entertaining the guests The bar was packed, so to not disturb Jack and Tanya, Jimmy quietly turned around and walked out.

<u>C.U. JIMMY AS HE'S SCANNING THE BAR AND ANALYZING THE CROWD.</u>

VOICEOVER (JIMMY)
THOUGHT
The heck with it. I'll get some fast food.

Jimmy hopped in the limo and drove to a fast-food place where he got a bite to eat and a beverage. By the time he got back to the restaurant, Jack was finishing up and called him saying they were on their way out.

TANYA
Jack, can you please take me back to the Casino where
so I can pick up my car.

JACK (a.k.a. Boris Potemkin)
Sure, no problem.

After that night, Jack took Tanya to dinner more and more often. Then one night after dinner at a swank restaurant up on the top floor of a hotel, Jack asked Tanya if she would like to go over to his condo nearby and listen to some music.

Tanya, feeling a little lubricated and happy, responded positively.

TANYA
Certainly.

Tanya didn't know what to expect, she had seen a few guys' *dumps* before, but was open-minded; plus, this guy Jack could afford a Limo, so it shouldn't be too bad.

As they entered Jack's condo, Tanya, who had a powerful sense of smell, discovered the very pleasant odor, and the well-kept look.

TANYA
You have got a nice place here, Jack.

JACK (a.k.a. Boris Potemkin)
Thank you.

TANYA
You're welcome, Jack.

JACK (a.k.a. Boris Potemkin)
What kind of music do you want to hear?

TANYA
Something light and easy, please.

Jack put on some light Jazz. Soon with a very expensive sound system Tanya was listening to her favorite tunes which Jack was more than happy to play for her as he kept her glass filled with Louis XIII Cognac.

<u>JAZZ MUSIC FOR THE SOUNDTRACK IF IT CAN BE LICENSED:</u>

<u>Bill Evans Trio, BBC studio, London, March 19th, 1965 (colorized) (youtube.com)</u>

Tanya started feeling really hot after the 3rd or 4th Louis XIII. Boris Potemkin, being a master in analyzing human emotion and estimating intentions knew that Tanya was well lubricated, and the time was right for transcendence into a physical event that he knew she was ready for.

When Boris attempted to kiss Tanya, she welcomed his touch and before long they were intertwined in passion and lust and moving forward into a slowly evolving relationship, that both parties benefitted from on many levels.

On that dreaded day a couple of years later when they were enjoying the ambience of each other's presence and touch, Jack was grateful that Tanya had been available on such short notice. Before she arrived earlier, he had written her a letter and placed a check with a large sum of money assigned to it written out to her, with a business card of his attorney with instructions to see him if she had any problems cashing it.

Jack that morning gave his attorney the power of attorney with a legal contract to dispose of all his assets and directed he send the proceeds to Tanya. That information and a copy of the contract was attached to the letter he would give her later. After Boris reached a point of exhaustion and begged Tanya to please give him a break, his phone rang as he was expecting.

JACK (a.k.a. Boris Potemkin)
Hello.

JIMMY
Jack, I've been instructed to pick you up at 2:30 and
take you to the airport.

Boris instantly knew it was Jimmy's voice and responded

JACK (a.k.a. Boris Potemkin)
I'll be ready.

In a while Tanya regrettably said:

TANYA
Jack, I must leave now and go to work.

JACK (a.k.a. Boris Potemkin)
I understand.

Tanya got up and very efficiently dressed, then bent over to kiss Jack on the forehead then he suddenly reached over and grabbed the envelope he had been waiting to give her.

JACK (a.k.a. Boris Potemkin)
Here Tanya, this is for you. Please do not open it until
you get off work tonight.

Tanya smiled, suspecting it was some kind of gift, then kissed him on the forehead again and smiled and left.

Exactly at 2:30 Jack was out front, dressed in a suit and tie, freshly shaved and ready to go. He had no luggage as he was aware he wouldn't need it where he presumed, he was going.

Jimmy pulled up, got out of the car and walked around and opened the car door in a highly choreographed manner Jack was used to.

Just before Boris got into the Limo, he handed Jimmy two envelopes.

JACK (a.k.a. Boris Potemkin)
The first envelope is for you. The second one I'd like
you to give to Alex over at Caesars Palace, this is
something I owe him.

JIMMY
Thank you, Jack. I'll make sure Alex gets the envelope.

The Limo was soon heading down I-15 and turned off at the airport exit and was soon pulling up in front of Jim's Air Service, a private plane support center that provided the wealthy quick and unobtrusive access to their private jets. Two men wearing sunglasses were there waiting for JACK (a.k.a. Boris Potemkin).

These two FSB agents knew Boris Potemkin (a.k.a. Jack) by sight and nodded and he followed them out to the Bombardier Jet that was originally designed as a corporate jet to haul up to 20 passengers, had been retrofitted to haul only eight passengers with extra fuel tanks so that they could fly non-stop to just about anywhere in the world.

The two men stepped at the side of the access door to the jet that was open with a very attractive flight attendant at the doorway. Boris Potemkin climbed up the stairs into the jet and was soon followed by the two FSB goons that were taking him back to Moscow.

The plane soon left on a flight directly over the North Pole to Moscow.

Jimmy headed north on I-15, got off at the strip, drove up to the VIP Valet parking attendant.

JIMMY
Could you please ask Alex to come here? I have
something for him.

Within 2 minutes of the summons, Alex appeared at the valet stand and instantly
recognized Jimmy who immediately handed him the envelope.

JIMMY
ALEX, this is from Jack. He owes you this money and
appreciates all that you have done for him in the past.

ALEX
Is Jack busy with his liquor store or a girlfriend? That
Tanya bitch is hot stuff.

JIMMY
Alex, I'm only telling you this because Jack liked you.
I could get in a lot of trouble informing you so do us
both a favor and forget you ever knew Jack. You will
not be seeing him again.

VOICEOVER
Alex knew the kind of business Jack was in. Something
bad happened to him, he knew that for a fact, and he
was glad Jimmy gave him the word.

Without another word, Jimmy got back into the Limo and drove off.

Alex soon discovered Jack had just paid him handsomely for his services and
immediately went to Guido and paid off his gambling debt in its entirety.

Guido had some ideas that Alex was involved in some crooked dealings, but he was
glad Alex finally paid off his gambling debt and soon coached him.

GUIDO
Alex, you can do well here in Vegas for yourself if you
stay the hell away from the dice.

Alex was truly tired of losing his ass knowing the odds were always against him.

ALEX
I've lost interest in gambling. I always lose so there
is no point.

GUIDO
That's good you understand that. You will make a lot
more money working with the house.

VOICEOVER
True to her promise, Tanya did not open the envelope until she got back to her condo. Shortly after opening it the tears rolled down her cheeks. Jack was the nicest man she had ever met.

Jack's departure caused Tanya great sadness. Jack was her savior, he put her in position to rebuild her life and one day get back her kids.

***

EXT. DAY. BAKER CALIFORORNIA.

As the Caravan got near Baker CA the seedy little town that had a half dozen gas stations and fast-food joints, was also the turn off on CA 127 towards Death Valley.

Gus called Roger who was riding shotgun in the white SUV.

GUS
Roger, we are going to pull over here at Baker to get
some coffee and take a restroom break.

ROGER
Yea, I could use a cup of coffee.

The two CIA SUVs pulled into Denny's parking lot, and everyone got out of the two SUVs.

ROGER
I like their coffee here

Beverly responded as she was feeling like she wanted a cup of Java too.

BEVERLY
Works for me.

When they entered Denny's, the waitress asked:

DENNY'S WAITRESS
How many?

BEVERLEY
Six please.

A moment later.

DENNY'S WAITRESS
This way please.

The waitress gave them a corner booth that had good observation of the restaurant and the parking lot in the direction of their parked SUVs.

Moments later the waitress appeared and asked if anyone wanted coffee, there were five *YES* answers.

CRYSTAL
I need to use the ladies' room.

Since Crystal was sitting on the outside of the booth easily got up and started walking to the lady's room.

BEVERLY
Me too.

Beverly followed Crystal.

To Vance's surprise Sandra (a.k.a. *Wánměi De Huā*) got up and followed the two female CIA agents to the lady's room.

Vance had no idea what the women had to say in the lady's room, but when they came back it was a lot of giggles and looks at Vance.

While the women were gone, Gus noticed 4 dudes in the parking lot who looked a lot like guys they saw at Boulder City.

GUS

> Roger, do you see those guys in the parking lot? Do
> they look familiar?

ROGER

> They kind of look like the dudes yesterday with the
> cyborgs with big guns.

GUS
That's exactly what I was thinking.

Gus and Roger watched as the men walked into Denny's Restaurant and were seated at the opposite end of the building near the restaurant entrance.

As hard as they tried, the *Měngjiàng Yún -Rén Spies* were not good at hiding the fact they were doing some sort of reconnaissance on Vance and the group.

The waitress came back and took orders. When she got to Vance he requested:

VANCE
I would like a Patty Melt Sandwich, please.

The rest all ordered hamburgers and fries to go along with their coffee except for Sandra (a.k.a. *Wánměi De Huā*) who indicated she wasn't hungry.

BEVERLY
Doesn't Sandra ever get hungry?

Beverly wondered why it seemed Sandra (a.k.a. *Wánměi De Huā*) never ate.

Vance responded in a way the women thought he was joking. Sandra just politely smiled.

VANCE
Oh yes, about once a month.

In due time everyone finished eating the quick meal and they got up to depart. Before anyone else could, Vance grabbed the check and carried it up to the counter and paid the bill.

As the group passed the four men, Gus felt nothing but evil. He swore to himself:

VOICEOVER (GUS)
THOUGHT
These four guys must be Aliens.

Sandra on the other hand knew precisely who they were, telepathically talked to their leader without giving away they were having a conversation.

SANDRA (a.k.a. *Wánměi De Huā*)
Are you here as part of my security detail?

MĚNGJIÀNG YÚN -RÉN SPY
Yes, Madam Empress, please do not expose us; it's in
your best interest.

SANDRA (a.k.a. *Wánměi De Huā*)
Of course. Could you please do me a favor?

MĚNGJIÀNG YÚN -RÉN SPY
Madam Empress, your command is our desire.

SANDRA (a.k.a. *Wánměi De Huā*)
Report to Drago that I'm having an excellent time.

Without giving any facial indication, the leader of the *Měngjiàng Yún-Rén* Security Detail responded:

MĚNGJIÀNG YÚN -RÉN SPY
Madam Empress, your message has been sent and received with a response from Drago that she is happy that you are pleased.

Beverly, a trained body language observer was able to catch the looks between Sandra and the *Měngjiàng Yún-Rén Spy*.

Vance's escort group and Sandra (a.k.a. *Wánměi De Huā*) piled into the two CIA SUVs and drove over to the Shell Gas station across the street along Baker Blvd.

Gus got out and started filling his gas guzzler and Beverly driving the white SUV pulled up behind the black SUV and got out and started filling up the gas in that car as well.

Right after Beverly put the nozzle into the tank access and put the nozzle on unattended filling walked over to Gus and said in a low voice:

BEVERLY
Sandra knew who those 4 dudes were that walked into Denny's.

GUS
Why do you say that?

BEVERLY
They made mysterious eye contact. We need to press Sandra (a.k.a. *Wánměi De Huā*) for confirmation.

GUS
They looked familiar. I think they are some of the guys who showed up and disarmed the people that pulled the guns at us at the helicopter ride business.

BEVERLY
Did you ever decide what that was about?

GUS
I think they were going to kidnap our special guests.

BEVERLY
Who do you think they are working for?

GUS
I'm not certain, but while I was out front of the hotel, I got a flash tweet from General Brazile that said, the Tall Whites who apparently are doing surveillance on us, think those were Grey Hybrids.

BEVERLY
You know those rumors of Grey Hybrids have been debunked.

GUS
The official party line sure, but in my private discussions with General Brazile, gave me the impression it hasn't been debunked and just because we never found a body or made an arrest, does not prove that hybrids are not amongst us.

BEVERLY
Well, whoever it was took those dudes away; we'll never know who they were.

GUS
I have my suspicion of who both parties at Boulder City are.

BEVERLY
Who do you think they were?

GUS
I think the guys who pulled the guns on us are Wogar Grey Hybrids and the others were *Měngjiàng Yún-Rén* sent down here to provide some protection for Sandra (a.k.a. *Wánměi De Huā*).

BEVERLY
Whoever they were didn't expect someone to come
along and upset their plans.

GUS
Maybe through Sandra (a.k.a. *Wánměi De Huā*) we
can establish some identity and confirmation and stop
speculating?

BEVERLY
I took some pictures of their car while we were driving
over here, but I didn't get any pictures of them.

GUS
They will probably be coming out soon, make sure we
get some pictures of them.

As Gus predicted the four men were hot on their heels. What they didn't know was
the CIA SUVs were loaded with cameras that Boris' *Locksmiths (plumbers)* failed to
recognize because they were built into the car body and without major disassembly
you would never know they existed.

The volume of the fake spare tire allowed considerable computer processing
power that interfaced with the various devices throughout the car on some
special wireless circuits.

The wireless signals were not operating on common frequencies. Since the
distances were short and power requirements low, they could pick frequencies
that were not expected by potential adversaries and out of the range of
industrial or commercial noise.

Cash in Advance (a.k.a. CIA) car network designers had unlimited budgets,
and even though there were only a dozen car people recruited out of Detroit as
prototype builders, they created numerous innovations that always provided
extraordinary capability for a more dangerous and ever-changing world.

Beverly now getting into the shotgun seat of the white SUV and Roger shifting
over as driver, all she had to do is run a CIA designed Surveillance APP on her
cell phone that now commanded the equivalent of a year 2024 supercomputer
mounted in the fake spare tire and battery operated.

Time is usually at the essence in surveillance in the field. The Surveillance APP
man machine interface was fine tuned to reduce operator intervention.

Beverly could talk to the cell phone giving commands or she could click on a few icons with her finger touch pad performance and achieve even quicker results.

As such Beverly was in a surveillance control mode and the car always presented a 360-degree picture of what's around them, all she had to do is select a target area to allow the surveillance APP developed a specific visual interrogation of that area or that equipment.

Beverly touched the I-phone display pane that showed the four possible *Měngjiàng Yún-Rén spies* approaching their car, and then simply applying slight pressure on the iPhone image for the top of the car made that object the source of the inquiry.

The automated system took over from there and did logical operations such as getting an ID on the car, license plate, owner, etc. It also zoomed in on any occupant getting in and out of the car and identified them or if they could not be identified with facial detection software, logged them into a hold file for later evaluation.

When the four *Měngjiàng Yún-Rén Spies* emerged from Denny's Restaurant and got near their car, the Surveillance APP already made the logical deduction that since they were closer to this car than any others, they were the expected occupants and started filming them in high-definition multiple wave lengths.

In a very short period when the processors started providing information the Surveillance APP created, the CIA SUV was in motion.

ROGER
Did you get a good identification on those guys?

Beverly
Still working on it.

VOICEOVER
SURVEILLANCE APP MESSAGE
Failed to identify.

Beverly swung into action to do some manual operations that might derive some useful information. First thing Beverly did was a comparison with the few pictures they managed to get back in Boulder City, and immediately the computer gave the prompt:

VOICEOVER
SURVEILLANCE APP MESSAGE
Match Confirmation.

BEVERLY
Yea these are the same people we saw back in Boulder
City

Beverly immediately hit the send button which routed the images whether deemed important or not, through Q-division who would keep General Brazile and if necessary, X-division duly informed.

Then suddenly, she got a very strange prompt:

VOICEOVER
SURVEILLANCE APP MESSAGE
Check Infrared and Ultraviolet.

Beverly clicked on the prompt that immediately reoriented the display to show these other wavelengths.

Beverly now saw the picture made no sense at all.

BEVERLY
This is crazy. Their infrared and ultraviolet displays have nothing that even slightly resembles a human body!

ROGER
Maybe there was a malfunction?

BEVERLY
Can't be. There are some other people in the background and their images look normal with expected heat signature for a sunny hot desert day.

ROGER
Let me see.

Beverly held the I-phone in an orientation where Roger could keep an eye on the road and glance over at the I-phone at the same time.

Roger swore as he saw exactly what Beverly had seen. Roger then subtlety said to himself

ROGER
Holy shit Batman.

BEVERLY
What the heck.

ROGER
Send that to Gus and Crystal, copy Q and General Brazile.

BEVERLY
What do you think?

ROGER
I think they're some kind of cyborgs or something with holographic capability.

BEVERLY
One thing is certain, they're not humans.

ROGER
That's all we need is another group of aliens showing up, we can't handle the ones already here. And the Wogar Greys are proving they're probably not really looking out for us.

BEVERLY
You have been listening to Struyograb too much; remember their competing entities looking out for their own interests.

ROGER
Yes, but their track record is a hell of a lot better than the Wogar Greys who still refuse to provide any evidence of what they did with the abductees other than claiming they're on their home planet and do not wish to return to earth.

BEVERLY
You must admit, the Greys at least kept the Azcarian Reptilians from taking over Earth back in 1972.

ROGER
That's probably because they want it themselves.

Crystal riding shotgun, got her notification of important incoming message clicked on message, then immediately opened it up and displayed pictures attached.

Crystal read Beverly's report, and then about the same time she received a response from General Brazile who had read Beverly's report:

<u>C.U. CRYSTAL'S IPHONE SHOWING GENERAL BRAZILE'S TEXT.</u>

GENERAL BRAZILE (TEXT)

> *X Division is setting up a technology scan in Barstow. Should be in place by the time you get there. Turn off I-15 on the exit ramp for East Main Street, then drive about ¼ mile across the overpass and pull into the Union 76 Gas station and wait until the blue van pulls in at Starbucks next to you. They will follow you into Los Angeles and do their sniffing on the way.*

Crystal unexpectedly made an announcement.

CRYSTAL

> Gus, we need to stop in Barstow. I will give you directions when we get up there.

Gus realizing he was in a dynamic fluid situation unfolding knew something was up and up at Barstow he would learn more, but listened as Crystal, a master interrogator started in.

CRYSTAL

> Sandra (a.k.a. *Wánmĕi De Huā*), did you know who those Aliens were back at the Denny's restaurant?

Sandra (a.k.a. *Wánmĕi De Huā*), was not prepared for any confrontation or inquisition at first deflected her question as if it was irrelevant, but Crystal exhibited a very determined interrogator.

Probing Crystal's mind Sandra (a.k.a. *Wánmĕi De Huā*), determined Crystal was a complex woman and her interrogation of Taliban fighters in Afghanistan proved Crystal could be a ruthless bitch. Sandra was shocked that Crystal's memories revealed an incident in Afghanistan.

On one occasion, Crystal threatened to cut the penis off a Taliban who refused to talk after he was captured when he had infiltrated a base with his partner who had just blown up 20 Americans before killing himself and an Army General in the process. As the blood started coming out and he was starting to feel the excruciating pain, fear struck him, he started talking.

Sandra was horrified when she probed and observed Crystal's graphic memory. She knew what Crystal and Gus knew via telepathic investigation then admitted:

SANDRA (A.K.A. *WÁNMĔI DE HUĀ*)
They are part of my security detachment keeping an
eye out for me.

As the SUV continued Southwest on I-15 towards Barstow, Crystal asked Vance and Sandra several questions.

CRYSTAL
Sandra, how did you meet Vance?

SANDRA (A.K.A. *WÁNMĔI DE HUĀ*)
My Chamberlain Drago introduced Vance to me after
I showed some interest in the story of how they found
him almost lifeless out in deep space in an emergency
escape pod.

CRYSTAL
Vance, how did you end up in space?

VANCE

It's a long story, but about fifteen years in the past, I was abducted by Mergenky Space Federation (MSF) from my back yard in Southern California.

The MSF took me to their City Quom on the planet Gwaba where I lived and experienced life with the Mergenky and my new family that began there until a fateful day where my circumstances changed.

Because of my desire to experience space travel as part of my entry into Mergenky society, I was allowed to be part of the MSF. In the beginning, I was a crew member aboard a Scout Class Spacecraft that had a dual purpose. One of which was exploration of the universe and the second purpose as a Scout Spaceship observing the enemy Anarchie as well as conducting special operations.

I went on a seven-year trip aboard the Mergenky Scout Spacecraft S1 to the Andromeda Galaxy. I became fully qualified as an MSF Officer and eventually I was assigned as Navigator to an MSF Battle Cruiser involved in the 2nd Jeeapa War.

The Mergenky Battle Cruiser I was assigned as navigator, was destroyed in a confrontation with the Anarchie in the vicinity of the Planet Jeeapa during the major space battle.

I was found in a Mergenky Emergency Escape Pod almost lifeless by the *Měngjiàng Yún-Rén* who rescued me and saved my life.

The *Měngjiàng Yún-Rén* took me back to their planets to decide what to do with me.

After being with the *Měngjiàng Yún-Rén* who were curious about me, I was introduced to Sandra (A.K.A. *Wánměi De Huā*) and after a while we became close friends.

The distance to Barstow did not take too long as they cruised along slightly above the speed limit, but had other cars flying past them at 85 mph.

CRYSTAL
Highway Patrol is out in force issuing tickets.

GUS
Sure are, in fact one of them just put his lights on me.

Gus pressed the switch indicator labeled *emergency lights* then suddenly a Highway Patrol emergency light panel popped up flashing on the roof of the SUV just like a patrolman's car would from a hidden cavity in the specialized design roof top.

The Highway Patrolman pulled alongside the SUV, Gus rolled down his smoke glass window and waved his U.S. Marshall's badge at the trooper while Crystal followed suit. The patrolman knowing Marshalls always monitored their frequencies while driving any major highway grabbed his microphone.

HIGHWAY PATROLMAN
Driver of the black SUV please identify yourself.

Gus responded by providing his Federal Badge number.

GUS
Hiway Patrolman, my Federal Badge Number is Sierra
Foxtrot Lima Niner Two Seven Alpha.

The patrolman's laptop screen facing him suddenly popped up a picture from the inquiry and the image matched the driver. The patrolman turned off his lights and then moved forward at a higher speed, obviously out to get some more speeders.

Gus pressed the *emergency lights* switch indicator control again and the lights receded into the recess and went off.

The trucker following Gus at a good pace blocking the view behind him of cars who missed the light show said to the 2nd driver in the cab who was there for long haul non-stop, spoke.

TRUCK DRIVER
WTF is that all about.

TRUCK DRIVER 2nd DRIVER
That's some kind of unmarked car; I'd give him plenty
of room.

The remainder of their travel to Barstow went off without any further incidents. Within minutes before the SUVs was almost at their turnoff and Crystal announced:

CRYSTAL
Take the next exit is East Main Street, turn off here and
make a left turn at the light.

Gus pulled into the gas station and within 5 minutes a Van pulled into Starbucks parking about 30 feet away. The Spook in the Van got out and approached the two CIA SUVs lined up at the pumps.

Gus recognized the man from X-division whom he worked with on some projects in the past, a guy named Jeff. The other man who got out on the other side of the Van, Gus also recognized, Gary.

Both these CIA X-DIVISION members were awesome people who could skin a cat in a New York minute and keep your ass out of trouble when you needed help the most.

Jeff had no problems locating the cars since the satellite tracker kept him informed of their current GPS coordinates. Jeff approached Gus.

JEFF
Long time no see stranger.

GUS
Sure, has been.

Gus nodded toward Gary.

GUS
Where did you find this character?

JEFF
Probably at some god forsaken cat house out in
Honolulu.

GUS
I can imagine.

JEFF

Yea that's where he told me you were quite the dancer.

GUS

What can I say. We sure had some good times together.

JEFF

Yep, it sure can separate the men from the boys and tell you who your friends are.

GUS

Well Jeff you may not realize this, but I first worked with Gary long before I met you.

JEFF

Yea, he can tell you about our little project in Groton.

GUS

Did it have anything to do with black boxes?

JEFF

You might say that. Probably that is where he screwed up his back too.

GUS

How did that happen?

JEFF

Just like Ron, you had a reputation for damaging people.

GUS

Don't say it's so?

JEFF

The Box Kicker (a.k.a. logistician) Ron you gave a bad back too, likes you. He said you helped him get on disability and will never have to work again.

GUS

I hear he now works on his T-bucket car, lifting engines out of it.

JEFF
Okay, so back to business now, just pretend like we don't exist.

GUS
Alright.

JEFF
We'll do all the technical analysis and send in the reports.

GUS
Alright.

JEFF
We are not expecting any trouble, but we do have a couple bruisers in the back of the van that not only operate the equipment but are pretty good with a gun.

GUS
We'll be stopping at Universal Studios, then over to Disneyland. Something to do with a sentimental attachment our guest has.

JEFF
What about tomorrow?

GUS
Vance wants to go down to San Diego to check out his former digs and if he finds the nerve maybe go visit someone he used to know.

JEFF
Okay.

GUS
Any special instructions?

JEFF
When you check into a hotel, make sure you park a little away from the buildings in a more open area to make it easier for us to park nearby.

GUS
All-night vigil?

JEFF
No, unlike you DD/P guys, we work in shift work. We have agents in Los Angeles who will relieve us around bedtime and keep an eye on things until we are ready to continue in the morning.

GUS
Alright then. I suppose we better get this show on the road.

JEFF
Go ahead and head out, we're going to grab a Starbucks, we'll catch up with you.

Soon the SUV Caravan was back on the road. This time Crystal was driving, and Gus was now riding shotgun so that he could catch up on all his emails and put together his latest status report which by direction now went to Brazile, Q, and X-divisions.

<u>C.U. GUS TYPING OUT SITREP MESSAGE DURING VOICEOVER.</u>

VOICEOVER
GUS EMAIL SITREP
Have tentatively identified aliens following us and who disarmed attackers at Boulder City. Based on an interview with primary guest, believe they are a Měngjiàng Yún-Rén security detail.

***

This latest report started to solidify the big picture General Brazile was starting to form. Now his only concern is what the implications might be.

VOICEOVER (GENERAL BRAZILE)
THOUGHT
Could these Aliens have an intergalactic event right in our own solar system?

A thought that did not please General Brazile in the least bit, and since about all he had available to deal with Aliens was pretty much spit balls.

Colonel Jones responded as he read the reports with General Brazile.

COLONEL JONES
The more Struyograb shows us, the less faith we had
that Grak was telling him anything near the truth,
and their behavior was becoming increasingly more
suspect.

***

The Caravan continued down I-15 and eventually turned off on the I-210 and made their way to the CA134 that took them right up to Universal Studios. They made a bee line to VIP Valet parking, and with a couple of Vance's $100 bills, the parking attendants were very gracious and arranged for a couple golf carts to carry them to the heart of the attractions where they got off thus saving a lot of time and escaped a lot of crowds.

Vance and Sandra were walking around the park holding hands and taking it all in for a few hours, and as the thrill wore off Vance announced:

VANCE
I've seen enough. I think it's time to go.

After loading back up in the SUVs they made their next journey down the CA101 to I-5 then on to the Disneyland Hotel, where they would spend the night and see some of the sights.

INT. DAY. DISNEYLAND HOTEL AND PARK.

The group all checked into their rooms then, as agreed, met down in the lobby where they made their way to the Monorail which took them over to Disneyland theme park attractions.

VANCE
Let's take the steam train around the park.

SANDRA (a.k.a. Wánměi De Huā)
Sounds like fun.

Sandra responded respectfully and walked with Vance to the main train station exhibit near the entrance and soon was on their way to obtain a quick look at numerous attractions that brought back a lot of Vance's memories.

Wánměi De Huā probed Vance which exposed gut wrenching sadness Vance felt when he lost his former life on planet Earth prior to his abduction by the Mergenky such a long time ago.

Having been considered as deceased all these years, Vance knew it would be pointless to contact his former relatives, who already had evolved from the reality he was gone forever and didn't want to open any new wounds by his sudden reappearance.

Unlike the terrestrials who had to get there the hard way, the *Měngjiàng Yún-Rén* were teleported.

All afternoon long, X-division was not getting any readings. It was like trying to find a needle in the haystack.

Jeff and Gary who followed the group into the park at a distance had some handheld instruments disguised as fancy cameras. Still no readings or any sign of aliens. Gus would have been pleased to know that his group even managed to lose the Grey Hybrids that had been following along loosely and would have completely lost them had Grak not been sending the mother ship secret reports relayed to the Grey Hybrids that he got from an insider mole at Area 51 who apparently was not only getting paid by the Grey Aliens but also the Russian FSB.

GUS

Vance, do you want to go on any of the rides?

VANCE

No, I just want to walk around and look at everything.
Sort of looks like the same way it was the last time I
was here over 20 years ago.

GUS

Doesn't change much here in Legacy Park, all the new
stuff goes into California Adventure.

VANCE

I suppose I got to ride Space Mountain, at least once.

ROGER

The lines are kind of long, give me all your park-
passes, and I'll get us all a Fast Trak ticket for later,
that way we don't waste our time in line.

Moments later Roger came back with tickets that would be good in about ½ an hour.

Sandra (a.k.a. Wánměi De Huā), probing the minds of people getting off the Space Mountain ride, came up with a few ideas of her own.

Disneyland would be investigating for months some of the claims of the riders as Sandra (a.k.a. Wánměi De Huā), probed deep in their minds and planted visions of surreal space battles and celestial objects that were suspended close to the rides that gave riders an impression they never dreamed of.

Vance was clearly animated in what he observed and as he got off the ride explained.

VANCE

Disneyland sure made a heck of an improvement; it
was just like I was back out in space on the Mergenky
Scout and the Mergenky Cruiser I almost died on.

GUS

Vance, what do you want to do next?

VANCE

Let's go to a restaurant down by the riverboat with an
outside view for the fireworks.

GUS

It's more like a laser show now with only a few
fireworks.

It's not hard to bump into people unexpectedly at Disneyland. Because of the actual proximity, someone performing surveillance can themselves become surveilled.

Gus wearing an ear bud was suddenly contacted by Jeff.

JEFF

Hey Gus, this is Jeff. I'm up in Disney Security
monitoring the park, and we have discovered those
four guys from those pictures you sent, are now tailing
you.

GUS

That's nice to know.

When Gus responded his voice was picked up by his hidden microphone sewn into his shirt color and wired into a pack on his side that looked like a cell phone carrier.

JEFF

Gary and one of the technicians are closing in behind
those four guys to see if they can get some readout.

The *Měngjiàng Yún-Rén Spies* held their distance.

GUS
I'm not worried about those guys; they're just here
protecting Sandra (a.k.a. Wánměi De Huā). It's the
other guys I'm worried about."

JEFF
No sign of any Hybrids.

GUS
Ok, thanks for the status report.

The group made their way over to the steamboat exhibit and a restaurant that would
give them comfortable viewing of the laser fireworks and water show.

<u>INT. NIGHT. DISNEYLAND RESTAURANT. OUTDOOR SEATING NEAR THE
STEAMBOAT EXHIBIT.</u>

BEVERLY
Looks like we arrived just in time, the restaurant is
starting to fill up fast.

GUS
We are lucky to get seating for 6 in this restaurant with
such a good view.

VANCE
I'd say the $200 paid for that reservation is what did it.

Vance smiled.

Vance and everyone were in a good mood, so much so they took the liberty of
exchanging some of that excess Vance's Vegas money for more draft beers.

The waitress came up to the table after clearing the plates away, announced to the
group:

WAITRESS
You all must leave soon to make way for more guests,
and you are not permitted to hang out during the light
show.

VANCE
Excuse me miss, could you come over here?

After Vance requested, the waitress approached and Vance put a $100 bill in her hand, she smiled and walked away.

A while later another waitress came by.

SECOND WAITRESS
Do you all want dessert?

GUS
That's a great idea, will keep the staff from bugging
us for a while.

The waitress left and came back momentarily with dessert menus which she gave one to each of the members of the party.

BEVERLY
I'll have the chocolate mousse.

CRYSTAL
Me too.

ROGER
I'll have cherry pie with vanilla ice cream.

GUS
Give me apple pie and ice cream.

VANCE
Just vanilla ice cream.

SANDRA (A.K.A. WÁNMĚI DE HUĀ)
I'll skip desert, thank you.

The orders were in; the manager was cooling his heels.

No sooner than after they finished the desserts and the dessert dishes were removed and the table cleared, they were once again invited to leave.

Vance tried to put another $100 in the waitress hand, but she explained:

WAITRESS
The manager is pissed and wants you all to leave,
some of the people in line are complaining you are
sitting here too long.

Vance feeling a little wired from the alcohol announced to the waitress:

VANCE
Let me go talk to the manager.

WAITRESS
It's not going to do you any good, he's an asshole.

Vance expressed his feeling to the very attractive young Latino lady.

VANCE
I like your attitude

Vance followed the waitress over to the far end of the restaurant where the manager was dealing with an irate customer probably going through the same routine being ejected and they had great seats for the laser light show and fireworks that just started.

Right about the time he was going to talk to the manager, nature called, and Vance needed to seek the rest room quickly. So instead of attempting to bribe the manager, Vance asked:

VANCE
Sir, can you please tell me which way to the men's room?

DISNEYLAND
RESTAURANT MANAGER
Out to the left and around the corner.

Vance thought he would use the restroom then come back and confront the manager with a much larger bribe. This was worth at least $500 to him.

Most of the crowd was moving in the direction opposite of what Vance was traveling, so he made quick progress to the restroom.

<u>INT. NIGHT. DISNEYLAND RESTROOM</u>

Vance felt very satisfied after he relieved himself. As he was washing and drying his hands there was a weird guy in there, who he made eye contact with and appeared kind of, staring at him.

The laser light show was a perfect distraction for the snatch and grab. Grak was a brilliant thinker and planner and figured the best place to attempt the kidnap would be at some venue with lots of people around which would even the odds. Grak was still pissed about his missing Hybrids and was convinced the Tall White Struyograb was somehow mixed up in all that.

Vance decided to leave the restroom immediately in haste, not feeling too safe, especially after what happened yesterday. Just as soon as he hit the restroom door, he was stunned and immediately unconscious.

<u>EXT.CGI.NIGHT *GREY ALIEN PLANETARY ROVER SPACECRAFT* VTOL DESCENT DOWN AND VANCE IS ABDUCTED. 20 SECONDS.</u>

The *Grey Alien's Planetary Rover Spacecraft* came down vertically, the planning was perfect.

 As soon as the four Grey Hybrids carried Vance out of the restroom, he was lifted vertically into the Grey's *Planetary Rover* Spacecraft . The Grey's *Planetary Rover* used antigravity propulsion which protected everyone inside from G forces allowing a fast getaway.

As soon as Vance was lifted aboard, and access hatch shut *the Grey's Planetary Rover* rose vertically extremely fast via anti-gravity into the semi overcast and disappeared in seconds. The bright lights from the Disneyland laser light show blinded the public to their rear point and few if any saw the *Planetary Rover* perform its abduction mission to abduct Vance.

By the time Vance was nabbed, Grak had figured out he would be a bigger asset than the *Měngjiàng Yún-Rén Empress* traveling with him for several reasons.

Since Vance was an Earthling, he wouldn't cause an intergalactic war with these beings, and secondly the *Měngjiàng Yún-Rén Empress* traveling with Vance appeared to have great attraction for him, so there was some connection there and a possible bargaining chip. Grak would play his hand when the time came.

After a few minutes, even though the light show was neat, Gus became slightly concerned when Vance did not reappear. So, when the waitress came by again, Gus asked the waitress:

GUS
Did you take my friend to the manager?

WAITRESS
Yes, he was talking to the manager just a while ago.

GUS
Can you take me to your manager; I want to know
what happened to our friend.

The waitress escorted Gus to the manager, where he still was minutes after Vance
approached him

GUS
Excuse me sir, there was a gentleman the waitress
brought to you a short while ago; he was going to talk
to you about our table.

DISNEYLAND
RESTAURANT MANAGER
There was a gentleman who approached me with her
but all he asked me was where the restroom was.

GUS
What did you tell him?

DISNEYLAND
RESTAURANT MANAGER
Around the corner to the left.

GUS
Thank you.

Gus followed Vance's footsteps taken maybe 10 minutes previously by now, into the
restroom, it was deserted. The mystery was starting to unfold. Gus went back to the
table and Vance still was nowhere to be seen, and it should not have been any problem
for him to get back here easily since the access was not through the crowd.

About that time GUS's cell phone pager went off. It was a red alert. Jeff was calling.

It was kind of too noisy because of the music and sound effects with the laser show so
Gus excused himself and went back to the same bathroom where it was nice and quiet.

GUS
Yes Jeff, what is it?

JEFF
You will not believe it, but we just watched a spacecraft
of some sort come right down near where you are a
few minutes ago on the video monitor. It appeared
they grabbed someone, are you guys all, ok?

Gus
Dammit!

JEFF
Something wrong?

GUS
Vance is missing! Exactly where did you see this person lifted into the spacecraft?

JEFF
Probably 20 feet from coordinates where your GPS indicates your location.

GUS
Alert General Brazile, those entities we had problems with a couple days ago probably abducted Vance.

Gus went back to the table and slumped down, chin resting on his upper torso shaking slightly as if he were saying *no*, repeatedly.

Roger started to get concerned.

ROGER
What's going on Gus,

GUS
They got Vance.

ROGER
Who?

GUS
Most likely it was the same people that were probably trying to get him a couple days ago.

Sandra (a.k.a. Wánměi de Huā) sensing Gus quickly discovering everything he was thinking went into a mild rage internally upset that someone would kidnap her beloved Vance and through her mental telepathy transceivers notified Drago:

SANDRA (A.K.A. WÁNMĚI DE HUĀ)
(TELEPATHICALLY)
Return me to the Royal Yacht immediately!

In front of Gus, Beverly, Roger and Crystal, Sandra (a.k.a. Wánměi de Huā) dematerialized in about a second and was suddenly gone.

ROGER
What do we do now that all our guests are gone?

GUS
That's one hell of a good question.

Gus set smoldering and taking personal responsibility for the disaster that just occurred.

The implications could be enormous. Initial indications are this is a very advanced race, and someone near and dear to a very high up VIP, was just kidnapped in of all places Disneyland! This is going to be very bad for their careers.

BEVERLY
May I make a suggestion?

GUS
Sure.

BEVERLY
It's obvious Vance and Sandra (A.K.A. Wánměi de Huā) are both gone and no longer near Disneyland. I suggest we check out of our hotels, have the X-division or Q guys take care of the SUVs and fly back to Area 51, S-4 where we can start putting a plan together or at least a brief.

CRYSTAL
I vote for that too.

ROGER
I agree Beverly, excellent idea. X-Division has offices at Burbank Airport, we can drop off the SUVs there and get a jet to take us back to S-4.

GUS
I know it's going to be rough for all of us, but even with the best backup with X-division here, we are just too inferior to deal with the forces involved in all this activity.

In 30 minutes, the group efficiently checked out of their hotel rooms without disturbing a thing. The maids were a little confused in the morning and wondered who cleaned the rooms!

The two CIA SUVs followed I-5 up to Burbank and got off West Burbank Blvd. then drove to North Buena Vista and tuned onto West Empire Ave.

And there that little unobtrusive building right across from the west side of Runway 33, X-division had their rented offices. The others they shared the building with were also considered shady characters and each group purposely looked the other way and never stuck their nose into each other's business. It was the perfect match.

Gus and Beverly driving the two cars, pulled up in some reserved parking spots. Within minutes, Jeff and Gary pulled up in the van and got out.

JEFF
You guys heading back North tonight?

GUS
Yes. A plane is due in 15 minutes.

A short time later while they were talking, a Gulf Stream 650 came down on Runway 33 landing to the North which they could see from their vantage point.

GARY
That looks like your plane now

GUS
Probably is.

Gus handed the SUVs keys to Jeff.

GUS
Here's the keys to the vehicles. You'll be getting
instructions on how to ship them first thing in the
morning.

JEFF
Probably shipping in a truck auto-carrier?

GUS
More than likely, we obviously will not need them for
a while.

Just as Gary thought, the Gulf Stream moved down near where they were standing about half a block away and did a 180 turn to prepare to promptly leave.

GUS
It looks like it's time to go.

GARY
Have a safe trip.

GUS
Thanks, good seeing you again.

GARY
Likewise.

***

INT. SPAC. *MĚNGJIÀNG YÚN-RÉN ROYAL YACHT* CONTROL ROOM.

The situation on the *Měngjiàng Yún-Rén Royal Yacht* now reconfigured as a Command Ship, exhibited frantic activity and great apprehension gripped the Royal Court. The four security men were standing in front of Drago trying to explain what happened. They were all in their *Měngjiàng Yún-Rén* green winged forms.

The bright green energy beings were extremely intelligent, these four security men were by far the best in the galaxy, so possible Aliens snatching Vance in a place like Disneyland did not make sense and the consequences were very troubling as it was quite apparent that *Wánměi De Huā Shèngdà Dá Qiè Sī* was outraged.

Wánměi De Huā outwardly appeared troubled and nearly heartbroken. Her spirit was severely impacted, and the vibrations of her soul obviously would create a huge crisis within the Empress Royal Court.

No doubt which hunts, and *Měngjiàng Yún-Rén* punishment were anticipated. And if Vance was harmed or disappeared forever, there would be no telling the extremes that *Wánměi De Huā* might inflict.

The immediate crisis centered on the knowledge that the Rén came in peace. They didn't bring an Armada with them. They had no intentions of terrifying this sector of space, so they faced a dilemma. They don't have the firepower to threaten anyone, and even if *Wánměi De Huā Shèngdà Dá Qiè Sī* was not satisfied real soon by the return of Vance, there is no telling what she might order. Drago also had one other lingering fear.

VOICEOVER (DRAGO)
THOUGHT

What if Vance chooses to stay on Earth? It seems a similar crisis would manifest serious consequences.

Therefore, it now appeared there was no other possible course of action for the present time, we need to find Vance!

When Drago received *Wánměi De Huā*, she could tell the Empress was shaken up and very emotional. The situation was very tough on her. Drago knew that based on the telemetry from *Wánměi De Huā's* implants, she had never experienced anything like the intensity of fusion with Vance. It was quite apparent this crisis was one that surpassed probably any Royal Court scenario in over 100,000 years.

Drago was very tough and vindictive. Under normal circumstances the four security men would have been incinerated for their failures, but Drago was also pragmatic and realized they were the best the *Měngjiàng Yún-Rén* had on this mission. She would save the punishment for later as she needed their services now to handle this crisis.

If Drago destroyed these security men, it would take a couple weeks to bring in replacements, which didn't seem a wise idea since immediate action was needed now and the source of the conspiracy was probably down on Earth, which these *Měngjiàng Yún-Rén* security agents would be highly useful in discovering who and who was involved

DRAGO

My dear Empress *Wánměi De Huā*, I assure you we are taking immediate action to try to locate and rescue Vance.

WÁNMĚI DE HUĀ

Drago, I know you are doing your best, but I can't help feeling sad because of all this.

DRAGO

May I suggest you go to the *Měngjiàng Jīngshén Néngliàng Spirit Room* and do some meditation; it may help you resolve some of your anguish so that in

days to come you can think more clearly to help you
make better decisions.

WÁNMĚI DE HUĀ
I shall go meditate, please keep me informed of any
new developments or leads that turn up.

Wánmi de Huā flapped her wings and flew down the hallway towards *Měngjiàng Jīngshén Néngliàng Spirit Room*

Drago was convinced and now spoke to the Chief Interrogator:

DRAGO
The Wogar Grey Hybrids we have in custody were
involved in the initial attempt to kidnap, may have
more information than we have been able to extract
out of them.

Měngjiàng Yún-Rén Royal Yacht However, their brain patterns were unlike
humanoids and are very difficult to sense.

DRAGO
What does that mean?

CHIEF INTERROGATOR
The classic interrogation techniques are not working.

DRAGO
I'm expecting a briefing, momentarily from the
chief scientist looking into the problem with mental
telepathy of these Grey Hybrids.

CHIEF INTERROGATOR
This problem is quite extraordinary and something we
have never come across before.

The chief scientist brought along in case there were new discoveries during the trip,
approached Drago who was in the control room of the command ship.

DRAGO
What took you so long?

CHIEF SCIENTIST
My staff has only limited resources on this ship which

is more of a social vessel vice experimental scientific research ship.

DRAGO
What seems to be the issue?

CHIEF SCIENTIST
It took a while to verify the specimen's DNA because such activity was not expected so we are short types of equipment necessary for examinations. We had to use older methods which are painfully slow.

DRAGO
What did you do?

CHIEF SCIENTIST
One of the eight captured Grey Hybrids was selected for the laboratory work. His body was examined thoroughly, and DNA samples were taken.

Drago, who was getting impatient with the doctor who could spend the next 30 minutes explaining the basic details interrupted.

DRAGO
What did you find out?

CHIEF SCIENTIST
It took us a day, but finally we had the DNA fully analyzed and broken down. These humanoids are different than most others we tested who usually have 23 sets of genes; these humanoids have 30 sets of genes, which are rather unique.

DRAGO
What does that mean?

CHIEF SCIENTIST
It means that most likely these are hybrids; the extra genes are there because the person has a little of its old characteristics left purposely.

DRAGO
Why do you think they did that?

CHIEF SCIENTIST
I would speculate it allows them to live in an alien
atmosphere but also exist in a new one.

DRAGO
Which means?

CHIEF SCIENTIST
Earth is not their native atmosphere, they are
physiologically able to exist on Earth as part of an
insertion for purposes yet to be discovered, but at the
same time can live and flourish on their native planets.

DRAGO
Why would they go to such extremes to make this
hybrid, unless they are used as spies?

CHIEF SCIENTIST
They were part of some mission when they were
captured, so it appears their purpose is clandestine
activities without giving away who they represent.

DRAGO
How many alien races have we discovered on Earth
and how many of them are not humanoid?

CHIEF SCIENTIST
Thus far, we know of only three out of eight alien
races now on earth are humanoid, the rest are reptilian,
amphibian, or aquatic origin.

DRAGO
Are there any chances of them being aquatics?

CHIEF SCIENTIST
No, we already tested that. They have no means to
breathe underwater like our special services people
who have the implants that allow them too.

DRAGO
So, are they either reptilian or amphibians?

CHIEF SCIENTIST
Most likely, yes.

DRAGO
And torture can't derive the information we need?

CHIEF SCIENTIST
No.

DRAGO
Why is that?

CHIEF SCIENTIST
When we raise the level of pain to the point most
people would break, these hybrids simply pass out.

DRAGO
What is the reason do you think?

CHIEF SCIENTIST
Their mental functions have been carefully designed
as if they were expected to be captured and tortured.

DRAGO
What can we do about it?

CHIEF SCIENTIST
Our only hope is a mental probe, once we can figure
out how to deal with the strange brain structure they
have.

***

INT. CGI. SPACE. WOGAR GREY *COLONY CLASS PLANETARY CONQUEST VESSEL/ MOTHER SHIP. PLANETARY ROVER ARRIVING AT HANGER. 20 SECONDS.*

The Wogar Grey *Colony Class Planetary Conquest Vessel/ mother ship* now following Pluto offset and behind by about 50 million meters was on the alert as its Grey's *Planetary Rover* Space craft approached for docking.

Not knowing what to expect, and realizing the kidnapping could place them at risk, the Grey Alien Commander Zorgjeck prepared for the worst.

Grey Alien crews in the fleet were placed on high alert at the beginning of the mission, with the knowledge they may have to abandon this position and fall back to the nearest star system, Alpha Centauri's red dwarf, Proxima Centauri, where they could better defend themselves by hiding from infrared probes and would be closer to reinforcements.

<u>INT. INT. SPACE. WOGAR GREY *COLONY CLASS PLANETARY CONQUEST VESSEL/ MOTHER SHIP.*</u>

Vance, still sedated and unconscious, was carried out of the *Planetary Rover* now aligned to the artificial gravity the moon-size mother ship created so that inhabitants could live a normal life.

Vance was soon wheeled in a self-propelled carrier into what could be described as an incubator that also contained other abductees, some of which were going into the materials recycler and turned into human compost that added to waste products to provide agriculture cells required to sustain the multitudes of caretakers and shock troops that would soon be used in planetary conquest.

Most Earth Abductees went through a deep psychological transformation as they awoke in the incubator and realized they were abducted by aliens. Quite often it was kids ranging from four years old to teenagers. In many cases it was females used in their hybrid breeding program.

Vance slowly came to as the aftereffects of the neurotic ray, applied at a lower dosage than what would be used in battlefield conditions where great slaughters occurred.

Back on Earth when Vance was being abducted and as Vance walked towards the door at the Disneyland restroom, he didn't see the Grey Alien Hybrid pull up the neurotic ray and zap him from behind.

The Grey Alien Hybrid was quick on his feet and grabbed Vance as he crumbled so that he would not sustain any injury from rapid acceleration to the tiled floor and the effects of terminal velocity hitting zero instantaneously.

When Vance was fully awake and alert, he looked at the large black-eyed creatures staring at him.

VANCE
Who the hell are you?

The Grey Alien nearest Vance responded.

WOGAR GREY ALIEN
Hello Vance

Vance tried to move but quickly discovered he was restrained.

VANCE
What am I doing here?

WOGAR GREY ALIEN
Our leader has determined your presence aboard this interplanetary assault command ship would prevent the various forces now engaged with Earth from interfering with pending operations.

VANCE
What does that mean, and you speak English so well.

WOGAR GREY ALIEN
Thank you, Vance, I've studied English for the past 81 years.

VANCE
Why is that?

WOGAR GREY ALIEN
When you Americans first exploded an atomic bomb, we knew time was running out for our plans.

VANCE
Which is?

WOGAR GREY ALIEN
Your planet would be better off with us managing it. You earthlings squander too many natural resources that would be better utilized by civilizations such as ours.

VANCE
So, what you are really saying is planetary conquest.

WOGAR GREY ALIEN
We would rather look at it as planetary rescue.

VANCE
What does that mean for the people living there?

WOGAR GREY ALIEN
Earth people will be thinned out in large numbers.
We'll keep enough of them alive for slaves until we
get most of the construction projects completed?

VANCE
What kinds of projects?

WOGAR GREY ALIEN
We must build a habitat for 10 billion Wogar Greys
who will inhabit the planet eventually as we relocate
them to Earth.

VANCE
So, you are Wogar Greys?

WOGAR GREY ALIEN
Yes. Our civilization is Wogar Greys, but on Earth
your people call us Greys.

Vance suddenly heard a lot of hissing and barking from the Wogar that indicated they
were conversing with one another in their native language.

WOGAR GREY ALIEN
Vance, our leader has said you are wanted in the control
room. You have neurotic shackles on, in a moment we
are going to let you stand up and walk with us to the
control room.

VANCE
Sure, I would like to meet your leader.

WOGAR GREY ALIEN
If you should think of suddenly doing anything
bold or irrational, our security detail following us
has great natural reflexes and they thoroughly enjoy
manipulating the neurotic shackles.

VANCE
I would think advanced civilization that can put a ship
like this out in space has good restraints.

WOGAR GREY ALIEN
Vance, neurotic shackles which can become extremely

painful if they raise the power levels up to battlefield
conditions, so please do not attempt anything and
follow our instructions and you will be treated
humanely.

Vance, having been around several aliens and dealt with and participated in several
crises, was calm and reflective and realized he would be rescued in due time responded.

VANCE

I do not plan on resisting. I know I'll be eventually
rescued so you do not have to worry about me
becoming violent.

WOGAR GREY ALIEN

Thank you for your cooperation. Your treatment will
be enhanced by how you conduct yourself.

The Grey Alien led Vance out of the incubator chamber and noticed several Earth
people there bound in neurotic shackles staring at him in almost utter disbelief.

After walking down, a hallway Vance guessed must have been 300 feet long, they
entered an average size room and when the door shut automatically behind them,
Vance felt slight gravity effects which led him to believe the room was moving.

In a brief period, Vance suddenly felt the opposite gravity he had just experienced,
almost as if he was on an airplane that suddenly was forced downwards in an air
column giving a sense of weightlessness.

When the gravity sensation suddenly ended, the large doublewide door opened in two
sections sliding in the opposite directions and exposed a large cavern probably the size
of a football field inhabited by hundreds of busy Wogar Greys monitoring all kinds of
displays and engaged in very professional conduct.

VOICEOVER (VANCE)
THOUGHT

*This must be the Grey Alien command center for this
ship.*

Vance followed along his captors at least 100 feet to an area that had an exposed glass
window that appeared to be pointed towards a central section of the solar system. The
first thing Vance noticed:

VOICEOVER (VANCE)
THOUGHT

*This appears to be Saturn with its rings, but in far
more vivid color and detail than what I have seen even
in photographs in the past.*

As the Grey Aliens led Vance up to a peculiar looking section, a large cylinder device suddenly swiveled around. This strange device appeared to have a seat and several gadgets and a Grey in uniquely designed attire.

VOICEOVER (VANCE)
THOUGHT
This Grey Alien is wearing attire that is different than what the rest of the Greys are wearing. He must probably be their commander.

The Wogar Grey Alien stood up and approached Vance and his Grey Alien escort group and with the most arrogant facial features.

WOGAR GREY
SUPREME COMMANDER
ZORGJECK
Is Grak here yet?

GREY ALIEN
He'll be here momentarily.

WOGAR GREY
SUPREME COMMANDER
ZORGJECK
It looks like you got our guest here without damaging him.

GREY ALIEN
The neurotic ray we used to stun him and knock him unconscious was set to low power, and his physiology perfectly matched the power setting.

WOGAR GREY
SUPREME COMMANDER
ZORGJECK
How did that work out for the abduction?

GREY ALIEN
Only one application was necessary to render him helpless, which enabled us to get him in our *Planetary Rover* very efficiently.

WOGAR GREY
SUPREME COMMANDER
ZORGJECK
I take it he's been informed why he's here.

GREY ALIEN
Yes.

WOGAR GREY
SUPREME COMMANDER
ZORGJECK
He seems to be calm for someone who understands his civilization is about to be wiped out.

GREY ALIEN
Yes, we've never encountered a Human with his disposition before.

WOGAR GREY
SUPREME COMMANDER
ZORGJECK
He might be worth further study, perhaps some Earth people will be far more useful than what we expected.

GREY ALIEN
No doubt any survivors would be inclined to go along with our plans, especially when they discover our low tolerance for disobedience.

WOGAR GREY
SUPREME COMMANDER
ZORGJECK
Vance, why are you so different than those Earth people we have in the incubator who are always displaying a neurotic transcendence?

VANCE
Sir, I believe I've not been introduced to you.

WOGAR GREY
SUPREME COMMANDER
ZORGJECK
Not that it matters Vance, I'm Zorgjeck, the Wogar Supreme Commander.

VANCE
It's always helpful to know who you are talking with.

Vance, then a deep long bow out of respect that gave a unique impression to the Greys including Zorgjeck.

WOGAR GREY
SUPREME COMMANDER
ZORGJECK
Vance, I asked a question, all I expect from you is answers.

Suddenly at the nod of Zorgjeck, Vance felt incredible pain radiating throughout his body.

Vance assumed the neurotic shackles must have been kicked in for a little demonstration of the power that Zorgjeck now held over him.

Vance quickly regained his composure as his Mergenky training kicked in and allowed his mental powers to overcome the pain and quickly transition to a very calm and decisive posture.

VANCE
Those other Earth people you abducted have never seen aliens before; they were not mentally prepared for all this.

WOGAR GREY
SUPREME COMMANDER
ZORGJECK
And you have?

VANCE
I've been to a couple galaxies and have seen a lot, nothing surprises me anymore.

Suddenly, a slight noise erupted down the hallway from where they were all conversing. Zorgjeck appeared to look past Vance at someone who was arriving. Vance turned around and saw someone he least expected, Grak whom he had met at area 51.

As Grak came close he bowed his head momentarily.

GRAK
Your Excellency.

WOGAR GREY
SUPREME COMMANDER
ZORGJECK
Grak, I see our plans are moving along quite efficiently.

GRAK
Yes, your Excellency they are.

WOGAR GREY
SUPREME COMMANDER
ZORGJECK
Now that we have effectively neutralized this new group of aliens, we are now able to carry out the next phase of the Earth invasion plan.

GRAK
Yes, I expect to send an emissary to the *Měngjiàng Yún-Rén* to get their cooperation of non-interference as we move our shock troops to Earth.

WOGAR GREY
SUPREME COMMANDER
ZORGJECK
When do you expect this to happen?

GRAK
Tomorrow. No doubt Struyograb will confront me in front of General Brazile, I'll then suggest they mediate a meeting between myself and *Měngjiàng Yún-Rén Empress Wánměi De Huā*, who now appears to have returned to the *Měngjiàng Yún-Rén Royal Yacht*.

WOGAR GREY
SUPREME COMMANDER
ZORGJECK
In case the *Měngjiàng Yún-Rén* do not go along with our plan, are they a threat to our fleet?

GRAK
No, the *Měngjiàng Yún-Rén* have only brought their *Měngjiàng Yún-Rén Royal Yacht*, a diplomatic ship. They have no firepower with them.

WOGAR GREY
SUPREME COMMANDER
ZORGJECK

How long would it take for *Měngjiàng Yún-Rén* to get
a sizeable force here?

GRAK

Based on our intelligence reports, due to their vast
distance to the other side of the galaxy, it will take up
to three weeks at the minimum for the *Měngjiàng Yún-Rén* to send a powerful force here.

WOGAR GREY
SUPREME COMMANDER
ZORGJECK

That should give us plenty time to wrap up the invasion
and be poised to repel any attack.

***

INT. SPACE. MĚNGJIÀNG YÚN-RÉN ROYAL YACHT

Wánměi De Huā suddenly came out of the trance she had developed while
meditating. Suddenly the answers came to her.

WÁNMĚI DE HUĀ

During my meditation, I sought your mental guidance
with telepathic questions, and thus was informed of
what you have discovered with the Greys.

DRAGO

Based on Intel just arrived, it was now probable the
Wogar Greys kidnapped Vance and is holding him as
a hostage.

Having been trained by the best Generals in the Galaxy, *Wánměi De Huā* knew exactly
what her next move should be.

WÁNMĚI DE HUĀ

Drago, the Tall Whites had just deployed a reserve
force to the war zone from their stop over rest and
recreation on Earth.

DRAGO

What does this have to do with Vance's problem?

WÁNMĚI DE HUĀ

If we could compel the Tall Whites to turn their fleet
around, we could create a Mexican standoff with the
Greys as people on Earth would say.

DRAGO

Alright, what then?

WÁNMĚI DE HUĀ

We can then scramble a Fleet to Earth and another one
to the threatening Grey Dominion to shift the leverage
in our favor.

Wánměi De Huā's natural leadership ability was starting to surface. Drago suddenly
getting a flood of telemetry from Wánměi De Huā's implants knew something had
stirred her and it might lead to a crisis sooner than Drago was willing to handle.

Before Drago could contemplate her next move Wánměi De Huā suddenly flew down
the corridor leading into the command center, then rematerialized into a figure that
was unfamiliar.

DRAGO

What's the significance of your new image?

WÁNMĚI DE HUĀ

During my deep mental probes of Vance who is a
historian, I came across this brilliant man named
Napoleon, who had tactical mastery.

DRAGO

Did Napoleon give you some ideas about how to
proceed?

WÁNMĚI DE HUĀ

Yes. I know what I need to do now. I'm going to
transport down to earth and talk to the Tall White
named Struyograb to convince him to turn his relief
force back for our use.

DRAGO

I advise you against returning to earth until this ordeal
is over, please let me handle it.

WÁNMĚI DE HUĀ
Thank you, Drago, for your support, but I must now
take matters into my own hands.

DRAGO
What then can I do to help

WÁNMĚI DE HUĀ
Transport me and the four security men who
allowed this kidnapping to General Brazile's office
immediately.

DRAGO
Why those four men?

WÁNMĚI DE HUĀ
I'm sure the security force wants to redeem themselves
and can be useful to me as well as provide protection.

DRAGO
No doubt.

WÁNMĚI DE HUĀ
Have them fully armed. I'm ready to leave immediately.

Drago understood she was helpless to defy the Empress. As the role of chamberlain, it
was not permissible to have any conflict with the Empress.

VOICEOVER (DRAGO)
THOUGHT
*In circumstances such as this terrible ordeal with
Vance, it was better the Empress have a temporary folly
than a long-term rupture and subsequent destruction
of me, as current chamberlain.*

Not that Drago was concerned about her own position and authority and power, she
was more concerned about the survival of the *Měngjiàng Yún-Rén*. Without Drago's
constant advice and support, *Wánměi De Huā* could make a series of fatal blunders
that would put them all at risk.

With *Měngjiàng Yún-Rén* efficiency, the four security men were armed and ready to
go in a few moments.

INT. DAY. AREA 51 GENERAL BRAZILE'S OFFICE.

And within seconds General Brazile was in a semi state of shock and surprise when the Five beings materialized right in front of him while he was discussing with Colonel Jones the previous day's events. Those events included Boyd Bushman, Vance's abduction, and the sudden disappearance of *Wánměi De Huā Shèngdà Dá Qiè Sī*.

To make matters worse, here the princess was in front of him dressed up and damn near looking like Napoleon!

***

Colonel Jones had just given a verbal report of his mission.

FLASHBACK:

Colonel David Jones left Area 51 aboard the *Company's* Gulf Stream 650 and flew down to the Naval Air Station at Fort Worth Texas.

EXT. DAY. FORT WORTH TEXAS, NAVAL AIR STATION.

As the Jet landed heading north into the wind, Colonel Jones observed 20 or so C-130 four engine turboprop planes parked near the runway. This was a major hub for that type of aircraft that was the backbone of the Marine Corp tactical lift operations.

C-130 Built for short runways with lots of guts in those turboprops, the 60-year-old design first test flown in the 1950s and later used in the Vietnam War had proved their worth.

 C-130 may be the first military aircraft in the inventory to ever last 100 years of service life, because the design was so practical and allowed efficient cargo deliveries which could be men or material; there was not much that could be improved upon except changing out the power plant and electronics which was an ongoing concern.

Already this C-130 plane design had been previously fitted with 15 different types of turbo props. Colonel Jones, coming from the test center at Groom Lake, was well informed of the *antigravity device* now being tested that would virtually give these planes an almost vertical lift.

Lockheed feared the V-22 Osprey built by Boeing and Bell Helicopter would eventually lead to the retirement of the KC-130 but wanted to keep their footprint in the small military cargo plane business when they pondered the antigravity they had pioneered in the TR-3B design.

Out amongst the group of C-130 and KC-130s, Colonel Jones spotted one of the variants coming off the retrofit facility with the hardware to allow future antigravity capability.

This plane would soon be flown up to Area-51 where it would get the conversion package put on by Skunk Works personnel who were the only ones cleared for the antigravity devices.

Pilots were handpicked and given appropriate levels of security clearances that were to fly all the test flights. To date there have not been any crashes because they were still in the preliminary stages of the tech insertion conversion process.

The next dilemma Colonel Jones knew that would manifest is when the production lines started operating and refitting of the entire fleet concerned security. How the hell would they keep something like this secret?

Those thoughts suddenly ended as the plane pulled over to the tarmac area near the North-West gate of the Naval Air Station and the door suddenly was opened by the crew and Colonel Jones realized it was time to disembark to the waiting Limo that pulled up.

Colonel Jones was wearing a business suit, and the Limo crew were all agency staff personnel assigned to Q-Division which he was a part of supporting General Brazile.

The man in a suit wearing sunglasses merely said:

Q-DIVISION AGENT
Good morning Mr. Jones, this way please.

The Q-Division Agent opened the passenger door for Colonel Jones then shut it after he got inside, then opened the door to the shotgun side of the Limo and hopped in which momentarily the Limo then sped off over and out of the Gate as it headed for Lockheed Martin Aeronautics Company located at One Lockheed Blvd, just West of the Naval Air Station.

EXT. DAY. FORT WORTH TEXAS Lockheed Martin Aeronautics Company, One Lockheed Blvd.

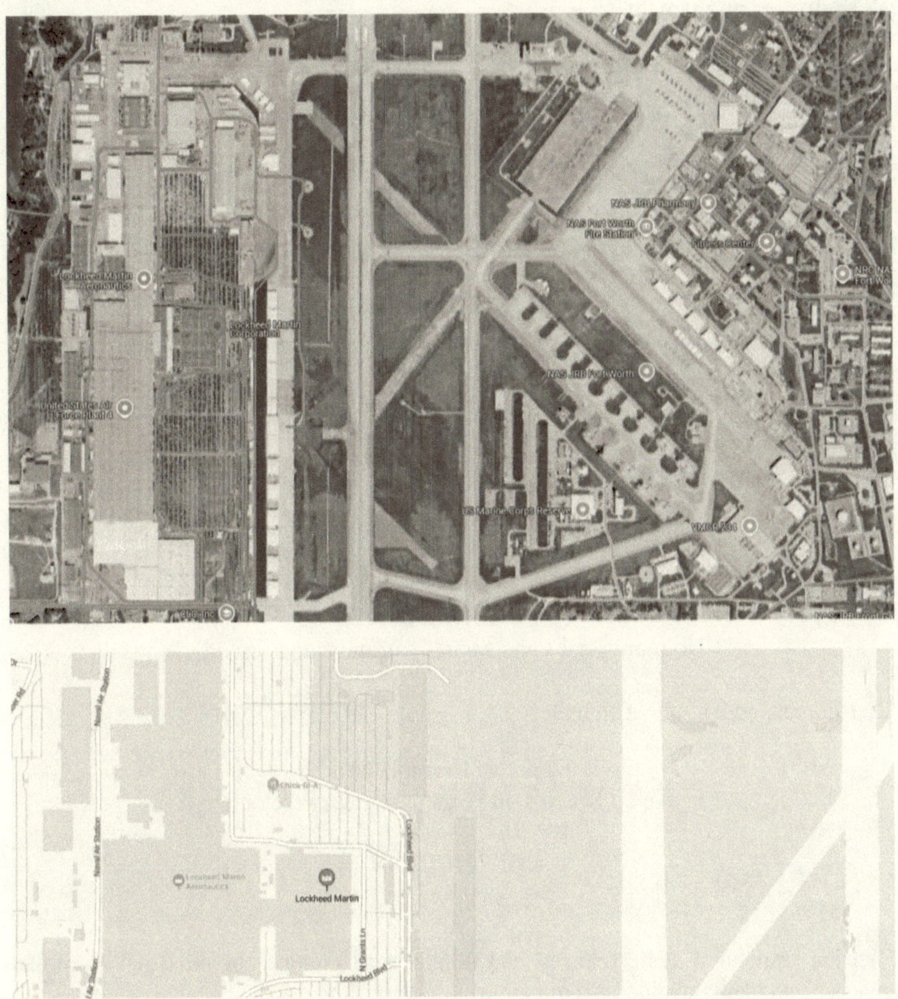

Due to the priority of the situation, it was decided Colonel Jones would take Boyd's former supervisor and mentor with him, who was also retired but agreed to meet at Lockheed facility then go over to Boyd's home to make one last plea for him to shut up about Aliens and hand over all the Alien pictures.

Otherwise, X Division was going to come in and sanitize Boyd Bushman's home. That meant searching his home and removing all materials of interest and probably giving Boyd a poisonous enema like that was administered to Marilyn Monroe many decades ago because just as done to Marilyn Monroe in the 1960s according to various researchers claimed she wouldn't shut up about JFK and his brother Bobby, whom she allegedly had affairs with.

Colonel Jones knew Dietrich von Braun, a direct relative of the world-renowned missile designer. He was getting old and fable looking, but still had a sharp mind even in his early 80s.

Dietrich greeted Colonel Jones when he got out of the Limo while Dietrich standing curb side in front of the Lockheed building and ready to depart to Boyd's home located in a Fort Worth Suburb not too far away.

DIETRICH von BRAUN
Morning Davy.

COLONEL JONES
You are looking good, Dietrich.

DIETRICH von BRAUN
Thank you. It was all made possible with my vegetarian
diet.

COLONEL JONES
No more steaks and sexually promiscuous braud's?

Dietrich responded with a chuckle.

DIETRICH von BRAUN
I gave up Braud's 40 years ago, steaks are optional.

COLONEL JONES
Shall we go?

Dietrich responded as he realized bad things were going to befall Boyd Bushman unless he suddenly decided to cooperate.

DIETRICH von BRAUN
Might as well get this over with.

After they were both in the Limo driving off towards the freeway, Colonel Jones asked:

COLONEL JONES
Was Boyd always this way?

DIETRICH von BRAUN
No, he was a company man and team player until the M21 crash, and the program was canceled. He became bitter then.

COLONEL JONES
Interesting.

DIETRICH von BRAUN
We didn't know he was stealing pictures and had friends on the inside giving him stuff they shouldn't have.

COLONEL JONES
Did you ever figure out who they were?

DIETRICH von BRAUN
We think we did with perhaps the exception of one guy we could never crack.

COLONEL JONES
Who was that?

DIETRICH von BRAUN
Robert Lazar.

COLONEL JONES
He seems like he's playing ball now.

DIETRICH von BRAUN
Yea it's amazing how people can change their attitude when *Cash in Advance* comes along and greases their palms, especially after being unemployed and hungry for a while.

COLONEL JONES
Robert Lazar certainly hasn't been in a position in over 30 years to give Boyd any materials.

DIETRICH von BRAUN
True, but we don't know how much he got away with before we busted him.

The Limo eventually exited off I-820 onto West Point Blvd and in a minute or two turned South on Chapple Creek which the Limo took just before turning right on Vista Heights Blvd where Boyd lived.

The houses were all crammed together with little space between them. But at least they had front and rear yards, unlike many urban settings where land was scarce.

The Limo pulled up in front of Boyd's home. All the homes in the neighborhood had at least 2 car garages and few cars were parked on the streets.

COLONEL JONES
This area looks abandoned.

DIETRICH von BRAUN
It appears that way because everyone is at work.

COLONEL JONES
Working class?

DIETRICH von BRAUN
Most of the people that live here require two incomes
including their wives working to cover their expenses.

COLONEL JONES
I can imagine the cost of living is high here because of
all the nearby employment driving up prices.

DIETRICH von BRAUN
Come back at 5:00 p.m. and you will see the curbs full
of cars.

Dietrich led the Colonel up the sidewalk to Boyd's home.

COLONEL JONES
I wish it didn't have to come down to this.

DIETRICH von BRAUN
I feel the same way; Boyd was a good engineer on the
A-12 program and various other assignments where
he groomed Ben Rich up for his position at the Skunk
Works.

The doorbell rang. Nobody answered.

268

DIETRICH von BRAUN
Are you sure he's home?

COLONEL JONES
Yes, our agents in the car across the street assure me
he is inside.

DIETRICH von BRAUN
Maybe he's taking a nap.

COLONEL JONES
Yea, ring it a few more times.

Another minute passed and just as they were starting to turn away, they heard:

BOYD BUSHMAN
Okay, okay, I'm coming!

Then the door opened.

BOYD BUSHMAN
Dietrich, what the hell are you doing here?

Boyd Bushman eyeballed him and saw he had a man in a suit behind him.

Dietrich responded in a not so happy manner.

DIETRICH von BRAUN
Boyd, I need to talk with you, if you don't mind.

BOYD BUSHMAN
Well come on in.

As Boyd Bushman closed the door behind the 2 men, he asked:

BOYD BUSHMAN
Can I get you guys a cup of coffee?

Colonel Jones who knew that because of his blood pressure meds he'd have to piss like
a Russian Racehorse if he had that coffee now responded:

COLONEL JONES
That won't be necessary Boyd, but thanks for the offer.

Boyd realizing this was more of a formal meeting than what he desired in retirement asked:

BOYD BUSHMAN
What is it you want to talk about Dietrich?

DIETRICH von BRAUN
Boyd, you were just up in Las Vegas at a UFO conference and according to Mr. Jones here, you may have shown uncleared people some Q-clearance pictures.

BOYD BUSHMAN
Is that so?

DIETRICH von BRAUN
Boyd, we believe that you have illegally obtained Q-clearance pictures. from an unknown source.

BOYD BUSHMAN
What's your point Dietrich?

DIETRICH von BRAUN
Boyd, you should know that when we had to retire you, it was because you were getting yourself into trouble back then.

BOYD BUSHMAN
You're talking about the Geek who turned me in that didn't have a fricking clue about what I was doing?

DIETRICH von BRAUN
You were never able to explain what items you took from the filing cabinet we had under surveillance.

BOYD BUSHMAN
Well, if you had a decent filing system and complied with records management regulations, you'd know what I took. I'll tell you what I told you back then, those were Girl Scout pictures.

DIETRICH von BRAUN
Boyd, you know that's BS.

BOYD BUSHMAN
Since you could never show what I took because of
your crappy filing system, I guess you will never know
for sure now, will you?

COLONEL JONES
Our agent in the audience saw the picture of the Grey
Alien you put up on the power point.

BOYD BUSHMAN
How do you know that's the truth?

Colonel Jones reached into his pocket and pulled out a picture of Boyd standing at the podium with a pointer aiming at the Grey Alien on the presentation screen and handed it to Boyd Bushman.

COLONEL JONES
Does this look familiar?

The conversation declined from there and when Colonel Jones felt he had done enough and had tried his best, he simply announced:

COLONEL JONES
Okay Boyd. Thank you for your time, we'll be going
now.

Colonel Jones then turned towards Dietrich and nodded at him conveying it was time to leave.

The two men hopped in the Limo that quickly sped back towards the Lockheed building were Dietrich got out and Colonel Jones continued his way to the Naval Air Base Northwest gate and was driven up next to the awaiting Gulf Stream that would have him back in Groom Lake in a couple hours.

***

INT. DAY. AREA 51, S-4 GENERAL BRAZILE'S OFFICE.

Colonel Jones met with General Brazile immediately upon return from Texas.

GENERAL BRAZILE
Did you get our problem with Boyd settled?

COLONEL JONES
No, he's never coming around.

GENERAL BRAZILE
That's it, contact X-Div and give them their marching
orders.

COLONEL JONES
Does that come with MJ-12 permissions?

GENERAL BRAZILE
It's always better to ask for forgiveness than
permissions in deals like this.

COLONEL JONES
I'll notify X-Div to start the project right away.

GENERAL BRAZILE
Put that on the back burner, we got bigger fish to fry.

COLONEL JONES
What's that?

GENERAL BRAZILE
We might be in the middle of an intergalactic war
sooner than we realized.

He then went on to brief Colonel Jones on Wánměi De Huā's recent appearance and
her strange Napoleon Uniform attire.

COLONEL JONES
So, what did she want?

GENERAL BRAZILE
It's obvious she wants Vance back or *hell hath no
mercy* for a woman losing her lover.

COLONEL JONES
Is Vance a more important person than we realized?

GENERAL BRAZILE
If we don't find Vance soon, things will unravel
quickly. The President's not going to like what we
have to say, in a scheduled briefing in 30 minutes.

When *Wánměi De Huā* visited General Brazile not long before Colonel Jones returned,
he claimed he didn't know where Struyograb was presently, but he had no knowledge
Wánměi De Huā had such awesome powers to read General Brazile's mind.

After *Wánměi De Huā* politely left, dematerializing in front of him, with her four bodyguards she instantly rematerialized in the new tall black building inside the Area-51, S-4 complex.

Since they arrived and were behind the guards at the front entrance nobody saw them arrive. The last person Grak wanted meeting Struyograb was the *Měngjiàng Yún-Rén* and had convinced General Brazil to keep them away from the Tall White claiming it would lead to conflict as the Tall Whites attempted to disenfranchise the Wogar Greys.

The Air Force receptionist outside Dr. Struyograb's office had been instructed he was not to be disturbed as he had been busy attempting to communicate with the Tall White Task Force Commander now in route to the war zone that would take him another eight months to arrive, most likely just in time to stave off the next push they expected the Azcarian Reptilians to make.

As the pretty young female blonde Air Force Sergeant suddenly saw the five *Měngjiàng Yún-Rén* come from nowhere and the one leading the group wearing a strange attire.

Sandra (A.K.A. Wánměi de Huā) could easily come out of a late 18th century painting of Napoleon's attire with a blue top jacket that opened to white lapels showcasing a field marshal crest and a couple medals to commemorate the victory at Austerlitz, red cuffs and golden Epaulettes for shoulder boards, also wearing tightly fit white trousers tucked into knee high riding boots. The other four simply looked like well-dressed men often seen in the Cash in Advance offices.

SANDRA (A.K.A. WÁNMĚI DE HUĀ)
I need to talk with Struyograb.

FEMALE
AIR FORCE SERGEANT
He's not available right now, and can't be disturbed.

It's an emergency.

FEMALE
AIR FORCE SERGEANT
Everything around this place is always an Emergency;
people need a break now and then.

SANDRA (A.K.A. WÁNMĚI DE HUĀ)
I will not be delayed.

FEMALE
AIR FORCE SERGEANT
I'm sorry, and is this some kind of joke?

The Air Force Sergeant looked at *Wánměi De Huā* thinking Grak was up to some trick as he was always a nemesis towards Struyograb.

SANDRA (A.K.A. WÁNMĚI DE HUĀ)
No this is very serious, just tell him, Wánměi De Huā Shèngdà Dá Qiè Sī is here to see him and it's a very urgent matter.

FEMALE
AIR FORCE SERGEANT
He's not going to be happy; I have my instructions.

SANDRA (A.K.A. WÁNMĚI DE HUĀ)
I'm sure he'll find our visit quite a welcome experience.

FEMALE
AIR FORCE SERGEANT
I would normally not do this, but I'm only doing it because you got that costume on, and I want to know what the joke is.

SANDRA (a.k.a. WÁNMĚI DE HUĀ)
You will find out shortly this is not a joke if I must lay waste to sections of Planet Earth as I eradicate the Wogar Greys and take my revenge.

FEMALE
AIR FORCE SERGEANT
No reason to get hysterical about this lady, I'll contact him now even though I think this will somehow get me in hot water.

The security guard pressed a button on her console.

FEMALE
AIR FORCE SERGEANT
Dr. Struyograb, you have visitors in the lobby. I suggest you come right away.

Struyograb was just finishing up with the Task Force Commander.

STRUYOGRAB
I will get back to you shortly.

VOICEOVER STRUYOGRAB
THOUGHT
*I wonder who that could be; I told the watch not to
disturb me. It could be one of General Brazile's people.*

A moment later as Struyograb walked out into the hallway towards the reception area his jaw just about dropped when he saw who was there and what she was wearing!

Struyograb almost started to drop to his knees just like he did just a few days before when she read his mind.

WÁNMĚI DE HUĀ
Formalities are not necessary; we need to talk right
away.

STRUYOGRAB
Yes, this way please.

Struyograb guided the five into his office and shut the door behind.

The pretty security guard was somewhat struck at Dr. Struyograb's demeanor, as he could be a complete asshole with a short fuse.

Within moments General Brazile also knew via the surveillance video, his worst nightmare was coming true, *Wánměi De Huā* had found Struyograb and was now in Struyograb's office!

STRUYOGRAB
I didn't expect to see you any time soon.

WÁNMĚI DE HUĀ
I wouldn't be coming to you if this wasn't an
emergency.

STRUYOGRAB
What kind of emergency, your Empire is so strong
why would you humble yourself to seek me out?

WÁNMĚI DE HUĀ
Well as you know, we *Měngjiàng Yún-Rén* did not
arrive with an armada, we came in peace.

STRUYOGRAB

Few civilizations have ever seen you come in peace or rarely at all, that I must say was quite a surprise.

WÁNMĚI DE HUĀ

We planned this to be a brief stop and then we would leave. We have no special interest in this sector of the Galaxy.

STRUYOGRAB

I don't recall hearing of the Měngjiàng Yún-Rén to this area in all our recorded military history.

WÁNMĚI DE HUĀ

That's because we have not been here in 900,000 years.

STRUYOGRAB

So, your Excellency, what may I be of service to you?

WÁNMĚI DE HUĀ

It will take two weeks to bring our *Měngjiàng Yún-Rén Fleet* here. But they're on the way and if this doesn't turn out well, I shall order them to lay waste to Earth and the Wogar Grey.

STRUYOGRAB
You mean the Greys?

WÁNMĚI DE HUĀ
Precisely?

STRUYOGRAB
What have the Wogar Greys done to you?

WÁNMĚI DE HUĀ

My special partner Vance was abducted by the Wogar Grey's.

STRUYOGRAB

For what purpose could that abduction possibly serve?

WÁNMĚI DE HUĀ

I see Grak has done an excellent job of deceiving you too.

STRUYOGRAB
I'm sorry. I'm not following you.

WÁNMĚI DE HUĀ
We have means of discovery, which eclipses any technology you have. Have you seen Grak lately?

STRUYOGRAB
No, but I usually try to avoid him, not track where he goes.

WÁNMĚI DE HUĀ
I think if you make an inquiry with General Brazile you will discover he can't confirm Grak's whereabouts for over the past 48 hours.

Struyograb was now suddenly getting very interested in what he was hearing.

STRUYOGRAB
How would Grak manage to Kidnap Vance right under your noses and for what purpose?

WÁNMĚI DE HUĀ
I believe the Wogar are preparing for the planetary conquest of Earth and want to make sure I stay out of the mix.

STRUYOGRAB
By holding Vance hostage.

WÁNMĚI DE HUĀ
Precisely.

STRUYOGRAB
And what am I supposed to do about it?

WÁNMĚI DE HUĀ
In two weeks, no doubt, my fleet will be here and wipe out the Wogar, but I don't want to lose Vance between now and then.

STRUYOGRAB
We don't have the manpower here to counter such a Wogar move.

WÁNMĚI DE HUĀ

Your reserves just left Earth two days ago heading to the war zone, they will not be there for another eight months.

STRUYOGRAB

I can't confirm that, but if so, what difference does that make?

WÁNMĚI DE HUĀ

I've done some calculations and believed that if you turn them around now and send them back to Earth they can be here in less than three days after they make a loop around Alpha Centauri.

STRUYOGRAB

And what results are you expecting?

WÁNMĚI DE HUĀ

The best we could hope to achieve with that reserve force is a stalemate. A delay in time for my Fleet to get here to wipe out the Wogar Grey's if necessary.

STRUYOGRAB

You mean like in earth terms, a Mexican Standoff?

WÁNMĚI DE HUĀ

Exactly. That's precisely what I want; just delay them long enough to get my *Měngjiàng Yún-Rén Fleet* here to threaten the destruction of their mother ship, once we find it.

STRUYOGRAB

My superiors will absolutely deny such a move because those reserve forces are desperately needed in the fighting.

WÁNMĚI DE HUĀ

Once I finish off Grak, I promise to transport half your forces to the war zone in about two weeks. They will be there about seven months ahead of schedule.

STRUYOGRAB

That would be very beneficial.

WÁNMĚI DE HUĀ

I can also destroy some of the Reptilian Azcarian bases
to give you some breathing room, but other than that I
do not wish to intervene much further.

STRUYOGRAB

I'll send the recommendation to my superiors via
neutrino dispatch, but I will not have any answers for
at least 24 hours.

WÁNMĚI DE HUĀ

That may be too late to get your force back in time.
Also, you should be aware that Grak will most likely
hunt you down and personally kill you, so your own
neck is sticking out too.

STRUYOGRAB

How could you possibly protect me, as you stated you
don't have a battle fleet?

WÁNMĚI DE HUĀ

We have shields and speed unlike anything the Wogar
Grey has. We'll simply take you aboard and fly out
into deep space at such velocities they will never catch
up.

STRUYOGRAB
What if they attacked today?

WÁNMĚI DE HUĀ

We could transport you up to my ship and depart in
such velocities in just a few minutes from now if
necessary.

Wánměi De Huā could read Struyograb's mind and knew he had the administrative
authority to recall the Tall White's fleet.

Wánměi De Huā then sent telepathic orders to Drago currently in the control room of
the Měngjiàng Yún-Rén Empress Yacht now continuing its leisurely orbit around the
sun.

WÁNMĚI DE HUĀ
(via Telepathic Transceiver)
*Beam all of us in this room to the Empress Yacht
immediately.*

Momentarily Struyograb's mind started to feel strange and watched *Wánmĕi De Huā* 's molecules disassociate and observed her body disappear. Struyograb went blank for an unknown period then reassociated in the Mĕngjiàng Yún-Rén Empress Yacht. Struyograb regained his consciousness while wondering what was happening to him.

<u>INT. SPACE. *MĔNGJIÀNG YÚN-RÉN ROYAL YACHT* CONTROL ROOM.</u>

The *Mĕngjiàng Yún-Rén Royal Yacht* looked far different than anything Struyograb had ever seen before.

The *Mĕngjiàng Yún-Rén Royal Yacht* layout was simple and designed around esthetics and not combat. There were no multitudes of soldiers sitting at computer consoles that would be expected on Tall White or Grey Alien vessels.

Per *Wánmĕi De Huā* directive the crew of the Royal Yacht took on human forms because Struyograb was now in the control room.

Note to cinematographer:

Treat the following TELEPATHICALLY statements as a voiceover with C.U. but no lip movements.

Drago commented with curiosity.

DRAGO
(TELEPAHICALLY)
Wánmĕi De Huā, I see you brought a guest.

WÁNMĔI DE HUĀ
(TELEPAHICALLY)
Drago, I felt that under the circumstances, I should
bring Struyograb here.

DRAGO
(TELEPAHICALLY)
What's the purpose of bringing Struyograb here?

WÁNMĔI DE HUĀ
(TELEPAHICALLY)
If Struyograb sends off his neutrino messages to turn
the Tall White Fleet around, it's going to take a day
delay to get confirmation.

DRAGO
(TELEPAHICALLY)
I understand, *Wánměi De Huā.*

WÁNMĚI DE HUĀ
(TELEPAHICALLY)
Tall White's fleet is getting close to Alpha Centauri and will need to make the maneuver around Alpha Centauri within a few hours.

DRAGO
(TELEPAHICALLY)
Conducting a tactical turning radius maneuver?

WÁNMĚI DE HUĀ
(TELEPAHICALLY)
Yes. They will need to use Alpha Centauri to help turn around much quicker at high velocity to get them back to Earth promptly to help us deal with the Wogar Greys.

DRAGO
(TELEPAHICALLY)
What are your plans to help implement this maneuver?

WÁNMĚI DE HUĀ
(TELEPAHICALLY)
We are going to leave orbit of this solar system and get out to the Tall White's Fleet so that we can put Struyograb aboard the command ship to make sure they don't miss that opportunity to maneuver.

DRAGO
(TELEPAHICALLY)
And if they do not get turned around what happens?

WÁNMĚI DE HUĀ
(TELEPAHICALLY)
It could be another week for the next opportunity.

DRAGO
(TELEPAHICALLY)
Is this essential?

WÁNMĚI DE HUĀ
(TELEPAHICALLY)

I want the Tall White Fleet to be in position near space of Earth by the time the Wogar Greys arrive for planetary conquest.

DRAGO
(TELEPAHICALLY)
What's your expectations?

WÁNMĚI DE HUĀ
(TELEPAHICALLY)

If we can hold them off for two weeks, our *Měngjiàng Yún-Rén Fleet* will arrive here to deal with the Wogar Greys.

DRAGO
(TELEPAHICALLY)
Understand.

Wánmi De Hu used mental telepathy to instruct Struyograb what he was required to do which was a repeat of what she just informed Drago.

STRUYOGRAB
(TELEPAHICALLY)

There is nothing that says I'm going to agree to do that.

WÁNMĚI DE HUĀ
(TELEPAHICALLY)

You will do it. Otherwise, when our *Měngjiàng Yún-Rén Fleet* gets here and after we wipe out the Wogar; we'll hunt your Tall White Fleet down and destroy every ship in the convoy.

Wánměi de Huā threat put strain on Struyograb now showing and as they started speeding up, he noticed the velocity was incredible as the planets quickly zoomed past the ship as they headed in the same direction of where the Tall White Fleet was heading.

A high-resolution video screen in the *Měngjiàng Yún-Rén Royal Yacht* control room more than likely teen feet tall or greater suddenly displayed the view ahead of them in the direction they were traveling. Flashes on meteorites suddenly turning bright in front of them caused Struyograb to ask the question:

282

STRUYOGRAB
What is that we are seeing?

WÁNMĚI DE HUĀ
Those are asteroids and space debris that are being shoved out of our way so that we don't collide with them.

STRUYOGRAB
Why do they suddenly start glowing so brightly?

WÁNMĚI DE HUĀ
The beams that we strike them with has energy that is arriving so quickly its intensifying the heat of the asteroid's surface so quickly that none of it escapes or radiates into space quick enough so that additional shove beams arriving cause great heat to add.

The summation of the beams causes some of those objects to melt, others are becoming soggy becoming a plasma state and frequency controlled as they're being pushed out of our way.

Struyograb could see a bright star directly ahead of them get even brighter and fear struck him that they could run into it if they didn't change course real soon. Then suddenly, the Royal Yacht slowed down.

Wánměi De Huā announced telepathically in a very terse tone that left no doubt in Struyograb mind; he was dealing with a tough commander. He knew he was on the spot.

WÁNMĚI DE HUĀ
(TELEPAHICALLY)
Struyograb, your video is now being shown to your Tall White Fleet on your command channel which *Měngjiàng Yún-Rén INTEL* have studied and mastered.

Struyograb realized *Wánměi De Huā* was honest and never embellished anything realized the Fleet Commanders were now probably observing him.

Wánměi De Huā directed Struyograb using mental telepathy.

WÁNMĚI DE HUĀ
(TELEPAHICALLY)
Explain to the Tall White Commander we will be transporting you aboard the command ship in a few moments for consultations.

The Tall White Fleet Commander General Sperberzing was suddenly observed on the big monitor that had previously shown the stars and meteorites. Fleet Commander General Sperberzing appeared to be looking quite surprised to be viewing Struyograb.

TALL WHITE
FLEET COMMANDER
GENERAL SPERBERZING

This is rather a surprise. I take it you are on that ship that just popped up in front of us out of nowhere.

STRUYOGRAB

Yes, General Sperberzing, I'm aboard the *Měngjiàng Yún-Rén Royal Yacht* that has brought me to you for this emergency.

TALL WHITE
FLEET COMMANDER
GENERAL SPERBERZING

I have to say this is a rather big surprise, since we were communicating recently.

STRUYOGRAB

I will be transported aboard your command ship momentarily by the ability these aliens have which we've never encountered before.

Wánměi De Huā stated with more mental telepathy now appearing far tougher than Struyograb had ever seen before.

WÁNMĚI DE HUĀ
(TELEPAHICALLY)

Inform General Sperberzing, I'll be coming with you.

STRUYOGRAB

General Sperberzing, the *Měngjiàng Yún-Rén Royal Empress* will be coming with me.

Within a few seconds Struyograb felt a strange tingling as his body suddenly disappeared into a cosmic abyss then reappeared on the bridge of the Tall White Galaxy Cruiser and command ship standing a few feet away from General Sperberzing with *Wánměi de Huā* standing a couple feet away from him on his right.

TALL WHITE
FLEET COMMANDER
GENERAL SPERBERZING

Struyograb, you are the last person I would expect to suddenly appear like this, we obviously have a lot to talk about.

STRUYOGRAB

General Sperberzing, let me introduce you to *Wánměi De Huā Shèngdà Dá Qiè Sī* who is with me and is the leader of the *Měngjiàng Yún-Rén* people.

TALL WHITE
FLEET COMMANDER
GENERAL SPERBERZING

May I ask what is the purpose of this visit?

STRUYOGRAB

General, I'm ordering you to turn the fleet around and head back to Earth, as we approach the *Alpha Centauri A* star, you will do the space curve around it to fling your fleet back to earth as to not lose any velocity in the maneuver.

TALL WHITE
FLEET COMMANDER
GENERAL SPERBERZING

Why are we going back to Earth? These men and supplies are desperately needed at the war zone, the Azcarian Reptilians are decimating our ranks.

STRUYOGRAB

General Sperberzing, your men and material will arrive at the war zone ahead of schedule with the help of the *Měngjiàng Yún-Rén.*

TALL WHITE
FLEET COMMANDER
GENERAL SPERBERZING

That doesn't seem possible.

STRUYOGRAB

We'll discuss the details of how and why after you return to Earth's near space.

After repeating much that was discussed before, General Sperberzing acknowledged his new orders and gave the fleet the instructions on the maneuver they were just about ready to start making when *Wánměi De Huā* stated to Struyograb:

WÁNMĚI DE HUĀ
(TELEPAHICALLY)
General Sperberzing knows what he must do. I will
now take you back aboard my Royal Yacht and return
you to your office in Area 51.

STRUYOGRAB
Goodbye General Sperberzing. I'll see you in three
days or sooner hopefully.

Struyograb announced moments before he dematerialized on the Tall White Galaxy Cruiser and suddenly was back aboard the *Měngjiàng Yún-Rén Royal Yacht* heading back to earth in the fastest manner he'd ever experienced before.

***

<u>EXT. DAY. MARS. SECRET INTERNATIONAL DEFENCE AND SURVEILANVE BASE.</u>

The secret base on Mars had detected some kind of spacecraft going by but they were too far away to intercept or get a good identification of it.

Due to the Doppler associated with the 2 bodies going in opposite direction, Mars at 45,000 miles per hour verses the craft at 115,000 miles per second the differential speed of relative motion blurred any hopes of getting a good picture.

By the time of the detection a realization it was most likely an interplanetary ship, it was too late for satellites to get any visual on it.

Grak had managed to sneak out with the abduction ship and now he returned and was soon dropped off near Area-51, S-4 on a pathway he often took walks, so his sudden reappearance did not cause any undue concern of the security personnel who quickly identified him and pretty much ignored him as he wondered back to the tall Black Building where he lived and had an office.

Suspicions were up because nobody had seen Grak for a couple days. The last time anyone seen Grak was about the same time as Vance's abduction.

<u>INT. DAY. AREA 51. FOREIGN ALIEN CONSULATE BUILDING.</u>

Grak had a stack of messages, but by routine nature, he always erased any that came from Struyograb whom he detested.

Colonel Jones was too far down on the food chain to take seriously, as Grak felt worthy of only talking to Generals or diplomats sent by Presidential envoy.

Surveillance video had recorded Grak's entry and identified him. General Brazile had queued for an alert in the security system that he be notified when anyone or any security check made contact with Grak.

Already assuming Grak may have had a hand in Vance's abduction, General Brazile really didn't expect Grak to return to Area-51, S-4. When Grak did finally show up, it was highly unexpected.

Struyograb had not yet returned and was a couple hours away with the *Měngjiàng Yún-Rén,* so he and Grak had no confrontation. When General Brazile requested he come by his office, he had no concern that anyone had connected him to the abduction of the distinguished guest Vance.

Grak's plan was in perfect order and in just a couple more days when the Wogar Greys deployed their fleet to harvest Earth, Grak planned to personally make Struyograb regret every unkind word he ever mentioned. The bitterness he had for that condescending Tall White was too great to describe.

The phone rang, and Grak pressed the button for the speakerphone.

GRAK
Hello.

Since most of his calls came in from English Speaking people after several years, Grak had grown accustomed to speaking this terrestrial language which he had learned as an early phase Hybrid.

If anything could most describe Grak besides his evilness was his hybrid envy.

Grak often felt he was born 30 years too early and missed out on the 30-gene modification that would have got him out of his semi-amphibian physical appearance and make him totally humanoid.

Grak lusted for humanoid females but because of his awkward appearance felt the revulsion Earth women held towards him.

Grak was just thinking about how he would enslave at least 2,000 Earth Women during the planetary conquest and take out his pent-up desires on them. Then the caller snapped him back to reality.

GENERAL BRAZILE
Grak, this is General Brazile. I need you to come over
to my office for a few minutes.

GRAK
Sure, I'll be right over.

***

<u>INT. SPACE. TALL WHITE GALAXY CRUISER CONTROL ROOM.</u>

The Tall White's fleet had come within the gravitational pull of the star Alpha Centauri
-A, the larger of the three stars in that cluster which is the nearest solar system to Earth
only four point three light years away.

GALAXY CRUISER HELMSMAN
General Sperberzing, applying maneuver thrusts to
conform to track.

GENERAL SPERBERZING
Very well helm, maintain speed through the turn.

The lead ship of the Tall White Fleet acted as the main navigator for the fleet. Just
like a mother duck leading all her ducklings in a pond, the rest of the Tall White
Fleet navigated off constant vectors sent out which the mother ship's computers and
processed them to keep an absolute fixed relative position to the lead element to
prevent collisions and confusion.

The fleet's helmsman took pride in precision navigation and if plotted on a large scale
map the track would show the current maneuver around Alpha Centaury-A an absolute
perfect circle.

But to maintain the distance from the star and not be pulled in closer a certain amount
of thrust was required. If the auto-throttles maintained enough thrust, centrifugal force
would prevent getting closer to the star and at the same time the gravitational waves
had started pulling the space craft towards the star increased its velocity measurably.

The result is that after one last throttle increase at the precise moment would then break
the ships away from the star's electromagnetic and gravity fields as the centrifugal
force was too much for the star's gravitational waves to have any further effect on
direction. Hence, the ships were flung towards the Earth's solar system at a very high
velocity.

<u>EXT. CGI. SPACE. TALL WHITE FLEET MANUEVERING AROUND ALPHA CENTARI-A STAR. 20 SECONDS WITH DRAMATIC MUSIC DURING VOICE OVER.</u>

VOICEOVER

General Sperberzing understood from the briefing the Wogar Greys could launch the attack at any moment; hence, he planned to return as fast as possible to make sure he had good areas to maneuver his Fleet near Earth.

Examining the possible vector arrangement and tweaking it a bit, though incurring some risk of passing too close to the star, General Sperberzing determined he could shave off at least half a day on his return and possibly more if his nerve held up and he got his fleet very close to the star.

General Sperberzing's main fear of course was should there be a massive coronal ejection towards his ships, they would be instantly fired. The risk was great, but if he could arrive back to earth half a day earlier or even more so, in his heart he knew he could stave off disaster the despicable Wogar Greys were likely to inflict with planetary conquest.

General Sperberzing who normally only managed the bridge during battle stations, stayed in full vigilance on the Bridge during this maneuver. Several generations later new cadets at the space academy would be taught the history of the great Sperberzing maneuver which broke all records of a solar sling shot.

<u>INT. SPACE. TALL WHITE GALAXY CRUISER CONTROL ROOM.</u>

GALAXY CRUISER HELMSMAN
Increasing throttle settings 10%, in accordance with the flight plan.

GENERAL SPERBERZING
Very well helm, make reports every 10 degrees.

Damage Control Officer, keep a close eye on hull temperatures in the fleet in case we must open range from the star.

DAMAGE CONTROL OFFICER
General Sperberzing, we are carefully monitoring hull
temperatures throughout the fleet and will advise you
as soon as we see any troubling trends.

The helmsman did his modified repeat back then continued with the flight controls as specified.

GALAXY CRUISER HELMSMAN
Passing 90 degrees in the turn.

GENERAL SPERBERZING
Very well Helmsman.

General Sperberzing was starting to feel a little relief knowing he was now halfway through the turn and by the end of the day would be pointing at Earth and going at a velocity few had ever experienced.

***

INT. DAY. BURBANK AIRPORT. CIA X-DIVISION OFFICES.

Jeff was sitting at his desk at the X-Division Burbank facility when suddenly, the phone rang.

JEFF
Jeff here.

GARY
Jeff, this is Gary, do you have your bags packed?

JEFF
Always.

GARY
A plane will be arriving in about half an hour to fly us
down to Dallas. You'll be briefed on the way.

Colonel Davy Jones had made the calls. X-division was called into action. The DD/P boys wasted no time in picking out the *technical's* to carry out this job. It was one of those that had high risk at the same time; it's the sort of actions often taken when Cash in Advance DD/P was tasked to act.

Jeff, a loner, constantly on the road, lived and worked from one challenge to the next. He had pulled off some amazing jobs and almost 20 years later was thinking about the time Gus had him do some things out in Honolulu in which he said:

VOICEOVER (JEFF)
THOUGHT
I'll never do that again!

But at the same time, he knew Gus had managed a technical feat never considered or done before, partly due to Gus' thinking outside the box and partly due to his stubbornness.

Gus had a lot of back stabbers and people complaining about him, but it was all about jealousy that others didn't have the balls to attempt what Gus did and accomplish them within the impossible timelines they had to work under.

It was not beyond Gus to steal a forklift or a crane, whatever it took to get the job done. And even though Jeff may hesitate in admitting it, some of their current operating methods were carved out of Gus's hard working, hard drinking constant push, as if the world was coming to an end this weekend and it had to get done now.

No doubt this unknown mission, with little or no information other than flying into Dallas very well could end up like another one of those Gus escapades.

That would get some negative feedback, but as Gus had told him, no matter how badly it pissed the bosses and the *ungrateful sons of a bitches*, the fact remained— Gus made it look easy, which led to many other enterprising fools wiggling their way into the business and eventually turning some of it into a soup sandwich, as the term applies to the business when neophytes screw up projects.

In a while, Jeff heard a jet land through an open window since they were located near runway 33, as he was used to the air traffic noise. He didn't know that was his transportation, but within about 5 minutes his phone rang again and on the other end of the line he could hear Gary's voice saying:

GARY
Your ride is here.

Jeff then suddenly heard a click and a busy signal.

Jeff grabbed his grip, walked down a flight of stairs and turned right out the door and walked a half block and hopped on the Jet which immediately moved out onto runway 33 and took off.

***

INT. DAY. AREA-51 GENERAL BRAZILE'S OFFIC.

General Brazile said immediately made the announcement when Grak walked into his office.

> GENERAL BRAZILE
> Grak, we've been looking for you a couple days!

> GRAK
> General Brazile, you know I like taking walks.

> GENERAL BRAZILE
> Security cameras didn't show you leaving the base and only caught you walking back today.

> GRAK
> My body heat must not have triggered the infrared scanners to make the recording. We've had a couple hot days; no doubt the infrared wasn't working too well.

> GENERAL BRAZILE
> Ok well, we have got some things to discuss.

> GRAK
> Don't tell me about those wild Struyograb claims, he hates me and will say anything to make me look bad.

> GENERAL BRAZILE
> Struyograb hasn't complained about you.

> GRAK
> Well, then what is it?

> GENERAL BRAZILE
> Our distinguished guests are gone, one was abducted, the other has left in search for her companion.

> GRAK
> I've not seen *Wánměi De Huā Shèngdà Dá Qiè Sī* or her earth friend Vance since the day they arrived.

GENERAL BRAZILE

Do you have any idea what may have happened to the
Earth man?

GRAK

If anything, I'd say Struyograb shanghaied him for
their fleet that just left out of here a couple days ago.
When did you say he came up missing?

VOICEOVER (GENERAL
BRAZILE) THOUGHT

*Grak is one incredible schemer how amazing it was,
picking the same day the Tall Whites left to help cover
up his possible involvement.*

***

INT. CGI. SPACE. *MĔNGJIÀNG YÚN-RÉN ROYAL YACHT* ARRIVING 15 SECONDS.

Mĕngjiàng Yún-Rén arrived back in Solar Orbit. *Wánmĕi De Huā*, having spent the last couple hours talking with Struyograb had growing confidence in his claim; they only intended to use Earth as a midpoint stop to shuttle troops to the war zone. No planetary conquest was envisioned by the Tall Whites who viewed Earth's humans as an ally and not an adversary.

Struyograb having watched re-entry to the solar system and the flyby Jupiter knew they were close to the sun hiding their heat signature as well as probably recharging their power plant took the opportunity to say:

STRUYOGRAB

It looks like we are back in the solar system; now that
everything is planned, you might as well transport me
back to Earth.

WÁNMĔI DE HUĀ

The transporter wasn't too rough on you?

STRUYOGRAB

No, I only felt a slight tingling sensation.

Wánmĕi De Huā took note of that thinking that may pave the way to transport Vance if they could ever locate him. She had an idea to test the safety of transporting humans on the secretary she met today.

***

<u>INT. DAY. AREA-51 GENERAL BRAZILE'S OFFIC.</u>

General Brazile looked up at Colonel Jones after watching some of the security alerts.

GENERAL BRAZILE
Come with me, we need to go to Struyograb's office
right away.

This was not going to be a pleasant meeting, confronting the new aliens whom he had no power over, but the fear of them triggering a galactic war over earth put great fear into him.

It did not take long for the two men to ride the elevator up to the surface, walk outside and hop in General Brazil's HUMV parked in a shaded area provided by a car park with solar panels on top of it. It only took a couple minutes to drive over to the 20-story black building recently completed to administratively house the numerous aliens that were starting to accumulate as intensive negotiations continued which really meant Earths fate.

It was only a matter of time when some spark would set ablaze an inferno because the three humanoid and five non-humanoid alien races did not get along with each other and General Brazile knew they were all eyeballing the Oasis Earth and the exclusive rights to plunder it, a fact that Majestic-12 tended to want to keep to themselves.

The two officers in uniform, walked into the building and took the elevator up to the 4th floor got out and approached the attractive blonde security guard.

GENERAL BRAZILE
Sergeant, we need to talk with Struyograb right away.

SECURITY GUARD
You might as well go on in, he has five people with him
already. I'm sure he's more than ready for additional
visitors.

General Brazile walked past the security guard's desk down the hallway and turned to the door to Dr. Struyograb's office and let himself in with Colonel Jones right behind.

His office was empty!

General Brazile walked back to the security guard.

GENERAL BRAZILE
Did you see any of them leave?

SECURITY GUARD
No, sir. Nobody left.

GENERAL BRAZILE
Show me the video recordings of the entrance to his
office for the past two hours and put them in high-
speed playback.

The computerized security recording showed the aliens arriving but nobody leaving.

GENERAL BRAZILE
What the hell?

COLONEL JONES
They must have used their transporter device.

GENERAL BRAZILE
No shit Sherlock. How do you think they made it back
on the base and into my office without being detected?

General Brazile knew he was in for a rough day.

Just as General Brazile slowly unwinding from the surreal nature of his discovery of
the empty office and was about to leave, Struyograb rematerialized back in his office.

STRUYOGRAB
Hello General Brazile. Next time please knock before
you come in.

GENERAL BRAZILE
Whoa, where did you come from?

STRUYOGRAB
General we have some things to talk about.

***

<u>INT. DAY. DALLAS TEXAS LOVE FIELD.</u>

The corporate jet landed at Dallas Love Field then taxied over to a Business Aircraft
Service Facility, where the X-Div personnel departed the plane and were met by their
driver and coordinator, a gentleman named Mark.

Mark was one of those secret agents who said:

MARK
Let it be written and let it be done.

Mark had his sidekick with him, the ultra-spook, Joe, who was a MacGyver in action, could just about get anything done.

These two *technicals* were the guys you wanted on your team if you had some serious business like the Cash in Advance boys often did.

Mark and Joe were the tops in the DD/P world when it came to facilitating technical challenges. They also had their experiences with Gus who would be there to receive all the stolen goods when the job was complete. Gus may never know that something bad happened to Boyd.

Mark was driving, Joe was shotgun, and Jeff and Gary were in the back going over the plan:

Note to cinematographer:

During this next dialog the scene is shot inside Boyd Bushman's home as if this is a VOICE OVER.

GARY
Joe will temporarily cut power to the house. Jeff will then disconnect leads to temporarily severing all phone lines, just in case a burglar alarm was hooked up.

JEFF
Gary will operate the cell phone jammer and act as lookout.

GARY
Mark, who is good with hypodermic needles from his fiber optic days when we were tapping into communications cables, will give Boyd a shot of sodium pentothal while the others hold him down.

MARK
Then what?

GARY
Then we will lay him in his bed if he isn't already there and put the little pill in his mouth that would dissolve quick and put some very nasty drugs into his system

that would end it for him and not be traceable in an autopsy.

JEFF
Since Boyd has cancer and does not have much time left, the killer drug will be hidden by his cancer treatment drugs, and nobody should ever suspect foul play.

Everything went per plan. X-div finished poisoning Boyd and quickly searched his home and determined most of the area 51 pictures were in his study.

MARK
Good thing we got a van, this guy has a lot of pictures.

While the boys were loading up all the Alien stuff, Mark pulled the hard drive out of Boyd's computer and replaced it with an erased hard drive they pulled out of recycling center for such operations. They wanted the hard drive to go through to make sure they had all his contacts and any possible information he might have scanned.

After all the tasks were completed and all classified documents removed, the X-div guys drove to the Naval Air Base where Gus waited next to a Gulf Stream destined to fly back to area 51. Within 10 minutes the plane was loaded up and took off just as the sun was rising.

Mark drove the X-Div boys back to Love Field where they got back on the plane to fly them to Burbank, then Mark drove the van back to Oklahoma City where he returned it to a secret agent who worked for Haliburton, which the company had no knowledge they had an employee engaged in clandestine operations.

But it goes to show you men out of the oil patch tend to be talented in many respects.

Mark hopped on a plane and was back at Dulles in time to watch the sunset.

VOICEOVER (MARK)
THOUGHT
All in a day's work.

Several days later when people went to check up on Boyd because he missed his doctor's appointment and had not been seen, he still had a lot of junk in his home but none of it came from area 51.

***

<u>INT. INT. SPACE. WOGAR GREY *COLONY CLASS PLANETARY CONQUEST VESSEL/ MOTHER SHIP.*</u>

Vance was marched back to his incubation cell where he got frightened looks by some of the humans that were there. Every one of them exhibited some schizophrenia like behavior.

VOICEOVER (VANCE)
THOUGHT

If I ever get out of here alive, I'll come back and rescue them.

Vance showed no cowering characteristics. Some of the abductees in the incubation center had been there for 20 years as Vance soon learned. Unlike them he knew he had someone that would search the universe to find him and if he was harmed, the Wogar Greys would regret the day they were born.

One of the prisoners approached Vance who was still wearing the neurotic shackles.

ABDUCTEE

Did you come from Earth?

VANCE

Yes,

ABDUCTEE

When did they nab you?

VANCE

Hours ago.

ABDUCTEE

Are you here to be experimented on or are you going to be one of the teachers?

The man thought that because the new abductee had not received any rough treatment had been led away and returned in cheerful manner it could be anything.

VANCE

Neither I'm a hostage.

ABDUCTEE

Are you some sort of big shot?

VANCE

Not really, just someone important who cares a lot about me.

ABDUCTEE

Do you think you are going to get out of here alive?

VANCE

A lot sooner than you realize. How long have you been here and where did you come from?

ABDUCTEE

I've been here about 15 years. I lived in San Diego, California.

VANCE

Were you stuck in this room the entire time?

ABDUCTEE

No, I used to be one of the teachers, went to a lot of different locations on this ship.

VANCE

So, you know your way around?

ABDUCTEE

I know all the living areas quite well, have no idea what the control center or technology centers are like.

VANCE

What's your name?

ABDUCTEE

Well people back on Earth Called me Bud.

VANCE

Hi Bud, I'm Vance.

Vance held out his hand and shook hands with Bud.

ABDUCTEE (BUD)

The prisoners seemed to calm down by the sight of you Vance.

VANCE
They do seem to appear less frightened now.

ABDUCTEE (BUD)
Maybe you give them hope by your presence.

VANCE
When I get out of here, they have a chance to be taken
back to Earth.

***

Boris Potemkin arrived in Moscow the following day. He wondered if he'd be taken out and shot or sent to Siberia. After he got off the business jet, he was put in a Zil Limo and soon found himself at a Dacha out on the outskirts of Moscow.

<u>EXT. DAY. MOSCOW RUSSIA, DACHA OUT ON THE OUTSKIRTS OF MOSCOW.</u>

BORIS POTEMKIN KGB HANDLER
Today's your lucky day.

BORIS POTEMKIN
Why's that?

BORIS POTEMKIN KGB HANDLER
You get to stay in Brezhnev's Dacha.

BORIS POTEMKIN
This was Brezhnev's Dacha?

Brezhnev's Dacha image:

<u>The Brezhnev Dacha: Just Another Lavish Home? · The Russian Dacha: Highlighting the Deviation between the Famed and the Commonplace · The Urban Imagination</u>

BORIS POTEMKIN KGB HANDLER
Sure was.

BORIS POTEMKIN
It's not luxurious, but the architecture is astounding.

BORIS POTEMKIN KGB HANDLER
Yes, Brezhnev had good taste until his final years.

BORIS POTEMKIN
Died from aging?

BORIS POTEMKIN KGB HANDLER
No drug abuse.

BORIS POTEMKIN
Did Brezhnev like to get high?

BORIS POTEMKIN KGB HANDLER
No, he had medical conditions and got hooked on the
medical drugs.

BORIS POTEMKIN
Wonder why he picked this spot?

BORIS POTEMKIN KGB HANDLER
The pine forest hides it quite well from the main
highway that goes by but allowed him to get back
to the heart of Moscow rapidly. It's also close to a
hospital.

BORIS POTEMKIN
When did the KGB start using it?

BORIS POTEMKIN KGB HANDLER
Shortly after Brezhnev's death.

The handler's cell phone rang. He didn't have much to say.

BORIS POTEMKIN KGB HANDLER
We will go there right away.

Boris Potemkin KGB Handler then turned towards Boris and announced:

BORIS POTEMKIN KGB HANDLER
We leave now.

Boris expecting rough treatment and possibly death was surprised when the handler
opened the passenger door for him, and then shut it after Boris was seated in the Zil.

The spotless Zil's interior was unexpected for someone fearing his own execution.

The car traveled into the heart of Moscow. Soon they pulled up to Lubyanka Square in Meshchansky District of Moscow. The sight of the building in front of Boris was very familiar as he spent several years working in it and training for various assignments.

<u>EXT. DAY. MOSCOW RUSSIA, FSB (KGB) HEADQUARTRES. LUBYANKA BUILDING IN MESHCHANSKY DISTRICT OF MOSCOW.</u>

The car pulled up to a semi-decorated entrance, considered extravagant for Soviet Standards, but functional and reasonable for Western Standards.

The driver got out and opened the passenger door on the right side, which was nearer the steps to the front entrance.

As expected, a couple men were standing there waiting for him. As Boris climbed the top of the stairs, one of the men said:

FSB/KGB ESCORT
This way Boris, please follow me.

Boris followed the well-dressed man wearing a business suit. Following behind Boris was another man also in a business suit but wearing sunglasses and based on his build and large size suit coat most likely covering up some serious muscles or hidden weapons.

The FSB Escort led Boris to think this guy was a security man quite capable of dealing with someone. Boris could only speculate. The bruiser was there for Boris' benefit.

They took an elevator up to the 4th floor, exited onto a plush red carpet that had sickles and hammers every 25 feet or so along the hallway. The carpet was extremely clean and bright.

<u>INT. DAY. MOSCOW RUSSIA, FSB (KGB) HEADQUARTRES. LUBYANKA BUILDING IN MESHCHANSKY DISTRICT OF MOSCOW 4<u>TH</u> FLOOR OFFICES.</u>

VOICEOVER (BORIS
POTEMKIN) THOUGHT
Probably a lot of people don't come up here. What happens during the winter months when people's shoes got all messy with slush and ice that could not be helped walking around Moscow.

Boris was led into a spacious office that had an extraordinarily attractive secretary and personal assistant sitting behind a receptionist desk. Two bruisers sat in chairs about ten feet from her, who no doubt was part of a security force.

The receptionist was expecting Boris.

RECEPTIONIST
Mr. Potemkin, please go in; Alexander Bortnikov is
waiting for you.

As Boris walked into the office following the man who escorted him, he immediately
saw Alexander Bortnikov sitting at his desk.

General Alexi Shoygu was sitting on a sofa about 10 feet away with what appeared to
be a teacup sitting on the coffee table.

The big bruiser that had followed Boris shut the door and did not follow them in,
presumably would be waiting outside.

Another extremely attractive administrative aid shoved a chair that had been sitting just
inside and to the right of the double door right up in front of the desk, then Alexander
Bortnikov gestured:

ALEXANDER BORTNIKOV
Boris, please sit down.

Boris had no idea what to expect; his reception didn't appear raw in any manner and
his curiosity was building.

Alexander Bortnikov had a file folder and handed it to Boris. It was a report from the
latest Fort Worth Star-Telegram internet story about prominent Lockheed Engineer
Boyd Bushman

ALEXANDER BORTNIKOV
Boris, take a minute to look at this.

VOICEOVER
FORT WORTH STAR-TELEGRAM
*Boyd Bushman, a Lockheed Engineer who had worked
with Kelly Johnson and Mark Rich was found dead in
his home, apparently died of natural causes.*

*Police forced their way into the home after friends and
relatives called 911 saying he had missed his doctor's
appointment.*

*Boyd Bushman appeared to have died in his sleep.
Nothing in the home appeared to be disturbed and the
Burglar Alarm system was fully functional.*

Boyd Bushman had not been seen in public since returning from Las Vegas where he did a controversial presentation at a UFO conference.

BORIS POTEMKIN
Cash in Advance boys probably took care of him.

Boris acted quite surprised, and then handed the file back to Alexander Bortnikov.

Alexander Bortnikov looked at Boris in a solemn manner.

ALEXANDER BORTNIKOV
Now you know why we had to pull you out.

BORIS POTEMKIN
What makes you think the CIA suspected I had any involvement with Mr. Bushman?

ALEXANDER BORTNIKOV
The reason why I sent word back to cease any further contact with Mr. Bushman is we discovered intensive surveillance on him and several intercepts.

BORIS POTEMKIN
That's very interesting.

ALEXANDER BORTNIKOV
We find the UFO conferences a major source of Intel, because not all UFOs are aliens, some are American TR-3B or SR-72 craft that look so advanced, it's hard to separate them from Alien spacecraft.

BORIS POTEMKIN
Those aircraft can easily appear to be UFOs.

ALEXANDER BORTNIKOV
Our people sent into the Las Vegas UFO conference detected DD/P X-division people doing their usual snooping.

BORIS POTEMKIN
Over the years I did see a few there myself.

ALEXANDER BORTNIKOV
Dring the UFO conference a CIA's DD/P X-division Rep shut Boyd Bushman down as he was going through his laundry list of sightings while showing pictures stolen from area 51.

BORIS POTEMKIN
And that led you to believe I had blown my cover?

ALEXANDER BORTNIKOV
We had Boyd Bushman under surveillance to approach him to get some information on Alien entities characteristics that he or his contacts had encountered.

BORIS POTEMKIN
And what did you get?

ALEXANDER BORTNIKOV
The indication jumped out at our agent that Boyd Bushman was under severe scrutiny and when our agents followed him to the bar after you dropped him off after taking him to dinner; he was sitting two bar stools down from a CIA Q-division spy.

BORIS POTEMKIN
Sounds to me like that was just a chance encounter.

ALEXANDER BORTNIKOV
You are probably right. After Boyd Bushman got into a discussion with a lady sitting next to him, the Q division rep called in backup.

BORIS POTEMKIN
What did the backup do?

ALEXANDER BORTNIKOV
According to our agent doing the surveillance another Q division agent was called to the bar and there appears to be some clandestine actions that occurred afterwards.

BORIS POTEMKIN
Interesting.

ALEXANDER BORTNIKOV
The cars you broke into were Q-Division.

BORIS POTEMKIN
And the passengers?

ALEXANDER BORTNIKOV
There were 4 of them all together we have verified worked for DD/P, but there were 2 others that we have not been able to identify.

BORIS POTEMKIN
What do you expect of me?

ALEXANDER BORTNIKOV
We have another mission for you. Even though your involvement with Mr. Bushman was probably not a wise thing to do, we realize you were not provided with important information that might have altered your actions.

BORIS POTEMKIN
No doubt.

ALEXANDER BORTNIKOV
In the future, we'll modify our procedures and protocols to prevent similar risky activities.

BORIS POTEMKIN
Okay understand.

ALEXANDER BORTNIKOV
A couple more things, we plan on sending you back to the United States, but due to the crisis we find ourselves in, we must give you a new identity.

BORIS POTEMKIN
That seems reasonable.

ALEXANDER BORTNIKOV
Your past is behind you. You cannot ever go back. We can't risk you contacting Alex or your hot flame Tanya.

BORIS POTEMKIN
Alright.

ALEXANDER BORTNIKOV
Also, you are not permitted to meet or socialize with
Jimmy in any manner.

BORIS POTEMKIN
May I ask why?

ALEXANDER BORTNIKOV
At this point in time, we do not know to what extent
they may have been penetrated or compromised.

BORIS POTEMKIN
Jimmy is a solid guy, always did good for me.

ALEXANDER BORTNIKOV
Jimmy might be a double spy. We are working on that.

BORIS POTEMKIN
How about Tanya?

ALEXANDER BORTNIKOV
She's not in the business, but you were seen with her
and Jimmy knows all about her. If he's a double spy,
he's already reported her relationship to you through
his handlers.

BORIS POTEMKIN
You are going to send me back to Las Vegas?

ALEXANDER BORTNIKOV
That's correct sort of, at least near there.

BORIS POTEMKIN
Alright.

ALEXANDER BORTNIKOV
You know Vegas well but most of your activity will
be north of there and trips to Vegas will only happen
occasionally.

BORIS POTEMKIN
If my identity has been blown, how will I be able to operate in Las Vegas?

ALEXANDER BORTNIKOV
We'll give you a new identity, some plastic surgery, and when you go back to Las Vegas and to your new designated area you will no longer be bald.

BORIS POTEMKIN
Hair transplant?

ALEXANDER BORTNIKOV
Yes, our 5th directive technical staff has perfected the art of hair transplant because we must take bald people like you and change your appearance in a major way.

BORIS POTEMKIN
What's my focus?

ALEXANDER BORTNIKOV
Your new focus is Area 51. You will be spending a lot of time in a town called Alamo Nevada which is due east of Area 51 and routinely gets pilots, scientists, and employees who stay there.

BORIS POTEMKIN
Sounds like an ideal location to operate.

ALEXANDER BORTNIKOV
We've done some investigation and found a Dude Ranch there is for sale. You will be the new owner/manager.

BORIS POTEMKIN
Will I spend any time in Vegas?

ALEXANDER BORTNIKOV
Yes, you will have some assignments there as well.

BORIS POTEMKIN
You're not afraid I will run into Jimmy?

ALEXANDER BORTNIKOV
Jimmy will be transferred to New York City soon, where we can vet him better since we have several agents that work at the United Nations can do all the protocol's necessary to flush him out if he is in fact a double spy.

BORIS POTEMKIN
When do I leave to go back?

ALEXANDER BORTNIKOV
After the face lift, new hair, and training on your new identity.

BORIS POTEMKIN
Since I'm here, how am I going to buy that Dude Ranch at Alamo Nevada?

Alexander Bortnikov then handed Boris an envelope which he opened. It was the letter Boris wrote to his lawyer in Las Vegas.

BORIS POTEMKIN
How did you get this letter from my lawyer?

Boris was slightly pissed that he had been deceived and his arrangements he thought a legitimate lawyer didn't get accomplished. He felt sorry for Tanya who wouldn't take long to go through the cash and would have to rely on her job to survive a shitty life.

ALEXANDER BORTNIKOV
He's one of our agents too. He's going to be purchasing that Dude Ranch for you.

BORIS POTEMKIN
How is it funded?

ALEXANDER BORTNIKOV
Your Liquor Business had an immediate buyer; the proceeds not only covered the price of the Dude Ranch, but also some cash left over for upgrades.

BORIS POTEMKIN
I see. When do we start?

ALEXANDER BORTNIKOV
You will be driven now back to your Dacha where
you'll begin your transformation of your identity and
study the factoids you need to know.

BORIS POTEMKIN
Alright.

ALEXANDER BORTNIKOV
One last thing Boris. No matter how much you
think you want that beautiful woman, under no
circumstances approach Tanya.

BORIS POTEMKIN
Understood.

Boris felt an inner sadness he could not quite understand.

***

INT.SPACE. *MĚNGJIÀNG YÚN-RÉN* ROYAL YACHT CONTROL ROOM.

Wánmĕi De Huā began maintaining her vigilance in the *Mĕngjiàng Yún-Rén Control Room*.

As *Wánmĕi De Huā* received more INTEL reports from her spies that were sent back and forth to area 51 nothing new arrived to give her any assurances that anyone knew any more details of Vance's disappearance.

Wánmĕi De Huā positioned the Royal Yacht, now reconfigured as a command ship in a circular orbit offset from the sun which allowed surveillance on Earth as well as a clear view of the *Tall White Fleet* that were coming their way.

***

EXT. CGI. SPACE. TALL WHITE FLEET APPROACHING 15 SECONDS.

The *Tall White Fleet* had by now completed its 180 turn around the *Alpha Centauri-A Star* and the fleet was just breaking free of the star's gravitational field as its velocity had now more than doubled and was heading back toward Earth.

Because of the obtuse angle formed from the *Mĕngjiàng Yún-Rén Royal Yacht/ Command Ship* and the offset orbit around earth's sun, there was just barely enough deflection angle between the approaching *Tall White's Fleet* to where the star's glare no longer obscured the fleet and the light from the star actually illuminated it where from this position it was easily observed with the advanced optics the *Měngjiàng Yún-Rén Royal Yacht* deployed.

The maneuver had exceeded General Sperberzing expectations as based on star observations and plots which allowed them to accurately determine their position in space by angular velocity from Alpha Centauri-A and -B stars, as well as the third, a red dwarf showed they had easily doubled their speed, an accomplishment that would no doubt bring some fame.

From his position in space General Sperberzing could view earth, not with the greatest of resolution but good enough to detect explosions or attributes of any form of major armed warfare, especially nuclear weapons deployment. At least for the time being, the Wogar had not shown their hand, but it was estimated that such a planetary invasion was eminent.

INT. SPACE. TALL WHITE GALALXY CRUISER COMMAND SHIP CONTROL ROOM.

That realization came several hours later when the Tall White Galaxy Cruiser Sensors Operator reported via the Control Room Supervisor:

GALAXY CRUISER
CONTROL ROOM SUPERVISOR
General Sperberzing, we are getting indications of
Neutrino pulses radiating from Mars.

***

EXT. DAY. MARS. SECRET MARS BASE NEAR CYDONIA.

The secret Mars Base located near Cydonia was ever vigilant. Q-Division was the main interface between Area 51 operations and the secret Defense grid that had built bases on Mars and the Moon and was in the early stages of exploring Europa, the sixth-closest moon orbiting Jupiter.

The reason why the Moon Europa was picked for the defense grid expansion is the atmosphere was mainly oxygen, and the frozen surface was believed to contain a vast ocean below the frozen water-ice crust surface.

Weather on Europa was constant, and no evidence of any major storms existed which meant construction techniques could be simplified, and the first machinery scheduled to be sent was drilling rigs to access the vast oceans below the surface that would simplify power needs by hydrogen fuel cells.

Nitrogen and other substances would be shipped to modify the air and allow hydroponic plant growth and sustainment. This settlement would then provide another sector of space surveillance, making earth less likely to receive a surprise attack from that direction giving a tremendous boost to global security.

Until that Europa base was built, Mars played a critical role in the early warning of approaching dangers.

The *Wogar Greys* had delayed their invasion too long. Had they attacked just a year earlier, they could have hit Mars, knocked out its early warning, then waltzed into nearby Earth Space and quickly devastated the planet in a simple manner with superior firepower.

Unfortunately for the *Wogar Greys*, the Tall Whites entered the picture. As galactic battlefield conditions worsened for the Tall Whites who were practically the only alien race truly looking out for Earth. The Tall Whites had sent a stream of ships to Earth stopover and R&R which took eight months to get to Earth from their home planet.

This midpoint rest area for the Tall White troops, allowed them to spend time in real gravity and get over space sickness before getting back on their ships to continue another eight months towards the war zone.

The timing of the *Wogar Grey* attack was planned around the departure of the Great Tall White Fleet that had gathered around Earth as a staging area.

Between Earth and their home worlds, the Tall Whites could send ships and crews without much concern of danger, but once they left Earth and got nearer to the war zone, the threat of ambush was a distinct possibility.

Hence, the Tall Whites traveled in convoys for mutual protection in power by numbers. There would be no way a lone ship could survive long attacking this formation. On the other hand, with the numerous scouts and wide swath the fleet took, there would be no possible way an enemy concentration could sneak in on them unobserved. The convoy insured most if not all the ships would arrive intact at the war zone.

<u>INT. SPACE. GREY ALIEN COLONY CLASS PLANETARY CONQUEST VESSEL</u>

Wogar Grey Supreme Commander Zorgjeck discussed the attack with his Tactical Officer in final preparations to launch the attack.

WOGAR GREY
SUPREME COMMANDER
ZORGJECK

The Great Tall White Fleet traveled several days away from Earth with no hopes of returning in time to intervene.

TACTICAL OFFICER
The only issue they had was the possibility of intervention by this unexpected arrival of the *Měngjiàng Yún-Rén*.

WOGAR GREY
SUPREME COMMANDER
ZORGJECK
Now that we have Earth man Vance as a hostage who Grak reported is the companion of the *Měngjiàng Yún-Rén Empress*, I feel safe from any intervention by the *Měngjiàng Yún-Rén*.

TACTICAL OFFICER
The time is perfect to execute the Earth Invasion plan.

WOGAR GREY
SUPREME COMMANDER
ZORGJECK
I agree. Commence Earth Invasion Phase-1.

The Wogar Grey's *Colony Class Planetary Conquest Vessel* soon responded to Commence Earth Invasion Phase-1 orders.

<u>EXT. CGI. SPACE. GREY ALIEN COLONY CLASS PLANETARY CONQUEST VESSEL LAUNCHING ATTACK FORCE 45 SECONDS.</u>

The *Colony Class Planetary Conquest Vessel* began launching a group of ships whose main task was to hit Mars and hit it hard to knock out the surveillance of space in the direction of the arriving armada that would demand surrender of face annihilation.

It would take about six hours for those advance Phase-1 craft to do the damage perceived they were capable of.

Launching from such a vast distance would also facilitate obscuring their *Colony Class Planetary Conquest Vessel* position in space which meant they were less likely to be discovered and remain invisible and safe from any retaliatory forces.

CONTROL ROOM
LAUNCH COORDINATOR
Sir, Phase-1 Task Force has been launched.

WOGAR GREY
SUPREME COMMANDER
ZORGJECK
Launch coordinator, thank you for your report.

Supreme Commander Zorgjeck felt this attack on Earth would be a cake walk and in about another couple days, 80 years of planning and conquest would finally pay off.

Supreme Commander Zorgjeck would then be able to signal *to send the immigrant ships* that would carry 10 billion Wogar Greys to earth to not only provide them with material wealth but alleviate congestion they desperately needed.

Unlike America's early history of being built by immigrants while Europeans continued to live in luxury, the opposite would occur; the immigrant's lives would be greatly enhanced and superior to those remaining behind where every Wogar Grey City had the density of Calcutta, Beijing, New York, Guangzhou, Tokyo, or any other highly dense city on Earth.

***

<u>INT. SPACE *MĚNGJIÀNG YÚN-RÉN* ROYAL YACHT/COMMAND SHIP CONTROL ROOM</u>

WÁNMĚI DE HUĀ

The *Měngjiàng Yún-Rén* security men coming and going to Planet Earth were not bringing back any good news.

DRAGO
We will eventually get to the bottom of it, eventually
Grak will tip his hand. Then we'll know for sure.

WÁNMĚI DE HUĀ
But Vance is still hopelessly lost, and the consensus is
the Greys nabbed him.

DRAGO
We still are unable to get into the minds of the Hybrids.

WÁNMĚI DE HUĀ
Even if we did, the prisoners may not have the big
picture and were already prisoners when Vance was
kidnapped.

DRAGO
The prisoners most likely have no awareness of what transpired.

WÁNMĚI DE HUĀ
Chief Scientist, please come to the control room to provide a status report.

CHIEF SCIENTIST
The latest INTEL, however, does present an interesting piece of information that Grak is half hybrid.

WÁNMĚI DE HUĀ
How will that help us?

CHIEF SCIENTIST
Once we figure out how to mentally probe our prisoners, we'll find a way to get into Grak's head so that we can establish culpability and possibly figure out where he took Vance, if he was involved in the abduction.

WÁNMĚI DE HUĀ
Have you made any progress?

CHIEF SCIENTIST
Very much so, but we must peel back layer by layer neuro signals to allow our mental telepathy to fully grasp all the occurring thought processes in the being under observation.

Wánmĕi De Huā agonized over every detail.

WÁNMĚI DE HUĀ
Why is this taking so long?

CHIEF SCIENTIST
If the prisoners were pure Amphibian, Reptilian, or pure humanoid, it would be a simple matter.

But because they're hybrids, their mental pathways are far more complicated, and instead of doubling the number of layers to penetrate, it's much more.

These hybrids are one of the greatest challenges of my career.

WÁNMĚI DE HUĀ
Thank you for the report and please keep me advised if
you have any major discoveries or breakthroughs. You
may return to your lab.

The hours of disappointment crept by the intensity of the agony just would not dissipate. A solution must be found.

***

Halfway through the flight to Earth, the Greys experienced something they didn't anticipate.

<u>INT. DAY. MARS. CENTRAL SURVEILLANCE CONTROL ROOM.</u>

Mars' central surveillance operators were extra vigilant with additional officers monitoring performance around the clock so that any possible clues might be found.

The recent detection of a spacecraft passing by was still being analyzed even though there appeared to be no hope of identification; they, nevertheless, pursued the mystery, hoping to eventually come up with some identification or explanation.

Because of the recent surprise as well as instructions from Space command, the Russian and American technicians were cooperating far better than usual and their ever vigilance was at its very peak. The keen interest and interest the surveillance operators exhibited with their due diligence finally paid off.

The young Russian Surveillance Operator reported with a slight St. Petersburg accent.

MARS' CENTRAL
SURVEILLANCE OPERATOR
Sir, we have an incoming spacecraft!

MARS' CENTRAL
SURVEILLANCE OFFICER
Where at?

MARS' CENTRAL
SURVEILLANCE OPERATOR
Sector 24-85B.

MARS' CENTRAL
SURVEILLANCE OFFICER
That's almost sheer space, would not expect aliens to

come this way in such wide-open space if they didn't want to telegraph their position.

MARS' CENTRAL
SURVEILLANCE OPERATOR

Perhaps they don't know about our new capability the Tall Whites recently gave us.

MARS' CENTRAL
SURVEILLANCE OFFICER

That could be it. Which of the eight groups of aliens do you think this is?

MARS' CENTRAL
SURVEILLANCE OPERATOR

Based on pure numbers I would speculate its Greys until we could prove otherwise.

MARS' CENTRAL
SURVEILLANCE OFFICER

I'm sending a report to Q immediately, keep target information coming in frequent updates.

MARS' CENTRAL
SURVEILLANCE OPERATOR

The system logs all contacts every 30 minutes by default.

MARS' CENTRAL
SURVEILLANCE OFFICER

Well, change the settings to every 10 minutes.

MARS' CENTRAL
SURVEILLANCE OPERATOR

With all due respect sir, their distance in space and relative motion suggests whoever they are, are a long distance away. So, all you will get is a lot of redundant reports for a while.

MARS' CENTRAL
SURVEILLANCE OFFICER

Very well, leave it at the 30-minute marks, but when they get closer and start to see some positional drift, I want more frequent reports.

An hour later after reporting the intercepts to Q, the space coordinator asked the operators:

MARS' CENTRAL
SURVEILLANCE OFFICER
Any indications of drift or calculations of its trajectory?

MARS' CENTRAL
SURVEILLANCE OPERATOR

Sir, I hate to be the bearer of bad news, but I think they're coming right at us?

MARS' CENTRAL
SURVEILLANCE OFFICER
Any estimation of range?

MARS' CENTRAL
SURVEILLANCE OPERATOR

They're between us and Saturn, based on triangulation of the two satellites now in position to observe whatever this is.

MARS' CENTRAL
SURVEILLANCE OFFICER

Any possible identification or the makeup of the unidentified craft?

MARS' CENTRAL
SURVEILLANCE OPERATOR
Sensors indicate there are at least 12 vessels.

MARS' CENTRAL
SURVEILLANCE OFFICER
This may not turn out well.

General Brazile received the flash message from Mars command copied to him from the space command to advise him:

SPACE COMMAND MESSAGE
Based on the trajectory of the unidentified ships, we
believe the formation is heading for Mars and most
likely is an attack, going to red alert!

Another hour passed and suddenly the sensor operators declared:

MARS' CENTRAL
SURVEILLANCE OPERATOR
We now see these Alien Spaceships on planetary radar!

MARS' CENTRAL
SURVEILLANCE OFFICER
How far away are they?

MARS' CENTRAL
SURVEILLANCE OPERATOR
These Alien Spaceships just crossed the 250,000-mile
trip wire.

MARS' CENTRAL
SURVEILLANCE OFFICER
Estimated time of arrival?

MARS' CENTRAL
SURVEILLANCE OPERATOR
Based on optical tracker coefficients, expect them to
arrive in slightly less than an hour.

MARS' CENTRAL
SURVEILLANCE OFFICER
Spin up all missiles. Prepare to deploy Weapons!

<u>EXT. CGI. SPACE. WOGAR GREY EXPEDITIONARY FORCE ARRIVING AND
ATTACKING MARS. ONE MINUTE.</u>

Wogar Grey Attack Force ships either Fast Frigate Space Craft or Space Destroyers attacked defenseless satellites and destroyed them with powerful lasers.

Next attack is on all the ground-based sensors and anything observable needed to support people living and working on Mars.

The Wogar Greys attacked and blew up a lot of empty storage containers shipped to Mars with Cargo used in building the underground base. At the distances the Wogar Greys were shooting they could not really know what they were blowing up but since a couple of the containers stored hazardous materials such as paint, isopropyl alcohol, and various chemicals they provided good secondary explosions giving the Greys a false sense of destruction.

Anything of importance except for radar arrays and sensors was below ground in retrofitted abandoned Martian tunnels from ancient civilizations.

A huge surprise to the Greys who were overconfident, Earth's Secret Space Force missiles launched at them had no restrictions since there were no friendlies anywhere nearby. As such the missiles were allowed to attack any target they detected with their built-in radars and sensors.

<u>INT. DAY. MARS CENTRAL COMBAT CONTROL ROOM.</u>

WEAPON'S OPERATOR
Have lock on multiple targets.

WEAPONS OFFICER
We need to let them blow up a few things to make
them feel invincible. We'll wait until they get close
then we'll unload with SALVOS. We have no friendly
forces fire restrictions. Rules of engagement is to shoot
to kill with full permissions.

The weapons operator was getting nervous holding back, but he knew the scattered missile silos were well camouflaged, it would be impossible to identify them from space.

The time seemed to last a short infinite amount with Weapons operators feeling huge stress over delaying launch.

Suddenly looking at the overall picture, the Weapons Officer finally gave the orders.

WEAPONS OFFICER
Launch all weapons, full salvo authorized.

A wing of Grey Frigates and Destroyers were getting close to the surface and were battering away destroying any target of opportunity. They never expected their reception.

What looked like large rocks and boulders were camouflage devices. It took only three seconds for these camouflage devices to rotate out of the way via hydraulic pistons exposing the missile that was launched two seconds later after all interlocks were verified by artificial intelligence computational management.

A full salvo is 64 missiles flying random patterns with last targeting coefficients locked in before launch and before the Greys can destroy the 3D fire control radar. These were launch and forget missiles that had artificial intelligence, built in frequency skipping radars and powerful warheads that were small nukes of 10 KT range.

<u>EXT. CGI. SPACE. WOGAR GREY SPACESHIPS BLASTING MARS SURFACE
AND EARTH DEFENSES LAUNCH MULIPLE MISSILES. ONE MINUTE.</u>

Just as the Greys attacked and launched their missiles and gravity bombs, the Space
Force Defense missiles came at them in clouds. In quick succession a half dozen Grey
Frigates and a couple Grey Destroyers were destroyed or heavily damaged. It appeared
one of them crashed.

The Grey Wing Commander didn't know if there were more missiles but knew they
had done their job destroying the satellites and Ground Based Radars thus decided to
not risk any more ships and ordered the beat-up remainder of his air wing to return to
the *Colony Class Planetary Conquest Vessel.*

***

<u>INT. DAY. AREA 51</u>

GENERAL BRAZILE

For the first time in Global Space Command history, a
weapon was now being spun up and launched to deal
with an unknown Alien threat whose approach deems
it necessary to start thinking about self-defense.

COLONEL JONES

The personnel are relatively safe in the numerous
underground caves, but the sensors up on the surface
will be in direct path of enemy weapons.

GENERAL BRAZILE

It does not look good for us. We'll probably be blinded
shortly.

COLONEL JONES

Earth and Moon Base Forces are following along with
status reports coming in from Mars Central.

GENERAL BRAZILE

This is most likely a strategic attack to knock out
sensors, but the main path of the Invasion force will
most likely come via the same directions.

Clark Douglas entered General Brazile's office with emergency communications just
received.

CLARK DOUGLAS
Just as expected, receiving reports Mars Central is
being attacked!

GENERAL BRAZILE
How's Mars Central fairing from the attack?

Word is all the satellites have been knocked out and all, but one ground sensor was
damaged beyond repair.

GENERAL BRAZILE
Dammit!

General Brazile exclaimed as he feared the worst.

GENERAL BRAZILE
Casualty report?

CLARK DOUGLAS
Just coming in sir, appears to have sustained light
casualties.

Colonel Jones interrupted and explained:

COLONEL JONES
Those underground bunkers we build in all those
caves are well hidden and it would take one hell of a
hydrogen bomb to take them out

GENERAL BRAZILE
Any enemy spacecraft shot down?

CLARK DOUGLAS
Yes, however most of them were destroyed in space
which will make it hard to obtain wreckage, but reports
are one crash, not far from Cydonia.

GENERAL BRAZILE
Direct Mars Central to send out a scouting party
and report back as soon as possible what they find,
especially if there are survivors we need to know right
way, plus the identification of who they are.

The Grey's expeditionary force did their work and turned around heading back to their
fleet with reports.

***

<u>INT. SPACE. GREY ALIEN COLONY CLASS PLANETARY CONQUEST VESSEL</u>

WOGAR GREY
TACTICAL OFFICER

Commander Zorgjeck, the Expeditionary Force Commander, is here with a status report of their mission on Mars.

WOGAR GREY
SUPREME COMMANDER
ZORGJECK
How did it all go?

EXPEDITIONARY FORCE
WING COMMANDER

Commander Zorgjeck, all our Gun Sight Videos are being uploaded onto ships' computers.

WOGAR GREY
SUPREME COMMANDER
ZORGJECK

That may take a while. I need to know now what the results were. Give me your viewpoint of what happened in-situ.

EXPEDITIONARY FORCE
WING COMMANDER

We did a good job, but too many of our ships were destroyed and there may be a couple more sensors we were not able to knock out.

WOGAR GREY
SUPREME COMMANDER
ZORGJECK
Why didn't they get knocked out?

EXPEDITIONARY FORCE
WING COMMANDER

We were unaware there were sensors we missed until we were already a safe distance from the planet.

WOGAR GREY
SUPREME COMMANDER
ZORGJECK

I need to look at the Gun Sight Videos before we critique the mission.

EXPEDITIONARY FORCE
WING COMMANDER

Supreme Commander, we need permission to go back to complete the job.

WOGAR GREY
SUPREME COMMANDER
ZORGJECK

We can't wait for another round trip; we'll have to deploy the fleet a few hours behind you.

EXPEDITIONARY FORCE
WING COMMANDER

Understand Supreme Commander Zorgjeck.

WOGAR GREY
SUPREME COMMANDER
ZORGJECK

You must finish the destruction of their eyes and ears before we get to Earth's near space. We've already alerted them with your attack, so we have no choice; we must commence the main attack before they get time to set up a defense.

EXPEDITIONARY FORCE
WING COMMANDER

Sir, I need a dozen replacement ships for this next mission. Half of the ships that came back were severely damaged.

WOGAR GREY
SUPREME COMMANDER
ZORGJECK

I will give you twelve ships that were part of my assault force to bolster your force. Launch immediately!

EXPEDITIONARY FORCE
WING COMMANDER
Yes sir!

The Expeditionary Force Wing Commander turned around and marched smartly to the air wing on the Battle Cruiser currently moored in one of the *Colony Class Planetary Conquest Vessel* hangers where he and the others were soon launched to go back to finish the job.

***

EXT. SPACE. *MĚNGJIÀNG YÚN-RÉN ROYAL YACHT.*

One of the *Měngjiàng Yún-Rén Battlespace Coordinators* alerted *Wánměi de Huā*:

Měngjiàng Yún-Rén

Battlespace Coordinator

Your Excellency, the earth Federation's Mars outpost was just attacked.

WÁNMĚI DE HUĀ
It all now begins.

Wánměi de Huā received an INTEL report:

INTEL OFFICER
Intercepts indicate the attack was devastating knocking out all their satellites and most of their surface sensors, but one battery of sensors apparently was not damaged so they should be able to warn of a future larger pending attack.

WÁNMĚI DE HUĀ
Still no indication of who the attackers are?

INTEL OFFICER
There has been no identification yet, but apparently, there is wreckage of one ship on planet Mars.

WÁNMĚI DE HUĀ
Let's go there immediately and find out.

INTEL OFFICER
They're probably a little trigger happy about now that might be dangerous.

WÁNMĚI DE HUĀ
I'll take care of that.

***

<u>INT. DAY. AREA 51 GENERAL BRAZILE'S OFFICE.</u>

Wánměi De Huā used her mental telepathy interface to direct the ship to transport her to General Brazile's office. Once again arriving in her Napoleon uniform. Wánměi De Huā slightly spooked the three men present.

GENERAL BRAZILE
What brings you here Wánměi De Huā?

WÁNMĚI DE HUĀ
We know about the wreckage on Mars, how soon would it take your personnel to get to it?

GENERAL BRAZILE
I would think at least a couple of hours.

WÁNMĚI DE HUĀ
We don't have a couple of hours.

GENERAL BRAZILE
We are trying the best we can under the circumstances.

WÁNMĚI DE HUĀ
I'm taking my ship there now to look it over, call Mars Central and notify them I'm arriving there in about 15 minutes, and do not shoot. I will let you know as soon as we exit the area.

Knowing he was not in any position to say no to *Wánměi De Huā,* General Brazile simply responded:

GENERAL BRAZILE
I'll notify them right away.

General Brazile picked up his red phone. It was the interface to the high-speed neutrino communicator the Tall Whites had given them not long ago.

The buzzer on the Red Space command phone went off. Colonel Babcock picked up the receiver knowing someone very important was on the other end.

COLONEL BABCOCK
Hello, Babcock here.

GENERAL BRAZILE
This is General Brazile, you will have alien ships enter
Mars' atmosphere in about 15 minutes and proceed to
the Cydonia crash site of the intruder your boys just
shot down. Do not shoot repeat, do not shoot, those
are friendly.

COLONEL BABCOCK
Roger that General Brazile. Should I cancel the
wreckage pickup?

COLONEL BABCOCK
No. Proceed with that, I think the aliens are just going
to look, I doubt they will bring any debris back with
them.

EXT. DAY. *MĚNGJIÀNG YÚN-RÉN ROYAL YACHT.*

Right on schedule, the *Měngjiàng Yún-Rén Royal Yacht* was directly over the
planet Mars in orbit right above Cydonia.

The science officer came to the *Měngjiàng Yún-Rén* Royal Mother Ship bridge
in anticipation of immediate transport to the planet's surface but hesitated and
suggested:

MĚNGJIÀNG YÚN-RÉN
SCIENCE OFFICER
Empress *Wánměi De Huā* I recommend we take the
shuttlecraft in case we want to bring any debris back
with us to study.

Within moments they were floating towards the planet's surface on a trajectory that
would take them nearly a dozen feet from the crash debris field.

Upon landing the science officer stated:

According to readings, the atmosphere is compatible with our requirements, so no
breathing masks will be required.

The *Měngjiàng Yún-Rén* got out of the shuttle and walked over to the charred remains.

The four security agents were with them as requested by Drago in case something
unexpected occurred.

They became instantly handy as the science officer directed them to search through the debris to see if they could find any corpse or anything that would identify who they were.

In due time one of the security men said

MĚNGJIÀNG YÚN-RÉN
SECURITY OFFICER
Got a corpse over here.

MĚNGJIÀNG YÚN-RÉN
SCIENCE OFFICER

Put it in the shuttle so we can take it back up to examine it closer.

MĚNGJIÀNG YÚN-RÉN
SECURITY OFFICER #2
Found a second corpse.

MĚNGJIÀNG YÚN-RÉN
SCIENCE OFFICER
Bring it too.

Finally, just before they departed one of the Security Officers, announced:

MĚNGJIÀNG YÚN-RÉN
SECURITY OFFICER #3
I found some electronic devices.

MĚNGJIÀNG YÚN-RÉN
SCIENCE OFFICER

Put it on the shuttle. I think we found what we are coming for.

Within moments the shuttle was back aboard the *Měngjiàng Yún-Rén Royal Yacht*

that soon departed Martian Air Space and returned to its circular orbit offset from the sun. That orbit would remain on one side of the sun only exposing about one hemisphere but allowed continued observation of the returning Tall White Fleet, that had managed to maintain its velocity it achieved speeding up looping around Alpha Centaury A star.

Wánměi De Huā directed as the cargo was unloaded off the shuttle and placed in transporter carts that were self-powered and guided by command to the science labs:

WÁNMĚI DE HUĀ
Science Officer, please provide identification of these
beings as soon as possible.

MĚNGJIÀNG YÚN-RÉN
SCIENCE OFFICER
Your Excellency we will work hard on the
identification.

The science officer was able to get most of the details of the aliens' bodies by the upper
torso on one that remained intact and the lower on the other.

The science officer immediately went to work on DNA analysis which they were
getting good at and since they had a library of DNA identifiers of Wogar Grey Hybrids,
the scientist was able to streamline the procedure by simply comparing the various
genes to what they had recorded in their exhaustive investigation.

MĚNGJIÀNG YÚN-RÉN
SCIENCE OFFICER
Control, this is the Science Lab, we have confirmed
20 of the chromosomes match the Hybrids. I'm pretty
sure these are Grey Aliens.

That's all *Wánměi De Huā* needed to hear when she decided to drop in on General
Brazile who was still in his office with Colonel Jones and Clark Davis, thinking over
their situation.

***

INT. DAY. AREA 51. GENERAL BRAZILE'S OFFICE

General Brazile commented as *Wánměi De Huā* materialized a short distance away.

GENERAL BRAZILE
We are going to have to stop meeting like this.

WÁNMĚI DE HUĀ
I apologize for my uninvited presence, but I have some
information I need to tell you.

GENERAL BRAZILE
Which is?

WÁNMĚI DE HUĀ

We removed two bodies off the crashed ship on Mars and have confirmed via DNA they are Wogar Grey aliens. I suggest you bring Grak over so that we can have a little talk with him.

***

<u>INT. DAY. MARTIAN BASE.</u>

The Martian Base Commander was just informed:

MARTIAN MAINTENANCE OFFICER.
Sir, we have got good news. Not only do we have our radar in perfect working condition, but we also have a long-range scanner now operational again.

MARTIAN BASE COMMANDER
COLONEL BABCOCK
How did you pull that off?

MARTIAN MAINTENANCE OFFICER.
We cannibalized parts from four damaged scanners and were able to get one operational.

MARTIAN BASE COMMANDER
COLONEL BABCOCK
That's outstanding news. Report via the Q-channel logistics status. We are not in as bad of shape as I thought we would be.

No sooner than he got those words out, than another RED alert was broadcasted.

MARTIAN BASE COMMANDER
COLONEL BABCOCK
What now?

SURVEILLANCE OFFICER
Sir, we have what appears to be another group coming at us, probably coming back to finish off the job they didn't complete the first time.

He then turned to his assistant.

MARTIAN BASE COMMANDER
COLONEL BABCOCK
COMMO, send immediate priority message to Q this force is coming in for attack, believe they're going to put the finishing touches on us and be prepared for attack on planet Earth.

COMMUNICATIONS OFFICER
Right away sir.

MARTIAN BASE COMMANDER
COLONEL BABCOCK
WEPS has all the missile tubes been reloaded?

WEAPONS OFFICER
Yes sir.

MARTIAN BASE COMMANDER
COLONEL BABCOCK
Weps, I might have to give you a battlefield promotion. Your recommendation to have those missile tubes installed to allow reloading from under the tube is paying off serious dividends. The enemy will not know we can launch a full salvo at them.

WEAPONS OFFICER
Sir, I don't want to Tüte my own horn over that recommendation, and you know I took a lot of nasty feedback for making what at the time was considered a dumb idea from my peers insisting we could easily reload using a crane on the surface.

MARTIAN BASE COMMANDER
COLONEL BABCOCK
Weps, when this is all over, we'll have a critique and I'll be happy to state to the naysayers how the crane would be lying in a pile of destroyed equipment we had in all those warehouses.

WEAPONS OFFICER
Sir, I can't take full credit. The person who deserves a lot of credit is TMC Fields who recommended we use a rig like they develop to load torpedoes in a submarine.

MARTIAN BASE COMMANDER
COLONEL BABCOCK

Yea, that ingenious idea to have electric powered trucks with a rotatable hoist made it practical.

WEAPONS OFFICER

That former farm kid Bill Alvey recommended buying one of those new *Tesla Wheat Trucks* made it possible.

MARTIAN BASE COMMANDER
COLONEL BABCOCK

The lower hatch assembly was one of the most ingenious devices I've seen.

WEAPONS OFFICER

Yes, it provides a steel buffer and a three-inch high-pressure steel pipe connection to eject the missile out of the tube before the rocket engine kicks in.

MARTIAN BASE COMMANDER
COLONEL BABCOCK

Why do we eject the missile with high pressure air?

WEAPONS OFFICER

That eliminates tube maintenance after each shot. The only issue is the time it takes to unbolt that section of pipe to allow opening the bottom hatch and loading it.

MARTIAN BASE COMMANDER
COLONEL BABCOCK

How long does it take to unbolt that section of high-pressure pipe?

WEAPONS OFFICER

Because they use electric impact guns to unscrew them and a torque wrench putting it back together, the pipe is out of the way in five minutes or less and reinstalled in the same amount of time.

MARTIAN BASE COMMANDER
COLONEL BABCOCK

How long per reload?

WEAPONS OFFICER
Sir, safety is paramount. We have written procedures just like the nuclear power RPM's you used when you were a submarine officer.

MARTIAN BASE COMMANDER
COLONEL BABCOCK
How long per reload?

WEAPONS OFFICER
A typical timing on a reload is they remove the high-pressure-pipe, open the hatch. The missile technicians do a quick inspection of the tube and note any deficiencies.

After an officer clears that milestone in the procedure, they move the *Electric Weapon Carrier Truck* under the bottom missile tube reload hatch.

MARTIAN BASE COMMANDER
COLONEL BABCOCK
How do you correctly position the *Electric Weapon Carrier Truck* under the missile tube reload hatch?

WEAPONS OFFICER
The cement floor of the weapons magazine and Vertical Launch Matrix has guidewires that were laid into the concrete when it was poured for cart position sensors. The weapons carrier onboard microcomputers follow RF signals radiated out of those guidewires for perfect positioning. One set of guide wires steers the weapons carrier using a set frequency.

MARTIAN BASE COMMANDER
COLONEL BABCOCK
How does the *Electric Weapon Carrier Truck* know where to precisely stop?

WEAPONS OFFICER
Two additional wires installed in the floor at perpendicular and operating with different frequencies stop the *Electric Weapon Carrier Truck* precisely at the load position.

MARTIAN BASE COMMANDER
COLONEL BABCOCK
How long does it take for the weapons loading truck to line up to the missile tube?

WEAPONS OFFICER
From about 10 feet away from the load position to an exact stopping point usually takes less than a minute.

MARTIAN BASE COMMANDER
COLONEL BABCOCK
I take it they can then load the missile into the tube.

WEAPONS OFFICER
After the missile tube has been checked and cleared by an officer and gives permission to load, a fully tested missile that is powered up and operating via wireless is loaded.

MARTIAN BASE COMMANDER
COLONEL BABCOCK
Why is the missile powered up during the load? That sounds kind of dangerous.

WEAPONS OFFICER
All during the load the missile knows by its programming its being loaded and the warhead is remotely disconnected and safe via T/R relays.

MARTIAN BASE COMMANDER
COLONEL BABCOCK
What's a T/R relay?

WEAPONS OFFICER
It's a Transmit/Receive relay that allows the missile electronics to connect to the warhead to detonate it. The relay only closes milliseconds before detonation.

MARTIAN BASE COMMANDER
COLONEL BABCOCK
Why is the missile powered up during the load?

WEAPONS OFFICER
The missile has internal health checks because we do
not want to waste our time loading a dud.

MARTIAN BASE COMMANDER
COLONEL BABCOCK
How does it get loaded?

WEAPONS OFFICER
The *Electric Weapon Carrier Truck*, which is a
modified electric powered farm truck raises its hoist
fully vertical. *A Teflon Ring Assembly* is positioned on
the missile tube by the breach door (bottom) that will
allow the missile to easily slide into the missile tube.

The missile held in a carriage sleeve is shoved through the Teflon Ring Assembly
by telescoping hydraulic ram up into the launch position in the missile tube that has
Teflon rollers built into the sides of the missile tube for friction free movement.

MARTIAN BASE COMMANDER
COLONEL BABCOCK
How long does that take?

WEAPONS OFFICER
Typically, within three minutes after the *Electric
Weapon Carrier Truck* stops, the missile is lifted
strapped to a lifting rig until the missile is halfway in
the tube.

At this point in time the lifting straps are removed, and the lifting device ram shoves
the 4,000-pound missile the rest of the way to the launch position in the tube. That
takes about a minute.

MARTIAN BASE COMMANDER
COLONEL BABCOCK
What stops the missile from falling out of the tube?

WEAPONS OFFICER
Inside the tube are six steel levers that pivot 90 degrees
creating a platform for the missile to sit on that lock in
place with latches.

The lifting mechanism then slowly lowers the missile, usually just a couple inches
securing the missile into the cradle position sitting on the six steel levers. That takes
about half a minute.

The lifter hydraulic piston then lowers, and the *Electric Weapon Carrier Truck* then moves out of the way and an electric powered maintenance cart pulls in place that lifts the workers to finish preparing the tube.

The bottom tube hatch used exclusively for loading has hydraulic actuators that shut the *Breach Door Hatch,* and a locking ring just like on a torpedo tube turns into the locked position.

Two workers lift the high-pressure pipe in position and a third person starts two bolts at each end of the pipe to hold it in place. They have spare bolts so any with defects are scrapped. One man completes putting on the nuts and bolts while the other two men torque them using electric torque wrenches.

MARTIAN BASE COMMANDER
COLONEL BABCOCK

We have had some of those missiles we launched today in the missile tubes for weeks. How long will the battery last if the missile remains powered up?

WEAPONS OFFICER

When the missile is sitting in the cradle it has guide pin slots to ensure it is sitting perfectly in the launch position.

The missile tube hatch will not shut unless the missile is perfectly aligned. The missile tube has a couple scanners that optically align with the missile sitting in the cradle to give system health check before the hatch is allowed to be shut. As you can see the process is very quick.

MARTIAN BASE COMMANDER
COLONEL BABCOCK

That does not answer the battery question, I'm curious.

WEAPONS OFFICER

Because the missile sits perfectly in the cradle, electrical connections are made that allow the missile to use external power until launch to save its battery. Batteries have shelf life, and all missiles are unloaded and go through a maintenance cycle including battery replacement every six months.

MARTIAN BASE COMMANDER
COLONEL BABCOCK

What happens if the missile is not launched in a long period?

WEAPONS OFFICER
Under normal circumstances with power shut off and the missile in a stored position not expecting launch, some of the electronics remains powered up via external power to allow the onboard computer to do health checks until it's spun up ready to be launched.

MARTIAN BASE COMMANDER
How long does it take to spin up a missile?

WEAPONS OFFICER
If you look at the fire control technician's console screen, he's getting ready to spin up missile #64B. As soon as he hits the [ENGAGE] switch the hole process starts. Artificial intelligence will give the missile its target including the target's last known position in space or in the atmosphere.

The fire control technician selected the [ENGAGE] icon on the weapons control console missile selection GUI (graphic use interface).

WEAPONS OFFICER
As you can see commander, in less than one minute the fire control technician has a green status panel which says it's ready to launch.

MARTIAN BASE COMMANDER
COLONEL BABCOCK
How do you shoot that missile?

WEAPONS OFFICER
As soon as I give the Fire control technician launch authority, he will select [STANDBY] then [FIRE] icons. Then the missile will be launched and there will be a status such as [MISSILE AWAY] indicating the missile health checks were good and the missile was properly launched out of the vertical launch tube.

MARTIAN BASE COMMANDER
COLONEL BABCOCK
Do we receive any information on missile status after we launch it?

WEAPONS OFFICER
Because of the missile's wireless capability, it will
send telemetry indicating its functional status and
health checks high level status update momentarily
after launch then shut off for stealth.

We then rely on photonics trackers to observe what the missile does until it acquires
the target and two seconds before calculated impact it sends telemetry which is
abbreviated to the maximum extent possible giving the basics:

Health check okay.

Acquired Target.

Missile solar position.

Target's solar position.

Distance to target expected impact.

A snapshot of the target is sent unless it's fired with
full video selected.

MARTIAN BASE COMMANDER
COLONEL BABCOCK
What do you mean by full video?

WEAPONS OFFICER
Full video means that from time of launch until
detonation we get a live video stream from the missile
showing the target as it approaches it.

MARTIAN BASE COMMANDER
COLONEL BABCOCK
Why would you do that?

WEAPONS OFFICER
We normally do not do that but sometimes we do it
with a missile that we want to be a decoy.

MARTIAN BASE COMMANDER
COLONEL BABCOCK
How is it used as a decoy?

WEAPONS OFFICER
The transmitted telemetry draws the attention of enemy
close in weapon systems to help the other missiles get
to the target undamaged.

***

INT. DAY. AREA 51 GENERAL BRAZIL'S OFFICE

Grak soon arrived in General Brazil's office.

GRAK
Looks like you got quite a group here, General Brazil.

General Brazil held his hand out in the direction of an empty chair directly in front of his desk.

GENERAL BRAZIL
Grak, please have a seat.

GRAK
What's this all about?

GENERAL BRAZIL
Why did Wogar Grey just attack Mars?

GRAK
I don't know what you're talking about.

GENERAL BRAZIL
Don't play dumb, with the help of the *Měngjiàng Yún-
Rén* we have proof it was Wogar Greys who attacked
Mars and according to our sensors are coming back for
the knockout punch.

Wánměi De Huā was trying hard to penetrate Grak's mind. Just as the *Měngjiàng Yún-Rén* Chief Scientist had said, it was almost impossible to crack. But suddenly *Wánměi De Huā* discovered one pathway that allowed her to at least know when Grak was telling the truth or a lie.

Wánměi De Huā then walked in front of Grak and yelled:

WÁNMĚI DE HUĀ
You're lying. Where is Vance?

GRAK
I have no idea where Vance is.

Suddenly prompted from her telepathic interface implant, four *Měngjiàng Yún-Rén security men* materialized in and around the office all carrying what was either a gun or a laser pistol.

Wánměi De Huā then looked at General Brazile.

WÁNMĚI DE HUĀ
We have ways of making people talk. I will be
borrowing Grak for a while.

Suddenly Grak and the *Měngjiàng Yún-Rén* dematerialized and disappeared.

With Grak safely escorted to the science lab where he was restrained and subjected to *Měngjiàng Yún-Rén torture techniques* that would even make the Greys proud, Grak was having second thoughts about not divulging what he knew.

But Grak figured if he had the Vance card, they could not dispose of him. However, the pain was starting to become unbearable.

As promised the Greys Expeditionary Force Wing finished their job on Mars. Even though there were only a few casualties, the sensors were wrecked, and no possibility existed for repairs this time.

When INTEL presented the case to *Wánměi De Huā*, she responded.

WÁNMĚI DE HUĀ
It looks like we have only one option left.

Drago could almost predict what she would say and responded:

DRAGO
You will be putting us all in jeopardy going back to
Mars now.

WÁNMĚI DE HUĀ
We can always outrun them. We just need to give earth
the warning when it's coming and hopefully delay
them enough for the Great Tall White Fleet to return.

In due course of evets, *Wánměi De Huā* made another surprise visit to General Brazile's office where she announced:

WÁNMĚI DE HUĀ

My ship is orbiting Mars now. We'll let you know
when the attack is coming.

Before General Brazile could respond, she was gone.

Just like he promised the invasion force was only 2 hours behind. Zorgjeck was pleased when he received the report:

WOGAR GREY
EXPEDITIONARY FORCE
WING COMMANDER

All sensors knocked out. Earth is blind from that sector;
the moon is too far out of position and its sensors are
pointed in the wrong direction for the next eight hours.

WOGAR GREY
SUPREME COMMANDER
ZORGJECK

Thanks for the status report.

The Grey assault fleet was bearing down on Mars but paid no attention as it was focused on Earth. Earth had been warned in time, but the immense fire power of the Greys was just going to be too much for them.

***

INT. SPACE *MĚNGJIÀNG YÚN-RÉN ROYAL YACHT*

Wánměi De Huā, feeling helpless suddenly announced.

WÁNMĚI DE HUĀ

Let's give the Greys a distraction, if we can just delay
them a few more hours our plan will work.

DRAGO

Empress Wánměi De Huā, I must caution you that you
are just about to go over the line.

WÁNMĚI DE HUĀ

Remember we can sustain a lot more damage and out
run the Greys.

Drago knew it was useless to argue with *Wánměi De Huā* because she appeared wildly in love with Vance, and she would do anything for him. Drago no longer interfered and stood back and watched.

341

Wánměi De Huā was a smart tactician, she knew she could do some hit and run techniques and become a big enough pest they would have to send a sizeable force after her.

That technique might weaken their assault force enough to delay its handiwork.

<u>EXT. CGI. SPACE *MĚNGJIÀNG YÚN-RÉN ROYAL YACHT* ATTACKING GREY FLEET. TWO MINUTES, MAJOR SPACE BATTLE IAW DESCRIPTION BELOW.</u>

Soon the *Měngjiàng Yún-Rén Royal Yacht, operating in an attack mode,* danced into Wogar Grey Fleet formations and took out several heavily armed ships using advanced beam weapons.

The Wogar Greys were taken totally by surprise, and as predicted they sent a large group after *Měngjiàng Yún-Rén Royal Yacht* which *Wánměi De Huā* merely left behind.

Then *Wánměi De Huā* did the unthinkable, *an end around.*

The *Měngjiàng Yún-Rén Royal Yacht's* astonishing speed *Wánměi De Huā* was able to come around the back side and hit the Greys flanks unexpectedly and damaged another couple large assault ships and drew chase again.

This time *Wánměi De Huā* didn't go so fast as to draw the Grey Frigates and Destroyers far away from their formation.

Earth was not scratched as the Great Tall White fleet soon arrived in combat range. The plan worked they were now at a *Mexican standoff.*

The Greys could not afford a battle of attrition because had the Tall Whites discovered the location of the mother ship, it would require just about all the Wogar Grey forces to protect it.

Now that the fighting died down as the Greys and the Tall Whites summed each other up, *Wánměi De Huā* repositioned her Royal Yacht in a circular course offset from the sun as done before so that all attention could focus on the direction the Greys.

DRAGO

> Celestial maps showing precisely where Pluto was
> at the time during the Wogar Grey assault, and it
> appeared the three different formations the Greys sent
> out came from that direction.

Wánměi De Huā also had a suspicion that's where they were holding Vance. Therefore, she decided to get Drago's opinion about her next move.

WÁNMĚI DE HUĀ

I think I know how to get the truth out of Grak, which I'll do shortly, but it seems to me the Wogar Grey mother ship must be somewhere in the direction of Pluto.

DRAGO

Since that's the direction all these Wogar Grey Spaceships came from, that's a good logical deduction.

WÁNMĚI DE HUĀ

I think that if we transit out towards them, it will accomplish 2 things:

DRAGO
Such as?

WÁNMĚI DE HUĀ
It will possibly encourage them to give up Vance.

DRAGO
What if they feel they need to hold Vance as a hostage and refuse?

WÁNMĚI DE HUĀ

If not, we will draw back much of their assault force which will then give an advantage to the Tall Whites who could then force them to capitulate and leave the solar system.

DRAGO

It's a calculated risk, but right now it appears we have a stalemate; hence, the new dynamics would create uncertainty that could possibly make Greys reconsider the consequences of their foolish act.

WÁNMĚI DE HUĀ

I'm going to the science lab to see how far along the mental telepathy work is going.

Wánměi De Huā rematerialized into her bright green body, flapped her wings and flew down the corridor; then through the open tunnel door that was sealed during battle stations and serious combat if ever required which sometimes occurred when they unexpectedly came across the roaming space pirates.

As *Wánměi De Huā* reached the science offices her wings flapped to a stop, and she rematerialized as Sandra back in the Napoleon uniform. The facial and energy detectors immediately identified the Empress and the door to the science lab broke in half, the top part sliding up and the bottom half down below into a recessed cavity in the walls above and below that room.

Grak, who normally is a condescending semi-extrovert now had a rather fearful look. Having already received some of the stimulus provided by the science officer, including psychoactive injections, made Grak start to feel the *Měngjiàng Yún-Rén* seemed far more brutal than the Greys ever thought to be.

Měngjiàng Yún-Rén interrogation capabilities were certainly impressive, but the motives of such an advance race wasn't clear. They applied pain in the most reserved and useful manners necessary. They usually didn't have to extract INTEL via torture because their mental telepathy provided much faster and reasonably netted profitable results.

WÁNMĚI DE HUĀ

Ambassador Grak, I need to ask you a few more
questions. Did you participate in Vance's abduction?

GRAK
No.

Having discovered a neuropathway into Grak's thinking processes, Wánměi De Huā knew that was a lie.

WÁNMĚI DE HUĀ
Do you know where Vance was taken?

GRAK
No.

Another lie.

WÁNMĚI DE HUĀ
Do you know where the Wogar Grey mother ship is at
this moment?

GRAK
No.

Another lie.

WÁNMĚI DE HUĀ

It's only a matter of time before all this concludes. I promise you that if Vance is harmed you will receive pain every day and wish you were dead.

GRAK

Is that so?

WÁNMĚI DE HUĀ

We'll keep you alive just so that you can experience more and more pain until you eventually go totally insane.

GRAK

I'm an ambassador and if you do that to me your people will become the social outcasts of the Galaxy once it's learned what you did to me.

WÁNMĚI DE HUĀ

Well Ambassador, you didn't think this through.

GRAK

When my government finds out you detained a diplomat they will appeal to the Intergalactic Federation and you, *Měngjiàng Yún-Rén,* will be compelled to release me.

WÁNMĚI DE HUĀ

Nobody in the Galaxy knows you are here except maybe General Brazile.

GRAK

You think so?

WÁNMĚI DE HUĀ

General Brazile is not going to tell anyone a thing, because you burned your bridges with him when you lied about a lot of things and were one of the people who planned to attack Mars then do planetary conquest of Earth. Isn't that correct?

GRAK

No.

Another lie.

WÁNMĚI DE HUĀ
You can save the Grey a lot of disgrace and serious retribution by telling me exactly where Vance is, because I can wipe out all 400 billion Greys.

GRAK
I do not believe you can do that.

WÁNMĚI DE HUĀ
Your Grey Fleet is now in a stalemate with the Tall Whites. Your plan has already failed.

GRAK
I know I will get out of this somehow.

WÁNMĚI DE HUĀ
The only way you can get out of this now is to assist us. If you help us return Vance, then you will be released into the neutral sector of Zantam, where you can live out the rest of your disgusting life in seclusion. Otherwise, your terrible existence begins shortly.

GRAK
We'll see what happens. You may have underestimated us.

WÁNMĚI DE HUĀ
I will be back shortly after I find your mother ship. And when my Armada gets here in two weeks it will be blown out of the galaxy if Vance isn't released unharmed by then.

Wánměi De Huā left the science lab and dematerialized into her green form and flapped her wings and flew back to the control room and then took on her Napoleon-like form.

Wánměi De Huā using her mental telepathic transceivers to communicate with the ship, ordered:

WÁNMĚI DE HUĀ
(TELEPATHICALLY)
Take a course opposite of what the Greys had taken. That is probably where the mother ship and Vance are located.

EXT. SPACE. CGI. *MĚNGJIÀNG YÚN-RÉN ROYAL YACHT* BANKING AWAY FROM THE SUN. 15 SECONDS.

The *Měngjiàng Yún-Rén Royal Yacht* banked away from the Sun and increased speed as it started its high velocity transit.

The Tall Whites and the Greys both detected the high velocity ship but had no means of identifying it as it was moving along too swiftly. It was essentially traveling 20 times faster than what the Greys achieved on their way to Mars.

INTEL OFFICER
Empress *Wánměi De Huā* we have intercepted and decrypted Wogar Grey Fleet ships communications and now have new intel on their dispositions.

WÁNMĚI DE HUĀ
Give me a verbal report so that I can continue monitoring our sensors.

INTEL OFFICER
The Wogar Greys have a *Colony Class Planetary Conquest Vessel*, mothership, designed mainly as interplanetary conquest and exploitation and to set up space colonies.

WÁNMĚI DE HUĀ
What does it look like?

The *Colony Class Planetary Conquest Vessel* is a very large spheroid shape and has propulsion and can obtain some impressive velocities. We obtained a video of it through a Wogar Grey communications intercept.

WÁNMĚI DE HUĀ
Go ahead and put that image up on my display for just
a minute.

After *Wánměi De Huā* assessed the image, she ordered:

WÁNMĚI DE HUĀ
I've seen enough, go ahead and remove that image.
Can it maneuver well?

INTEL OFFICER
It's like a huge ocean-going ship. The Grey *Colony*

Class Planetary Conquest Vessel takes a long while to work up to maximum speed and has difficulties turning and more importantly stopping.

WÁNMĚI DE HUĀ
Can it protect itself?

INTEL OFFICER
The Grey Colony Class Planetary Conquest Vessel requires Combat Space Patrols providing area security and surveillance to keep out all would be intruders or take defensive actions if necessary. Its main firepower is an offensive weapon to attack planets with a large energy beam.

WÁNMĚI DE HUĀ
How are the *Planetary Conquest Vessel* Combat Space Patrols implemented?

INTEL OFFICER
The Greys employ three defensive rings for their Grey *Colony Class Planetary Conquest Vessel.*

The intercepted intelligence showed three defensive rings graphically on their sensor status displays in the Grey *Colony Class Planetary Conquest Vessel* control room.

WÁNMĚI DE HUĀ
Does this display offer them an advantage?

INTEL OFFICER
I'm going to put up an example one of their displays we intercepted and processed on your display screen on the upper right corner so it will not obstruct your view ahead.

WÁNMĚI DE HUĀ
Certainly.

INTEL OFFICER
You can see on your display; the Grey's outer green ring defense area designation is about three AU's radius from the *Colony Class Planetary Conquest Vessel.*

WÁNMĚI DE HUĀ
I've never heard of an AU before, what is it?

INTEL OFFICER
One astronomical unit (AU) defined by EARTH'S NASA is 150,000,000 km, the distance from Earth to the sun which takes light about 8 minutes to travel.

WÁNMĚI DE HUĀ
Why would Grey's use AU as a measure?

INTEL OFFICER
The Greys adopted using AU scaling for their earth mission since that is what Earth uses.

WÁNMĚI DE HUĀ
How would the Greys use this system if the *Colony Class Planetary Conquest Vessel* when transiting?

INTEL OFFICER
With the dynamic movement of the Grey Fleet patrol craft operating at three AUs on the Green ring after enough orbits around the mother ship, a track could be printed they would resemble a perfect sphere shape.

WÁNMĚI DE HUĀ
How do the Greys maintain a perfect spherical geometry based on the center of the mother ship?

INTEL OFFICER
Grey navigation systems compensate for forward motion traveling in elliptical geometries, but when plotted in relative motion and using automatic ranging tools for navigation vectors they appear to travel a perfect sphere around the Colony Class Planetary Conquest Vessel.

WÁNMĚI DE HUĀ
The bottom line is, how effective are these defensive patrols?

INTEL OFFICER
Because of the long distances and time to make orbits around the green ring, it was assumed to be very

porous and only have a 50% probability of detecting a threat.

WÁNMĚI DE HUĀ
Thus, the figure of merit is not very good.

INTEL OFFICER
The Yellow ring at two AUs from the center of the Grey *Colony Class Planetary Conquest Vessel* (Fleet's mother ship) is considerably less porous and has about 75% probability or figure of merit in detecting potential threats.

WÁNMĚI DE HUĀ
I think at those odds, we still have an advantage due to maneuver and speed.

INTEL OFFICER
The inner red ring is one AU from the center of the Grey *Colony Class Planetary Conquest Vessel* and is an absolute trip wire.

WÁNMĚI DE HUĀ
Since we'll be going inside that trip wire what should we expect?

INTEL OFFICER
If an enemy maneuvers inside the red ring zone, there was about a 100% probability of detecting the enemy but also a high probability an enemy could do damage to the Grey *Colony Class Planetary Conquest Vessel.*

WÁNMĚI DE HUĀ
This is all rather informative.

INTEL OFFICER
The trick to space warfare is to know your enemy trip wires and defensive ring geometries for several reasons.

WÁNMĚI DE HUĀ
I think I know this but tell me again.

INTEL OFFICER

First is to know their lethality of where you are at. An attacker would not get too bloodied crossing over the Green Zone, which means that distance can be at maximum velocity and hope the enemy doesn't get a lucky target of opportunity.

WÁNMĔI DE HUĀ

I think I know I'm not too concerned about the Green Zone; I want to hear about the yellow zone.

INTEL OFFICER

The Yellow zone was the tricky one, an attacker could quickly become a target of opportunity but if you slow down too much, the big Defensive line will be waiting for you in the Red Zone and your chances become remotely successful.

WÁNMĔI DE HUĀ

I do not plan on slowing down.

Wánmĕi De Huā, having 1,100 years of military training knew all the factors and rules of thumb as she applied her mental gymnastics and fabricated a penetration plan.

INTEL OFFICER

Secondly by knowing where the trip wires are, you will know what to expect at that time and can determine what specific actions you need to take.

WÁNMĔI DE HUĀ

I've studied how fleets of large size set up those artificial reconnaissance zones and trip wires, they also tend to move assets in to block your path to the real target.

INTEL OFFICER

Correct. In essence they inadvertently give away the most important information and that is, *where* the command ship is.

WÁNMĔI DE HUĀ

This is what I plan to do. We'll transit in the general direction then where resistance stiffens is most likely the direction to go, but attack via an end around once we established the target's location and disposition.

INTEL OFFICER

Pluto being 40 AUs away from the sun means the Greys are probably at least five AUs just beyond Pluto. They more than likely use the sun as a solar navigational anchor the Greys could easily index positions off.

DRAGO

How the Greys managed to hide out at that location 80+ years will soon become the mystery of the century.

WÁNMĚI DE HUĀ

Had we not come along with Vance, Earth may never have known before their demise.

INTEL OFFICER

Just like other Empires we observed, once the planetary conquest was completed, they simply move off to their next solar system and continue the mass migration through this part of the galaxy.

DRAGO

80 years' investment by the Greys is trivial considering some planets took several hundred thousand years.

WÁNMĚI DE HUĀ

From my studies about Mars which was undergoing planetary conquest 900,000 years ago had an unlucky break in that a nuclear holocaust soon vanquished those invaders. It was never truly established who set off the 2 huge Hydrogen Bombs that an Earth person Dr. Brandenburg reported as root cause for the extinction event.

INTEL OFFICER

In recent years Tall White Scholars researching the Mars extinction event concluded the Martians did it themselves.

WÁNMĚI DE HUĀ
How was it done?

INTEL OFFICER

After evacuating all they could manage to Earth on such short notice before the Martians set off the charges.

WÁNMĚI DE HUĀ
What were the results?

INTEL OFFICER
Those two huge nuclear blasts destroyed all life on
Mars, but also wiped out the invaders who were then
raping and plundering Mars society in the evilest
fashion.

WÁNMĚI DE HUĀ
The Martians chose death over Tyranny.

In about an hour the *Měngjiàng Yún-Rén* passed Jupiter at about 750 million kilometers
from the sun, as another hour passed and velocity increased, they soon passed the
distance of Saturn 10 AUs away from the sun.

WÁNMĚI DE HUĀ
Due to the continued speed increase as we are slowly
escaping the gravity waves of the sun, we've traveled
another 10 AUs to a total of 20 AUs about the distance
to Uranus, still no sight of any Greys.

DRAGO
Where do you think they are hiding?

WÁNMĚI DE HUĀ
They probably were so arrogant they sent most of
the Frigates and Destroyers they have which are now
facing down advanced weapons of the Tall Whites.

DRAGO
You expect their mother ship defenses will be
diminished as a result?

WÁNMĚI DE HUĀ
Yes, I think they overplayed their hand.

DRAGO
With this increase in speed, we should be passing
Neptune in 20 minutes.

WÁNMĚI DE HUĀ
Then 10 minutes after a Pluto fly-by and we will be in
the Green Zone.

The time crept up, so did the velocity.

> ### WÁNMĚI DE HUĀ
> This feels just like the Earthmen playing Chess, which
> Vance often enjoyed.

Pluto finally showed up on forward low power scanners not requiring much magnification to track it as they skipped past its atmosphere at velocities the Greys were not accustomed to.

> ### DRAGO
> If they have an outpost on Pluto, they have just
> received a wakeup call.

> ### WÁNMĚI DE HUĀ
> When we dipped slightly into the atmosphere, we left
> behind quite a shock wave.

> ### DRAGO
> No sign of any enemy ships or the Grey Mother ship.

> ### WÁNMĚI DE HUĀ
> It's most likely darkened out to avoid detection, but
> we can light it up with some artificial sunlight that will
> allow our infrared scanners to see it easily enough.

Wánměi De Huā then gave telepathic orders via her telepathic implants to the ship that immediately launched several Orbs shot out sideways at high velocity essentially provided a mini sun on each.

Even from Earth the orbs would be observed as a bright light as bright as the star Alpha Centaury or some recent comets. The glare would also hide the *Měngjiàng Yún-Rén* Royal Yacht at the same time light up anything in front of the ship and if there was a large mother ship it would no doubt be exposed.

***

<u>INT. SPACE. *COLONY CLASS PLANETARY CONQUEST VESSEL* CONTROL ROOM.</u>

The sudden bright lights caught the Wogar Greys completely by surprise at first didn't know what to make of them.

If things were not bad enough, the Grey Fleet was now neutralized in a stalemate with the Tall Whites.

Supreme Commander Zorgjeck made the fatal blunder of dividing his forces where he very may well be destroyed in detail.

Never in Wogar (Greys) history had they encountered aliens that could produce miniature stars.

Fear crept up on Supreme Commander Zorgjeck and he now contemplated ordering maneuvering the *Colony Class Planetary Conquest Vessel*.

It would take a while for the *Colony Class Planetary Conquest Vessel* to get up to speed, but it also meant leaving the assault force behind that in due time would wither away, a prospect Supreme Commander Zorgjeck did not relish.

***

EXT. DAY. MOSCOW RUSSIA. BREZHNEV'S PRIVATE DACHA.

The FSB (KGB) special directorate man arrived at the former Soviet leader Brezhnev's private dacha, now Boris Potemkin's temporary residence, with Boris briefing papers. These documents and identifications such as his new Nevada Driver's license, forged passport, and other documents that would allow Boris to get back into the United States and take over where he left off.

> VOICEOVER (BORIS
> POTEMKIN) THOUGHT
> *Poor Boyd Bushman Paid for his passion towards aliens and UFOs with his life.*
>
> *Also, poor Tanya. She is not as rich as I intended to leave her because that damn lawyer had been KGB all along and merely gave me the impression it would be handled.*
>
> *The other interesting sting was Jimmy. I truly believed that after all these years I could trust Jimmy and now I wonder, did Jimmy give the money to Alex?*
>
> *Lessons learned is, you can't trust anyone.*

Almost like going back to grammar school, the FSB tutor made sure Boris was well informed about his future project, gave him lectures and learning sessions, then tests, tests, tests.

At times Boris wanted to go to sleep and when the instructor saw he was having a narcolepsy moment asked:

FSB INSTRUCTOR
Would you like a stimulant?
VOICOVER
(During Boris Learning Session)

To assist in improving Boris's attentiveness and more efficiently accomplish the course work, which was essential and mandatory before they sent Boris back into harm's way, Borris would be shot up with stimulants if necessary.

Boris in some ways felt bad that he had been kicked out of Las Vegas. Boris knew Las Vegas was an important assignment, but now area 51 was taking on a new meaning.

The FSB (KGB) wanted a stronger footprint near Area 51 to increase data gathering and recruiting capability. Boris would not risk being Turned by attempting any recruitment.

Boris would be in a more important but passive role, like a manager, keeping an eye on and tweaking from time to time those agents sent in to do the dirty work, the bribing, recruitment, and if necessary dirty tricks.

There would always be a firewall between Boris and the recruits. None would ever know Boris was involved nor would they ever meet him in any role other than he was the nice guy new owner of the Dude Ranch in the out of the way slowly growing town of Alamo Nevada.

As it turns out that Dude Ranch that was north of town was outside city limits for a few good reasons, liquor license and call girls.

Pilots who spent a lot of time at Groom Lake were often seen utilizing the establishment. Pilots on TDY got some real nice per diem money for hotels and food.

Since there were not many hotels without the long drive into Vegas it was easy to justify staying at the dude ranch that was well within the per diem rates, and for a little extra, fringe benefits.

Even though BOQ living accommodations were available at Groom Lake the problem became when the staff upped the posture for the base (way above top secret), those guys were kicked off the base for a day or two and not allowed back in until the actions taking place were finished.

Such was the case with Have Blue, Have Orion, Have TR-3B, and alleged SR-75 test flights. There were 16 different Have projects, which led to frequent up postures.

The BOQ though did have high occupancy, because when the pilots with the lesser security clearances left, many of them simply headed to Las Vegas; the contractors with EG&G, AECOM, Lockheed, and other beltway bandits involved in Have test flights took up all the empty BOQ rooms for a day or two.

<u>EXT. DAY. ALAMO NEVADA DUDE RANCH.</u>

The former dude ranch owner never really capitalized well on the location and situation, and with the influx of more Aliens, up posture days were occurring at a higher rate.

But the other overlooked matter was some of those pilots were raised as farm boys and enjoyed riding a horse now and then.

One of the innovations Boris did once he eventually made it to Alamo, Nevada was he went to some of the neighbors who were noticeably upset about all the call girls coming to and from Vegas all the time, that he would clamp down on that if they would run horses for him and actually paid some of the locals in the area to act as guides to ride out in areas on horseback trail rides, picnics and fishing.

Once again, a Boris innovation paid off handsomely.

On one of those trips, a TR-3B pilot who thought he was going to razzmatazz his buddy who had told him he was going horseback riding that day, went out looking for him and without permission or authorization violated his flight plan and nearly got his buddy bucked off the horse after the TR-3B spoofed the horses the group was riding.

The pilot's buddy didn't even know the TR-3B program existed, as his clearance level was shy of the Q rating required to get anywhere near it; mainly because it utilized alien anti-gravity propulsion re-engineered from a downed Alien craft belonging to some Alien civilization not associated with the eight alien groups that had diplomatic space ports at Area 51, S-4.

Some of the civilians along for the ride got a couple pictures with their cell phones as the TR-3B banked and headed vertically into the cloud cover and disappeared.

Later that day, Boris called the room of the hotel guest he saw taking pictures and talked about photographing the strange encounter.

DUDE RANCH GUEST
ROOM 222
Hello

BORIS (a.k.a. MR. KEENEY)

Hi, this is the manager; you're the guy who got the picture of that cool UFO today?

DUDE RANCH GUEST
ROOM 222
Yea that's right.

BORIS (a.k.a. MR. KEENEY)
How would you like to have your room for free?

DUDE RANCH GUEST
ROOM 222
What's the catch?

BORIS

I love UFO pictures and if you are willing to email me copies of those pictures, your room which you reserved for the weekend is free.

DUDE RANCH GUEST
ROOM 222
You're joking?

BORIS (a.k.a. MR. KEENEY)

No, come out to the front desk and I'll give you a paid in full bill.

DUDE RANCH GUEST
ROOM 222
Be right there.

The Dude Ranch guest asked Boris as he arrived moments later.

DUDE RANCH GUEST
ROOM 222
So, what's your email address?

Boris handed the guest a business card.

BORIS
It's on the bottom of the card, just send it there.

DUDE RANCH GUEST
ROOM 222
Got it.

Then after a moment of time the guest announced, after he sent the pictures via his I-phone:

DUDE RANCH GUEST
ROOM 222
You should have it in your email now.

Boris was one step ahead of him and had already looked at one of the pictures and it was one damn good picture. That pilot screwed up good. The one group they never wanted to see, the TR-3B would have it in merely minutes from now.

Boris handed the paid in full receipt to the customer.

DUDE RANCH GUEST
ROOM 222
That's the fastest $500 I've made in a long time!

BORIS
I see UFOs but my buddies never believe me.

DUDE RANCH GUEST
ROOM 222
Thanks a million.

The dude ranch guest walked off thinking tonight would be a good night for a really good call girl since he had a lot more money left to spend than he expected, then said to himself:

DUDE RANCH GUEST
ROOM 222
THOUGHT
I might even throw a few dollars in the slot machines!

In a short while, Boris sent an email to his buddy in Switzerland, Robert Simmons that had the pictures attached and the subject line:

BORIS POTEMKIN
(Email)
I thought you might want to see this.

The subject line was a predesignated macro code word for: send this to Alexander Bortnikov.

VOICEOVER (BORIS
POTEMKIN) MESSAGE
*Taken from some guy at the dude ranch, thinks this is
some type of a UFO.*

That one picture ended up costing the FSB (KGB) about $50 million over the next month as there was enough detail in the picture taken at relatively close range and because of the sudden maneuver up vertical created a few moments of excellent photography opportunity which the amateur photographer got lucky. FSB now had a highly detailed picture of the TR-3B taken at close range.

Further picture enhancement with stochastic resonance and wavelet filtering brought out staggering detail. In essence the cost of the dude ranch paid for itself with just one picture, and the good part hadn't started yet.

***

EXT. SPACE. *MĚNGJIÀNG YÚN-RÉN* ROYAL YACHT

When the *Měngjiàng Yún-Rén* Royal Yacht finally got out to around the 50 AU distancing from the sun, it finally started detecting a visual on something that looked like a small planet, but sensor readings indicated something otherwise.

WÁNMĚI DE HUĀ
We may have missed it all together and misidentified
it as a distant Planet, but suddenly it started to move.

DRAGO
The object is increasing speed. That is most likely the
Colony Class Planetary Conquest Vessel making a run
for it.

WÁNMĚI DE HUĀ
Those two bright lights we put up probably shook them up.

DRAGO
That is not all, looks like we got company coming. Wogar Grey Supreme Commander Zorgjeck finally took more stress than he could stand and gave the orders to maneuver into deep space heading directly away from the solar system in a perpendicular reference to the galaxy.

Grey officer standing next to Zorgjeck stated:

GREY OFFICER
Sir, you are leaving our assault force stranded in the solar system.

WOGAR GREY
SUPREME COMMANDER
ZORGJECK
I cannot risk the destruction of this *Colony Class Planetary Conquest Vessel.*

The Grey sensors coordinator analyzed the possible scenario unfolding.

PLANETARY CONQUEST VESSEL
SENSORS COORDINATOR
The enemy may be coming towards us.

WOGAR GREY
SUPREME COMMANDER
ZORGJECK
Launch the defense grid immediately.

Supreme Commander Zorgjeck feared the obvious conclusion of those two sudden illuminations.

The Greys didn't quite know where the alien ship was coming from, but those Grey Fighters would move between the enemy and the mother ship as soon as it was detected, which as it was, would occur real soon.

***

WÁNMĚI DE HUĀ
As we approach those Grey Fighters, they will be
blinded by the artificial suns we put up, but once we
get past them if they detect us and swing around and
chase us.

DRAGO.
No doubt.

WÁNMĚI DE HUĀ
We will lose the initial surprise. But based on our
velocity, I doubt they can catch up to us, as it will be
too late. If we take enough of them out the mother ship
will have to surrender.

DRAGO
You should bring Grak to the control room/bridge and
let him watch us destroy the mothership.

WÁNMĚI DE HUĀ
I am not really interested in destroying their
mothership; I just want to get Vance back.

Suddenly, a voice emanating out of the audio system associated with the large display
panel announces.

MĚNGJIÀNG YÚN-RÉN
[AI ALERT]
Incoming communications intercept.

DRAGO
Show it.

Drago immediately monitored the video was split on the display with further prompting.

MĚNGJIÀNG YÚN-RÉN
[AI ALERT]
Multiple communications.

The Greys had no idea they were dealing with technologically advanced Aliens that
dwarfed them in ability and had the ability to real time unscramble and show all video
communications.

Wánměi De Huā said the obvious as the translations flowed across the bottom of the
screens.

WÁNMĚI DE HUĀ
The Grey commander was evidently reacting to a
report from a Gray Fighter who apparently spotted us.

DRAGO
The Greys are in full panic.

The translation sliding across the bottom of the screen continued:

VOICEOVER
WOGAR GREY
MESSAGE
*Your excellency Zorgjeck, the enemy just passed by so
quickly we had no time to respond, their velocity is
extremely high, doubt our weapons can catch the ship.*

Drago understood the *Měngjiàng Yún-Rén Royal Yacht's* current velocity might be
higher than what Greys had ever experienced.

DRAGO
That is understandable.

The ship's sensor system, fully robotized and controlled by Artificial Intelligence
communicating over the telepathic transceivers so as not disturb the large screen
activity stated and was repeated in the neurotransmitters of the *Měngjiàng Yún-Rén
Royal Yacht Control Room.*

ROYAL YACHT
ARTIFICIAL INTELLIGENCE
*All enemy fighters are now behind and trailing.
Negative range rate on rear mounted sensors indicates
they are opening.*

DRAGO
They will never catch up to us in time.

ROYAL YACHT AI
The Grey mother ship continues to increase speed.

DRAGO
The only thing the Grey Mother Ship is achieving by
increasing speed is to leave their escorts behind.

WÁNMĚI DE HUĀ

We will slow down and chase them a bit and let them
put a large gap between us and their escorts, and then
we'll confront them.

The confrontation was just about to begin.

WÁNMĚI DE HUĀ

Science Officer, have you been able to construct
Wogar Grey translators so we can converse with their
mother ship?

Answering from the science lab where he was slowly making progress with Grak, he
responded:

SCIENCE OFFICER

Yes, we now have real time translation via your
telepathic transceivers.

Wánměi De Huā announced after the range opened to the point, they were 30 minutes
in front of the escort ships left far behind.

WÁNMĚI DE HUĀ

I believe it's time we have a talk with them.

The next telepathic translator communique informed the control room of *Wánměi De
Huā's* intended actions.

WÁNMĚI DE HUĀ

Please translate and send my voice to the Wogar
Mother Ship when I communicate with them.

Wánměi De Huā communicated telepathically through her telepathic transponders (in
her implants).

Virtually without moving her lips she communicated and *Wánměi De Huā* saw Wogar
Grey Supreme Commander Zorgjeck real time display up on the control room large
screen on one side and she and what she was communicating on the other.

WÁNMĚI DE HUĀ

Your Excellency Supreme Commander Zorgjeck, we
wish to talk.

WOGAR GREY
SUPREME COMMANDER
ZORGJECK
What is it that you want?

WÁNMĚI DE HUĀ
You have something that belongs to me, and I want it
back.

WOGAR GREY
SUPREME COMMANDER
ZORGJECK
I have no idea about what you are talking about.

WÁNMĚI DE HUĀ
Do not try to stall; we can wipe out your escorts if they
attempt to approach.

WOGAR GREY
SUPREME COMMANDER
ZORGJECK
What is it you claim we have?

WÁNMĚI DE HUĀ
You have the Earth Person named Vance.

WOGAR GREY
SUPREME COMMANDER
ZORGJECK
We have no such person aboard.

WÁNMĚI DE HUĀ
Well, if that is the case, then since Vance's not aboard
your *Colony Class Planetary Conquest Vessel*; there is
nothing stopping me from destroying you.

WOGAR GREY
SUPREME COMMANDER
ZORGJECK
I doubt you can do that.

WÁNMĚI DE HUĀ
We have weapons you are not familiar with that will
make your ship disappear in seconds as if it just went
into a black hole.

WOGAR GREY
SUPREME COMMANDER
ZORGJECK
Is that so?

WÁNMĚI DE HUĀ

If you delay any further and claim Vance is not
onboard, I'm going to go ahead and destroy your ship
just to prove to you I'm not bluffing.

Zorgjeck knew his escorts were 30 minutes behind and might be too late to rescue him
needed to stall for time and wasn't about to hand over the alien but decided to say.

WOGAR GREY
SUPREME COMMANDER
ZORGJECK

Ok. If we have Vance on Board, we are not going to
release him; so, if you kill us, you kill him too.

WÁNMĚI DE HUĀ

I do not believe you have Vance onboard; therefore, I
think we will just go ahead and destroy your ship.

WOGAR GREY
SUPREME COMMANDER
ZORGJECK

No need to act hastily, I will have him on the bridge
with me immediately so you can see him.

The translation picked up him turning to an assistant:

WOGAR GREY
SUPREME COMMANDER
ZORGJECK

Bring that Earth Man Vance to the bridge immediately.

All *Wánměi De Huā* had to do was *think* it, and the telepathic translator ordered the
ship to transport Vance to the *Měngjiàng Yún-Rén Royal Yacht* vessel. Within a minute,
there was Vance.

Zorgjeck looked in horror as Vance dematerialized in front of him in about one second
Vance was gone.

Instantly Vance was on the *Měngjiàng Yún-Rén Royal Yacht* control room standing in
front of *Wánměi De Huā*.

366

Wánmĕi De Huā thinking ahead telepathically announced:

WÁNMĔI DE HUĀ
I do not think Grak will be of any use to us. We should
send him back to the Wogar Grey now, along with the
Grey Hybrids.

Vance remembering the abductees.

VANCE
There are about Twenty abductees on that Wogar
Grey ship; some are in decent shape; the others are in
horrible mental condition; why don't we trade Grak
for all those?

WÁNMĔI DE HUĀ
Science Officer, bring Grak and all the Hybrids to the
control room immediately.

The *Mĕngjiàng Yún-Rén* Science Officer had Grak, and the Gray Hybrids escorted to
the control room quickly.

Shortly *Wánmĕi De Huā* communicated to the Greys:

WÁNMĔI DE HUĀ
Your Excellency Zorgjeck, we have some of your
people we want to return to you now.

Wánmĕi De Huā held out her hand indicating Grak and the Hybrids.

GRAK
Zorgjeck, thank you for saving me.

VANCE
Not so fast, Grak.

Right after the *Mĕngjiàng Yún-Rén* removed Vance's neurotic shackles he
announced:

VANCE
There are 20 Earth people abductees I witnessed. We
want all of them returned; bring them to your control
room.

The Earth abductee prisoners were brought to the Grey *Colony Class Planetary
Conquest Vessel* Command Ship control room.

VANCE
After we get the abductees back, we will send over
Grak and your Grey Hybrids.

Moments later the abductees and the Grey's were swapped, and the *Měngjiàng Yún-Rén* were long gone by the time the Grey *Colony Class Planetary Conquest Vessel Escorts* arrived in near space.

The man Vance had met in the Wogar Grey *incubation center* was about the only one in the group that seemed happy to be away from the Greys. The rest almost seemed like Zombies.

VANCE
Ladies and Gentlemen, you will all be returned to
Earth and will be able to live your lives without fear of
the Greys anymore.

BUD (ABDUCTEE)
When you said you would soon be leaving and come
back to get us all, I did not believe you sir, but now I
am incredibly grateful.

VANCE
Most of these other people seem to not realize they are
going home.

BUD (ABDUCTEE)
After years of terrible treatment by Wogar Grey, they
probably have psychological wounds and will never
be the same again.

WÁNMĚI DE HUĀ
I have ideas that may help. Science officer, please take
them to your lab and see if you can help restore them
to their former lives.

The Science Officer looking at the abused individuals taking on a humanoid appearance so as not to upset their new guests led them to his science lab. The lab was large but somewhat small for a large group like this.

The science officer made do with what he had available.

Abductees who were comatose psychologically were merely sedated and put in makeshift sleeping platforms.

The other abductees were split into separate rooms accompanied by his lab assistant who also functioned as the ship's medical doctor, which was not deemed necessary for the *Měngjiàng Yún-Rén* but there mainly for Vance's needs.

A psychological and metaphysical triage was performed. The same advanced technology used to extend Vance's life one thousand years was put to practice to make repairs of damaged sections of abductee brains.

Those areas that contained memories of their horrible abduction and treatment by the Wogar Greys were permanently erased.

One by one those helpless humans were restored somewhat and after the science and medical staff completed the treatment, they were invited back to the Bridge where Vance had made a determination that in order to compensate these weary people from their many years of abuse, they would give them a wonderful tour of the solar system, visiting all the major planets except Mars which they passed by at a safe range as to not cause a scramble of the Earth Forces who were locked in great fear of a major galactic skirmish ready to unfold at close range with the Tall Whites and the Greys locked into a Mexican Standoff.

Amazingly by the time the *Měngjiàng Yún-Rén* ship returned to its solar orbit *Wánměi de Huā* noted:

WÁNMĚI DE HUĀ
Fifteen of the abductees appear restored to almost normal psychological health.

DRAGO
The others might take a while and probably should remain until the de *Měngjiàng Yún-Rén* Fleet arrives for the big showdown, by then all the remaining except possibly one should be ready to be returned to earth.

SCIENCE OFFICER
It is time to take the abductees back to earth now.

WÁNMĚI DE HUĀ
Vance and I will take the abductees aboard the shuttlecraft.

DRAGO
You need to take a security force with you.

WÁNMĚI DE HUĀ
Transport the security detail to the planet surface when we arrive there.

The *Měngjiàng Yún-Rén* put all the abductees in the slightly crowded shuttle craft.

Music overlay Melodies for the next two CGI's:

This music would fit in well during the sequence when the abductees are returned to Earth. The music that starts at the 1:18 mark exemplifies the extraordinary psychology a person would have under such circumstances. The melody portion at the 2:00 mark could be played to a viewer's loved one before giving a kiss and telling sweet lies.

<u>Valentina Lisitsa - Addinsell "Warsaw Concerto" - YouTube</u>

The cut in mark would be around one minute mark in the concerto. Then with special emphasis at the 2:25 mark in this performance.

<u>EXT. CGI. SPACE. *MĚNGJIÀNG YÚN-RÉN* SHUTTLE CRAFT DEPARTS THE ROYAL YACHT AND FLIES TO EARTH. 30 SECONDS.</u>

VOICEOVER
(During this video scene)
*For those Wogar Grey abductees who were mentally
fully coherent, this was the greatest moment in their
lives, rescued from living hell.*

<u>EXT. CGI. SPACE. *MĚNGJIÀNG YÚN-RÉN* SHUTTLE ARRIVED AT GROOM LAKE AND PARKED RIGHT IN FRONT OF BUILDING 27. 30 SECONDS (CONCATINATED TO PREVIUS CGI. 30 SECONDS.</u>

Vance then led the abductees out of the shuttle with two-thirds of them appearing extremely happy to be home on *Terra Firma*.

Much work remained ahead as the government would have to figure out how to integrate the abductees back into society without disclosure to the alien situation they just escaped.

Another issue is not all of them are Americans. To avoid exposing this to their country, they would receive a manufactured identity and be allowed to remain in the USA, which was fine for all of those in that situation.

As if it had been a repeat performance of their earlier arrival, the HUMV's and the rocket launcher vehicles slowly surrounded the shuttle.

General Brazile with Colonel Jones walked out of building 27 and approached the shuttle with great trepidation. Fear was in their eyes as they were in the crisis of dealing with two immensely powerful, nuclear capable alien races staring down at each other's gun barrels in nearby space.

General Brazile looked as if someone had just run over his dog or first born.

GENERAL BRAZILE

You did not pick the most advantageous time to come back.

VANCE

We thought it was important to bring you back all these abductees we managed to pry away from the Wogar Greys.

GENERAL BRAZILE

Did the *Měngjiàng Yún-Rén* kidnap Grak too?

VANCE

Yes, however Grak is on the Wogar Grey *Colony Class Planetary Conquest Vessel* mother ship traveling away from this solar system at high speed, I doubt he will be coming back soon.

GENERAL BRAZILE

What about all these spaceships orbiting Earth that are now starting to be discovered by amateur astronomers?

VANCE

You will have to figure out how to deal with that as well as all these people.

GENERAL BRAZILE

You can't leave your ship parked here. You must park it in the hanger, or it must depart. We are now under intensive satellite observation.

Without hesitation, the shuttle departed and went back to the *Měngjiàng Yún-Rén Royal Yacht*.

GENERAL BRAZILE

Colonel Jones, call over to transportation and get a Bus to pick up all these people; take them to the cafeteria, and cordon them off from any of the base inhabitants.

COLONEL JONES
Right away general.

GENERAL BRAZILE
I do not want them talking to anyone. I need time to figure out what to do with them.

VANCE
General Brazile, I would like to stay with these people until I find out what's going to happen with them.

GENERAL BRAZILE
As you wish, but what about that trip you wanted to take to see all your old sights?

VANCE
We'll just have to put that on hold until these people are taken care of.

GENERAL BRAZILE
As you wish, Vance.

In approximately twenty minutes, the group including the *Měngjiàng Yún-Rén security detachment* that had been transported down were on a couple busses and taken to the cafeteria that provided meals for not only the military, but also the civilian contractors working at Area 51.

The Area 51 cafeteria wasn't the best looking greasy spoon in the world, but it was a hell of a lot better than the treatment on the Wogar Gray's ship where each person present had lost 10 to 20 pounds and a few of them were senior citizens who were abducted as Children back when steam engines roamed the high rail of the ancient transportation system, were very thin and sickly looking.

The elderly abductee's bitterness was overshadowed by the fact they realized they could finish out their final days at home, even though the people they once knew were long gone.

After everyone who wanted to eat were fed, they were escorted out to the buses where General Brazile and Colonel Jones were having a private sidebar.

GENERAL BRAZILE
What Q division is faced with in dealing with these returned abductees can only be managed by the government's witness protection program. Nothing else could work.

COLONEL JONES

Since a few abductees had former spouses who were either deceased or remarried, bringing them back to their prior lives is impossible.

GENERAL BRAZILE

Q division has their hands full. But the un-daunting challenge will in time be overcome by their clever application of the same process we use to create spooks.

COLONEL JONES

Essentially, they will all be given new identification and decent pensions and handled by the Witness Protection Program people.

GENERAL BRAZILE

Those witness protection program experts have a good understanding of how these people will be able to live.

COLONEL JONES

The witness protection program has miserly compensation for numerous criminals they needed to protect to take down big, organized crime bosses.

GENERAL BRAZILE

Before abductee repatriation all unfolds, the immediate need is to get them all off the base and tucked away in a nearby hotel, where they can be watched and protected.

COLONEL JONES

There are not many nearby hotels and the few that exit in nearby towns are infested with bed bugs and hookers making a living off the Truckers that roamed up and down Highway 93.

GENERAL BRAZILE

I think I know one facility that has rooms to accommodate all of them in one spot.

COLONEL JONES
Where may that be?

GENERAL BRAZILE
Don't laugh, the Dude Ranch over at Alamo Nevada.

COLONEL JONES
I kind of like that idea.

***

<u>INT. DAY. ALAMO NEVADA. DUDE RANCH.</u>

Boris a.k.a. Mr. Keeney (Boris' new identity for this assignment), was delighted when the Air Force man came that day and wanted to know:

COLONEL JONES
How many rooms can we book for a large group?

BORIS (a.k.a. MR. KEENEY)
Depends on how many rooms and how long.

COLONEL JONES
Say, twenty-two rooms for two weeks.

BORIS (a.k.a. MR. KEENEY)
I suppose we could find the space, let me check my reservations.

It was getting towards that hot time of year when the tourists heading for sightseeing up the Extraterrestrial Highway were petering out. Hence the reservations were few and far between, but Boris, knowing the negotiations would soon commence, played coy with the officer.

BORIS (a.k.a. MR. KEENEY)
It will be tough to block off all 22 rooms for that many consecutive days.

COLONEL JONES
How much do you charge?

BORIS (a.k.a. MR. KEENEY)
Those rooms normally go for around $125 to $250 a day, as some have more features than others.

COLONEL JONES
Ok, how about I pay you, $250 a day for all the rooms, would that lock them in?"

BORIS (a.k.a. MR. KEENEY)
Certainly.

COLONEL JONES
Ok, they will be arriving in a while. Also, these people have some important roles, and we do not want them disturbed by other guests.

BORIS (a.k.a. MR. KEENEY)
Not a problem.

COLONEL JONES
One other item.

BORIS (a.k.a. MR. KEENEY)
Yes?

COLONEL JONES
What kind of dining facilities do you have here?

BORIS (a.k.a. MR. KEENEY)
Well as a Dude-Ranch we provide meals too. We usually have a country style barbecue every evening in fact.

COLONEL JONES
How is the food?

BORIS (a.k.a. MR. KEENEY)
We do so well with the Barbecue, which the town's people sometimes quickly visit and pay to receive the meals because they are that good.

COLONEL JONES
Okay, that will work simply fine. Put all the room charges on my credit card.

Colonel Jones handed Boris his special DOD credit card, then while Boris was printing out the contract, Colonel Jones called General Brazile.

COLONEL JONES
It is all set bring them over.

Boris handed Colonel Jones the guest registration sheet.

BORIS (a.k.a. MR. KEENEY)
Please sign here.

Colonel Jones signed the hotel contract.

BORIS (a.k.a. MR. KEENEY)
Do you have a list of names for the people?

COLONEL JONES
Yes, all the men are John Doe, and all the women are
Jane Doe.

BORIS (a.k.a. MR. KEENEY)
Are you some sort of wise guy?

COLONEL JONES
These people's identities are protected. I am sorry.
I cannot say any more about them, considering it a
government project with need to know.

BORIS (a.k.a. MR. KEENEY)
All right then.

COLONEL JONES
If you know what is good for you, do not advertise this
to anyone or discuss it with anyone.

Boris smiled.

BORIS (a.k.a. MR. KEENEY)
Certainly sir, I understand.

***

<u>INT. DAY. GUS AND BEVERLY HOME RESIDENCES.</u>

<u>SPLIT SCREEN. GUS ON ONE SIDE AND BEVERLY ON THE OTHER.</u>

Gus was working on reports for recent assignments when the phone suddenly rang. It
was Beverly on the other end.

BEVERLY
Their back.

GUS
Who?

BEVERLY
Our guests.

GUS
Vance included?

BEVERLY
Yep.

GUS
Where did they find Vance?

BEVERLY
Nobody knows, that is one of our assignments.

GUS
When do we start?

BEVERLY
Right now, a car will be pulling up in 10 minutes, grab
your grip, you will be gone a while.

***

<u>INT. DAY. ALAMO NEVADA. DUDE RANCH.</u>

After the Air Force officer (Colonel Jones) left, Boris started wondering:

VOICEOVER BORIS POTEMKIN
(a.k.a. MR. KEENEY) THOUGHT
I wonder, is this why Alexander Bortnikov put me here?

Forty-five minutes later, two blue Air Force buses following a couple of interesting
looking SUVs pulled into the Alamo Nevada Dude Rance parking lot.

The group was told they would be vacationing at this Dude Ranch for a couple of
weeks as preparations were being made to return them to society.

The government promised the abductees a pension if they kept their story out of the public eye.

As the cheerful group piled out of the bus, the first impression Boris had was they all seemed just like happy tourists and wondered.

VOICEOVER BORIS POTEMKIN
(a.k.a. MR. KEENEY) THOUGHT
What is the American government up to?

Boris, an astute INTEL collector, knew he would have to surreptitiously acquire photographic evidence for his reports realized suddenly how important his security cameras would play in that role.

An intelligence gatherer in a foreign country can never be put in a position to compromise himself by doing risky things such as getting caught taking pictures. Though that may have to be a risk he might soon have to take.

Colonel Jones handed the card style room keys out to all the John Does and Jane Does as each had a room number on the little envelope like holder each key had with it.

One by one they were taken to their rooms, and Boris was surprised few if any had any had luggage. At best, they had shopping bags with a few minor items.

Colonel Jones approached Boris (a.k.a. Mr. Keeney) to introduce Gus and Beverley.

COLONEL JONES
These two are the overall coordinators, Gus and
Beverly, any issues that come up please take it to them.

Boris noticed the four other men wearing suits and sunglasses following Vance and Sandra who followed the group in, asked, "

BORIS (a.k.a. MR. KEENEY)
Who are these guys?

COLONEL JONES
They are security people to make sure none of our
group hike far away and possibly get lost.

About that time, Boris realized *this situation really is quite unusual.*

The rest of the Q dream team who had reservations just driving in, followed the group moments later and purposely stayed in their vehicle until the lobby emptied out.

BORIS (a.k.a. MR. KEENEY)
May I help you?

ROGER
Yes. We are checking in. I have reservations; name is
Roger Smith.

BORIS (a.k.a. MR. KEENEY)
Sure, let me check.

In a brief time, the Q team back together was checked into their rooms, posing as two married couples.

VOICEOVER BORIS POTEMKIN
(a.k.a. MR. KEENEY) THOUGHT
It seems weird the two couples asked for queen beds.

Gus and Beverly had done undercover assignments together and were paired up and Roger and Crystal likewise.

A while later, the two couples departed in their Black and White SUVs and as they were driving off, Boris suddenly remembered the cars. At first it didn't make sense but as he thought deeper and deeper, it came back to him. Then a chill really went up his spine.

VOICEOVER BORIS POTEMKIN
(a.k.a. MR. KEENEY) THOUGHT
Those are the CIA people from back in Vegas!

Boris started trying to figure out why these CIA people were all here.

VOICEOVER BORIS POTEMKIN
(a.k.a. MR. KEENEY) THOUGHT
The crowd of people brought in with them, including senior citizens, just does not add up to being a clandestine type of team.

***

<u>INT. DAY. ALAMO NEVADA.</u>

As a collateral duty, Gus was asked to look around and help establish logistics for the abductees, but as it seemed Alamo Nevada was only going to allow them bare necessities at service station shops.

Gus drove around Alamo Nevada, looking to see if there was much in the way of shopping: there was not much, mainly just tourist trap stores selling useless junk made in China.

                              BEVERLY
              The closest place that has any good stuff is the base PX
              over at Nellis Air Force Base.

                                GUS
              Yes, but I doubt General Brazile wants visibility and
              must later cover up these people were there.

                              BEVERLY
              We can take four of them at a time to Vegas to go
              shopping.

                                GUS
              If we take them over to Groom Lake and put them on
              a plane down to Vegas, we can get a lot more shopping
              done at some place like Walmart.

After getting a good look at Alamo, Gus announced:

                                GUS
              If I wanted to settle down someplace and start a family,
              this would be it.

                              BEVERLY
              You can tell the people here do not have the big city
              problems; see kids walking around unattended.

                                GUS
              Ok well, let's head back over to the funny farm.

Gus then headed back to their charge of abductees.

                                ***

INT. DAY. ALAMO NEVADA. DUDE RANCH.

Boris had already emailed Robert Simons and had copied some surveillance film footage into a few short video files, with some discussion of what was in the package.

                    VOICEOVER (BORIS POTEMKIN)
              Exhibit A shows the group of people coming into the
              lodge and given their room keys.

Exhibit B is the registration 10 John Doe's and 12 Jane Doe's.

Exhibit C is two SUVs, were identical to the ones I had searched in Vegas on May 20th.

Exhibit D is the four CIA individuals I believe are agents and I observed in Vegas.

The man with the blue *Polo Shirt* and *Khaki Shorts* is the man who sat on the other side of me at the bar in Vegas.

The other gentleman is another who came in the bar and sat near me. The two women with them are probable agents.

INT. DAY. SWITZERLAND ROBERT SIMMONS CREATING EMAIL 20 SECONDS.

C.U. ROBERT SIMMONS TYPING ON LAPTOP.

C.U. LAPTOP CONTENTS (INCLUDING TEXT OF VOICE OVER ABOVE SHOWING EXIBITS A THROUGH D.

Twelve hours later Robert Simmons (aka Aleksandr Zubkov) in Switzerland sent an email to Alexander Bortnikov; it again had the subject; *thought you might like to look at these videos*.

INT. DAY. MOSCOW RUSSIA. LYBIANCA, FSB (KGB) HEADQUARTERS.

The communications technician quickly surmised this was an extraordinary submission, quickly and efficiently put it all on the laptop and brought along a long cord he could use to plug into the big screen video display mounted on the wall to the right side of the door in Alexander Bortnikov's office.

Just like clockwork, the secretary pressed the button on her control panel that had some predefined indicators such as: Messenger; VIP; Cleaning girl; Putin; Medvedev; General Alexi Shoygu, which simultaneously lit up and flashed on an identical one at Bortnikov's desk on a little panel that also was used as the stand to raise the flat screen monitor to a more comfortable viewing level.

If Alexander Bortnikov's pressed the flashing light, it would cause both lights on his and the receptionist's desk to go out, or he had one other button he could press at any time that said, cannot be disturbed.

That *DO NOT DISTURB* [Это не беспокоить] *lighted switch* also meant no entrance in the event he was looking at or discussing some highly classified information.

If an urgent need existed, the receptionist had to get verbal permission from the phone to let someone in.

Alexander Bortnikov expecting his routine briefing emails and videos from the communications technician pressed the flashing light, and the receptionist immediately directed the communications technician:

ALEXANDER BORTNIKOV
RECEPTIONIST
Please go in.

A moment later:

ALEXANDER BORTNIKOV
COMMUNICATIONS
TECHNICIAN

Sir, I have an interface cable to plug into your big screen to watch the videos on. They will be ok on the laptop but show quite a bit more on the big screen.

ALEXANDER BORTNIKOV

Thank you, go ahead and plug the cable in the big screen for me.

Moments later the briefing began, and it was all automated. First was Boris' Potemkin comments, then one by one the video fragments were played.

By the end of the videos, Alexander Bortnikov asked the communications technician:

ALEXANDER BORTNIKOV

Please disconnect the cable from the large screen, and you can take the laptop, I'm done looking at it for now.

Just as the technician was leaving the room, the light with General Alexi Shoygu's name on it started flashing. Alexander Bortnikov quickly pressed that lighted switch and within a moment Alexi Shoygu walked in his office.

ALEXANDER BORTNIKOV
Would you like something to drink?

GENERAL ALEXI SHOYGU
Sure.

Alexander Bortnikov pressed the [Attendant] light switch button on his control console.

A moment later, an attractive young lady, General Shoygu guessed was in her early twenties, walked in from the side door.

ATTENDANT
What may I do for you, Mr. Bortnikov?

ALEXANDER BORTNIKOV
Pour General Shoygu a drink, I would like one too.

The administrative aide Svetlana who was thoroughly trained in Bortnikov's idiosyncrasies, left the room momentarily and returned with a bottle of *Belver Bears Belvedere Vodka* on a sparkling shining silver tray and a couple of small crystal *Chinelli Swarovski Regina Vodka Glasses*.

The crystal vodka glasses could hold a full 2 ounces, but out of etiquette and protocols that Bortnikov had schooled the young lady, Svetlana only filled the two vodka glasses half full, then handed one to the General Shoygu and the other to Alexander Bortnikov.

ALEXANDER BORTNIKOV
That will be all for now.

Svetlana then left out the side door leaving the tray and bottle of vodka behind on the coffee table in front of the sofa where General Shoygu sat.

ALEXANDER BORTNIKOV
Excellent timing.

GENERAL ALEXI SHOYGU
Why is that?

ALEXANDER BORTNIKOV
I just got a report from our agent near Area-51. It appears something interesting is going on there.

GENERAL ALEXI SHOYGU
Anything related to the number of alien UFOs we've recently detected?

ALEXANDER BORTNIKOV
We do not know if there's a connection or not, but we'll soon find out.

GENERAL ALEXI SHOYGU
The reason I came over is I have something to inform
you of.

General Alexi Shoygu then took a deep swallow of the vodka and felt that pleasant sensation it quickly provided.

ALEXANDER BORTNIKOV
Go on.

GENERAL ALEXI SHOYGU
Our Zenit 17 Satellite just photographed an alien ship
landing in front of Building 27 at Groom Lake.

ALEXANDER BORTNIKOV
Another alien visit?

GENERAL ALEXI SHOYGU
We are trying to figure it out, but twenty-two people
dressed in what appear to be wearing lab coats got off
the spacecraft.

As far as we can tell by other photographs we obtained, those twenty-two people were taken to Building-44 which we believe is the base cafeteria.

And then after a while about the time it takes to eat a meal, these twenty-two people still wearing lab coats were bussed to the base PX, where apparently, they all got a change of clothes, got on a bus and left?

ALEXANDER BORTNIKOV
Any idea where they went from there?

GENERAL ALEXI SHOYGU
Unfortunately, we lost communications with the
Satellite for 15 minutes and by the time it was restored
the bus carrying the civilians was gone.

ALEXANDER BORTNIKOV
You could not find it anywhere on the base?

GENERAL ALEXI SHOYGU
No, we are going back over the video and still images
of the base, and even though other buses are on the
base, none of them moved from their parking locations
though out, just this one bus.

ALEXANDER BORTNIKOV
How about the alien ship, did it remain?

GENERAL ALEXI SHOYGU
No, as soon as the last person departed the spaceship left.

ALEXANDER BORTNIKOV
Were you able to track where it went to?

GENERAL ALEXI SHOYGU
No, it did not go into any sort of orbit, it simply zipped out into space and in a very quick period, was lost on any form of surveillance.

ALEXANDER BORTNIKOV
So, no destination, not even planets or moon?

GENERAL ALEXI SHOYGU
No, it simply disappeared into outer space.
Alexander Bortnikov had seldom had a day like today.

ALEXANDER BORTNIKOV
Later when I brief the Prime Minister, it will be clear the Americans had been withholding possible Alien involvement in violation of the secret *Solar Defense Force Agreements*.

General Shoygu responded feeling this alien business really felt unsettling.

GENERAL ALEXI SHOYGU
Add that to the strange reports we got from Russians manning the Mars site.

ALEXANDER BORTNIKOV
Right at the time our furthest outpost was attacked, the Americans have visitors from outer space.

Alexander Bortnikov had yet to drink the vodka Svetlana poured him, just made the mental connection! Twenty-two civilians off the alien space craft and twenty-two civilians carted around the base, and twenty-two people showed up at the Russian controlled Dude Ranch in Alamo, Nevada, was starting to add up.

Alexander Bortnikov then grabbed his Chinelli Swarovski Regina Vodka Glass and in one gulp swallowed all the Belver Bears Belvedere Vodka. Its pleasant sting as it went down added to the quintessential effect of intrigue and chemical equilibrium amplifying the results of both.

General Alexi Shoygu stood up.

> GENERAL ALEXI SHOYGU
> I have important matters to attend too, I thought you should be aware of recent activities.

> ALEXANDER BORTNIKOV
> Yes, thank you Alexi for coming by. We have much to investigate and I have some ideas which we will try out soon.

> GENERAL ALEXI SHOYGU
> I will be seeing you soon, Alexander. Thanks for the nice vodka.

> ALEXANDER BORTNIKOV
> My pleasure, I'll be sending you some new satellite requests to look at from the footage of the archives concerning those Area-51 visitors.

> GENERAL ALEXI SHOYGU
> I'll be waiting to hear from you.

Goodbye General.

***

<u>INT. DAY. ALAMO, NEVADA. DUDE RANCH.</u>

The next day, Mr. Durant who had a ranch right across the road from the Dude Ranch, came into the lobby, Boris (a.k.a Mr. Keeney) was sitting there at a computer terminal with the screen away from public viewing, and was as Durant assumed him to be, working on reservations or Dude Ranch matters.

> MR. DURANT
> Hello Mr. Keeney, are we going to have a horse ride
> today?

Durant had been getting anxious lately because as the horse rides declined, he was suddenly faced with the costs of maintaining the extra horses he bought and was now upset he was losing money on what he thought was a sure money maker.

BORIS (a.k.a. MR. KEENEY)
Mr. Durant, we have twenty-six new guests in a group
traveling together. I am going to contact their group
coordinator and find out how many want to go, hold
on.

Gus really caused Boris heavy stressful moments when the Air Force Colonel
introduced him and said he would be a coordinator for all the guests. Boris dialed his
room. He was glad the Russian plastic surgeons had done such an excellent job; the
American did not recognize him from Vegas.

Gus answered the phone.

GUS
Hello.

BORIS (a.k.a. MR. KEENEY)
Good morning Mr. Hall (or whoever your real name
is thought Boris), I'm calling to check how many of
your group would like to go on the horseback ride.
If you look through our Dude Ranch brochures this
horseback ride is one of the amenities we provide.

Gus not realizing he was at a Dude Ranch because it didn't look like one. Gus had not
gone through all the brochures to figure out what types of recreation were available.

GUS
Not sure, let me find out and get back to you.

BORIS (a.k.a. MR. KEENEY)
That would be great. We need to know in a half hour
from now so the horse guide can prepare the mounts,
and our kitchen prepares a box lunch he carries along
with pack horses including drinks.

VOICEOVER BORIS (a.k.a. MR. KEENEY)
THOUGHT
*I hope those horses don't crap all over the driveway
again. I usually get the chore of cleaning it up.*

Boris then got a sudden brilliant idea, he could also go along and use it as an excuse to
get a couple photographs, they might use in their future brochures for the guests. And
it would go way beyond the crappy surveillance photographs sent.

Talk about extraordinary luck. An Air Force pilot Dudley Brown who stayed at the Dude Ranch often, entered the lobby about then and as soon as Boris got off the phone with Gus.

DUDLEY BROWN
Good morning Mr. Keeney just thought I would come by and sign up for the horseback ride today if you are going to have one.

BORIS (a.k.a. MR. KEENEY)
Why certainly we are. I will add your name to the list Dudley, be back here in an hour.

DUDLEY BROWN
Thank you.

Dudley then headed out the door.

As Dudley Brown was leaving the Dude Ranch lobby and headed back to his room Boris started thinking.

VOICEOVER BORIS
(a.k.a. MR. KEENEY) THOUGHT
This could the guy on the horse ride the pilot spoofed that provided me all those wonderful pictures of the TR-3B. Will I receive such similar gifts today?

In the middle of Boris thoughts and contemplation the phone rang again. It was Gus on the other end.

GUS
Got a head count, have 12 of our guests plus me and my wife: make that 14 that want to go on the horseback ride.

BORIS (a.k.a. MR. KEENEY)
14 total, understand.

GUS
Lunch, drinks, and everything is provided.

BORIS (a.k.a. MR. KEENEY)
Absolutely, we all meet in the lobby in one hour.

When Boris (a.k.a. Mr. Keeney) hung up Durant then asked:

DURANT
So, does that mean fifteen horseback riders plus
normal staff?

BORIS (a.k.a. MR. KEENEY)
No, make that 16.

DURANT
How do you figure, got the Air Force guy and the 14
others.

BORIS (a.k.a. MR. KEENEY)
I'm going along too.

Boris yelled for his assistant Jessica who helped take care of the rooms and keep an
eye on the maids.

BORIS (a.k.a. MR. KEENEY)
Jessica!

Jessica was given notice and was quite surprised to learn that Mr. Keeney would be
going on the horse ride.

In about an hour, Gus, Beverly, Vance, Sandra (*Wánměi De Huā*) and 10 of the
abductees met in the lobby. Roger and Crystal were left behind to keep an eye on the
rest and make sure they did not wander away too far. Most of those remaining went to
the swimming pool.

The Pilot Dudley Brown showed up sporting a polo shirt, shorts, tennis shoes, pilot's
sunglasses, and wearing suntan lotion.

Mr. Durant led twenty horses all tied in a string to the saddle on the horse in front of
each of them, and the horses at the rear used as a pack horse with a strange looking
contraption carried on the back made from wood, came up the driveway.

To Boris' chagrin it did not take long for the animals to crap all over the driveway.
Jessica was there with a snow shovel and a wheelbarrow to perform one of the tasks
she would soon be getting used to performing.

After the horses were all gone, and the manure shoveled up, Jessica would take the
garden hose to the driveway and clean off any residue. On the return trip as agreed
upon by Mr. Durant and Boris (a.k.a. Mr. Keeney), the riders would be let off on the
road in front of the Dude Ranch to avoid having to clean the driveway twice in a day.

Mr. Durant said gave basic horse handling instructions to the group.

MR. DURANT
These horses are very gentle, don't kick them or hit
them and they will treat you right.

Interestingly, the only people with cameras were Beverly, Boris, and the Air Force pilot. One by one Durant untied the string of horses then helped just about each person up on the saddle and handed him or her the reigns.

During this time, the cook came out with a small wagon loaded with boxes that were put into Durant's contraption on the pack horse that now everyone realized was their box lunches. Then away they went.

INT. SPACE. *MĚNGJIÀNG YÚN-RÉN ROYAL YACHT.*

Back on the *Měngjiàng Yún-Rén Royal Yacht,* Drago was getting telepathic transceiver status from Sandra (*Wánměi De Huā*) and the two *Měngjiàng Yún-Rén Security Agents* on horses with the other guests. These two *Měngjiàng Yún-Rén Security Agents* had changed out of suits and into tourist clothes at Vance's suggestions so they would blend in better.

Drago gave the security team instructions:

DRAGO
This time we will not chance losing Vance again. Your
orders are to not let Vance out of your sight.

Report any attempts on Vance immediately as we have a security force prepared to be sent as backup immediately upon such an event.

Figuratively, though while Vance was alone with Sandra (a.k.a. *Wánměi De Huā*) in their Dude Ranch private room, they remained outside performing their ever vigilance getting Sandra's (a.k.a. *Wánměi De Huā*) telepathic status checks that conditions are normal.

EXT. DAY. ALAMO NEVADA DUDE RANCH.

The horses knew exactly where they were going. They also knew that up at the creek not only would they get a cool drink of water, but Durant had packages of grain stored up there in a little shed that contained fishing poles and gear and other essential items in case someone got lucky and caught a fish.

This was going to be an auspicious occasion because *Nevada Fish and Game* had just stocked the creek and pond with some nice trout which meant it would not be hard not to catch a fish today.

The group slowly rode up the leisurely path, over a couple hills and before long they were in sight of this lovely pond dead ahead. The horses were also in anticipation of a drink and that grain and had no indication they were going to slow down until they reached it.

As they pulled up to the picnic area, Mr. Durant got off his lead horse and explained:

MR. DURANT
Tie your horses up like this.

Mr. Durant then wrapped his reigns around the series of boards that appeared pounded by nails to fence posts.

This area looked like it could easily tie up 30 or 40 horses which during peak tourist season often did.

Mr. Durant got the grain out of about the time his hired hand walked up and started untying and leading each horse over to the creek one by one, so they could get a drink and then tied them back up as he systematically took care of all the horses who all seemed to have a good disposition.

Attached to each of the tied-down places were a strange looking run of boards that soon revealed their purpose as Mr. Durant gave each of the horses a helping of grain which the horses knew was in store for them. Durant then led the people over to a shed.

MR. DURANT
Each one of you go ahead and grab a fishing pole. We
want to see if any of you *City Slickers* can catch a fish.

With Mr. Durrant's assistant still working the horses nearby and knowing what to expect was grinning.

Before long Mr. Durant had schooled everyone including the women, how to put those big worms he pulled out of a bucket for them on the hook, then gave some simple casting instruction. Within 5 minutes as expected the first person got a hit and the next thing you know; Mr. Durant was there with a bucket half full of water and unhooked the fish and put it in.

Sandra (a.k.a. *Wánměi De Huā*), sensing all the abductees enjoyed this little recreation that was quickly restoring some of their mental health and cheerfulness, and realized they would easily re-integrate back into society. But would need some help for a while since America had changed a lot since some of these people were abducted as children.

Others who were abducted as adults to become teachers or surrogate mothers to the hybrids, would have to learn to cope with the fact their former spouse long ago assumed them dead or missing, would not be able to ever contact them again as they existed in the witness protection program.

Some of the women were better off because they had been living with an abusive husband, so their new lives under a full pension and protection, were going to be far better, plus they were older and more mature and having experienced such unbelievable reality with the Wogar Grey Aliens, would be very careful of picking a mate should they decide to do so.

After they had been fishing for a while, Mr. Durant's assistant started handing out box lunches and nice cold-water bottles and sodas if people wanted them.

When it appeared, everyone had finished eating their box lunches and were losing interest in fishing, Mr. Durant let them continue fishing for about another half hour when he announced:

MR. DURANT

My assistant Pedro Sandervol will be taking all the
fresh caught trout back to the Dude Ranch for us in his
ATV, and the trout will be on the dinner menu tonight.

About the time the Dude Ranch guests were on their horses and continuing the trek over the circular route. As they were a hundred yards away from the pond, they heard behind them Pedro starting up the John Deere four-wheel ATV with a couple buckets full of trout.

Up and down a couple more hills with Boris sticking to the rear, filling up his camera's memory, they came across a beautiful meadow which was the turning point of which would lead them back to the Dude Ranch when suddenly, a very strange screeching sound appeared. Once again, an air force pilot was hot dogging the TR-3B and this time Boris was there to catch it all!

The Air Force pilot Dudley Brown said to himself aloud:

Dudley Brown

I bet that was Bob Watson. Bob is going to catch all
kinds of hell now.

VOICE OVER (DUDLEY
BROWN) THOUGHT

*The General is going to be extremely displeased and
will probably ground Bob Watson's ass and put him in
a desk job.*

Boris (a.k.a. Mr. Keeney) did not know if it was a UFO but the U.S. Air Force markings on it clearly exposed who the real owner was.

VOICE OVER
BORIS (a.k.a. Mr. Keeney)
THOUGHT
I need to make a mental note of the two Air Force pilots
possibly involved, Dudley Brown and Bob Watson.

The loud noise the TR-3B made while banking had an impact on the abductees that was not good for their mental conditions. The TR-3B's very strange noise brought back horror to half the abductees present the *Měngjiàng Yún-Rén* had worked hard to treat.

Sandra (a.k.a. *Wánměi De Huā*) probing the abductees' minds did the best she could to calm the abductees down, but this Airforce Pilot stunt was a disaster for those poor miserable souls.

Sandra allowed her horse to drift slowly, allowing all the others to pass her up as she sampled each of the abductees riding beside her, until she finally was parallel to Boris near the end of the group. At the present time, Boris (a.k.a. Mr. Keeney) was thinking about Tanya, his long-lost love.

Sandra could feel the intense emotions in Mr. Keeney and the desire to see Tanya once again. Sandra continued the probing and then started layering thoughts in Boris supplanting his own, that might one day prompt Boris to seek out Tanya.

SANDRA (a.k.a. *WÁNMĚI DE HUĀ*)
Drago are you able to identify the aircraft that buzzed
us and shook up the Abductees?

DRAGO
Give me a minute, the Intel Officer will analyze all the
probe data directly over you.

While Sandra was waiting for Drago's response, she started manipulating Gus via telepathic insertions. It did not take long for Gus to realize Sandra (a.k.a *Wánměi de Huā*) was communicating telepathically with him.

SANDRA (a.k.a. *WÁNMĚI DE HUĀ*)
(TELEPATHICALLY)
Gus, I want you to send my complaint to General
Brazile about that aircraft buzzing us. It had U.S. Air
Force markings on it.

Gus was then informed:

> SANDRA (a.k.a. *WÁNMĚI DE HUĀ*)
> (TELEPATHICALLY)
> You do not need to respond to me verbally, just think
> of your answers and replies and I will understand.

This was a strange circumstance for Gus, but it also meant a huge security breach because no secrets were safe from *Wánměi De Huā*. He responded in thought.

> GUS (THOUGHT)
> Alright, I understand.

About that time Drago reported back.

> DRAGO
> The aircraft that buzzed you is a *top-secret spy plane*
> designated TR-3B. It just landed at Area 51 on runway
> 32 at Homey Airport with airport identifier and
> location. (ICAO: KXTA, FAA LID: XTA).

> SANDRA (a.k.a. *WÁNMĚI DE HUĀ*)
> (TELEPATHICALLY)
> Drago, any other information?

> DRAGO
> Homey Airport is considered to be located in Rachel
> Nevada, a town nearby. The TR-3B buzzed you at 1:15
> P.M. and landed at KXTA Homey Airport at 1:35 P.M.
> The pilot's call sign used was *JACK RABBIT.*

Wánměi De Huā with a photographic memory and telepathic transceiver recall capability then passed on that information to Gus and further stated:

> SANDRA (a.k.a. *WÁNMĚI DE HUĀ*)
> (TELEPATHICALLY)
> Pass on to General Brazile if the pilot with call sign
> *Jack Rabbit* buzzes us again, he will disappear.

> GUS
> Sandra, with the information you gave me I assure
> you that you will no longer need to worry about *Jack
> Rabbit.*

Around 3:00 P.M. it was time to head back to the Dude Ranch which suddenly appeared over the next hill.

Mr. Durant rode up to almost the North side of the Dude Ranch driveway where he stopped and dismounted. He then instructed all the riders:

MR. DURANT
Please stay on your horses. I will come back to each of
you and grab the reins and tie your horse to the line of
horses, so they do not wander away, and I must chase
them down.

Boris who ended up in front because he wanted to be the first to dismount then requested:

BORIS (a.k.a. MR. KEENEY)
Mr. Durant, before the riders dismount their horses, I
would like to take a group picture if you do not mind.

MR. DURANT
Make it quick, these ponies already smell the grain
back home; they know Pedro is waiting for them.

BORIS (a.k.a. MR. KEENEY)
Not a problem.

Boris (a.k.a. Mr. Keeny) then took a couple steps sideways and up to the side of the driveway and took several pictures and got detailed photos of everyone.

Gus was wise enough to turn away realizing those pictures could end up in the wrong hands, but not quick enough to avoid one picture.

Even though it seemed rather harmless at the time, Gus usually adhered to *rule number one* of the spy businesses: *avoid getting your picture taken.*

VOICEOVERR (GUS)
THOUGHT.
The pictures just taken were probably harmless.

The people who operated the business around Alamo had typically been here a long time and knew everyone. He made the mental note to investigate Mr. Keeney's background when he got the chance.

Mr. Durant went down the line of horses taking the reins, tying them to the saddle of the horse ahead, which these ponies were all used to, and offering to help people down. Most of the riders refused help and climbed down on their own. Other than the UFO looking plane setting their psychology back some, possibly requiring future clinical treatment, the group as a whole felt good.

MR. DURANT

Any of you that will be here tomorrow, be sure and sign up for the horseback ride. We take a different route each day; therefore, you will see something different as we take another route.

GUS

Will you stop so riders can go fishing again?

MR. DURANT

Yes. We will stop for a while to go fishing for new Dude Ranch guests that join us.

GUS knew he already paid out a lot of money for the Abductees to go on this horse ride that he sensed helped many until the Airforce jet spoofed them, but felt he should give Mr. Durant a nice tip and handed him a wad of folded up Cash in Advance.

Vance observed that transaction and Sandra (a.k.a. *Wánměi De Huā*) suggested he also give a tip with some of that left over Casino money. He added to the amount.

As Mr. Durant led his team of horses away, he could not feel more pleased for a couple of reasons: it would be a fat paycheck for the day's work, because the fee was $35 per person and that would pay for a lot of hay for his horses and some tamales for him and his assistant, who was a dedicated soul.

Halfway home, Mr. Durrant figured the two men probably have him $40 in tips and pulled out the wad of cash and was utterly shocked they paid him more than $1000 in generous tips. He now had the taste of what *Cash in Advance* felt like.

The group then went back to their rooms after Boris (a.k.a. Mr. Keeney), announced:

BORIS (a.k.a. MR. KEENEY)

Ladies and gentlemen, please do not forget happy hour starts at the pool in about 30 minutes. Drinks come with the room charge.

Just around time happy hour began, Beverly and Crystal were in one their rooms, putting on bathing suits to take in a swim to cool off and participate in happy hour.

Beverly and Crystal needed to make sure Abductees didn't get too polluted and get themselves into trouble. But they also thought that several women who had not seen a human male for quite some time, might be emotionally vulnerable, not to just some of the Abductees but also the other Dude Ranch clientele whom they knew little about or what their intentions were.

BEVERLY

I hope that one Dude is not back this afternoon, he's
acting like he's in extreme heat.

CRYSTAL

Yea we need to keep our female abductees away from
him, that's for sure.

BEVERLY

I suppose we could always ask one of those Androids
for help.

CRYSTAL

They are always eyeballing everyone; how do you
know they're not wanting a little action themselves?

Beverly and Crystal, who lately went out for runs together in the morning, were in fantastic physical shape. Beverly would be considered a plain Jane with her body, but Crystal was Crystal. She always made men turn their heads and do a double take.

Beverly on numerous occasions following Crystal at a distance while on a mission, as a rear guard, chuckled several times when she saw women give their husbands a nice elbow to the rib section as they turned around and took a 2nd or 3rd look.

Today would be no different as they walked out to the pool area in their stunning attire. Several men were immediately transfixed on this bosom blonde, whose aqua blue marine eyes were not only a perfect tone, but they seemed to reflect light almost as good as a mirror.

Crystal's CIA screener must have known right off those eyes would get her far, and he was right.

Beverly had a beautiful face, nice hips, but it's clear she wasn't destined to be a dancer at a strip club because she was shallow chested.

Beverly would have been an ideal middle school teacher or a librarian, plus she usually had a book in her hand in her spare time. Teaming up with Crystal was great because Beverly liked reading and Crystal liked driving, and as they were heading to their hotels or to Groom Lake, there wasn't much need usually for her to do the typical shotgun routine as they would on an actual mission.

Because of her vast reading including subject matter concerning people, traditions, geography, and history, Beverly was essentially a walking encyclopedia and very well may have the highest IQ of anyone in the DD/P.

Mr. Keeney was at the bar today, mixing drinks for the customers and keeping them entertained with jokes he usually found in various sources, but it also served the useful purpose of watching the staff prepare for the barbecue that would start serving around 5:30 p.m. and end at 7:00 when the extinguished the fire and took no more new orders.

Aside from the lovely Fresh Trout guests would eat tonight, as well as Chicken, steaks, burgers and even hotdogs were available.

It was sad to see that in many cases the only food parents could get the kids to eat was the hot dogs.

Sandra (a.k.a. *Wánměi De Huā*) always stayed close to Vance and now wore what appeared to be a two-carat diamond ring, just large enough to show she was taken, but not so large that it would seem implausible.

The security detail was loosely watching, and their drinks never got emptied. They always ordered what Vance drank and if it looked like Vance needed a drink, instead of making him wait for the server to come around and pick up orders, one of the security detail guys simply walked over and exchanged their full glass with Vance's empty.

As the clientele at the Dude Ranch were settling back taking it all in stride, enjoying this evening, including abductees getting in a swimming pool, in some cases for the first time in 40 years.

***

<u>INT. DAY. AREA-51. GENERAL BRAZILE'S OFFICE.</u>

About the same time over at Groom Lake, Bob Watson was standing at attention in front of General Brazile.

GENERAL BRAZILE

What possessed you to pull that stunt today, *Jack Rabbit*?

General Brazile using Bob Watson's call sign , *Jack Rabbit* added sting to the statement.

MAJOR BOB WATSON

May I have permission to talk sir?
GENERAL BRAZILE
Go ahead.

MAJOR BOB WATSON
You see Dudley and I have this little rivalry, and you recall you put Susan off limits, neither of us was allowed near her for 3 months. Well, I decided to return the favor he recently did for me.

GENERAL BRAZILE
Do you realize Major Watson; I have the authority to ground your ass right now for pulling that stunt?

MAJOR BOB WATSON
It will never happen again sir.

GENERAL BRAZILE
I would never have known about this stunt had you not buzzed several CIA agents and a VIP who was on those horses.

MAJOR BOB WATSON
I am sorry sir.

GENERAL BRAZILE
The CIA agent whom I know well, called me and said he damn nearly got bucked off his appaloosa pony. Others could have been injured.

MAJOR BOB WATSON
I assure you it will not happen again sir.

GENERAL BRAZILE
Alright Major Watson, this is what I am going to do. I am going to enter a page 13 comment in your service record. Even though you are a hot shot test pilot whom we expect more out of you.

MAJOR BOB WATSON
Yes sir.

GENERAL BRAZILE

I promise you this: One more screwup while I am in command here, I will ship your ass off to Greenland and let you cool off a bit. Do I make myself clear?

MAJOR BOB WATSON

Yes sir.

GENERAL BRAZILE

Major Watson, even though the TR-3B has been recently photographed and our new friends the Russians have been asking about it is sending our state department this wonderful picture of the TR-3B you were flying and asking if it's ours or an alien craft, the fact is it's still a top-secret Q clearance program.

MAJOR BOB WATSON

Understand sir.

GENERAL BRAZILE

Do not and I repeat do not ever fly anywhere your test plan does not specify. And for the record, our flight plans never take the TR-3B over any populated area below 50,000 feet. Do you understand, Major?

MAJOR BOB WATSON

Yes sir.

GENERAL BRAZILE

Dismissed.

Major Watson gave a sharp air force style salute, did a regulation 180-degree turn, as good as the best military parade performers, then marched out of General Brazile's office, which door had automatically opened and closed by the infrared monitors.

COLONEL JONES

Almost sounded like you were a little hard on Major Watson.

GENERAL BRAZILE

Its better *Jack Rabbit* got his ass chewed by me than the DOD just before they kicked him out of the program and probably out of the Air Force.

COLONEL JONES

Speaking for the Major, he is one of our better test pilots.

GENERAL BRAZILE

He might be a great test pilot, but pulling a stunt like this shows a character flaw which means Major Watson is no longer in the top 10% as far as I am concerned.

COLONEL JONES

I am sure Major Watson will work hard on re-establishing his credibility.

GENERAL BRAZILE

That is great but for now Major Watson down in the bottom 10% and has a way to go to get out of the shits. I want you to ride his ass hard for a while. Push him to the point he may crack, then back off a bit, then do it all over again.

COLONEL JONES

Sir, I promise he will never cross you again.

Colonel Jones knew General Brazile was one of the most vindictive pricks in secret black projects, but he had the absolute toughest job, being a Marine Corp General heading up the Technical Director Job of an Office of Naval Intelligence funded program in control of a bunch of Air Force pilots and CIA types that are former Air Force and Navy pilots.

***

Dudley Brown, sat down at the bar stool in the shaded outdoor bar overlooking the heated swimming pool that was open 10 months out of the year. He was enjoying his time off and like many others was mysteriously shuttled off the base for 48 hours while they up postured for an event most were not cleared.

The strange looking aircraft Dudley saw on the horse ride had to be the new jet Bob Watson was test flying but would not comment on since it was compartmentalized, and Dudley had no need to know.

Dudley assumed it was Bob Watson (a.k.a. call sign Jack Rabbit) who was scheduled to fly today, otherwise he would be at the swimming pool with him *coking and joking*.

Dudley really liked the arrangement here, the rates were very reasonable; booze came with the room and on days like today, got some unusual recreation riding horses and fishing.

Boris, always wanting Dudley to say more than he should, kept his drinks coming as rapidly as Dudley could take them.

In the brief time that Boris got to know Dudley in the few trips he made to Alamo, Nevada's one and only famous Dude Ranch. Boris learned quickly to keep the lad Dudley lubricated with booze because eventually, he slipped over the line and said more than he should.

Boris, being an excellent Intel gatherer, knew how to paste together the macro picture on a few of those slip-ups.

The FSB (KGB) knew the money used for all that extra lubrication was money well spent because a day didn't go by that some Air Force pilot or technician would be acting like Mr. Smarty Pants and divulge minor details, so they seemed that went into a mosaic that eventually created an image that was easily recognizable.

The treatment and handling of the Air Force test pilots was extraordinarily dumb because as the same guys showed up around certain dates, the FSB knew they were test flying something, especially when the dummies wore their green fight suits with command insignias on them out to places like the filthy truckers' hotels or the fun spots like the Dude Ranch.

Seldom did a week go by where Boris was reviewing the surveillance video to collect the uniform insignias for the designation of the commands the pilots worked for.

Boris was talking to Dudley he thought:

VOICEOVER (MR. KEENEY
a.k.a. BORIS POTEMKIN)
THOUGHT
Americans are so stupid when it comes to security.
They are almost as dumb as us!

Boris thought Dudley was well lubricated enough to probe him.

BORIS (a.k.a. MR. KEENEY)
Hey Dudley, what do you think about that UFO that
buzzed us today?

DUDLEY
That was not a UFO.

BORIS (a.k.a. MR. KEENEY)
How would you know that, Dudley?

DUDLEY
I am not going to tell you how or why.

Boris smiled as he took the information down to memory, once again celebrating a personal victory over an unlikely recruit, who did not know he had just been recruited and gave up the information for free.

BORIS (a.k.a. MR. KEENEY)
Okay.

VOICEOVER (DUDLEY
BROWN) THOUGHT
I sure hope Bob gets an ass chewing for today's actions. I wonder if General Brazile knows about it?

Half of the abductees on the horse ride were not doing well.

SANDRA (a.k.a. *WÁNMĚI DE HUĀ*)
(TELEPATHICALLY)
What is in store for tomorrow, there are a couple of people back in their rooms now that started having a tough time that maybe could use a little sightseeing trip tomorrow to get their minds off it.

VOICE OVER (VANCE)
THOUGHT
(*WÁNMĚI DE HUĀ OBTAINS
TELEPATHICALLY*)
I was looking at a brochure in the lobby and there's a thing about a mine museum tour at a place called Tonopah, Nevada, that says they have a bus that can take at least 20 passengers and are willing to pick up in Las Vegas if there are enough members of the tour group.

SANDRA (a.k.a. *WÁNMĚI DE HUĀ*)
(TELEPATHICALLY)
That sounds fun.

VOICE OVER (VANCE) THOUGHT
(*WÁNMĚI DE HUÁ OBTAINS TELEPATHICALLY*)
We are a lot closer than Las Vegas; I am sure they would pick us up.

SANDRA (a.k.a. *WÁNMĚI DE HUÁ*)
(TELEPATHICALLY)
I would like to know.

VOICE OVER (VANCE) THOUGHT
(*WÁNMĚI DE HUÁ OBTAINS
TELEPATHICALLY*)
Let us call them.

Vance grabbed the I-phone Gus gave him to use to make sure he never got lost again, had a GPS tracker in it so they could always determine his whereabouts, or he was last known to be.

Vance called the number for *Tonopah Mine Museum Tour* reservations. After 2 rings:

TONOPAH
LOST MINE MUSEUM
EMPLOYEE
Hello, this is the Tonopah Lost Mine Museum. How can I help you?

VANCE
Hello, I'm calling about your *Tonopah Lost Mine Museum* brochure I'm looking at in the hotel, says you guys have a bus that will carry up to 20 if the tour group is large enough you would send the bus.

TONOPAH
LOST MINE MUSEUM
EMPLOYEE
That is correct.

VANCE
Can you pick us up at the Dude Ranch in Alamo Nevada?

TONOPAH
LOST MINE MUSEUM
EMPLOYEE
Yes, we have picked up groups at the Dude Ranch in
Alamo. How many are in your group?

VANCE
I'll call you back with a head count.

TONOPAH
LOST MINE MUSEUM
EMPLOYEE
Certainly.

Vance and Sandra (A.K.A. *Wánměi De Huā*) then went and conferred with Gus who said he would go along but follow with their SUVs for obvious reasons.

SANDRA (a.k.a. *WÁNMĚI DE HUĀ*)
Gus, here is a list of individuals and the reason I feel
they needed a day trip.

GUS
Alright we will help prepare them for the short trip.

The next day the Bus arrived and a dozen abductees, Vance and Sandra, plus her security agents all hopped on the bus which left the dude ranch around 8:30 a.m. and made its way to Tonopah.

The bus with one of the CIA SUVs following, retraced some of their path from Groom Lake as they passed through Ash Springs, Crystal Springs, then Rachel on the Extraterrestrial Highway.

<u>EXT. DAY. WARM SPRINGS, NEVADA. ROADSIDE BAR/RESTAURANT.</u>

45 minutes after passing Rachel they pulled into Warm Springs. That is when Vance asked the driver:

VANCE
Could you please stop so the group can get drinks, and
they could use the restroom if needed?

BUS DRIVER

Sure, no problem.

The place was just about abandoned, only a couple buildings still stood and about 100 Harleys were parked outside of one that had just been reopened after many years of neglect. Before anyone got off the bus, Gus came up to the passenger entrance. The driver had been watching the two SUVs follow them.

When Gus well dressed in a polo shirt and shorts and sneakers, banged on the door, Vance informed the driver:

VANCE
He is with us.

The driver opened the bus door.

GUS
Let me go inside first to make sure the place is ok.

The driver announced:

BUS DRIVER
I have never stopped here before, but I have heard
rumors there were a lot of drugs, booze, and bimbos
which might not be appropriate for the clientele on the
bus.

The bus driver thought most of the people on the bus appeared to be very meager people.

GUS
We'll check it out and make sure your passengers will
be safe.

Roger, who always liked a good scrape followed Gus in who went up to the self-serve counter checking out food and drinks they could get. Shortly upon arrival at the bar several bikers walked up behind them, looking for trouble.

BIKER
Hey punk, what do you want?

GUS
I am not sure, maybe a soda.

BIKER
Oh yea, I think I got something you want.

Gus realizing the Biker was going to sucker punch him let his natural reflexes take over resulting in a Gyakuzuki to the biker's solar plexus. About that time, the biker's two buddies decided they were going to join in.

Roger decided he would have to prevent the bikers from hurting Gus and gave a round house kick to one of the two which only accomplished getting another 5 bikers up to go after the dudes fighting their buddies.

Through the open door, the people on the bus could hear crashes and obviously something bad was not going on. Sandra, not feeling good about the situation with her acute hearing directed her four security men:

> SANDRA (a.k.a. *WÁNMĚI DE HUĀ*)
> Go in and see what's happening and protect Gus and
> Roger.

> VANCE
> I should go too.

> SANDRA (a.k.a. *WÁNMĚI DE HUĀ*)
> Please stay here Vance, my security detail can handle
> it easily.

At first it looked like something out of a science fiction movie, all four *Měngjiàng Yún-Rén security men* were off the bus in approximately one second and at the entrance to the greasy spoon in another 1.47 seconds as if in a time warp, where they appeared to shift down via quantum steps of space time and entered the establishment.

By then, Gus and Roger had both been hit hard and the security guys watched a group of men with tire irons and baseball bats approaching the two CIA men who had already taken down a dozen bikers.

Gus had felt the security guys were acting kind of funny when they wore identical clothes matching what Gus was wearing, but that was all part of their plan for distraction and dispersion.

Unbeknown to the bikers, if they thought Gus and Roger were a problem requiring a tire iron and baseball bats, they hadn't seen anything yet like they were about to witness.

Nor had the Bikers ever witnessed a security detail that was the toughest in the galaxy ever perform.

As the bikers were swinging the bats and the tire irons at the new arrivals, the *Měngjiàng Yún-Rén security detail* simply grabbed them in midflight then twisted the men around about 30 times like a tornado hit them and flung them at the next group approaching.

One of the bikers late to get up halfway intoxicated announced aloud:

INTOXICATED BIKER
I'll be damn never saw anything like that before!

When suddenly thirty Bikers were lying unconscious on the floor the rest decided they wanted no part of these guys.

Gus wiped off his bloody lip.

GUS

Roger looks like they don't have the flavor of soft drinks we wanted.

ROGER

What a shame, I was looking forward to a nice soft drink.

The two CIA men then turned and walked out and headed back to the SUV.

The *Měngjiàng Yún-Rén* security guards didn't budge, they stood there in a Zenkutsu-dachi stand with fists in the Don Shin position ready for anything.

Unlike humans with milli-second response and awareness with a 240-degree vision, the *Měngjiàng Yún-Rén* security detachment essentially had a full 360 because they could telepathically notify the others within one microsecond of observing a movement.

Just as if they were cued in the 4 security guards who had not broken a sweat, walked to the entrance and just like they were in a time speed up warp were at the bus in 1.4 seconds which was probably 30 yards away. For well over a couple minutes, none of the bikers stirred. Then slowly one at a time the moaning and groaning commenced.

It is safe to say several of the bikers that day gave up the notion of ever harassing strangers again.

The security detachment notified the *Měngjiàng Yún-Rén Royal Yacht:*

SECURITY DETACHMENT VIA
TELEPATHIC TRANSCEIVER

People associated with Vance are injured and need medical attention.

<u>INT. SPACE. *MĚNGJIÀNG YÚN-RÉN* ROYAL YACHT CONTROL ROOM.</u>

Drago immediately transported the science officer and his assistant who suddenly appeared next to Gus and Roger who were leaning over the car sweating and feeling aches.

<u>EXT. DAY. WARM SPRINGS, NEVADA. ROADSIDE BAR/RESTAURANT.</u>

MĚNGJIÀNG YÚN-RÉN
SCIENCE OFFICER
(TELEPATHICALLY)
What happened?

SANDRA (a.k.a. *WÁNMĚI DE HUĀ*)
(TELEPATHICALLY)
They took part in a terrestrial brawl that sometimes
occurs with low life's but that thanks to the security
detail they were basically ok, just bruised a bit.

Gus appeared mildly shocked to see a doctor and nurse suddenly materialized appearing out of nowhere, did not know what to say when the doctor announced:

MĚNGJIÀNG YÚN-RÉN
SCIENCE OFFICER
Let me look at that lip.

GUS
Why?

MĚNGJIÀNG YÚN-RÉN
SCIENCE OFFICER
I can treat it.

The *Měngjiàng Yún-Rén* science officer who was medically trained, reached in his bag and pulled out a silver bottle, then squeezed a little of the contents onto Gus' lip which immediately took away the pain.

The *Měngjiàng Yún-Rén* Science Officer then he took a probe out of his hand carry bag and used it to place a light blue beam on Gus' wound which could only be described as time lapsed photography watching the wound heal.

The doctor then swept the entire body with a blue beam and Gus suddenly announced:

GUS
I feel like a million bucks.

Roger also received similar treatment, and then suddenly without any warning the two-medical people dematerialized and disappeared.

The old biker who was partly inebriated watched most of what went on, sat down, and informed his friend:

OLD BIKER
I need another drink.

Moments later, the bus and two CIA SUVs pulled out back out onto Extra Terrestrial Highway and within 5 minutes 2 sheriffs who had been just been driving nearby and responded to a 911 call made by the owner who was afraid the bikers would trash the place and put him out of business again, pulled in, walked over to the bar and saw a bunch of bodies still lying on the floor.

SHERIFF TRAVIS
What the hell happened here?

BAR OWNER
Not sure exactly, but a bus and a couple SUVs pulled in and when the clean cuts on the bus walked in here, a few bikers decided to mess with them, and the next thing you know we had mayhem.

DEPUTY SHERIFF
CHESTER WEST
That must have been the bus and two cars, we just
passed Sheriff Travis.

SHERIFF TRAVIS
Yea we better go pull them over and get a statement,
some of these guys look banged up bad and there is
some damage to the joint.

The two Sheriffs hopped in the cop car, turned on the lights and the siren then headed out on the Extra-Terrestrial Highway. The Sheriff Travis drove 90 miles per hour as if he loved to do it didn't take long to catch up with the bus and SUVs.

The bus driver knew they probably wanted a chat, so he pulled over and stopped.

Both Roger and Gus put up their flashing lights at the same time and had the bus not stopped they would not have either.

Gus rolled down his window and when the Sheriff approached pulled out his U.S. Marshall's badge.

                    SHERIFF TRAVIS
                    You guys' Feds?

                    GUS
                    Yep.

                    SHERIFF TRAVIS
What the hell did you do back at that Warm Springs
dump?

                    GUS
As you can see by what we left behind, those bikers
decided to attack us. We would have cuffed them
all, but we only have one set piece here and decided
we'd just leave them '*as is*' since they probably regret
assaulting us now.

                    SHERIFF TRAVIS
If you don't mind, I want to call the Liaison Office and
I have their phone number to verify who you are.

                    GUS
                    Sure, not a problem.

Sheriff Travis dialed his U.S. Marshall's Liaison.

After a couple rings.

                    U.S. MARSHALL'S LIAISON
                    U.S. Marshall's Liaison how may I help you?

                    SHERIFF TRAVIS
Sheriff Travis from Tonopah Nevada. I got a U.S.
Marshall here, a Mr. Vandyke according to his badge;
need to verify it.

                    U.S. MARSHALL'S LIAISON
                    Where's Mr. Vandyke at?

                    SHERIFF TRAVIS
                    East of Tonopah, Nevada.

Looking at the GPS tracker U.S. Marshalls kept in their cars, the liaison man responded:

U.S. MARSHALLS LIAISON
Yep, that is our agent, is he having any problems?

SHERIFF TRAVIS
Oh no, he just took care of some scumbag bikers for
us, just wanted to confirm he is one of the good guys.

U.S. MARSHALLS LIAISON
Yes, he is one of our special agents.

SHERIFF TRAVIS
Ok thanks for your assistance.

U.S. MARSHALLS LIAISON
You are welcome, Sheriff Travis. Please call us back if
Mr. Vandyke needs any assistance.

Phone conversation ended.

SHERIFF TRAVIS
Looking at what you guys left behind at Warm Springs
looks like you are as good as they say you are, and I
don't see any bruises.

GUS
That is the way we like it.

SHERIFF TRAVIS
Stay safe Mr. Vandyke and if you are up in this neck
of the woods and run into assholes, you do not have to
do all the work yourselves. Here is one of my business
cards for the next time you run into trouble.

GUS
Thanks Sheriff Travis.

SHERIFF TRAVIS
You are welcome Mr. Vandyke.

The Sheriff gave the bus driver the thumbs up, then went back to his car and as soon
as the bus and 2 SUVs pulled out, the Sheriff's car turned around and headed back to
Warm Springs.

***

<u>EXT. DAY. TONOPAH NEVADA.</u>

The *Lost Mine Museum* tour bus finally pulled into Tonopah around 11:15 A.M. and the guests were getting a little hungry and thirsty.

> ROGER
> Too bad we could not get them a drink back at Warm
> Springs.

> CRYSTAL
> Well, you tried.

Crystal had a smile having seen some of the action from the passenger side window.

> ROGER
> I'd probably be dead now if those four aliens had not
> come in and rescued us.

> CRYSTAL
> Yes, it's good to have them on your side in a bar fight.

The bus turned off highway 6 onto US-95 heading north then a short distance pulled into a decent size parking area next to what the driver said was the best restaurant in town, with the SUVs right behind.

<u>EXT. DAY. TONOPAH, NEVADA *EXTRATERRESTRIAL GRILL*</u>

Everyone seemed to need to go to toilet to the same place at the same time and use the facilities as they shuffled into the *Extraterrestrial Grill*, right downtown Tonopah. One of the tallest buildings in town, a hotel, was within eyesight of where they were.

> GUS
> Tonopah is a larger town than I imagined.

> BEVERLY
> You never were here before?

> GUS
> No, I spent most of my time either in Las Vegas or at
> Groom Lake.

> BEVERLY
> Our guests seem to be responding positively to the trip.

GUS
The wide-open area is an enormous difference to being
trapped in the bowels of a ship for 10 or 20 years in a
helpless state not knowing you would ever be returned.

BEVERLY
I suppose so.

GUS
You have not been fully briefed, but I think you have
the right to know because of your involvement. All of
them owe Vance their lives.

BEVERLY
How so?

GUS
After these Abductees are sent on their way soon,
we'll be back at Area-51, and you will be read into the
SAP information then you will know why.

BEVERLY
Something serious?

GUS
I can't say much more until you are read in, but I know
you will be utterly shocked as to what transpired.

BEVERLY
Is this somehow related to Vance's abduction?

GUS
Yes.

BEVERLY
I kind of wish I had not asked that question.

***

The manager of the restaurant was all smiles.

EXTRATERRESTRIAL
GRILL MANAGER
It's a dream come true, big crowd all at once and they
ordered the entire menu.

*EXTRATERRESTRIAL
GRILL* COOK
Yea I'd like to have more days like this.

EXTRATERRESTRIAL GRILL MANAGER
Kind of weird the 4 guys ordered but didn't touch their
meals.

EXTRATERRESTRIAL GRILL COOK
They're all dressed exactly alike too, and like that
other man.

EXTRATERRESTRIAL GRILL MANAGER
Yea. It's kind of weird.

Vance still carrying far more money than he needed to pick up the tab. The manager
and the waitress were even more delighted with a $400 tip each.

Soon they all loaded up on the bus. The driver was very happy he got a nice meal out
of the deal, took them a short distance to the museum.

As expected, the guests did not stay in the mine shaft long and appeared they were
ready to head out.

BEVERLY
The guests didn't seem to like the mine shaft.

Gus
Being cooped up on a spaceship for 10 or 20 years
probably makes them not too fond of tight places.

On the way out of town, retracing their path on Highway 6, Gus saw the Sheriff's car
leading a couple of ambulances into Tonopah.

Gus waved at the Sheriff who then waved back giving each other a thumbs up.

GUS
I guess that means it is safe to go by the bikers' bar.

An interesting sight appeared as the bus and SUV caravan passed Warm Springs. Most
of the motorcycles were gone. By the time they got back to Alamo, it was slightly
passed the start of happy hour. Vance settled with the driver.

The fare for the bus and the museum visit was paid up in Tonopah, but one thing was
left, and that was a nice tip, which the driver got, as well as a box lunch to eat on the
way home.

***

<u>EXT. SPAC. WOGAR GREY *COLONY CLASS PLANETARY CONQUEST VESSEL* MOTHER SHIP CONTROL ROOM.</u>

By the time the Wogar Grey mother ship passed 50 AUs from the sun out into deep space heading for Tau Ceti star system about 11.887 light years away, Grak had just about convinced the Supreme Commander Zorgjeck:

GRAK

If we turn around now and enter the solar system and come within one AU (astronomical units) of Earth, we will tip the balance of power with the Tall Whites.

WOGAR GREY
SUPREME COMMANDER
ZORGJECK

I am not convinced we can defend ourselves from the *Měngjiàng Yún-Rén* ship.

GRAK

If we do not turn around now, your shield spaceships will be marooned forever in space.

WOGAR GREY
SUPREME COMMANDER
ZORGJECK
That is regrettable.

GRAK

But it is avoidable if we turn back now. Besides, the Tall Whites would never expect you to bring a ship the size of a small planet or moon into the solar system.

WOGAR GREY
SUPREME COMMANDER
ZORGJECK

What if they detect their Sun wobble from our gravity synthesizers?

TACTICAL OFFICER

According to theory, our gravity machines produce a toroidal shaped field and would only exert maybe 15% of its gravity towards the Sun, so any disturbance should be minimal.

WOGAR GREY
SUPREME COMMANDER
ZORGJECK
You do not think Earth scientists are not monitoring their sun and detect a resulting wobble?

TACTICAL OFFICER
Since Earth's sun does a certain amount of wobble already due to the complexities of the NINE planets orbiting, they may miss a subtle change.

WOGAR GREY
SUPREME COMMANDER
ZORGJECK
How would we approach Earth?
TACTICAL OFFICER
We should not make the same mistake the next time.

WOGAR GREY
SUPREME COMMANDER
ZORGJECK
What should we do differently this time?

TACTICAL OFFICER
You should not deploy the defense grid until the enemy ships get into the red defense zone.

WOGAR GREY
SUPREME COMMANDER
ZORGJECK
Such a plan is highly risky.

TACTICAL OFFICER
The defense grid will be able to help defend us, and we'll then be able to more effectively target the *Měngjiàng Yún-Rén* ship with our *Plasma Cannon.*

WOGAR GREY
SUPREME COMMANDER
ZORGJECK
Yes, but based on their extreme velocity, we will have to get a lucky shot to hit the Měngjiàng Yún-Rén ship.

TACTICAL OFFICER

I understand this is not the same as shooting inferior planets like Earth where all their craft move very slowly to galactic standards then it is like swatting a fly with a large hammer with the firepower of our *Plasma Cannon*.

WOGAR GREY
SUPREME COMMANDER
ZORGJECK
What do you have in mind?

TACTICAL OFFICER

If we can box them in, using our defense grid assets for one base and recall the planetary assault force to form the other sides of a reinforced U pattern we might be able to delay them enough to where our *Plasma Cannon* can get a solid hit on the Měngjiàng Yún-Rén ship.

WOGAR GREY
SUPREME COMMANDER
ZORGJECK

I think we would be better off continuing to the Tau Ceti star system, which has five planets ready to harvest and nowhere near a civilization or Alien involvement like on Earth.

GRAK

But it will take us several years to get there and we will have squandered such a huge treasure giving up on Earth.

WOGAR GREY
SUPREME COMMANDER
ZORGJECK
That's regrettable but seems necessary.

TACTICAL OFFICER

Please, turn this ship around. We should go back; the distress calls have already started.

GRAK

If we turn now, we can save 90% of the defense grid.

Wogar Grey Supreme Commander Zorgjeck was feeling the stress and knew he could not underestimate the possibility Grak, and the Tactical Officer might assassinate him if he did not give into their demands.

WOGAR GREY
SUPREME COMMANDER
ZORGJECK

Very well, helm, reverse your course. I will be in my
stateroom. I have a lot to think about.

Everyone now felt a strange sensation aboard as the centrifugal and galactic gravitational and cosmic waves as well as the steering mechanism for such a huge object caused complex gravity coefficients out of the generators and the rippling effect throughout the ship could be felt.

The *Wogar Grey Colony Class Planetary Conquest Vessel* speed was decreasing in the turn as drag was needed on one side otherwise it would take weeks to turn around. The type of maneuver they were making was rarely used because it was elevated risk. If completed successfully, the course reversal could be completed within an hour at this velocity.

Just like Grak predicted, the Earth People and Tall Whites had all concluded the Wogar (Grey's) mother ship was departing the solar boundaries and heading into deep space for another conquest somewhere else.

When the assault force started a tactical withdrawal in the direction of the last known *Wogar Grey Colony Class Planetary Conquest Vessel* position, the Tall Whites were getting increasingly convinced the threat was over.

That is everyone except Sandra (a.k.a. *Wánměi de Huā*) who would volunteer to help emergency ship parts and materials that would allow the Mars Base to restore their sensors just in case the Greys were not done.

***

<u>EXT. DAY. ALAMO NEVADA DUDE RANCH.</u>

During happy hour, Dudley got a drink and walked over to Crystal and started to initiate a conversation that quickly gave Crystal the impression Dudley was a hungry wolf on the prowl.

Having known Beverly for several years, they had facial expressions and little hand signs they worked out not only for professional behind enemy lines but also for moments like this.

Both women were amused this military guy whom they figured out was a test pilot was working so hard now to try to get to first base.

Beverly and Crystal were polite to Dudley, but he wasn't one to give up.

DUDLEY
How long are you gals going to be here?

BEVERLY
Probably a couple weeks.

DUDLEY
Is that so?

BEVERLY
Yep.

DUDLEY
I must go back to the air base tomorrow, maybe I'll
come back here next week; see you gals again.

BEVERLY
We will be here waiting for you.

Dudley got up and walked back to the bar.

DUDLEY
Give me another one pal.

MR. KEENEY (a.k.a. BORIS)
Strike out again Dudley?

DUDLEY
Does not hurt to try.

Boris informed Dudley as he poured another rum and coke:

MR. KEENEY (a.k.a. BORIS)
They are with those two dudes. You are wasting your
time.

DUDLEY
That's a shame, I wouldn't mind getting it on with the
blonde.

MR. KEENEY (a.k.a. BORIS)
I heard you tell the ladies you are leaving in the morning.

DUDLEY
Yep, heading back got a test flight tomorrow?

MR. KEENEY (a.k.a. BORIS)
Oh really, what do you test?

DUDLEY
It's just more experimental shit and it's on a damn slow cargo plane.

MR. KEENEY (a.k.a. BORIS)
Is this a new kind of plane?

DUDLEY
No, just a modification of an old flying museum.

MR. KEENEY (a.k.a. BORIS)
Interesting, well you know the Air Force is still flying our B-52s since the 1950s.

DUDLEY
That's true, and they were on the drawing board right after WW2 and were being built for the Korean War that ended just about time the plane was coming operational.

MR. KEENEY (a.k.a. BORIS)
Wow! did not know that.

DUDLEY
I have flown most of the big planes and being stuck on this prop job kind of irritates me.

MR. KEENEY (a.k.a. BORIS)
I see. Hopefully, they will give you a better plane you deserve to fly much better stuff.

DUDLEY
Thanks.

MR. KEENEY (a.k.a. BORIS)
Where are you flying this plane too?

DUDLEY
I'll fly down to Texas on a transport, then pick it up
and fly it back here for the test flights.

MR. KEENEY (a.k.a. BORIS)
Shouldn't you know how well it is working before
flying here? That is a long flight it seems.

DUDLEY
That is just straight flying; we will not take it through
its paces till we get it up here. I'm just ferrying the
plane up here for now.

Boris was really feeling good, he now had found another recruit, and he thought there
would be no action in Alamo Nevada!

The next day the FSB greatly increased the interest of the Russian Air Force in what
was going to happen at Groom Lake and would be poised to watch it with the next
Zenit 17 Satellite soon to be put in position over Area 51.

***

<u>INT. DAY. FSB HEADQUARTERS, ALEXANDER BORTNIKOV'S OFFICE SUITE</u>

The General Shoygu indicator was blinking on the intercom display panel, which Alexander Bortnikov pressed and about 30 seconds later, the receptionist opened the door.

ALEXANDER BORTNIKOV'S
RECEPTIONIST
General Alexi Shoygu is here sir.

ALEXANDER BORTNIKOV
Thank you.

Alexander Bortnikov's receptionist held the door open as General Shoygu walked in and took his expected sofa position left of Alexander Bortnikov's desk.

Just like on a typical meeting between the two men, the administrative aide soon arrived with a bottle of Belver Bears Belvedere Vodka on a sparkling shinning silver tray and Chinelli Swarovski Regina Vodka Glasses then poured two glasses and served the two men, then left the room.

ALEXANDER BORTNIKOV
Thanks for coming over right away, to discuss this
American C-130 transport aircraft.

C-130 CARGO PLANE

GENERAL ALEXI SHOYGU
We will have a Zenit 17 Satellite in position and keep
a look out for prop driven craft flying around Area-51.

The only time they usually come in there is delivering freight, but the C17s and C5s and C-141s are usually the big jets that go there.

ALEXANDER BORTNIKOV
What is your take on them test flying an old 50-year-old C-130 design prop powered plane?

GENERAL ALEXI SHOYGU
We can assume they modified the propulsion system.

ALEXANDER BORTNIKOV
Why would they do that to an old plane?

GENERAL ALEXI SHOYGU
With 20/20 hindsight, they have already modified the propulsion system for the C-130/KC-130 a dozen times already.

ALEXANDER BORTNIKOV
What more could they possibly achieve?

GENERAL ALEXI SHOYGU
Aircraft such as the C-130 based Specter Gun Ships could benefit by more speed and horsepower. It could be a fuel saving move.

radical departure for that old cargo plane?

GENERAL ALEXI SHOYGU
Ok, this might sound kind of wild and many people in the Air Force would laugh at me for even suggesting it, but since you asked I'll comment.

ALEXANDER BORTNIKOV
I know you are a man with a lot of common sense. I highly value your input. Tell me.

GENERAL ALEXI SHOYGU
If the Americans have succeeded in building an anti-gravity machine which we know they have been working on, it could have a revolutionary impact.

ALEXANDER BORTNIKOV
Very interesting Toast to you.

Alexander Bortnikov suddenly had a big smile as he lifted his glass and took the entire contents in one swallow.

GENERAL ALEXI SHOYGU
Spasibo i vashemu khoroshemu zdorov'yu. (thank you and to your good health).

Then general Shoygu swallowed the contents of his Chinelli Swarovski Regina Vodka glass that seemed to liberate his tongue a bit for the continuation of the discussion.

ALEXANDER BORTNIKOV
General Shoygu, we must start thinking creatively, or we get caught setting on our thumbs which means we must constantly play catchup.

GENERAL ALEXI SHOYGU
Alexander, I agree completely. Our country needs to start being initiative-taking instead of reactive all the time.

ALEXANDER BORTNIKOV
Ok General Shoygu us think about this, how much antigravity do you think they could install on a cargo plane like the C-130?

GENERAL ALEXI SHOYGU
It is interesting that you asked me this because this is precisely what I asked our top engineers just recently when we started looking into the TR-3B after we got those GRU reports. Our scientists think the Americans have achieved 89% anti-gravity.

ALEXANDER BORTNIKOV
Is that based on empirical evidence?

GENERAL ALEXI SHOYGU
No, we have an incredibly beautiful GRU agent who has seduced one of their top scientists who was the principal researcher on the anti-gravity device.

ALEXANDER BORTNIKOV
Ok General, thinking about the impact of anti-gravity, what would be the significant impact on aircraft design?

GENERAL ALEXI SHOYGU
It would be huge, totally revolutionize air transportation.

ALEXANDER BORTNIKOV
What would be the major structural changes to aircraft?

GENERAL ALEXI SHOYGU
My engineers suggested the wings could be shorter and much thinner and turn into simply flight control surfaces since the body itself would produce enough lift to keep flying.

ALEXANDER BORTNIKOV
How thin?

GENERAL ALEXI SHOYGU
A few inches thick.

ALEXANDER BORTNIKOV
Really?

GENERAL ALEXI SHOYGU
Aircraft designers could triple the amount of fuel a plane could carry with the weight reduction.

ALEXANDER BORTNIKOV
How about speed?

GENERAL ALEXI SHOYGU
Thinner wings mean much faster performance.

ALEXANDER BORTNIKOV
This could be huge!

GENERAL ALEXI SHOYGU
Yes, now start thinking what happens when they put
that capability on B52s, B2s, C17s, V-22s and more
importantly Helicopters.

Alexander Bortnikov pressed the button, and the administrative aide came back in, and
she knew as he nodded, she was to pour a refill set of Belver Bears Belvedere Vodka.
Then another toast:

ALEXANDER BORTNIKOV
Na zdorovye!

GENERAL ALEXI SHOYGU
Na zdorovye!

ALEXANDER BORTNIKOV
Let us talk helicopters, explain that angle to me.

GENERAL ALEXI SHOYGU
Certainly.

ALEXANDER BORTNIKOV
I cannot see the helicopter angle.

GENERAL ALEXI SHOYGU
Just like the airplane wing can be thinner, the rotor
on the helicopter can be thinner and less horsepower
required lifting it.

ALEXANDER BORTNIKOV
Interesting.

GENERAL ALEXI SHOYGU
The biggest advantage would be stealth.

ALEXANDER BORTNIKOV
Why is that?

GENERAL ALEXI SHOYGU
Helicopters are very noisy, and easy to hear from
the ground, that's what hurt the Americans during

the Vietnam War and our Army in Afghanistan. If a helicopter had 89% anti-gravity, it could deliver its troops with 89% less noise.

ALEXANDER BORTNIKOV
Speed improvements too, no doubt.

GENERAL ALEXI SHOYGU
This is probably a Lockheed plan to compete with Boeing with the V22.

ALEXANDER BORTNIKOV
Please explain.

GENERAL ALEXI SHOYGU
With an AGD (anti-gravity device) installed the V22 would no longer be needed because the KC-130 and C-130 could probably take the role of most V22 missions.

ALEXANDER BORTNIKOV
C-130 can carry far more cargo as well. But the V22 can take off vertically.

GENERAL ALEXI SHOYGU
Yes, but in doing so they burn up so much fuel they cut the range down significantly, forcing them to deploy closer to the battlefield.

ALEXANDER BORTNIKOV
What is the big picture we need to think about C-130 modifications?

GENERAL ALEXI SHOYGU
With the AGD, and a new wing design, the C-130 / KC-130 could go 1000 miles further with a combat load with a cruising speed perhaps 100 knots faster. That would make the V22 instantly obsolete.

ALEXANDER BORTNIKOV
One more question, General, what would be the runway requirements of a C-130 with an AGD?

GENERAL ALEXI SHOYGU
Football field length possibly, depending on the load.

ALEXANDER BORTNIKOV
Amazing.

GENERAL ALEXI SHOYGU
As soon as we get the Zenit 17 Satellite moved over
Area-51 in the next day or so, we should be able to
catch the Americans doing test flights.

Because of operational security Alexander Bortnikov could not tell General Shoygu they had already started recruiting the actual test pilot for the C-130.

Then Alexander Bortnikov pressed the button one more time and the administrative aid Svetlana came in and refilled their glasses with more Belver Bears Belvedere Vodka. Then one last toast.

ALEXANDER BORTNIKOV
Na zdorovye!

GENERAL ALEXI SHOYGU
Na zdorovye!

***

<u>INT. DAY. ALAMO NEVADA DUDE RANCH</u>

The witness protection program experts were systematically coming in and interviewing *Abductees* staying at the Alamo Nevada Dude Ranch.

In a few cases, Gus or Roger transported Abductees to Las Vegas where the probability of relocation was high. The abductees were there to get their new identity as well as several days of learning and practicing their cover stories.

The elderly who had been abducted 50 or 60 years ago were the easiest to deal with because there would not likely be anyone looking for them.

The elderly Abductees were immediately transported to a high-rise building in Florida that was built to provide safe existence for former CIA and Mob people who worked under cover for DD/P through many years.

By the end of the first week only eleven of the original abductees were left which allowed Sandra (a.k.a. *Wánměi de Huā*) to work on them and improve them to the point they would be functionally aware and fit in on the witness protection program.

The American government mental health experts were amazed at the rate of recovery but none of them knew it was all due to Sandra's (a.k.a. *Wánměi de Huā*) unique telepathic abilities.

The consensus was the Abductees being out in the country setting and being exposed to the vast openness experienced by road trips and the horse rides, was the catalyst that brought them back, but in later years trying to treat Post Traumatic Stress Disorder (PTSD) in other abductees, it didn't work, and they were never able to figure out why.

***

Boris received his new instructions from Moscow. They were going to send expert help to improve the recruitment of the C-130 pilot, Dudley Brown.

The new *guest* Rich was quiet, kept to himself, but when Dudley Brown returned, the *guest* was seen more frequently at the bar and talking with Dudley, who amazingly had similar interests. The interviewer had an easy time figuring out what made Dudley tick.

Dudley, a highly intelligent and dynamic person, had broad interests and sports was one of them. Amazingly Rich and Dudley seemed to like the same teams!

Dudley was an open book, and his Achilles Heel was women.

As Rich sucked Dudley increasingly into the recruitment he eventually took him down to Vegas and took him around where he introduced him to some call girls that Dudley had no idea were working girls.

Since Dudley was only interested in one-night stands, he never bothered to attempt contact them again. Rich realized that was a very inefficient way since Dudley was often coming and going and simply could not go to Las Vegas since he often had to fly the next day.

That's when Rich started bringing the call girls to the Dude Ranch. He had to pay these women a lot of money to get them to travel so far and not ask any questions.

Call girls can be patriotic. Their means of an income have nothing to do with their loyalties and Rich was aware of that fact. So, Rich had to very carefully play the role that Dudley was his very good buddy, and Rich liked the Dude Ranch to get the hell away from Las Vegas and sin city as much as possible and breathe clean air and feel the open country.

Rich being a master controller knew better than to bring the same call girl out more than 2 or 3 times. In many cases after the 3rd trip the call girl didn't want to come back anyway because their business in Vegas was so much easier to do and it was straight forward.

Then one day, the *shit hit the fan*, literally. Of all the people that show up working for Rich was Tanya!

At first Boris is in utter shock, then he was somewhat bitter and got mad especially when he had surveillance equipment in the special room he gave at discount to Dudley, he almost cried watching Dudley having his way with Tanya, who was screwed out of all that money he thought he had arranged for her, forced her to resort to this kind of behavior to make ends meet.

VOICEOVER (BORIS)
THOUGHT

Jimmy let me down and my Lawyer the FSB (KGB)
operative had also not only screwed me over, but also
forced Tanya into becoming a call girl to survive when
she should have been living like a well-kept woman.

The problem Boris now faced is he had no way of finding Tanya, but he wanted to reach out to her. He agonized every day since he first saw her again. And due to his wonderful plastic surgery and hair transplants, she had no idea who he was.

Boris knew that, just like the other call girls, Tanya probably would not be coming back. Then an amazing thing happened, Boris was doing the bookkeeping for the dude ranch which was one of those evil necessities of keeping out of the interest of the Internal Revenue Service was transferring the billing of the telephone bills to the accounting information he would be handing over to the CPA, then it hit him right between his eyes.

VOICEOVER (BORIS)
THOUGHT

Phone calls leaving Rich's room to Vegas, and based
on the days and number of them it seemed to match the
volume of call girls coming in.

It had been three days since Tanya had been at the Dude Ranch; so, Boris went back three or four days and copied all the phone charges to Rich's room and then took them to his own personal room where in his spare time he called them with his room-phone.

Its evident Rich was avoiding using his I-phone calling the call girls to avoid NSA and police intercepts and was using the room phone.

Boris was now slowly sinking into a state of mind where he did not care any longer. Even though Boris' FSB masters had instructed him to never attempt contacting Tanya something was driving him. Sandra's (a.k.a. *Wánměi de Huā*) telepathic thought insertions now guided Boris' activity.

That mental stimulus to violate stipulations Alexander Bortnikov no longer mattered. If Boris had to defect to the West, he would.

VOICEOVER (BORIS)
THOUGHT
*The CIA is always looking for guys like me to be
double agents.*

One by one, he called them. Even though he had plastic surgery and hair implants, his voice was the same. And after numerous conversations with Tanya, he knew she would remember his voice.

Boris dialed the first number, at the other end an answer.

STRANGER.
Hello.

The voice did not match Tanya's voice which had unique qualities and some ethnicity to it, so Boris hung up.

Boris dialed the next number and got a New Yorker accent. No good.

Again, Boston accent.

Again, Atlanta southern peach.

Again, African American.

Again, Hispanic.

Again, plain Jane with a Texas accent.

Just when Boris was about to give up all hope the voice sounded familiar.

TANYA
Hello.

VOICEOVERE (BORIS) THOUGHT
It is Tanya!

At first, Boris was so stunned and scared he could not talk.

TANYA
Hello?

Then click and dial tone.

Tanya looked at the caller's I.D. and quickly determined it came from the Alamo Nevada Dude Ranch.

Tanya's Phone rang again, same caller I.D.

TANYA
Rich?

This time Boris found the bravery to follow through.

BORIS (a.k.a MR. KEENEY, a.k.a. JACK)
No, this is Jack.

Suddenly it was quiet, and Jack thought he could hear someone crying at the other end.

BORIS (a.k.a MR. KEENEY, a.k.a. JACK)
Tanya?

After he heard her sucking air up her nose, possibly wiping her tears as well, Tanya finally spoke.

TANYA
I thought you were dead.

BORIS (a.k.a MR. KEENEY, a.k.a. JACK)
In a way, I was.

TANYA
Your lawyer said you died.

BORIS (a.k.a MR. KEENEY, a.k.a. JACK)
He was told to do that.
TANYA
Why did you tell him to tell me you were dead?

BORIS (a.k.a MR. KEENEY, a.k.a. JACK)
It was out of my control; I wasn't given any options.

TANYA
Are you organized crime or something?

BORIS (a.k.a MR. KEENEY, a.k.a. JACK)
Probably worse than that.

TANYA
Why are you calling me now?

BORIS (a.k.a MR. KEENEY, a.k.a. JACK)
I missed you terribly.

TANYA
I see you are up in Alamo at the Dude Ranch; it shows
up on the caller I.D.

BORIS (a.k.a MR. KEENEY, a.k.a. JACK)
Yes, I own this place.

TANYA
Jack, where do we go from here?

BORIS (a.k.a MR. KEENEY, a.k.a. JACK)
I'm going to get out of this business one of these days
soon and when I do I want you to go away with me.

TANYA
Where do you have in mind?

BORIS (a.k.a MR. KEENEY, a.k.a. JACK)
I am not sure it's going to be difficult, but if you're
willing to take some risk with me, we can go
somewhere and restart our lives.

TANYA
What about my kids?

BORIS (a.k.a MR. KEENEY, a.k.a. JACK)
They can come along too.

TANYA
I will think about it, you left me alone too long and
things were not working out well for me.

BORIS (a.k.a MR. KEENEY, a.k.a. JACK)
It will be difficult for me to see you, but I want you to
know I've changed my appearance. I have hair now
and my face is different.

TANYA
What do you look like now?

> BORIS (a.k.a MR. KEENEY, a.k.a. JACK)
> Remember when you were at the Dude Ranch a few
> days ago, and you were sitting at the bar talking with
> Dudley?

> TANYA
> Oh yes.

> BORIS (a.k.a MR. KEENEY, a.k.a. JACK)
> I was the bartender that served your drinks.

> TANYA
> You did not say much.

> BORIS (a.k.a MR. KEENEY, a.k.a. JACK)
> I was in a state of shock.

> TANYA
> When can we meet again?

> BORIS (a.k.a MR. KEENEY, a.k.a. JACK)
> I've had a few trips to Vegas lately; I'll try to get down
> there to see you again.

> TANYA
> Okay, Mr. Bartender, I will be waiting for you.

***

<u>EXT. DAY. AREA-51. IN THE COCKPIT OF C-130.</u>

It seemed like a normal day at Area 51, and since they were flying a cargo plane that seemed rather innocuous, the security was not nearly as tight as when the TR-3B was tested and soon the ATR-4, (Advanced Tactical Reconnaissance) designed to fly out into space from a runway like TR-3B.

> DUDLEY
> Okay Ralph, are you ready to try this?

> RALPH
> Ready when you are.

The center console of the C-130 had a round dial about the diameter of a coffee cup. It was the encoder wheel for the anti-gravity device. The flight plan today was to do a series of takeoffs with various levels of anti-gravity.

RALPH
AG (Antigravity Gravity) set for 20%.

DUDLEY
Roger that, here we go.

Dudley pushed the throttles forward with flaps deployed. Normally, when the C-130 rolled down the runway, it used about a mile before it went airborne with no antigravity applied.

The plane was unloaded which would also get it airborne quicker but by the time they hit the 2500-foot mark they were going up, but to their surprise their vertical velocity was amazing.

The modified C-130 then got up to around 1000 feet, the flaps were raised slightly, and they circled the airfield then came back around, getting in position to do a normal landing.

RALPH
Taking the AG down to 0%.

DUDLEY
Roger that.

RALPH
Flaps fully deployed.
The plane then came down, made a normal landing and Dudley taxied the plane back to the starting point to the next flight where they would again take off runway 14E which was the shorter runway than 14W also pointing towards the north is seven miles long.

Despite what many people think, the extra-long runway gives test pilots of experimental aircraft the ability to land if there was a propulsion problem or if there is a mechanical defect such as one of the two engines on an SR-71 flameout.

The C-130 pulled back out on 14E.

RALPH
Adjusting the AG to 30%.

DUDLEY
Roger that.

On board flight controllers recorded all the cockpit conversations and the plane was all wired with telemetry devices. Only normal crew members and two Lockheed guys who were network and communications experts were there mainly to ensure the entire electronics suite worked properly and to take any corrective actions required.

All the brains were on the ground in processing rooms set up for the test and evaluation.

To maintain absolute secrecy, orders were to minimize talk with the control tower that could be picked up by police scanners or other devices. Telemetry was also strictly controlled for similar measures.

Area-51 leadership was concerned about the Russians or Chinese finding out what they were doing. The C-130 cargo plane communicated and transmitted telemetry via lasers to several aiming points. The laser device sending the information was programmed by the servers in the computer racks on board.

The data rate was high, and all aircraft performance got shipped down via these laser pathways in segments depending on where the plane was in its flight. Only a few gaps existed, mainly while the plane maneuvered as it went around the box pattern which best describes the flight path (box with rounded corners.)

When Dudley received permission to proceed, the permission was sent via the laser to the plane which lighted an indicator on the dashboard again, done to avoid surveillance by the Russian satellites or sensitive receivers the FBI had found in hotels over at Tonopah spying on nearby Area 52.

Dudley shoved the throttle forward and at about 2000 feet the plane left the ground, Dudley made the comment which was recorded.

DUDLEY
I can feel greater uplift.

This was really getting exciting now, Dudley had never experienced anything like it before and he had flown a lot of large aircraft.

The 40% AG settings got them airborne at 1500 feet. Fifty percent AG allowed them to leave the surface at 1200 feet. At 60% AG, the C-130 went airborne at 900 feet.

DUDLEY
I felt a much stronger sensation of lifting.

At 70% AG, airborne at 600 feet. Now Dudley was starting to feel strange as the implications were now just starting to set in. At 80% AG, air born at 400 feet. Finally, at 89% AG, they went Airborne at 300 feet, the length of a football field.

Then came landing tests. They were far more interesting than takeoff because there was no need to increase throttle with full flaps, establishing a much shorter required runway.

The next day was to be straight level flight at cruise speed. The trim of the airplane became strange, and the angle of attack significantly altered as if the center of gravity was too.

Flying the eight-mile-long racetrack simply by flying around the long runway, the fuel consumption printouts being recorded were far different than a normal C-130 aircraft. The gas mileage spiked upward enough to get the Lockheed engineers jumping up and doing *high-5s*.

Dudley announced in the most inquisitive manner.

DUDLEY

Based on fuel consumption, I bet the Boeing V22 boys
are not going to be happy when they find out what they
are up against.

RALPH
There is a downside to all this.

DUDLEY
Such as?

RALPH

We will have no excuse to land in Hawaii on our way
to Guam to take on more fuel. Say goodbye to the
grass skirts.

The next day, Dudley was back at the Dude Ranch, jovial, that he just helped make history. After Boris lubricated him up a bit, even without mentioning the type of aircraft or the anti-gravity device installed, confirmed what the GRU was reporting to General Shoygu that Zenit 17 Satellite observations showed that based on the position of the plane's shadow from the angle of the sun, the C-130 was taking off and landing in much shorter distances.

When they did the straight and level flights, the next day they flew that circuit around runway 14W all day long. The reduction in fuel consumption was unprecedented and caused the Russian aerospace scientists many long hours of calculations to figure out how antigravity would impact lift and other factors.

***

<u>INT. DAY. MOSCOW RUSSIA. LUBYANKA BUILDING. FSB (KGB) HEADQUARTERS. ALEXANDER BORTNIKOV'S OFFICE.</u>

With a good shot of Belver Bears Belvedere Vodka the toast.

ALEXANDER BORTNIKOV
Na zdorovye!

GENERAL ALEXI SHOYGU
Na zdorovye!

ALEXANDER BORTNIKOV

General Shoygu, it's all coming together, your theory is coming close to being proved.

GENERAL ALEXI SHOYGU
It sure seems that way.

ALEXANDER BORTNIKOV

We now know they got something, that's causing the effects that you suggest matches what theoretical anti-gravity would have on the aircraft.

GENERAL ALEXI SHOYGU

Thanks to frequency convolution and time lapsed satellite images of the propellers, we have established that on some of their test flights, engine RPMs were significantly lower than expected.

ALEXANDER BORTNIKOV
That is quite remarkable.
GENERAL ALEXI SHOYGU

What we discovered to be highly serious was the C-130 landing at 60 mph within 300 feet.

ALEXANDER BORTNIKOV
The implications must be huge.

GENERAL ALEXI SHOYGU

When we start observing American refits CH53 transport helicopters with anti-gravity machines, then we'll really have problems.

ALEXANDER BORTNIKOV
Why is that General?

GENERAL ALEXI SHOYGU
It's a cheap way to extend their combat range more than 1000 miles.

ALEXANDER BORTNIKOV
Can you imagine American Marine assaults launched 1000 miles further away?

GENERAL ALEXI SHOYGU
How would you know what direction they're coming from?

ALEXANDER BORTNIKOV
Our satellites will see them.

GENERAL ALEXI SHOYGU
Not if they're all destroyed. If we ever have a conflict each country will blind the other.

ALEXANDER BORTNIKOV
What fears me the most is, the Americans deciding to modify their helicopters in the same way.

GENERAL ALEXI SHOYGU
That would tip the balance in the battlefield because American helicopters could then carry much heavier loads and travel more indirectly towards insertion points.

ALEXANDER BORTNIKOV
Hopefully they will just stick to the C-130s.

GENERAL ALEXI SHOYGU
We need to get some performance data from our Agent in Area 51.

ALEXANDER BORTNIKOV
It's obvious I need to send in another agent to assist recruiting the C-130 pilot, from the reports I'm getting we are getting close to where we can start blackmailing him. Therefore, I'm sending in another agent that will help with that final phase.

GENERAL ALEXI SHOYGU
What do you expect that spy to obtain?

ALEXANDER BORTNIKOV
After she gets done with the pilot, we'll have complete control over him and get actual C-130 antigravity performance data and technical specifications.

GENERAL ALEXI SHOYGU
Perhaps the spy can obtain technical manuals and pictures of the anti-gravity device if one exists.

ALEXANDER BORTNIKOV
Based on these C-130 observations and the TR-3B, how could one not exist?

***

Pictures of the individuals described in this section are to be shown during the voiceover. Anastasiya Pushkin's picture will be who is selected to perform the role in the movie.

VOICEOVER.
The Russian FSB (KGB) spy Anastasiya Pushkin was an incredibly attractive blonde with beautiful blue eyes, perfect breasts and hips.

Anastasiya Pushkin was another deep cover FSB mole who was inserted in America as a college student and was educated at Harvard where she graduated from Harvard with double master's in communications and political science.

The U.S. government lost track of Anastasiya; thus, she just stayed since she had obtained a green card while working on her master's and was firmly planted and finished going through the naturalization process a half dozen years after arriving to make her stay permanent.

Since the FSB wanted time to indoctrinate Anastasiya more deeply, Anastasiya was brought back to Russia where she earned her PhD in communications at Saratov University, as well as training her in advanced studies of seduction.

The thought of applying Anastasiya FSB talents towards the seduction of men somehow enticed her to apply herself more.

Because of Anastasiya's superior intellect and drive, she wanted to be the next Margarita Konenkova who had worked for the NKVD (as formerly know before the creation of the KGB) and considered Soviet Union's top spy ever who did among other things, seduce Albert Einstein whom the Russians thought had the secrets to America's new atomic bomb.

Margarita Konenkova

As part of her training in the handicraft of using her natural talents, Anastasiya read Einstein's nine love letters that Konenkova's family recently sold at auction in New York at Sotheby's auction house that were eventually given to the University of Jerusalem and are part of all of Einstein's letters between the two.

Albert Einstein

In Anastasiya's analysis of photocopies of the letters she knew the extent of Einstein's seduction, but what most of the rest of the world didn't know, Anastasiya also read numerous Konenkova detailed status reports in the KGB archives provided to her.

Anastasiya naturally drew the conclusion men always thought with the little head while they tried to reason with their big head.

Margarita Konenkova married the noted Russian sculptor Sergei Konenkova, who created the bronze bust of Einstein at the Institute for Advanced Study at Princeton which gave her frequent access to the world's top scientists assigned there during WW2.

Sergei Konenkova

Since most of those scientists explored the universe with their "little head" almost as often as their "big head," the job of Margarita Konenkova (code name Lukas) was to influence Oppenheimer and other prominent American scientists whom through her husband's work she frequently met at Princeton Center for Advanced Study.

J. Robert Oppenheimer

Robert Oppenheimer admitted such in a book Special Tasks,' [The Memoirs of the Soviet Spy Master, Pavel Sudoplatov and His Son, Anatoly].

Pavel Sudoplatov

Anastasiya didn't take long to figure out how Margarita Konenkova influenced the scientists.

Margarita Konenkova succeeded in introducing Einstein to the Soviet Vice Consul, Pavel Mikhailov, who further manipulated Einstein, and Einstein refers to him in his love letters to Margarita Konenkova.

What really enthralled Anastasiya was NKVD files that described the secret relationships Margarita Konenkova had with Sergei Rachmaninoff.

Sergei Rachmaninoff

Margarita. Konenkova was also known to have had an affair with the famous emigre artist Boris Chaliapin. Boris Chaliapin an artist for Time Magazine when he illustrated more than 400 covers including Queen Elizibeth, Jawaharlal Nehru, Richard Nixon, and many other prominent people

When Margarita Konenkova was finally recalled to Moscow in 1945 because the OSS was on to her, she received the highest Soviet awards.

In the special section of the KGB archives that gives official notice to the top Russian spies in a beautiful display, Margarita Konenkova is on top of Lavrenti Beria.

Lavrenti Beria

Margarita Konenkova is also recognized as more important to Soviet Espionage than Elizabeth Bentley; Rudolf Abel (who was traded for Gary Powers, U2 SPY PLANE PILOT); Harry Hopkins, Alger Hiss, Kim Philby from British MI5; Anthony Blunt (Part of the infamous Cambridge Five group of British spies) who also served in MI5.

[Queen Elizabeth II rescinded her cousin Blunt's knighthood in 1979].

Elizabeth Bentley

Others on the official notices at lower levels below Margarita Konenkova accolades include Morris and Lona Cohen an American couple who ran the Rosenberg's before the Cohen's fled to England to avoid arrest later swapped in a spy trade; and Ethel and Julius Rosenberg who died for Mother Russia; along with Richard Sorge, who was considered the top spy in WW2, who was executed by the Japanese in 1944.

Richard Sorge

Note: Richard Sorge provided Stalin with the crucial INTEL that Japan had no intentions of attacking Russia, so that Stalin was able to move 18 divisions to the Moscow defense and counterattack that otherwise were being wasted in the far east via the Trans-Siberian Railway. Sorge also provided Stalin with the exact time and date of the start of Operation Barbarossa, Hitler's invasion of Russia. Even though Stalin was forewarned by 6 months, he refused to believe Sorge's reports.

Margarita Konenkova's KGB archives citation reads:

Margarita Konenkova is the very most successful spy Russia has ever produced.

That is until now that Anastasiya Pushkin aimed to surpass Margarita Konenkova and all the rest.

***

<u>**EXT. DAY. ALAMO NEVADA DUDE RANCH.**</u>

Sitting at water's edge kicking her feet in the swimming pool slowly, making obvious gestures to *hot dog* Dudley, the sting was set. In due time, Dudley approached and invited Muriel Barber (a.k.a. Anastasiya Pushkin), to the Bar for a drink and some conversation.

DUDLEY
Hey, what brings you to a Dude Ranch of all places?

MURIEL BARBER
(a.k.a. ANASTASIYA PUSHKIN)
I like horses, and I plan on going on the Horse Ride
tomorrow.

Dudley made the mental note to sign up for another horse ride.

DUDLEY
Nice, so am I.

The suntan lotion seemed to add a texture to Muriel Barber's (a.k.a. Anastasiya Pushkin) skin that along with the French perfume *Chaud de Chienne* designed to stimulate the male libido, had increasingly expected results.

Muriel Barber (a.k.a. Anastasiya Pushkin) had scientifically tested the French *Chaud de Chienne* perfume and proved on several small headed guinea pigs.

MURIEL BARBER
(a.k.a. ANASTASIYA PUSHKIN)
Are you enjoying your vacation?

DUDLEY
I'm not on vacation; I just have a couple days off
between my next flight.

MURIEL BARBER
(a.k.a. ANASTASIYA PUSHKIN)
Are you a pilot?

DUDLEY
Yes, I fly out of Nellis Air Force Base

Technically Dudley's statement was correct but used as every pilot's cover story because under no circumstance were they ever allowed to divulge they worked at Area-51.

MURIEL BARBER
(a.k.a. ANASTASIYA PUSHKIN)
What kind of planes do you fly?

DUDLEY
Mainly I fly multi-engine transport planes.

MURIEL BARBER
(a.k.a. ANASTASIYA PUSHKIN)
I see, that must be fun.

DUDLEY
It gets boring at times. How about yourself?

MURIEL BARBER
(a.k.a. ANASTASIYA PUSHKIN)
I'm an investment banker, specializing in international
investments.

DUDLEY
Wow, I bet you make a lot of money?

MURIEL BARBER
(a.k.a. ANASTASIYA PUSHKIN)
More than I need.

Muriel smiled.

After they polished of their second drink, Dudley suggested:

DUDLEY
Why don't we get in the water and cool off a bit?

MURIEL BARBER
(a.k.a. ANASTASIYA PUSHKIN)
Sure, why not?

After they swam around a bit, Muriel swam to the side of the pool with her right arm
out over the cement on the side of the pool, as Dudley swam up to her and copied her
posture with his left arm on the cement only a few inches away. Muriel could tell back
at the bar her stimulation was working; her seduction was as great as any beautiful
flower is to a bee searching for the splendid nectar.

DUDLEY
You're a beautiful lady.

MURIEL BARBER
(a.k.a. ANASTASIYA PUSHKIN)
You're a handsome guy.

DUDLEY
I like you.

MURIEL BARBER
(a.k.a. ANASTASIYA PUSHKIN)
I like you as well.

Dudley put his right hand on her side, then slid it down to her buttocks and caressed them. Muriel smiled. Dudley, whose passions were now intensely elevated, pulled Muriel closer and attempted to kiss her.

Anastasiya pushed away from Dudley and said to herself:

VOICEOVER MURIEL BARBER
(a.k.a. ANASTASIYA PUSHKIN)
THOUGHT
*I'm going to make Dudley work real hard for it. Desire
is always a much stronger weapon than gratification.*

Allowing Dudley to pull Anastasiya closer briefly was only for the purpose of determining the extent to which Dudley was aroused, which Anastasiya now confirmed, and she could see the agony of desire in Dudley's eyes.

MURIEL BARBER
(a.k.a. ANASTASIYA PUSHKIN)
I would like to get out of the pool now, if you don't
mind.

Muriel then with incredible strength for a woman hoisted herself up on the cement edge of the pool and in the process purposely bent over so that Dudley would see more of the exposed part of her breasts that barely hid the area that she knew would eventually cause Dudley to lose control and fall into the nice spider web she was weaving for him.

Muriel walked back over to the bar and asked Boris who was bartending again.

MURIEL BARBER
(a.k.a. ANASTASIYA PUSHKIN)
Do you have any good expensive vodka?

> MR. KEENEY (a.k.a. BORIS POTEMKIN)
> Sure, I have some Gray Goose, but it's not out here;
> we normally do not give it out during happy hour, only
> served during dinner as guests order it.

Muriel had a slightly disappointed look on her face.

> MR. KEENEY (a.k.a. BORIS POTEMKIN)
> But for you, I will go get a nice glass of it for you; be
> right back.

Moments later Boris returned with two beautiful Baccarat Abysse Vodka Glasses filled with Gray Goose vodka.

Muriel noticed the second glass

> MURIEL BARBER
> (A.K.A. ANASTASIYA PUSHKIN)
> Are you going to toast me?

> MR. KEENEY (a.k.a. BORIS POTEMKIN)
> No, I poured a glass of Vodka for your friend.

Boris then handed Muriel the glass of Vodka, and then as Dudley sat down, handed one to Dudley.

MURIEL BARBER
(A.K.A. ANASTASIYA PUSHKIN)
Cheers.

Muriel swallowed the entire contents in one drink.

VOICEOVER (ANASTASIYA)
THOUGHT
Dudley and I will soon we shall be saying:
Na zdorovye!
Na zdorovye!

The timeline was shrinking for when Muriel knew she would have Dudley in her spell.

MURIEL BARBER
(a.k.a. ANASTASIYA PUSHKIN)
That barbecue smells good.
The fumes permeated the pool area signaling *time for dinner*.

As per plan Boris had drugged Dudley, with a sophisticated Russian invention that would soon have Dudley sleeping like a kitten. The combination of the great food and that last drink made Dudley extremely sleepy, then he suddenly announced:

DUDLEY
I'm going to my room to change, getting kind of cold.

As the sun was reaching the horizon, Dudley went to his room and was not seen for the rest of the evening as he climbed into his bed after getting out of his swim trunks and had just put on his underwear.

VOICEOVER (DUDLEY)
THOUGHT
I'll just take a little cat nap.

Dudley slept until 8:00 the next morning when the phone rang. It was Boris (Mr. Keeney).

MR. KEENEY (a.k.a. BORIS POTEMKIN)
Hello, Dudley?

DUDLEY
Yes, what do you need?

Dudley said then looked at his watch and said to himself:

VOICEOVER (DUDLEY) THOUGHT
Oh my god, slept all night.

MR. KEENEY (a.k.a. BORIS POTEMKIN)
Dudley, you indicated yesterday evening you wanted
to sign up for the trail ride, just wanted to confirm you
wanted to go.

Remembering suddenly Muriel saying what she did about coming to the Dude Ranch
to ride horses, responded.

DUDLEY
Yea sure, sign me up.

MR. KEENEY (a.k.a. BORIS POTEMKIN)
We'll be leaving in about 30 minutes.
DUDLEY
Thanks, I'll be there.

Dudley then hung up.

Just like Dudley's last trail ride, the cavalcade got underway with Boris's assistants
shoveling the dropping the horses left behind cussing them.

Dudley assumed the horses knew exactly where the grain was as they approached the
fishing area and dismounted as he experienced the previous week. This time instead of
having all those strange people that acted like they hadn't been anywhere in 20 years;
they had some new enticements including Muriel who gave Dudley several smiles.

Muriel's long sleeve white shirt with the cuffs rolled up was the perfect match for her
blue jeans that seemed to conform to her body almost like sweatpants. Dudley rode
close to Muriel and when they dismounted, he helped tie up her horse and became very
helpful with the fishing pole.

DUDLEY
Ever go fishing before?

MURIEL BARBER
(a.k.a. ANASTASIYA PUSHKIN)
Never.

DUDLEY
Okay, I'll help you. Hold my fishing poll while I put
your bait on and show you how to cast your line.

Soon Dudley and Muriel's lines were in the pond and the bobbers bobbing up and down as the trout were nibbling in the large fat worms.

As Mr. Durant, their guide, figured it would not take long for the well-stocked pond to give some of these new *anglers* the time of their life.

And just as expected, Muriel's line jerked hard, and she shrieked.

MURIEL BARBER
(a.k.a. ANASTASIYA PUSHKIN)
I think I caught one! What do I do now?

Dudley sat his fishing pole on the ground. Dudley reached out for Muriel's rig.

DUDLEY
Here let me help you.

In the matter of moments, he had his arms wrapped around her showing and helping her manipulate the fishing pole to bring in the catch. Anastasiya's (a.k.a. Muriel Barber) *Chaud de Chienne* perfume was not only intoxicating, the *Chaud de Chienne* perfume had Dudley's hormones raging.

The *Chaud de Chienne* perfume Anastasiya's (a.k.a. Muriel Barber) applied that morning in preparation for today's events, was loaded with pheromones that had been purposely elevated by KGB chemists to help produce the desired effect.

Anastasiya's (a.k.a. Muriel Barber)knew the trigger point was coming soon, but she had to hold off and make Dudley work extra hard for it. It was just like a cat playing with a mouse before it killed and ate the mouse.

After the Dude Ranch guests finished their box lunches and drinks and showed no more interest in fishing, Mr. Mr. Durant knew it was time to get back on the horses and continue the ride. The horses were well fed and watered at the pond and were in a reasonable mood.

As Dudley had experienced in the past, the horses knew the path well that took them along the expected route.

Just as the horse ride group swung to the North Dudley looked out and saw a C-130 propeller driven Air Force cargo aircraft flying off at the distance. He knew what it was and who was flying today.

Today instead of flying the course around runway 14L at Groom Lake, the plane was flying over to Nellis Air Force Base. Since it was just a dumb slow cargo plane, it would not stick out since it was only doing level straight line flying as to get more miles in quicker to help baseline the fuel consumption rate at the various AG settings on the plane.

The test pilot he knew had taken to the air around 06:00 a.m. this morning and it was already after lunch around 1:00 p.m. almost and the plane was going after one more of its big elongated 50-mile loops, to get the ultimate figures on fuel savings with the Artificial gravity turned on at 89%, max amount.

Dudley could not help but follow the plane's progress as it continued flying that 50-mile racetrack that was already allowing the C-130 to shatter all fuel performance records of any aircraft in the Air Force, with one exception: TR-3B.

Muriel continued to pour on the charm throughout the rest of the horse ride and by the time they got back to the Dude ranch and turned all the horses over to Mr. Durant, Dudley was beyond ready.

MURIEL BARBER
(a.k.a. ANASTASIYA PUSHKIN)
Shall we go for a swim and cool off?

Dudley appeared eager and ready.

DUDLEY
I would love to.

Before long, they were back at the pool; first taking in a couple drinks then got into the water together and swam around in small strokes essentially treading water.

Muriel went to the side of the pool and Dudley followed her.

Just as Anastasiya (a.k.a. Muriel Barber) knew, Dudley would put his arm around her waist, and she smiled in the most seductive manner which led to Dudley pulling her closer.

She could feel he was ready and did the unexpected, wrapped her legs around him allowing her to feel his strong erection for verification. Dudley's physical response gave a clear and compelling signal that Anastasiya (a.k.a. Muriel Barber) drove his endorphins into stratospheric highs.

Unexpectedly Anastasiya (a.k.a. Muriel Barber) released Dudley then pulled herself to the concrete. , then walked over to the bar stool that had her towel and personal effects.

MURIEL BARBER
(a.k.a. ANASTASIYA PUSHKIN)
Mr. Keeney, any chances I can get another glass of that
Gray Goose Vodka?

Boris, who Muriel (a.k.a. Anastasiya Pushkin) had brought into her planning, knew that he was being sent for the drink to provide her and Dudley a moment of privacy so she could close the deal.

Boris poured the Gray Goose vodka into the nice Baccarat Abysse Vodka Glasses and waited for Muriel (a.k.a. Anastasiya Pushkin) signal she would give by placing her hand on Dudley's shoulder.

MURIEL BARBER
(a.k.a. ANASTASIYA PUSHKIN)
Dudley let's have another drink then go to your room
for a while and get to know each other better.

DUDLEY
I would like to get to know you better Muriel.

Muriel placed her hand on his shoulder, which now stimulated Dudley beyond his emotional boundaries as he felt the fabric of his self-control slowly slipping away.

Boris left and came back momentarily and served the expensive Vodka which the two downed, then Dudley and Muriel (a.k.a. Anastasiya Pushkin) went to his room where as a professional seductress Muriel (a.k.a. Anastasiya Pushkin) flicked her bikini top off exposing her breasts, and her bikini bottoms that exposed the essence of a woman that Dudley normally would never get a chance to have in his lifetime, had he not been *recruited*.

Muriel who knew precisely how to handle amateurs and guided Dudley to the bed and told him *lay down*, then she proceeded to assist removal of his swim trunks and proceeded to further elevate his blood pressure that seemed to diminish his awareness as she further amplified his hormones to an explosive result.

The drugs that Boris placed in Dudley's Vodka were now just starting to take effect and Dudley now slipped in a semi-comatose state. When Muriel thought Dudley was fully unconscious, she slapped him a couple times to attempt arousing him to make sure. Dudley didn't budge.

Muriel (a.k.a. Anastasiya Pushkin walked over to the phone and called Boris who had a telephone ready at the pool bar.

MURIEL BARBER
(a.k.a. ANASTASIYA PUSHKIN)
He's ready.

The Russians are the experts in blackmail, nobody does it better. That's why they selected Guy Burgess, Kim Philby, Donald Maclean, and Anthony Blunt to train and deploy them as spies, because they were known homosexuals. Homosexuals make far better blackmail conduits than straight people because in that era the stigma of being exposed as a homosexual was a powerful inducement in homosexual honeypot schemes.

Dudley had been given a room on the side of the Dude Ranch main building complex where people could come to his door from the south side without much exposure to people in the pool since the stairway semi hid Dudley's room entrance from most of the pool area.

A tall black male with a Hispanic woman appearing as Dude Ranch house keepers often not completely done cleaning the rooms till just around happy hour time had the cleaning cart in front of Dudley's room and let themselves in with a master key. The Hispanic woman carried in what appeared to be cleaning supplies; and so, did the tall black male.

The woman Guadalupe Hernandez was a professional photographer who often worked for a particular private detective, along with Leroy Johnson former distinguished college football star who ended up hooked on drugs and failed NFL urinalysis after abnormal behavior during a game.

Leroy had recently become an inspiring porn actor. As a porn actor, he was paid more while filming with homosexuals. The private detective who hired them simply said:

PRIVATE DETECTIVE
The man in the room being set up by the beautiful
woman in the bikini, was a wealthy guy going through
a nasty divorce in Virginia that still has alimony and
wants pictures available for court.

As Leroy with Guadalupe's assistance positioned Dudley in a variety of positions, Leroy made it look good as they shot up several rolls of film that showed Dudley in compromised positions with what appeared to be a black male homosexual prostitute or Gay friend.

Dudley, being completely out of it never came to until the next morning, and then smiled as he remembered the exquisite experience he had with Muriel. He had to (shit, shower, and shave S/S/S in military vernacular) and get ready to head over to Groom Lake.

Dudley, now somewhat romantically attached to Muriel, knew which room she was in and went and knocked at her door. It was around 8:00 a.m. so the horses were out front to pick up their riders for the day's ride.

Dudley walked into the Dude Ranch Lobby and approached the front desk.

DUDLEY
Mr. Keeney, have you seen Muriel Barber this morning?

MR. KEENEY (a.k.a. Boris Potemkin)
Yes, she checked out an hour ago.

DUDLEY
Really?

MR. KEENEY (a.k.a. Boris Potemkin)
Yep.

DUDLEY
Did she say where she was going?

MR. KEENEY (a.k.a. Boris Potemkin)
Sure, back to Boston.

DUDLEY
Damn, any way you can give me her contact information?

MR. KEENEY (a.k.a. Boris Potemkin)
Absolutely not, this is a Dude Ranch, remember.

Dudley limped like a kid that just lost his pet dog to his room, got all his belongings, did the automated checkout like he always did, then walked out to the parking lot located on the side of the complex.

Just as he was about to get in his Jeep, a Limo pulled up. The window rolled down, and the black man wearing an expensive suit in the back said, excuse me sir this is for you, handed the package to Dudley with his name Dudley Brown written on the package, then pulled away and then headed down the highway south, most likely on its way back to Vegas.

Dudley opened the package, there was a small note from Muriel.

MURIEL BARBER
(a.k.a. ANASTASIYA PUSHKIN)
MESSAGE
Dudley, I'm sorry I could not be there when you woke up but here are some pictures and some instructions for you to follow if you don't want these pictures delivered to General Brazile's office in Area 51.

A contact phone number that is automatically routed number to Bern Switzerland you are required to contact within 48 hours, or the pictures will be delivered via special courier to General Brazile.

Dudley felt the noose slowly tightening around his neck. As he looked at the pictures that anyone would believe he was a willing participant in, including photo etching smiles on his face overlaid on top of the contrived pictures.

No one would ever be able to prove they were not legitimate. His security clearance and his career were now in jeopardy.

It was plainly stated what they wanted, pictures, technical manuals and anything related to the anti-gravity machine on his C-130 cargo plane.

Dudley knew he was now in the deep shits of an espionage case, a classic recruitment and manipulation. Muriel or whoever she was knew her business well.

The note also said all the paper including the pictures was heavily impregnated with a phosphor substance and burned quickly if Dudley wanted to get rid of the pictures right away, and the envelope had a half dozen old style matches that could be lit on just about anything.

Fearing that he might be searched driving on to the base he found a camp site along the Extraterrestrial Highway that was vacant with nobody around.

Dudley, put the papers except for the phone number he put in his wallet into the barbecue then lit it. Just like the instructions promised, the highly impregnated phosphor on all the pictures and the instructions burned very efficiently and hot, and in the span of 1 minute nothing was left but ashes.

Dudley then got into his Jeep then drove on Highway 6 to the Northwest Entrance to the base and drove down to the BOQ where he would change into his flight suit and get picked up in a couple hours by service personnel that would take him near hanger 27 where the plane awaited him.

Today's testing involved how much they could load on the plane. The limit wasn't the tires, the limit was stress on the wings and the plane's turbo props could not operate with 100% throttles for the entire flight to keep airborne; otherwise, the turbo props would simply fail after a short lifespan.

Hence it was expected that if they overloaded the plane, with the help of the antigravity device the plane could handle if it as a normal load and not overwork the turbo props.

Today they would use runway 14L, the 7-mile-long runway.

Having compiled the flight characteristics with an empty plane, they loaded it with 150% of maximum takeoff weight. The plane took off at 89% maximum antigravity and the length of runway required was measured on several back-to-back test flights.

The C-130 aircraft was now flown with 80, 70, 60, and 50% AG settings and in each occurrence had successful takeoffs and landings. Since they were looking at the high-end loading, there was no need to go down to the lower AG settings.

The following day Dudley finally had the nerve to call the number that ultimately got forwarded to Switzerland via some elaborate fancy KGB tricks to avoid logging the real destination of the phone call.

Dudley was instructed not to call the number ever again and directed to check in at the Dude Ranch on his next break period which the Russians had developed a crude calendar suggested would be in a few days.

A cell phone would be delivered to him via UPS to use for the next time, then was to be discarded and would be replaced by another phone at that time.

Upon receipt of the phone, it said press the "PRESS ME" AP then instructed, *Hold the phone up for a selfie picture* which Dudley did. A moment later the phone rang.

Dudley
Hello.

MURIEL BARBER
(a.k.a. ANASTASIYA PUSHKIN)
Hello Dudley.

It was clearly Muriel's voice at the other end.

DUDLEY
It's you, I should have suspected.

ANASTASIYA PUSHKIN
(a.k.a. MURIEL BARBER)
Well Dudley I don't like your attitude and first thing
first, never mess with a bitch that owns you.

Dudley didn't know what to say, he was decimated and almost ready to cry.

ANASTASIYA PUSHKIN
(a.k.a. MURIEL BARBER)
What did you bring for me?

DUDLEY
Nothing, I haven't decided exactly what I'm going to
do.

ANASTASIYA PUSHKIN
(a.k.a. MURIEL BARBER)
Ok, Dudley, let me make this straight. We got assets
in place in high places that can simply walk in and
place your portfolio on General Brazile's desk when
we direct him to do so.

DUDLEY
Is that so?

ANASTASIYA PUSHKIN
(a.k.a. MURIEL BARBER)
Yes, and I seduced his dumb ass too.

DUDLEY
So, what makes you think you can force me to spy?
Maybe I'll just go turn myself in.

ANASTASIYA PUSHKIN
(a.k.a. MURIEL BARBER)
Ok Dudley if you do that, then you better get signed
up in the witness protection program, because if you
double cross me I'll make sure you die a very painful
slow death.

DUDLEY
We will see.

ANASTASIYA PUSHKIN
(a.k.a. MURIEL BARBER)
Leroy says he wants to have fun with you the next time
you are awake.

DUDLEY
You are a sick bitch.

ANASTASIYA PUSHKIN
(a.k.a. MURIEL BARBER)
Bitch yes, sick no, so now I'm going to reiterate my

shopping list and if you're a good boy, I might even let
you have some sweets.

DUDLEY
I would never touch you now.

ANASTASIYA PUSHKIN
(a.k.a. MURIEL BARBER)
When you deliver those plans of the antigravity
machine to me, you'll want to taste the splendid nectar,
and I'll certainly want to give it to you. It's all part of
doing business.

DUDLEY
I'm not even sure I can get access to any plans.

ANASTASIYA PUSHKIN
(a.k.a. MURIEL BARBER)
Don't keep momma waiting too long, she wants her
milk, MEOW!

Click, then no dial tone was heard.

***

The *Měngjiàng Yún-Rén* Fleet was due in less than a week. However, as the Greys slowly pulled out heading towards Pluto presumably going after their mother ship, the Tall Whites were now displaying the probability they too may pull out at any time and head for the War Zone as planned.

Wánměi De Huā pleaded with them to stay, but about three days prior to *Měngjiàng Yún-Rén* Fleet arrival, the Wogar Greys were all, but gone, last remnants of their assault fleet were drifting at forty AUs just past Pluto now heading in the direction of the Tau Ceti star system, which was the apparent direction last seen of the Wogar Grey mother ship.

Not much longer than that the Tall Whites made the decision to proceed to the war zone, leaving earth behind and delivering the desperately needed men and materials there.

As the long range Wogar Grey *Colony Class Planetary Conquest* mother ship approached closer to the forty AU limit, she had recovered 75% of her assault force and 90% of her defense grid. With more expected to be found by search parties.

Zorgjeck felt that soon he would be almost right where he started minus a small attrition from recent operations.

But what was different this time is, the plan and the Wogar Grey *Colony Class Planetary Conquest Vessel* was now back in the solar system and had not been detected by prying eyes, nor would it until they sprang the trap on the *Měngjiàng Yún-Rén* spaceship that had interfered and single handedly wrecked their plans and their timetable.

<u>INT. DAY. ALAMO NEVADA DUDE RANCH.</u>

Wánměi De Huā worried the Tall Whites' departure would unravel the tenuous defensive posture, informed Vance.

> *WÁNMĚI DE HUĀ*
> I'm going back to my Royal Yacht to confer with
> Drago about our military situation here. I want you to
> stay here where you will be safe with the bodyguards
> who are ordered not to let you out of their sight.

> VANCE
> Sure, don't take too long.

Wánměi De Huā flapped her green wings, flew over to Vance where she momentarily did a brief fusion, dissolving into his body and leaving him with a euphoric like state. Wánměi De Huā then rematerialized in her green *Měngjiàng Yún-Rén* elf like form and suddenly dematerialized completely as she transported to the Royal Yacht now configured as a Command Ship on high alert.

***

<u>INT. DAY. ALAMO NEVADA DUDE RANCH.</u>

Boris was at the Bar serving happy hour drinks to Vance, Gus, Roger, and Beverly, while Crystal was doing laps in the pool working on her shape. The phone rang. It was Tanya.

> TANYA
> Hello.

> MR. KEENEY
> (a.k.a. BORIS POTEMKIN, a.k.a. JACK)
> Howdy.

> TANYA
> Did you decide when you can get down to Vegas?

MR. KEENEY
(a.k.a. BORIS POTEMKIN, a.k.a. JACK)
Looks like it could be tomorrow.

TANYA
Great I'm looking forward to seeing you.

MR. KEENEY
(a.k.a. BORIS POTEMKIN, a.k.a. JACK)
Where are you staying now?

TANYA
Promise you will not laugh?

MR. KEENEY
(a.k.a. BORIS POTEMKIN, a.k.a. JACK)
Sure.

TANYA
Circus-Circus.

MR. KEENEY
(a.k.a. BORIS POTEMKIN, a.k.a. JACK)
Why the hell are you staying there? That place has
turned into a family style vacation place.

TANYA
My mom brought my kids by for a couple of days,
thought they could have fun here.

MR. KEENEY
(a.k.a. BORIS POTEMKIN, a.k.a. JACK)
Oh, I see.

TANYA
And don't worry honey, they are leaving tomorrow
morning; she's flying them back to Phoenix so we can
have some privacy.

Boris had been put on the alert that he would be delivering a package the next day.

It was do or die time for Dudley. If he didn't deliver something useful tomorrow he would be outed and then probably kicked out of the military when the mole in General Brazile's office delivered the promised package showing Dudley in the compromised positions with what would appear as his black gay lover.

Anastasiya Pushkin (aka Muriel Barber) now performing her roles down in Acapulco Mexico would use Rich, the other FSB agent who had been recruiting Dudley as the pickup man.

Rich would get the materials from Dudley over at Tonopah, then drive them down to Alamo Nevada, and place them in one of the guest rooms.

Boris would then access the guest room, pick up the package and drive it down to McCarran airport where a private air firm had a jet heading to Acapulco Mexico where Anastasiya would take the package and analyze its contents then carry it to Moscow.

*** *** ***

INT. SPACE. *COLONY CLASS PLANETARY CONQUEST VESSEL BRIEFING ROOM.*

In the briefing room of the Grey *Colony Class Planetary Conquest Vessel*, Supreme Commander Zorgjeck informed the pilots of the strike force and the defense grid that would be deployed.

The three-dimensional briefing room like an auditorium capable of holding several thousand pilots had multiple level in a circular layout of seating to allow maximum closeness of the briefers to the pilots

WOGAR GREY
SUPREME COMMANDER
ZORGJECK
All the details have been encoded into the simulation
software holograph shows all the timing and the new
guidelines of how ship captains are to deploy.

Supreme Commander Zorgjeck in his dress uniform with a white cape and sword and Commanders top hat gave the impression of power and deliberateness.

Nobody in the room knew who designed Supreme Commander Zorgjeck's hat, but it looked like a Russian Fleet Admirals hat.

WOGAR GREY
SUPREME COMMANDER
ZORGJECK
Our *Colony Class Planetary Conquest Vessel* is speeding up now and in about an hour we will reach the trip wire of 20 AUs from the sun. The assault force will be launched at that time as Earth view will be obscured by Jupiter in the direction we are traveling.

Supreme Commander Zorgjeck delayed speaking for a couple minutes while the simulation holograph displayed the Wogar Grey Alien Fleet maneuvering IAW the plan. Supreme Commander Zorgjeck nodded at the Tactical Officer who was standing beside him to give out the grizzly details.

WOGAR GREY
SUPREME COMMANDER
ZORGJECK
Our *Colony Class Planetary Conquest Vessel will* slide into Jupiter's orbit where it would easily be misidentified by astronomers for a while.

WOGAR GREY
SUPREME COMMANDER
ZORGJECK
We will have several hours of this ruse until Earth astronomers start trying to figure out which moon is showing since its appearance did not match the expected orbits of the existing moons.

The Gray's briefing room crowded with pilots and commanders of the multitudes of ships could see the automated plan simulation on the large holographic display in front, with a beautiful voice of a female Grey explaining details as it manifested in simulation on the screen. Then the Tactical Officer continued.

TACTICAL OFFICER
Assault Force flight plans are loaded and verified in all assault force ship's computational suites, that will get your ships into position at exact timing. This is just an indoctrination of what to expect as you will get to that P-Point in autopilot.

WOGAR GREY
SUPREME COMMANDER

ZORGJECK

However, once in place, due to the dynamics of the battlefield, each commander might have to take personal initiative as scenarios arise that were not predicted.

TACTICAL OFFICER

Should the Alien *Měngjiàng Yún-Rén* ship show itself for battle, the plan is to box in the ship to slow it down so we can hit it with our *Colony Class Planetary Conquest Vessel Plasma Cannon.*

WOGAR GREY
SUPREME COMMANDER
ZORGJECK

The extreme fire power that *Plasma Cannon* can exert devastating destruction on slow moving targets not capable of sustaining extreme speeds like the *Měngjiàng Yún-Rén* exhibited.

TACTICAL OFFICER

Without the help of a high powerful telescope, the *Colony Class Planetary Conquest Vessel* will appear most likely as Calisto, one of Jupiter's moons.

WOGAR GREY
SUPREME COMMANDER
ZORGJECK

We do not know if any of the Martian sensors have been brought back online. However, it is felt by INTEL the Mars sensors cannot be repaired in time for our attack.

TACTICAL OFFICER

Therefore, we should be able to slip in without being observed and wipe out the Moon's defense grid and sensors.

WOGAR GREY
SUPREME COMMANDER
ZORGJECK

After we finish wiping out Earth's Moon sensors, we should be poised to attack Earth and apply staggering losses so that the Earth forces immediately surrender their planet.

TACTICAL OFFICER
Based on no reaction coming from Earth yet as our *Colony Class Planetary Conquest Vessel* continues its slow orbit from behind Jupiter staying out of view from the Earth we will be operating with complete surprise and INTEL has no indication the *Měngjiàng Yún-Rén* ship is around nearby.

SUPREME COMMANDER ZORGJECK
Ship's Captains, that concludes your briefing. Good luck and man your ships and prepare for immediate deployment.

As soon as the *Colony Class Planetary Conquest Vessel* slowly eased out from behind Jupiter and was now visible to powerful earth telescopes, Supreme Commander Zorgjeck ordered:

SUPREME COMMANDER ZORGJECK
Launch the assault force.

The colony class planetary conquest vessel captain asked Colony Class Planetary Conquest Vessel Sensor Operator:

COLONY CLASS PLANETARY
CONQUEST VESSEL
CAPTAIN
Still no sign of the *Měngjiàng Yún-Rén* ship?

COLONY CLASS PLANETARY
CONQUEST VESSEL
SENSOR OPERATOR
None yet.

WOGAR GREY
SUPREME COMMANDER
ZORGJECK
As soon as all the assault ships clear the hanger bays, deploy the defense grid.

COLONY CLASS PLANETARY
CONQUEST VESSEL
CAPTAIN
Yes sir.

EXT. CGI. SPACE. ASSAULT SHIPS LEAVING THE COLONY CLASS PLANETARY CONQUEST VESSEL MULTIPLE HANGER BAYS. 30 SECONDS.

Spread around the circumference of the massive structure were nodules fastened to the hull. They were self-sealing and separated from the hull in the event they were breached in battle would not cause a hull breach.

The crews were in their assault or defense craft and all conditions indicated go. ready to launch, the support personnel relocated into airtight temporary service nodules which had access via airtight hatches they could egress back into the mother ship.

The air in the hanger was sucked into storage tanks leaving a near vacuum then large panels slid open exposing the craft to the vacuum of space.

The assault craft which were not pressed for time would simply be shoved out at a few feet per second using electromagnet repulser's built into both the mother ship and the craft.

Later when they returned for docking operation, the electromagnets would be reversed and instead of repelling they would be attracting at controlled deaccelerations that very smoothly docked the vessel.

The sliding doors would then shut and once airtight was achieved with a 14-PSI test, the crews would then exit their craft and walked through a passage to a ship access door that had an isolation chamber that opened then shut after they entered, then opened a second door on the other side which prevented air leaks of any kind.

Even though the Wogar Greys could manufacture their own air, it was an energy drain, and thus avoided losing air as much as possible.

The ships for the defense grid had electromagnetic catapults. Here the time was critical if they were to be launched.

The main difference between the assault ships hanger bays and the defense grid hanger bays, is the nodules mounted on the hull. Those nodules containing defense grid fighters were more pronounced and extruding out more in a hyperbolic shape.

The defense grid ships were mounted on a launch structure that had electromagnets along its length and the craft had guide struts that kept the ships perfectly straight and kept an air gap of approximately an inch between the crafts skin and the launch apparatus.

The combination of the fighter's small electromagnets that were simply for stability and the electromagnets of the launch mechanism propelled the defense ships out reaching 12 Gs by the time they reached separation from the ship.

Drones could be launched from either type of deployment Hanger bays.

The initial wave drones' that were part of the assault force were sent out launched at 2000 Gs and reached incredible velocities and since they were all over the surface of the mother ship, there were always drones to launch during an initial salvo towards an enemy that was not wiped out first by the Colony Class Planetary Conquest Plasma Cannon.

The Grey strategy was to knock down all the enemy air assets, get the mother ship in planetary orbit, and then blast the inhabitants with the plasma cannon into submission.

After the planet surrendered and all factions disarmed the population was collected in concentration centers, where they would be evaluated as fit for use as slaves or designated and rendered as food supply to the Greys and the inhabitants who never knew they were eating their own after the bodies were processed in the protein converters.

The lessons of Admiral Kimmel and General Short commanders during the Pearl Harbor attack, was long forgotten in in the present circumstances as the consensus was the Greys were leaving with their tail between their legs.

VOICE OVER

Nobody in Earth Defenses had the common sense to
ask the question:

What if the Wogar Greys attacked again?

Even Tall White's Noble defenders were also lured into a vigilance lapse and readily left the day before on their own priorities. No doubt that had the Tall Whites suspected Zorgjeck had a trick up his sleeve, they then would have chosen another course of action.

The reality was the Tall Whites didn't need to leave the day before because the *Měngjiàng Yún-Rén Empress* promised to get them to the war zone quicker than planned.

The truth of the matter, Earth would have been caught with its pants down, had *Wánměi De Huā* not made that fateful trip up to discuss the situation with Drago.

INT. SPACE. *MĚNGJIÀNG YÚN-RÉN ROYAL YACHT CONTROL ROOM*

Shortly after *Wánměi De Huā* arrived in the control room Drago announced:

DRAGO

Our sensors have picked up some strange emanations
coming from the direction of Jupiter.

Concern soon struck Wánměi De Huā.

> WÁNMĚI DE HUĀ
> It's very unfortunate the Tall Whites hastily left
> yesterday; this could be the attack I was afraid of.

> DRAGO
> Our capabilities are limited, there is no way we can
> defend the planet.

> WÁNMĚI DE HUĀ
> What can we do?

> DRAGO
> I suggest you get Vance and the security detail men
> back as soon as possible so that we can leave if
> necessary.

Wánměi De Huā communicated telepathically via her telepathic transceiver to the ship.

> WÁNMĚI DE HUĀ
> (TELEPATHICALLY)
> Bring the Vance and the security detail men back
> aboard Royal Yacht immediately.

Vance was on the rear horse of today's Dude Ranch trail ride. He was getting to like riding horses and fishing in the morning, swimming and drinking in the afternoon, and after he gave feedback to the Dude Ranch chef about the menu loved eating those fish tacos during happy hour and barbecue time.

One of the Dude Ranch guests observed one of the security detachment guys in her peripheral vision disappear and suddenly realized Vance was gone!

> DUDE RANCH GUEST
> (FEMALE)
> Oh my God!

Others riding along looked back and saw three horses with no riders on them.

Mr. Durant looked back and with equal concern.

> MR. DURANT
> Where the hell did those guys go?

DUDE RANCH GUEST
(FEMALE)
The guy riding beside me just disappeared!

The woman nearly freaking out demanded:

DUDE RANCH GUEST
(FEMALE)
I want to go back to the Dude Ranch.

The Dude Ranch female guest then tried to turn her pony around who wasn't obliging because that wasn't the correct direction for the grain.

The woman got furthermore flustered as the horse did not react to her steerage.

Gus, who was with the group near the lead also turned back to look at all the commotion.

VOICEOVER (GUS)
THOUGHT
I'll be damned.

Gus pulled his cell phone out of his pocket, holding the reigns by one hand called Roger whom he knew was reading a book sitting near the pool under the shade.

Roger knew it was Gus calling on the caller's I.D.

ROGER
Hello.

GUS
Roger, we have a problem. Vance and his two bodyguards just disappeared like Sandra (a.k.a. *Wánměi de Huā*) did at Disneyland.

Roger looked around and added:

ROGER
I'll be damned, and the two guys they left here that were by the pool disappeared too!

GUS
Contact General Brazile right away and explain just what happened.

ROGER
Will do.

Click and then dial tone was heard.

***

INT. SPACE. *MĚNGJIÀNG YÚN-RÉN ROYAL YACHT CONTROL ROOM.*

Vance and the four-security detachment *Měngjiàng Yún-Rén* suddenly materialized next to Wánměi De Huā who had once again put on her Napoleon uniform. Vance was not expecting any of this.

VANCE
What's going on, do we have some kind of emergency?

Drago, who was getting more concerned responded.

DRAGO
We are getting some emanations around the area of Jupiter; we fear the Wogar Greys may be getting ready to attack Earth again.

VANCE
That's quite convenient for them since the Tall Whites left yesterday.

WÁNMĚI DE HUĀ
And not in a position to offer any help before the damage is done.

VANCE
Are we going to get confirmation so that we can warn Earth?

WÁNMĚI DE HUĀ
Are you reading my mind.

VANCE
I wish I could.

WÁNMĚI DE HUĀ
Well in due time you will be able to.

VOICEOVER (WÁNMĚI DE HUĀ)
THOUGHT
As *soon as you agree to leave Earth with me and
return to the Měngjiàng Yún-Rén*

As *Wánměi De Huā Shèngdà Dá Qiè Sī* consort, Vance would be required to get all the normal implants their royalty must have for telepathic communications and personal safety.

All diplomatic activity anywhere near the *Měngjiàng Yún-Rén* worlds were telepathically communicated and would put Vance at a disadvantage if he did not have the implant to give him the capability that important *Měngjiàng Yún-Rén* were normally equipped with.

Wánměi De Huā telepathically gave the ship and Vance simultaneously, the steering commands so that Vance would know what she was doing.

Drago stood back allowing Empress Wánměi De Huā to act because she knew this experience would no doubt be good for her; plus, Drago understood, she could always intervene if necessary.

Vance could tell by the image on the large screen in the very simple control room which was essentially fully automated, that stars and planets appeared to be moving in various directions which conveyed to him the awareness the ship had transitioned to a high-speed maneuver and was gaining speed very rapidly.

Not wanting to tangle with the Wogar Greys by herself and no armada to support her, *Wánměi De Huā* was not going to get boxed in for any major weapons including a *Plasma Cannon* kill shot.

Even though *Wánměi De Huā* didn't at the present time know the Wogar Grey *Colony Class Planetary Conquest Vessel* had such a plasma cannon, she was quite aware they had to have some sort of deadly weapon they just had not revealed. Therefore, at high speed and a wide birth she went blasting by like a steaming hot Sirocco.

Due to the hull static generated by the excessive speed that occurs near a star that has more debris than typically found in deep space, plus the meteorite repellent they had to perform along the way, meant the *Měngjiàng Yún-Rén* ship lost its stealth. This was expected but by traveling at safe distance and high speed, the counter threat was diminished.

***

<u>INT. SPACE. *COLONY CLASS PLANETARY CONQUEST VESSEL* CONTROL ROOM.</u>

The Wogar Greys detected an ion wake from the *Měngjiàng Yún-Rén* ship.

TACTICAL OFFICER
Your excellency, we are picking something up on the
scanners going at high speed.

WOGAR GREY
SUPREME COMMANDER
ZORGJECK
It must be the *Měngjiàng Yún-Rén*, get ready to lock it
on and fire the plasma cannon.

TACTICAL OFFICER
Due to the distance and velocity, focusing the plasma
cannon on the precise area of the target for the kill shot
was almost impossible, only a lucky shot will get it.

*COLONY CLASS PLANETARY
CONQUEST VESSEL* SHIP'S CAPTAIN
Your Excellency, we have no range information on
such short notice due to lack of distance calculations
that will take at least another five minutes.

EXT. CGI. SPACE. WOGAR GREY *COLONY CLASS PLANETARY*

CONQUEST VESSEL SHIP FIRING 15 SECONDS.

TACTICAL OFFICER
The first shot from the Wogar Grey *Colony Class
Planetary Conquest Vessel Plasma Cannon* fell
woefully behind the *Měngjiàng Yún-Rén* ship.

Even trying to lead the ship and fire produced similar results; it was trying to shoot a
needle in a haystack with no clue which haystack to shoot at.

***

EXT. CGI. SPACE. *MĚNGJIÀNG YÚN-RÉN ROYAL YACHT.*

The flyby produced the results *Wánměi De Huā* wanted, to make determination if there
was a threat and where was it?

Wánměi De Huā was also mildly depressed knowing that a large *Grey Colony Class
Planetary Conquest Vessel* had a terrible weapon on it that would devastate poor Earth,
making it an almost absolute certainty they would be conquered and in short order the
conquest would be complete.

Furthermore, once that moon-size *Colony Class Planetary Conquest Vessel* got in Earth's orbit with their Grey Fleet deployed in a defensive position it was not likely the Tall Whites could ever rescue them since their ships were not fast enough to avoid the plasma cannon.

As *Wánmĕi De Huā* maneuvered her command ship putting Jupiter and the Wogar quickly behind them, she started the end around to get back near earth to warn them on something they had no ability to defend.

Wánmĕi De Huā looked at Vance and her heart melted; suddenly feeling helpless to save his civilization that may be completely wiped out by the end of the day.

In doing so, *Wánmĕi De Huā* probed deep into his mind to feel all his experiences when she came across his memories of Vickie and the Jeeapa campaign and how Vickie had delayed the Anarchie just long enough so that Vance's Scout Class Ship which he was assigned as a crew member could survive.

As *Wánmĕi De Huā* explored the tactics Vickie did at *Jeeapa*, it suddenly made sense to her. These tactics were different than the hit and run tactics she employed during the Greys initial assault.

Wánmĕi De Huā could do a similar feat such as what Vicki did; that would also provide enough of a delay that hopefully her *Mĕngjiàng Yún-Rén Fleet* would arrive soon enough to rescue Earth.

Knowing the *Wogar Colony Class Planetary Conquest Vessel Plasma Weapon* might get a lucky shot *Wánmĕi De Huā* immediately informed the ship via her telepathic transceiver to communicate to the fleet via their neutrino system and give a status report as well as direct them in the event she and the ship are destroyed to rescue Vance whom she soon planned on kicking Vance off the ship in the shuttlecraft and sending him out of harm's way.

But also, when *Wánmĕi De Huā*'s Fleet arrived, since the battle would be underway, and Earth most likely partially devastated by then. She wanted her fleet to wipe out the Greys and leave no quarter for any of them. She wanted no trace left of their existence if it came to that.

Drago, reading her mind, which was naturally assumed, unanimously supported her decisions and was growing prouder by the moment of her Empress *Wánmĕi De Huā* now showing the skills and leadership she had vested a dozen centuries in developing.

Wánmĕi De Huā knew she had little time to share with Vance and decided:

WÁNMĚI DE HUĀ
(TELEPATHICALLY)
Vance, I'm going to take you with me to see General
Brazile to give the General a final warning before we
implement Earth's defense plan.

Vance then responded:

VANCE
Let me stay with General Brazile. If Earth is wiped
out, I want to be with him when it happens.

Wánměi De Huā suddenly emotionally struck by Vance's reply would not commit to
letting him stay but announced:

WÁNMĚI DE HUĀ
We are close enough to Earth to Transport down,
we must leave now because I must be back in a few
minutes to commence the attack.

INT. DAY. AREA 51. GENERAL BRAZILE'S OFFICE.

Within probably a second, they dematerialized and reappeared in General Brazile's
office who was just then discussing a few issues with Colonel Jones and his civilian
advisor Clark Douglas.

Wánměi De Huā announced immediately upon arrival:

WÁNMĚI DE HUĀ
Hello General Brazile.

GENERAL BRAZILE
This is not appropriate for you to just pop in here like
this any time you wish. I wish you would first arrive
at my secretary's office and ask permission to see me.

WÁNMĚI DE HUĀ
I'm sorry General, this is an Emergency. Earth is just
about to be attacked.

GENERAL BRAZILE
What?

Vance then spoke.

VANCE

General the Wogar Greys have commenced a new attack and will be hitting earth probably in a couple hours based on their speed and current position around Jupiter.

GENERAL BRAZILE

I thought the Grey's all departed the area.

VANCE

They did but most likely, Grak convinced them to come back.

General Brazile asked knowing it would be impossible to resist the Greys.

GENERAL BRAZILE

What can we do about it?

WÁNMĚI DE HUĀ

Try to distract them from Mars, get your Lunar forces ready; if you can kill a few of their assault ships, you might be able to delay them enough so that our fleet can get here in time to deal with them.

GENERAL BRAZILE

Colonel Jones, send out red alert, man battle stations.

COLONEL JONES

What do we tell them.

GENERAL BRAZILE

Inform the Lunar Base and Mars Base, we will send clarifying information shortly but warn the Lunar and Martian bases they are under imminent attack by superior forces and to do the best with what they got.

COLONEL JONES

They will be slaughtered.

GENERAL BRAZILE

Most likely but go ahead and send the directive now.

COLONEL JONES

Yes sir.

WÁNMĚI DE HUĀ
I'm sorry but we must leave now.

***

<u>EXT. CGI. SPACE. *MĚNGJIÀNG YÚN-RÉN ROYAL YACHT* CONTROL ROOM.</u>

Vance was about to request not to be taken away at that moment, they both dematerialized and rematerialized in *Wánmĕi De Huā's* personal quarters for a tender private moment.

WÁNMĚI DE HUĀ
I'm sorry Vance, I must do this; I would not feel like
living if something happened to you.

Wánmĕi De Huā then transformed into her green elf like form flapping her wings and slowly dissolved into Vance's body as she performed a short fusion and very strong emotional binding then exited his body rematerializing with her Sandra (a.k.a. *Wánmĕi de Huā*) image in the Napoleon uniform.

Vance suddenly disappeared and quickly found himself inside the shuttlecraft now leaving the ship heading far away from earth at high speed with his own security detail aboard.

Vance's shuttlecraft was vectored towards the approaching *Mĕngjiàng Yún-Rén Fleet* still too far away to intervene, but suddenly aware Vance was on his way, so high speed escorts were sent out to intercept the shuttle and transport him to the highly armored vessels that would be a serious match for any Wogar Grey ships that were dumb enough to attack them.

Some of the Wogar Grey assault ships detected the shuttle as soon as it was high-speed leaving behind a large ion wake, and gave chase for a while but saw the ship was slowly pulling away; realized further chase was pointless, returned to formations now approaching Mars for the first knockout punch.

Just like before, most of the staff on Mars in the deep underground caverns only received minor injuries as the onslaught began. As soon as the Greys got near orbit of the planet unexpectedly several weapons were fired at them, and as inferior as the Earth-designed weapons might have seemed, they made their mark destroying a few major Wogar Gray ships like *Wánmĕi De Huā* hoped they would.

Meanwhile, *Wánmĕi De Huā* back on the bridge with Drago started her maneuvers. Just like Vickie had done, she pointed her lasers and danced the ship in high-speed random turns that accomplished distracting the Grey's assault force which enabled the Earth's Martian force to knock out a few more Wogar Grey assault ship assets.

Not far behind the assault force came the Wogar Grey Colony Class Planetary Conquest Vessel and once it got into position, its plasma cannon wiped out any more offensive capability left on Mars and the planet was suddenly quiet, though most of the inhabitants were still alive thanks to the great planning and design of their underground fortifications.

The Wogar Greys would have to land on the planet and perform a wide search of underground caverns to locate and wipe out any living beings, something they would do later after they finished off the moon and got the Earth to capitulate.

Wánměi De Huā distractions were eating up a lot of time for the Wogar Greys.

Every half hour *Wánměi De Huā* could delay the Greys, giving a chance for her fleet to arrive before the Greys had a chance to wipe out most of the population of Earth which she assumed was in store.

Such imperialism is always the case when bastard civilizations pick on the weak and defenseless souls often found in the outer galactic solar systems.

The *Colony Class Planetary Conquest Vessel* tried shooting at the *Měngjiàng Yún-Rén Royal Yacht,* but the *Vickie Maneuver* that *Wánměi De Huā* now performed seemed to avoid all the kill shots, though one time they came close to getting a lucky shot.

There were enough Wogar Grey ships available to both deal with the *Měngjiàng Yún-Rén* and now move to the next phase of the operation, taking out the Moon bases which were far more plentiful in scope than on Mars.

<u>EXT. CGI. SPACE. LUNAR FORCES BATTLING WOGAR GREY SPACE ARMADA WITH *COLONY CLASS PLANETARY CONQUEST VESSEL SHOOTING A PLASMA CANNON. 45 SECONDS.*</u>

During the Lunar phase of the battle, it quickly turned into a slug match and if it were not for the plasma cannon on the mother ship, the lunar force might have been able to delay the invasion all by themselves.

Supreme Commander Zorgjeck slid the *Colony Class Planetary Conquest Vessel* into Earth's orbit not far from the Moon. Its presence had effects on Earth's tides just like the moon and in some areas caused coastal flooding with tidal waves. People hearing reports from TV and radio were outdoors watching the newly arrived moon and the glittery like flashes on the surface of the moon which was massive destruction going on.

It would take the planetary conquest vessel at least 30 kill shots to completely take down all the moon defenses, and then it could concentrate on the final phase of the battle destroying Earth's defenses.

EXT. CGI. SPACE. *MĚNGJIÀNG YÚN-RÉN ROYAL YACHT* CONTROL ROOM.

Drago observed the Lunar slaughter.

DRAGO

It appears their plasma cannon is mounted only on
one side of the mother ship.

Within a second after further telepathic communications between Drago, *Wánměi De Huā*, and the automated ship via the telepathic transceivers in their implants, the *Měngjiàng Yún-Rén Royal Yacht* leaped into great velocity also performing zigzag courses in the process.

WÁNMĚI DE HUĀ

If we hit them from behind it will force them to turn
away from the moon to give the lunar bases some
breathing room.

Wánměi De Huā soon had the *Měngjiàng Yún-Rén Royal Yacht* slightly exceeding light speed which caused the strange appearance of strobing impulse images as if the ship would appear and disappear in a quantum manner with the spaces of the strobes slowly expanding as the ship increased velocity.

Měngjiàng Yún-Rén could withstand far more G forces than humans and the ship's navigation system was fine tuned to almost reach those G forces as it banked into the turn that put it squarely behind the *Colony Class Planetary Conquest Vessel*.

As the *Měngjiàng Yún-Rén Royal Yacht* got close *Wánměi De Huā* fired a salvo then banked hard as she and the ship could take it knowing she would soon be a target from at least 50 nearby Wogar Gray assault craft.

EXT. CGI. SPACE. *COLONY CLASS PLANETARY CONQUEST VESSEL.*

Explosions and hull breach warnings were suddenly showing on damage control displays and as the sensors showed the alien ship now shooting behind the *Colony Class Planetary Conquest Vessel.*

WOGAR GREY
SUPREME COMMANDER
ZORGJECK

Helm, come around I want to point the plasma cannon
in the direction of the *Měngjiàng Yún-Rén ship.*

***

<u>EXT. CGI. SPACE. SPACEWAR BETWEEN WOGAR GREYS AND EARTH WITH HELP FROM *MĚNGJIÀNG YÚN-RÉN ATTEMPTING TO SAVE EARTH. 45 SECONDS.*</u>

The *Měngjiàng Yún-Rén was* now speeding away, jerking as it went.

The huge moon size ship didn't turn very fast and by the time it had done a 180 degree turn, the *Měngjiàng Yún-Rén Royal Yacht* had maneuvered which now placed it another 60 degrees off the *Colony Class Planetary Conquest Vessel* plasma cannon's direction as *Wánměi De Hu* continued on a long circular course to attempt getting out of range of any weapons and a kill shot from the plasma cannon.

The smoldering wreckage side of the *Colony Class Planetary Conquest Vessel* now faced the moon, was no longer firing plasma bursts and enough moon assets were still firing away actually landing good hits when a small tactical nuke hit a weak spot and put on some serious damage.

WOGAR GREY
SHIP'S ENGINEER

Your excellency Zorgjeck, we have some major hull breaches in sector G on our ship; we must break off the attack and move out to safety so that our damage control teams can do repairs before fire spreads to our Cerelium Reactors!

WOGAR GREY
SUPREME COMMANDER
ZORGJECK

Very well, maneuver back towards Jupiter and hide on the darks side of the planet.

Supreme Commander Zorgjeck knew Jupiter would hide the *Colony Class Planetary Conquest Vessel* from Earth.

WOGAR GREY
SUPREME COMMANDER
ZORGJECK

After we get the damage contained, we'll go back to finish off the moon, then hit Earth with a few kill shots in places like Washington DC, Moscow, Tokyo, London, Paris, and Beijing, that should force Earth to capitulate.

<u>INT. SPACE. *MĚNGJIÀNG YÚN-RÉN HIGH-SPEED ESCORT.*</u>

The *Měngjiàng Yún-Rén High-Speed Escorts* which rescued Vance and were carrying him were getting close and seeing the damage being inflicted on the Moon. Vance on the bridge of one of the ships pleaded:

VANCE
We need to go help them before it's too late.

MĚNGJIÀNG YÚN-RÉN
HIGH-SPEED ESCORT
CAPTAIN
Your excellency Vance, we will do as much as we can.

<u>INT. SPACE. *MĚNGJIÀNG YÚN-RÉN ROYAL YACHT.*</u>

Wánměi De Huā soon received the notification on her large control room screen That *Měngjiàng Yún-Rén High-Speed Escorts* were arriving momentarily, and they safely had Vance aboard.

WÁNMĚI DE HUĀ
(VIA TELEPATHIC TRANSCEIVER)
Why did you bring Vance back, I didn't want him near
the battle zone!

MĚNGJIÀNG YÚN-RÉN
HIGH-SPEED ESCORT
CAPTAIN
(VIA TELEPATHIC TRANSCEIVER)
Vance insisted we get here quick because of the
situation that your ship might be in danger.

Wánměi De Huā then ordered her *Měngjiàng Yún-Rén High-Speed Escort*s to attack the Wogar Greys and sped up to join the fray.

Realizing the timing was simply unfortunate, and the situation so grave, *Wánměi De Huā* realized she could not order the Rén ship with Vance aboard to leave the battle until the present emergency was dealt with, then gave that ship's captains his orders to join the battle including specific directions:

WÁNMĚI DE HUĀ
Help but minimize exposure for Vance's safety.

Drago articulated the pending crisis snapping Wánměi De Huā back to temporal reality.

DRAGO

The Wogar Greys were inflicting great damage to the lunar bases even without their planetary conquest vessel's plasma cannon, and without immediate help would soon be completely wiped out.

WÁNMĚI DE HUĀ

The approaching *Měngjiàng Yún-Rén High Speed Escorts* do not have enough firepower to take out Wogar Grey ships.

Drago now responded as a new type of battle began.

DRAGO

Nevertheless, our *high-speed escorts* diverted the Wogar Grey's attention from the Moon and are giving the moon bases a little breathing room.

Wánměi De Huā spoke within a short while after the *Měngjiàng Yún-Rén High Speed Escorts* arrival; then continued speaking.

WÁNMĚI DE HUĀ

The Wogar Greys are no longer fighting primitive Humans. They now faced a galactic threat as good or if not better than the Tall Whites.

DRAGO

Our *Měngjiàng Yún-Rén High-Speed Escorts* have shifted the momentum of the battle.

WÁNMĚI DE HUĀ

They give me hope we can delay long enough for the Fleet to arrive.

Drago received more battle reports.

DRAGO

Planetary assets launched by earth containing tactical nukes wiped out a few additional Wogar assault cruisers as well. One of the *Měngjiàng Yún-Rén High-Speed Escorts* was damaged by the Wogar Greys.

WÁNMĚI DE HUĀ

They at least had obtained a growing stalemate which

the Wogar Greys would soon learn is not a good thing
for them, because after the Měngjiàng Yún-Rén Fleet
arrives, the Wogar do not stand a chance.

DRAGO

The Wogar Greys appear to be conducting a tactical
withdrawal.

WÁNMĚI DE HUĀ

The Wogar Greys could no longer assert themselves
in the battle space with overwhelming superiority and
they realized the plan was no longer sustainable.

DRAGO

The Wogar Grey Fleet did a tactical withdrawal to
take care of their immediate concern of defending the
mother ship now licking its wounds.

WÁNMĚI DE HUĀ

It appears the Wogar are starting on a deep orbit behind
Jupiter.

DRAGO

Probably think the planet afforded them a margin of
safety, at least removes a possible attack from 180
degrees from their position

The Rén followed the Wogar to the near proximity of Jupiter, but they understood the
Wogar Grey's plasma cannon was still in working order, so the ship was still deadly.
The Rén did not let up, they pursued and attacked and drove in close range when
suddenly, the first Rén was obliterated by the plasma cannon. Before the *High-Speed
Escort* Vance was on could get out of the way, they too were hit but not destroyed.

Wánměi De Huā almost predicting this mishap came by in high speed and with quick
consultations with the ship's captain, fearing a kill shot any minute transported Vance
back to her ship. Predictably the Rén ship Vance just got off just in time, as it also
disappeared into a sparkling inferno just like the one before.

Suddenly the battlefield had flip-flopped back with the Wogar Greys now with the
momentum.

<u>INT. SPACE. WOGAR GREY *COLONY CLASS PLANETARY CONQUEST VESSEL*</u>

Zorgjeck was notified:

SHIP'S ENGINEER
Your Excellency Zorgjeck, it will not be long before getting the ship repaired and functionally able to continue the attack.

WOGAR GREY
SUPREME COMMANDER
ZORGJECK
What's the status of the fleet?

SHIP'S ENGINEER
The only thing we will lack is one-third of the defense grid catapults on the backside; otherwise, we are just about ready to proceed.

WOGAR GREY
SUPREME COMMANDER
ZORGJECK
Status report?

SHIP'S ENGINEER
All damage is temporarily repaired, we are ready to recommence attack, your Excellency.

WOGAR GREY
SUPREME COMMANDER
ZORGJECK
Very well, let's return to the Moon: we need to finish Earths Moon off now.

***

INT. SPACE. *MĚNGJIÀNG YÚN-RÉN ROYAL YACHT.*

Wánměi De Huā pulled back out of range at high speed to figure out her next move. Her fleet was getting closer and if she could just delay another hour, they would arrive in time to save 8 billion Earth people from slaughter.

WÁNMĚI DE HUĀ
The best we can do is distract them now, Vance. I'm sorry; we may not be able to save your Earth.

VANCE
Wánměi De Huā, you tried your best; you did all you could do.

DRAGO
No doubt Zorgjeck will be facing his plasma cannon
at the moon again; we can try to hit him from behind
like we did before.

Drago said as she too recognized the slaughter was not far off.

EXT. CGI. SPACE. SPACE BATTLE SYNCHRONIZED WITH FOLLOWING
VOICEOVER.

VOICEOVER
*Wánměi De Huā telepathically commanded the ship
with instructions to do a similar attack, but this time
peeled off a little sooner and headed into a different
direction that now appeared to contain fewer Wogar
Gray ships thanks to their attrition.*

*Wánměi De Huā came in for the attack, hit the
planetary conquest vessel in a good spot setting off
massive fires, but this time a random shot from one
of the Grey's assault cruisers managed to hit the
Měngjiàng Yún-Rén Royal Yacht starboard propulsion
cyclotronic reactors. The speed was suddenly cut.*

INT. SPACE. *MĚNGJIÀNG YÚN-RÉN ROYAL YACHT.*

DRAGO
We are now sitting ducks.

Drago's prime directive in protecting the Empress prompted her to say:

DRAGO
Wánměi De Huā, you and Vance must leave the
emergency escape pod immediately, or you both may
soon perish.

EXT. CGI. SPACE. *MĚNGJIÀNG YÚN-RÉN ROYAL YACHT* LAUNCHING ESCAPE
POD 15 SECONS.

Drago's evacuation order to the automated ship's systems programmed to protect the
Empress as a higher priority than any other function designed for such an event soon
had *Wánměi De Huā* and Vance deposited in the escape pod that was ejected into
space at extreme speed and shot out in the direction of the approaching fleet who were
immediately notified:

The emergency pod was coming their way with the Empress and her Consort Vance aboard.

The escape pod attained above light speed velocity rather quickly, didn't have meteorite sweepers so it had to maneuver to avoid collisions, was a rough ride that Vance hoped he never went through again.

It was not long before the fleet picked up their escape pod and transported the inhabitants aboard the fleet commander's battle cruiser.

Meanwhile Drago realizing they could not outrun the Wogar Greys did some quick calculations that if she turned now while the Grey *Colony Class Planetary Conquest Vessel* was turning to get in a kill shot at her she barely had enough time to slip in behind it again with her port propulsion system still online and hit the ship with maximum damage possible. At the same time, Drago transported all the *Měngjiàng Yún-Rén on the Royal Yacht* down to Area 51 where they may have a chance to survive.

Because of the damage Zorgjeck was now dealing with that was worse than before, he had no choice but to once again disengage and head for the dark side of Jupiter again to commence further repairs.

<u>EXT. CGI. SPACE. WOGAR GREY *COLONY CLASS PLANETARY CONQUEST VESSEL RECEIVING DAMAGE FROM THE MĚNGJIÀNG YÚN-RÉN ROYAL YACHT* ATTACK. 30 SECONDS.</u>

The Wogar Grey *Colony Class Planetary Conquest Vessel* was slowly picking up speed as propulsion was unaffected by the damage.

Drago made her supreme sacrifice knowing she had done everything expected of her developing the Empress who was now quite capable of continuing without her, guided the ship right at the moon size vessel and as the *Měngjiàng Yún-Rén Royal Yacht* got closer, and her powerful lasers fired away but was also making a beautiful target of her own ship.

While Drago's pumped in ample amounts of critical damage to the Wogar Grey *Colony Class Planetary Conquest Vessel*, Drago did not waver course and was taking numerous direct hits which soon knocked out all hope of steerage and at the velocity going even with just one engine created a fiery crash just moments later set off a huge explosion that rocked the Wogar Grey *Colony Class Planetary Conquest Vessel* and frightened Zorgjeck and everyone on it.

The Grey's *Colony Class Planetary Conquest Vessel* velocity had picked up quite a bit but soon the Engineering department reported:

SHIP'S ENGINEER
Your excellency Zorgjeck, we have lost the means
to steer ship, and the steering mechanism is not
functioning!

Having pointed at Jupiter with the intention of changing course to obtain an orbit, they were now on a collision course with Jupiter and had no means to steer. But Zorgjeck knew he could just slow down; however, that also presented a problem: without steerage he would not be able to hide anywhere in the solar system and the hunter might soon become the hunted, especially if the Tall Whites came back.

Zorgjeck now feared out loud:

WOGAR GREY
SUPREME COMMANDER
ZORGJECK
This ship was no longer in any kind of conditions to
deal with the Tall Whites and the day of reckoning was
now occurring

The control room was stunned by Zorgjeck's statement

WOGAR GREY
SUPREME COMMANDER
ZORGJECK
Slow us down since we can't control our course.

SHIP'S ENGINEER
Sir, the auto-throttles are stuck wide open.

WOGAR GREY
SUPREME COMMANDER
ZORGJECK
What does that mean?

SHIP'S ENGINEER
Sir, recommend you transfer your staff to one of the
battle cruisers via a shuttlecraft.

The *Colony Class Planetary Conquest Vessel* continued to speed up as the throttles were stuck wide open. Zorgjeck with Grak in toe boarded the Wogar Grey shuttlecraft and it was launched and soon picked up by the Wogar battle cruiser called in for the rescue operation.

Zorgjeck ordered the ship's captain:

WOGAR GREY
SUPREME COMMANDER
ZORGJECK
Follow along with the Planetary Conquest Vessel in
case they were able to restore steering. I will go back
aboard and retake command of it.

The Wogar Grey *Colony Class Planetary Conquest Vessel* continued to slowly add to its speed, which was now at a velocity not seen since its interstellar transit 80 years ago. As Jupiter grew larger and larger it appeared the initial navigation coefficients that steered the mother ship on its present course had picked what appeared to be exactly the center of the planet.

<u>EXT. CGI. SPACE. WOGAR GREY *PLANETARY CONQUEST VESSEL CRASHING INTO JUPITER 45 SECONDS.*</u>

In due time Zorgjeck watched in pure horror as the *Planetary Conquest Vessel* with 400 million Greys aboard including a vast Army planned for planetary conquest and brutal and savage extermination of the Earth people went right towards Jupiter's planet surface.

The *Planetary Conquest Vessel* started smoldering as the ionosphere started burning away the protrusions sticking out first and a stream of smoke trailed the fastmoving object as it slammed into the planet surface below the thick cloud cover.

<u>EXT. CGI. JUPITER PLANET SURFAC. *NEPAPOLIUN GIANTS' VILLAGE.* WOGAR GREY *PLANETARY CONQUEST VESSEL* CRASHING. 15 SECONDS.</u>

The planet Jupiter *Nepapoliun Giants* observed the crash from 50 miles away and within a few seconds the shock wave hit them, wiping out most of them out.

The primitive silicon-based *Nepapoliun Giants* had liquid methane and nitrogen in their circulatory systems had mainly gone undetected in the solar system and those that survived merely thought it was another rock from outer space that arrived every few years that wiped out some of the herd.

The *Nepapoliun Giants* viewed comet strikes like Americans think of a tornado in Oklahoma, doing some damage, but not really impacting life on Jupiter.

Nepapoliun Giants were just now going through its 16th Century and dealing with its own Galileo like problems and growing civil unrest.

<u>EXT. CGI. VICINITY OF EARTH.</u>

Shortly when the huge *Měngjiàng Yún-Rén* Space Armada arrived the remaining Wogar Greys offered to surrender, expecting harsh treatment from barbarian-like creatures.

All the Wogar Greys were transported off their ships which were immediately towed to the sun for destruction and the Greys were given a ride home to their planet in a couple of weeks instead of the 18 years it would have taken them.

As the Wogar Greys were released to their home world, by direction of the Empress, the Greys were warned that if they ever ventured into the Gamulin Solar System again, the Wogar Grey Home World would pay a terrible price.

Now it was getting down to Vance's decision point. Should he leave or should he stay, but as he pondered the question, he suggested to *Wánměi De Huā* they go back to Earth for a short while and help deal with the remaining abductees, just a few left that had not transferred to the witness protection program.

***

Boris met up with Tanya and rekindled the flame at the Circus-Circus Hotel and Casino that wasn't so bad after all. Perhaps Tanya's presence created such an environment that it really didn't matter.

TANYA
When are you going to tell me why you disappeared?

BORIS
Alright, but your life will be in danger if they know
I told you, but I do plan on leaving the organization
soon as I think I know a way out.

TANYA
Are you into organized crime?

BORIS
It's far worse than that. That's why we can't see each
other again until I get resettled, and I will call for
you then. After that we'll spend the rest of our lives
together.

TANYA
Are you sure?

BORIS
Yes. And this time I'm a little smarter not to trust my

former attorney, I'm already planning, and got a Swiss
bank account set up so when I quit and move, I will
have cash to sustain us.

***

Dudley called the designated number the next day. At first, he got an answering
machine and as he started to leave a message a voice came on.

ANASTASIYA PUSHKIN
Hello Dudley, just wanted to make sure it's you.

DUDLEY
Okay, I photographed the entire tech manual to the
C-130 with an anti-gravity device, have the file on my
smart phone.

ANASTASIYA PUSHKIN
Excellent, Rich will see you tomorrow at Tonopah and
you can give it to him there.

DUDLEY
That's not going to work, you owe me one.

ANASTASIYA PUSHKIN
What do you mean by that?

DUDLEY
After you come to the Dude Ranch tomorrow and give
me what I want, I'll email you the J-peg files.

ANASTASIYA PUSHKIN
I can't do that.

DUDLEY
Then I'll just go tell the General tomorrow that I'm
homosexual and want out of the Air Force and explain
to him a spy ring is trying to blackmail me and see
what happens.

For the first time in her life, Anastasiya Pushkin was confronted with a situation where
she was losing control.

Anastasiya Pushkin didn't mind having sex with Dudley, because it wouldn't be the
first or the last time, she went the extra mile to achieve the kind of results that even
Margarita Konenkova would admire.

But, based on FSB Intel reports, Anastasiya Pushkin didn't feel safe returning to Nevada. She would call Rich right away and demand he go spend some extra money and get an outstanding call girl to settle Dudley down.

VOICE OVER (ANASTASIYA
PUSHKIN) THOUGHT

But dealing with the immediate crisis that if Dudley has the entire technical manual photographed, it might be worth the risk because that's probably all that Alexander Bortnikov really needs to know for now.

Besides, they have numerous other ways of stealing the technology through many useful idiots willing to sell out their country in America.

ANASTASIYA PUSHKIN

Alright Dudley. I will come and visit you tomorrow, but in the future, you will have to fly down to Acapulco to see this Pussy Cat and bring me the kinds of presents I want if you expect to get any more.

DUDLEY
I'll bring nice gifts.

Dudley had done some soul searching and now he was mad. It turns out Rich was using him too. He had no idea his buddy was all part of this!

Dudley was developing a plan in his head. Since he was hopelessly lost now because he attended numerous INTEL briefings on security and reporting requirements.

The Russian FSB would never let you go until they sucked all the blood out of you, blackmailing you to keep providing what they wanted. If you ever crossed the Russian FSB, either they would kill you or arrange for your arrest. So, the name of the game was to never get involved with them in the first place.

Dudley was now starting to see the Russian FSB recruitment techniques were far more complex than he ever imagined, and his Air Force Intel Security briefers apparently didn't know jack shit on how ruthless the Russians really operated.

VOICEOVER (DUDLEY)
THOUGHTS

American boy scout approach just can't come close to dealing with these evil pricks.

> *Russian INTEL out class us Americans so badly it is
> not even funny.*
>
> *Americans get a lucky break now and then, but by
> sheer luck only!*

Dudley would take matters into his own hands and already resigned himself to the fact his Air Force days were numbered anyway, as he felt the cold steel of his pistol he now gripped in his hand.

***

The next day Vance and Sandra (a.k.a. *Wánměi de Huā*) returned. There were only five of the original twenty-two abductees left. The witness protection program had processed all the rest.

Because these remaining five Abductees were making such good progress with their psychiatrists who were shuttled in to treat them, thinking their psychoactive drugs were doing the trick.

In the future psychiatrists treating Abductees would become disappointed and not have such successes with abductees like these twenty-two who truly were repaired only by *Wánměi De Huā* extraordinary mental capabilities.

The government up till now considered Mr. Keeney (Boris) a decent person, who ran a professional organization and seemed keen on a lot of things. The witness protection program that dealt with him and asked for his cooperation and silence was delighted in how he conducted himself as if he was a team player.

As such Boris had a couple of their business cards, and they fit well into his plans. He knew he could not run away from the FSB (KGB). They would travel to the ends of the earth to hunt him down and kill him if he defected.

Boris knew his only way out was via America's witness protection program and a change of I.D. It was kind of ironic; the same forgers who worked making documents for the DD/P were also hard at work for the witness protection program.

But for Boris' situation, things unfolded quite quicker than he ever anticipated.

Out of the blue the following afternoon Dudley reappeared and seemed somewhat nervous as Boris thought he should be.

Anastaysia Pushkin (a.k.a. Muriel) had flown into McCarran on a private jet and drove herself up to the Dude Ranch.

It was not long before Anastaysia went into Dudley's room, and she performed one of her best acts ever. Anastaysia almost made Dudley believe that she was in love with him and would soon arrange for him to come down to Acapulco and live lavishly with her.

But Dudley had seen the light and was now going to deal with Anastaysia and Rich. After he finished up what he thought he was owed for the grief that woman Anastaysia put him through.

Dudley looked out the window as he shifted the blinds a bit and saw Rich nearby working the grill for the expected afternoon Dude Ranch barbecue.

Then he sat down in a chair beside the bed that Muriel was laying on going through her cell phone looking at some of the JPEG files that Dudley had given her.

The fact Dudley had just had sex with a Russian spy means he was now in over his head.

Anastaysia only paid attention to the first couple of pages of the tech manual that looked legitimate; then shut off her phone believing she had the entire manual.

Dudley was essentially a nice guy and one with a sense of humor. There was no way he was going to hand over the antigravity system tech manual to Anastaysia.

Instead, Dudley photographed a couple of the first 3 or 4 pages that included an index, and then copied the 1957 C-130 operating manual! No antigravity or classified data was attached.

DUDLEY
What's your real name if you don't mind me asking?

Looking at the pathetic weak American whom she had no respect for and only did her performance to get the technical manual, coldly responded.

ANASTASIYA
Not that it matters, my name is Anastasiya.

Anastasiya then got up and went to the bathroom.

Dudley heard Anastasiya flush the toilet and the bathtub filling up as if it appeared she was cleaning herself up which she intended to do, then put her clothes on and leave right afterwards with no plans to ever see Dudley again.

Anastasiya didn't need any more interactions with Dudley. She thought she now had priceless blackmail material, and Dudley was just another useless pawn in the game of espionage she had checkmated in her superior strategy and manipulations.

Dudley knew it was time; she wasn't expecting his move and if she knew martial arts, there would be no way she could defend herself now. Underestimating Dudley, Anastasiya didn't even lock the bathroom door.

Dudley put his ear up to the door, heard her splashing in the bathtub as she was cleaning herself, he then opened the door and as soon as she looked facing the gun barrel, Dudley started shooting with his semi-automatic pistol, emptied the clip in Anastasiya then ejected the clip and put a new one in.

As expected, her assistant agent Rich was outside cooking, heard the gunshots coming from the room, then walked over, knocked on the door and when nobody answered put the master room key and walked in. Dudley was waiting for Rich and as soon as he stepped in the room—bang-bang-bang—Rich was laying on the floor dead!

Dudley having solved the Russian spy case, sat down on the bed, put the gun up to his head and suddenly there was darkness.

Gus, hearing someone firing weapons, flew out of his room, and Boris stood there at the Grill just staring, now realizing his plans had just been altered.

Gus holding his pistol in the air saw Boris with spatula in hand and told Gus,

BORIS
The shooting came from the room with the door open.

Gus nodded and carefully walked over to the open door expecting a possible assailant.

Gus looked inside the open door and observed a man lying on the floor in a pool of blood and another on the bed also bloody from a gunshot wound.

Gus, realizing he and his guests could not be associated with this mess and needed to clear out suddenly recalling the Sheriff he met after the bar fight, he pulled the business card out of his wallet, then called it on his cell phone.

SHERIFF TRAVIS
Hello.

GUS
Sheriff Travis this is Gus, remember U.S. Marshalls,
met you up near Warm Springs on Hiway 6 after the
biker bar incident a while back?

SHERIFF TRAVIS
Oh yea, you did a great job on some of those ole boys,
we had to take them to the hospital. It's been quiet
ever since!

GUS
Sheriff Travis, we have a major problem here at the
Dude Ranch in Alamo, a couple people shot, probably
dead; you need to come right away and bring an
ambulance.

SHERIFF TRAVIS
You have anything to do with that mess?

GUS
Nope, this one is not on me, just a concerned citizen
reporting what appears to be a homicide.

SHERIFF TRAVIS
Ok, we'll be right over.

By the time Sheriff Travis and his deputies showed up along with a couple ambulances,
a crowd was gathered outside staring at the open door to the room clearly seeing a man
lying on the floor and one on the bed. Gus had grabbed a couple lawn chairs and put
them in front of the door to keep out anyone before law enforcement arrived so as not
to disturb the evidence.

Dudley left a suicide note behind in his room at the BOQ which investigators found
the next morning as they searched the BOQ room for evidence.

In the suicide note envelope labeled *to General Brazile*, Dudley explained what all had
happened and apologized for creating a disgrace for the Air Force, and said what he
had copied and turned over to the Russian spy was the useless 1957 manual that one
third of the major countries on the planet had since they flew the plane now.

Dudley also reported General Brazile had a Russian Mole working for him according
to Anastaysia the female spy blackmailing him that he intended on killing.

The next day, the witness relocation program agents showed up and met Boris who
they had counted on his cooperation in the past were suddenly taken in when Boris
announced:

BORIS POTEMPKIN
I'm a Russian Spy and I would like to defect but want

to be allowed into the witness protection program. I would like to speak to someone in the CIA.

Since the witness protection program (WPP) agents often had to deal with the CIA, especially in this case of the abductees, already knew Gus was on hand, and worked directly for DD/P.

WPP AGENT
We know just the guy you need to talk with.

When they had their private meeting in Gus's room with Roger attending, Gus at first spoke.

GUS
I'm not sure what to make of it all

BORIS POTEMKIN
The FSB (KGB) altered my appearance. But if you recall you were at the Top of the World Restaurant, CIA was observing Boyd Bushman talking to a bald Russian Spy that was having dinner with Boyd Bushman; that was me.

The mere mention of Boyd Bushman got Gus' attention.

GUS
I can't promise you anything, and know time is at the essence because the FSB will no doubt discover something isn't right here, will be sending in the Calvary to figure out what's going on and your situation becomes tenable at best.

BORIS POTEMKIN
I understand completely.

GUS
Roger, take Boris over to your room while I call Langley for instructions.

In about 30 minutes, Gus knocked on Roger's door and was invited in immediately.

Boris sitting on a chair and Roger on his bed facing them obviously deep in discussion before Gus arrived, looked up.

BORIS POTEMKIN
Any good news?

GUS
Langley agrees to hide you via the witness protection
program, but they want you to stay put here a while.

BORIS POTEMKIN
Why is that?

GUS
Langley is sending a couple agents to provide you
security and allow you to continue your business and
in about a month we figure we'll be able to use you as
a double spy.

BORIS POTEMKIN
Why the delay?

GUS
We'll arrange for what looks like your death in a tragic
accident. Then we'll move you somewhere with a
change of identity.

BORIS POTEMKIN
I've waited this long. I suppose another month won't
hurt, but if I fully cooperate and help, I want one other
thing.

GUS
What's that?

BORIS POTEMKIN
I have a girlfriend down in Vegas, Tanya; I want her to
come with me.

GUS
She can't, unless she's your wife.

BORIS POTEMKIN
I'm sure she'll agree to that right away; we'll go
through one of those drive through weddings in Vegas.

GUS
This is getting kind of complicated, but I suppose the DD/P boys can arrange to get your wedding license made out to your new identities.

***

An Area 51 Rep arrived days later from General Brazile's group.at the Dude Ranch to confer with Gus about what all went on.

GUS
The last of the abductees were moved out of the Dude Ranch.

AREA 51 REP
No more psychiatrists and no more government people coming with them.

GUS
The airman's death had to be publicized so that they could create a controlled story of the murder suicide, which made it look like the two men were fighting over the woman.

AREA 51 REP
What other option did they have?

GUS
Not many.

AREA 51 REP
Dudley was in a way a hero as he chose to die rather than compromise with evil.

GUS
Eventually the spy ring would have got what they wanted, had Dudley not stepped in and sacrificed himself.

AREA 51 REP
That was a beautiful woman he killed.

GUS
Even more it blends in well with the cover story.

AREA 51 REP
Have the FSB guys left yet?

GUS
You mean the individuals who came to reclaim her body to take her home to Illinois?

AREA 51 REP
Yes.

GUS
They thought they were clever, but we know they delivered the two dead spies to Moscow and had private burials, though one of our informants.

AREA 51 REP
Who was that?

GUS
Can't tell you, he's now in the witness protection program.

AREA 51 REP
So, what do you know about that FSB guy that was killed in the high-speed chase out by Warm Springs?

GUS
Charred remains burned beyond any possible recognition.

AREA 51 REP
He's the guy that ran the Dude Ranch?

GUS
Sure was.

AREA 51 REP
Well thanks for giving me the report, will make sure that General Brazile gets it.

GUS
You're welcome, Mr. Douglas.

AREA 51 REP
Call me Clark.

GUS
Sure thing, Clark.

Gus was smiling as Mr. Douglas left knowing he had just started the new project on their double spy Mr. Clark.

With Boris assistance, Langley Inspector General's office had been briefed by Gus about their Russian Double Agent who had corroborated about a Mole in General Brazile's office. General Brazile was flown to Langley then briefed on Clark Douglas and Boris Potemkin and the entire Anastasiya Pushkin affair.

***

INT. DAY. FSB HEADQUARTERS, ALEXANDER BORTNIKOV'S OFFICE SUITE

The special FSB Communications Technician had the laptop in hand as he entered the reception area, the receptionist announced:

ALEXANDER BORTNIKOV'S
RECEPTIONIST
You may go in now.

Alexander Bortnikov, read Boris final report on the laptop. Laying on his desk was a report sent in by his agent Clark Douglas, who also independently reported much of what Boris's report stated concerning Anastasiya Pushkin and Dudley Brown.

Clark Douglas had information on how Boris was killed in the car wreck when a fuel truck pulled out in front of him on the 2-lane road and was instantly incinerated as the truck trailer caught on fire from the side impact and immediately went up in a wall of fire.

EXT. DAY. HIWAY NEAR ALAMO NEVADA CAR CRASH INTO GASOLINE CARRIER TRUCK AND EXPLOSION. 20 SECONDS.

Gus' friend Sheriff Travis investigated the staged incident that utilized one of the new Google self-driving cars with a cadaver as a driver and the self-driving truck with a cadaver as the truck's driver they obtained to appear as the truck driver who also was burned beyond recognition. The Sheriff was starting to like the Cash in Advance boys that rescued his Sheriff's department yearly budget.

***

Vance and his entourage finally got the road trip going.

After a stop in San Diego so he could look over some of his former life and visit familiar places like Point Loma, Ocean Beach, Scrips Ranch, Mira Mesa, Miramar, and Ballast Point, they were heading up I-15 to Salt Lake City and the next day checking into their hotel in Yellowstone Park.

After seeing some of the sights, Sandra (a.k.a. *Wánměi de Huā*) now realized what Vance saw in his life here, and other than the recent adventures, was a sweet life.

SANDRA (A.K.A. *WÁNMĚI DE HUĀ*)
Vance, do you want to leave and go home with me?

VANCE
It only takes 3 weeks to get here; I can come back and visit in the future. After we finish Yellowstone, it's time for us to go home

They entered their hotel room then shut the door; it was fusion time again.

Paul D. Escudero
August 2024

BACKGROUND INFORMATION ON THE DEVELOPMENT OF AREA-51

The City of Las Vegas never sleeps. One of the most amazing situations exists for that baron landscaped area. Las Vegas is located near the most secret location in America, Area 51.

Picked out by Kelly Johnson as a test site for the U2 Spy plane test flights, was once considered the most useless piece of real estate in America and diminished in value furthermore by numerous nearby nuclear tests.

The need for absolute secrecy made the site very palatable for CIA officials, and particularly Richard Bissell, who sanctioned the U2 test flights there.

In the 1950s the surrounding areas accessible from highway U.S. 95 or U.S. 93 but laid into a valley hiding its occupants, added to the features that Kelly Johnson and his assistants from the Skunk Works thought were ideal.

The short comings of the prospective base not having much of anything was quickly overcome by the knowledge Tonopah was nearby so Lockheed's men involved with the U2 could initially have a place to stay and eat that didn't take long to travel to and from.

Las Vegas initially was too far away for a daily commute, but when the logistics arm of a Belt Way Bandit, EG&G suddenly in the mix, all logistics problems were solved and with the arrival of rapidly advancing Jet technology, the Boeing 737 Jets EG&G purchased forming the Janet Airline used as a commuter plane wasn't far behind.

Unmarked Janet Airlines Jet.
Initiated by EG&G to fly passengers from Las Vegas to
six locations including Area-51 and Area-52, Burbank,
Vandenberg AFB, and Edwards AFB.

The Brilliance of the Boeing 737 use paid off because PhDs involved in the research around the U2 and subsequent A12, and future high-performance aircraft could sustain themselves indefinitely living in Los Vegas with their families. The University of Las Vegas also provided education for family members and a future group of highly skilled workers needed at the Area 51 facility.

During the 1950s three events occurred that put great fear in President Eisenhower: Sputnik the first satellite put in space by the Russians, and the supposed Bomber Gap, and the very first actual deployment of a Russian ICBM.

Because of Russia's extremely large areas stretched over 11 time zones including Siberia, the Russians had vast potential launch points for their new ICBMs that theoretically could fly over the North Pole and hit American Targets in 15 to 30 minutes.

U2 and later A12 developments were rushed into development. CIA director Allen Dulles agreed the U2 could be funded by DD/P (Deputy Director of Planning) at the time Frank Wisner, who had delegated U2 and A12 development to Richard M. Bissell, Jr.

America needed aerial surveillance for Russian military and weapons testing. The recent propaganda put in newspapers around America describing the Bomber Gap, turned into raw political them verses us in Congress which some experts claim may have impacted the 1956 presidential elections.

Eventually the bomber GAP was debunked by U2 flights.

Richard M. Bissell, Jr., understood that, given the extreme secrecy enveloping the U2 project, the flight test and pilot training programs could not be conducted at Edwards Air Force Base or Lockheed's Palmdale facility.

The Groom Lake test facility was, therefore, established in April 1955 by the Central Intelligence Agency (CIA) for Project Aquatone, the development of the Lockheed U2 strategic reconnaissance aircraft.

Richard Bissell, who later was fired by John F. Kennedy, because he took over from Frank Wisner as DD/P after Frank's nervous breakdown around 1959, ended up as the fall guy for the flawed operation the Bay of Pigs Incident.

Even though Kennedy's withdrawal of fighter jet escorts doomed the B25's flown by CIA men, caused the ultimate failure of the mission, he needed plenty of scapegoats. Richard Bissell was the first head to be lobbed off.

A year after being fired over the Bay of Pigs Incident, Richard Bissell was back in the Oval Office getting his picture taken with Kennedy while receiving the Presidential Medal of Freedom, for his development of the U2 and the A12 (the forerunner of the

SR-71 super-fast spy plane).

It was the U2 flights that first photographed Russian missiles in Cuba that led up to the Cuban Missile Crisis. Hence, the U2 at that time provided the most important warning the Pentagon had received in our nation's history.

It's been stated by historians that had U2's not found the Soviet Union's missiles in shipment, they would soon have been camouflaged and we wouldn't know they existed or how to find them if we did. Kennedy, unfortunately, was dead a short time later.

The CIA and the Air Force concurred with Kelly Johnson's choice for the location of the U2 test fights and were delighted to discover the Groom Lake base soon had some other highly classified activities surrounding it which means they would not be alone, nor pay for all the base security out of their own budget. The other entities would be able to help maintain the base and provide a lot of security.

The original airfield on the Groom Lake site began service in 1942 as Indian Springs Air Force Auxiliary Field and consisted of two dirt 5000-foot runways. The airfield was originally built for bombing and artillery practice; large bomb craters are still visible in the nearby vicinity.

Kelly Johnson named the area "Paradise Ranch" to encourage Lockheed workers to move to this base that the CIA's official history of the U-2 project would later describe as "the new facility in the middle of nowhere.

On 4 May 1955, a Lockheed and government survey team arrived at Groom Lake and laid out a 5,000-foot north-south runway on the southwest corner of the dry lakebed and built a base support facility, initially consisted of little more than a few shelters, workshops and brought in trailer homes in which to provide temporary housing for the on-site team.

The CIA did not fail to realize there was a mining town nearby named Tonopah. With the mines slowly going out of business there was high unemployment, and the wages the Cash in Advance boys (as CIA is often referred to) would pay them more than they were earning as miners.

As time passed and other situations and scenarios evolved. Underground facilities that would shield their images and electromagnetic emanations from possible spy satellite Passovers enhanced the need for more underground caverns that could have very high security. It was a win/win having all that mining expertise nearby.

Area 51, a number picked out by the CIA because it was next to Area 15 nuclear test site, was chosen to mislead anyone who would try to penetrate and obtain information.

The first U-2 arrived on 24 July 1955, on a C-124 Globemaster II cargo plane from Burbank, accompanied by Lockheed technicians in a Douglas DC-3 Air Transport sent to Area 51 from Lockheed's Burbank, California Skunk Works offices.

Eventually security concerns made it necessary to fly personnel to Nevada on Monday mornings and return to California or Las Vegas on Friday evenings. Also, it was probably done so they could convince people who didn't want to leave California to not quit the project and find numerous lucrative jobs without the need to live in Nevada.

For a while permanent military and CIA personnel lived in Tonopah and eventually a BOQ (bachelor officer quarters) and BEQ (bachelor enlisted quarters) facilities were built on the base for a small, limited number of military personnel who were needed for around the clock staffing of security and other requirements.

Very few service personnel ever volunteered to come back after their typical 3-year tour was complete, mainly due to the isolation and constant surveillance in their personal lives.

Since the Air Force was supplying the CIA test pilots, they arrived in small numbers and since Wright Patterson was running out of storage space for wrecked UFOs and dead alien corpses, CIA quickly determined some extra buildings could be set up to provide the facilities needed to store and analyze the alien technology and dead aliens often recovered in crashes for alien technology exploitation and development.

Because of the possible Soviet Bomber Gap, and the new threat from Soviet ICBMs, America suddenly found itself in an unprecedented arms race that further concerned Eisenhower who believed half of it was propaganda, and eventually coined the phrase Military Industrial Complex.

Around this time, the Navy had developed the nuclear "Regulus" missile program. The Regulus was a cruise missile launched from a submarine that flew below radar as a remotely guided drone to the target. The missile would be launched a great distance from the Target, fly the distance but near its destination such as Vladivostok or Petropavlovsk, would be guided and controlled by a Regulus guidance submarine, of the SSN-578 Skate Class.

The flaw in this system is it took 2 submarine crews to launch 1 weapon. Only one nuclear powered launcher existed, USS Halibut and its reliability was questionable, and several diesel electric submarines including USS Grayback about the time Lockheed engineers conceived of a new type of weapon Polaris.

Regulus history:

<u>Regulus missile submarines - Wikipedia</u>

Regulus Patrols conducted:

<u>Encyclopedia of WW3: USN Regulus Deterrent Patrols (generalstaff.org)</u>

It quickly became apparent to Admiral Burke that solid-fueled ballistic missiles had advantages over cruise missiles. Hence, with his leadership the Navy quickly determined the obvious advantages solid rocket-fueled Polaris ballistic missiles had over cruise missiles in range and accuracy, and unlike both Jupiter (Air Force Missiles) and Regulus Cruise Missiles, the Polaris were able to be launched from a submerged submarine, improving submarine stealth and survivability.

At the project Nobska conference in 1956 with Admiral Burke, nuclear physicist Edward Teller stated that a physically small one-megaton warhead could be produced for Polaris within a few years, and this prompted Burke to abandon the Regulus and Jupiter programs and concentrate on Polaris.

In December of that year Admiral Burke later was instrumental in determining the size of the Polaris submarine force, suggesting that 40-45 submarines with 16 missiles each would be sufficient. Eventually, the number of Polaris submarines was fixed at 41.

The whole program was sold to the President by Charles A. Lindbergh after he took a two-week VIP cruise on USS Swordfish (SSN-579) off the California coast, just returning from a 6-month Western Pacific deployment.

Although their wives, girlfriends, and plenty of cold beer was waiting for them on the beach, and Lindbergh knew it, the Swordfish crew professionalism quickly outshined the negative propaganda the Air Force was using while attempting to prevent the program from ever starting.

The Air Force only wanted Air and Ground based missiles along with all the unlimited budget money under their control. Lindbergh, a Brigadier General in the U.S. Air Force Reserve spoke favorably about the proposed Polaris program which convinced Eisenhower to endorse the program to congress.

The CIA suddenly had another tie into area 51. The W47 and W58 nuclear warheads designed for the Polaris Missiles, were designed and tested not far from area 51. The logistics involving those tests which "beltway bandits" like EG&G provided increased the footprint of area 51 in a major way. EG&G built buildings and facilities there. It's not been determined if EG&G had any involvement in General Brazile's vast underground complex; however, the likelihood is great.

EG&G, formally known as Edgerton, Germeshausen, and Grier, Inc., was a United

States defense contractor providing management and technical services. The company EG&G was involved in contracting services to the United States government during World War II and conducted weapons research and development after the war. Its close involvement with some of the government's most sensitive technologies has led to its being cited in conspiracy theories related to DOD black projects. The revelation they flew large numbers of employees routinely to area 51 on Janet Airlines greatly added to the mystery.

Vance never worked directly for EG&G before he was abducted by Mergenky Aliens. But Vance often worked with EG&G personnel on a variety of projects. In numerous cases EG&G handled most of the logistics, but also provided several people working on weapons systems and provided engineering services to develop testing devices that could be hooked up directly to launchers and other systems to vastly speed up and streamline testing needed to certify the equipment and components.

In 1931, MIT professor Harold Edgerton (a pioneer of high-speed photography) partnered with his graduate student Kenneth Germeshausen and started a small technical consulting firm. The two were joined by fellow MIT graduate student Herbert Grier in 1934. Bernard "Barney" O'Keefe became the fourth member of their advanced technology group.

The group's high-speed photography was used to image implosion tests during the Manhattan Project. The same skills in precisely timed high-power electrical pulses also formed a key enabling technology for nuclear weapon triggers. After the war, the group continued their association with the growing military nuclear effort and formally incorporated Edgerton, Germeshausen, and Grier, Inc. (EG&G) in 1947.

Because of the mounting security concerns about the various secret projects now sharing area 51 due to its unique location and isolation, led to the Joint Chiefs deciding to put one of the major services in charge of security and after bitter in-fighting, the Navy won out even though a former Army General was now president (Eisenhower). The Office of Naval Intelligence was given the enormous task of all security for area 51.

Eventually dead aliens and the UFOs were skirted out of Wright Patterson Airforce base and New Mexico to foil several congressmen's attempts on raiding and disclosing to the public the facilities Alien involvement. The location where the nuclear secrets were kept was above their security clearances.

Hence, the CIA was ordered by Majestic 12 to get every scrap of Alien evidence and ship it out to Area 51 where it would be protected from people like Senator Church of Idaho who were not cleared and could not get access.

The fear of future congressional actions then led to the brainstorming which influenced the decision for the creation of several underground facilities for alien related storage that would have only one access through a nuclear boundary, and at the same time, building 27 was envisioned.

Since former "Navy Air Dales" were on the staff, the idea of a large carrier-like elevator was envisioned to move the alien spacecraft in and out of the building, especially for cooperative test flights with the Greys, and later the Tall Whites.

The novel idea of an underground multi-level hanger to obscure satellites from the size and scope of the operation was quickly sold. EG&G boys stepped in and helped make it happen, just like many other black projects they very successfully supported.

When Majestic 12 and the Joint Chiefs initially made the determination, the U.S. had to commence re-engineering all the alien hardware they were quickly collecting, a person was chosen to oversee the efforts.

It didn't take long for Dr. Edward Teller to be chosen as the overall technical director. He subsequently made recommendations of people that he felt would be ideal in alien reverse engineering, and subsequently wrote a letter of recommendation for Robert (Bob) Lazar who was immediately hired by the Office of Naval Intelligence and sent out to Area 51.

Bob Lazar ostensibly worked on reverse engineering Extraterrestrial Technology at a Site Called S-4, in The Emigrant Valley and Old Kelley Mine Area Near the Area 51 Test Facility. In due time, Robert Lazar had worked in building 27 when all his problems began.

***

AUTHOR NOTE:

This is a work of fiction. There are no facts or individuals attributed to the characters or events that took place in this work of fiction. Any resemblance to persons or names was strictly coincidental. If there are names used in the text that seem like they identify individuals, they were randomly selected, and the work of fiction does not relate to anyone I may have known in my lifetime.

In my professional working career, I had the opportunity to work with some incredibly talented individuals. There is no way I could ever repay them for all their dedication and major contributions to projects I worked on and may have played key roles which assisted me greatly. We had fantastic teams. They know who they are, and I do wish those individuals happy lives and good health in their remaining days.

Some of those who know me also know people we worked with who we all admired are no longer with us. To those mentors and people who played a major role in my development, which manifested some incredible experiences and the many individuals who supported me throughout my adult careers in many ways I thank them.

A small sample of names were used that do relate to notable public figures that have been involved in organizations that have committed espionage, as well as others who are well known by many regarding UFOlogy.

It is public knowledge that Robert Lazar and Boyd Bushman gave revelations of Alien or UFO activity including discussion on area 51, section S-4 and described aliens and craft.

If you take the time to google submarine UFO pictures you will see images that also appear in Boyd Bushman's YouTube videos.

You will also discover I published a Novel concerning such matters:

https://www.barnesandnoble.com/w/submarine-
alien-adventure-trepang-incident-paul-d-
escudero/1145688870

Any discussion in the screenplay is strictly fiction and speculation or embellishment of what the characters may or may not have done in real life.

This being a work of science-fiction does not imply anything any person might have done or said but randomly selecting the various names provided certain flavoring to the story.

UFOlogists have their critics of course and the government will never *confirm nor deny* any of their claims.

In some cases, it's not that the government in general is trying to discredit them, though I sense there could be some of that going on too, but the probability is that if their allegations have merit that also means so few have ever been made aware because of tight security requirements imposed. Hence, few would have any direct knowledge to either make a comment or form an opinion.

I do believe it is worthwhile to watch YouTube videos or listen to replays of events such as interviews with Art Bell, George Noory and others associated with UFO's or Alien situations discussed various highly sensational incidents.

My personal assessment of Art Bell and George Noory who did many interviews of individuals associated with UFOlogy is very high and hold them with great respect and admiration. The way Art Bell and George Noory interviewed various guests about UFOs and related topics always seemed fair and open-minded and allowed those persons to tell their story.

Art Bell and George Noory guests guided in an expert fashion to streamline the process to get the essential information out in a limited period constrained by a few hours has been an ongoing exceptionally good form of journalism.

A good journalist reports the news or facilitates the news instead of crafting or spinning the news to support some agenda.

I do not agree or disagree with any of their assertions, any UFOlogists or notable individuals associated, because I have no direct personal knowledge of their activities and would not have any way to vet them.

I do not find myself as a skeptic to their public disclosures as I chose to remain open-minded and allow our representational government to keep us informed on Aliens and UFOs.

51 REASONS TO ASK 51 QUESTIONS is a work of fiction hints the government may not be fully forthcoming in disclosing all they know about UFOs (UAPs), and we do see in published work sighting Government sources, heavily redacted documents.

65 years later why should something remain undisclosed and so heavily redacted?

This considerable amount of redaction on documents released in FOIA requests (Freedom of Information Act requests) simply doesn't help the government's case.

In my opinion all that government redaction goes a long way to establish that Boyd Bushman as well as Bob Lazar portrayed or mentioned in this science-fiction are just as credible as the government.

If you do decide to follow up and google those names and watch their YouTube videos do so with an open mind and ask yourself:

What if UFOlogists are telling the truth?

I submit, there is no reason to believe Bob Lazar and Boyd Bushman were not telling the truth even if you already have your mind made up with internal bias based on your upbringing.

The existence of Extraterrestrial life has been an ongoing debate for a while. It's expected that no person associated with *UFO Classified Information* or government entity will ever confirm UFOs and UAPs have alien crews, at least not in my lifetime.

Only an alien arrival in a large city in broad daylight would force the government's hand.

I put the Kennedy assassination conspiracy theory in mainly to make the assertion the main purpose of the assassination was to prevent alien disclosure.

That insertion was to flavor the story.

Numerous books have provided information suggesting those mentioned and their alleged involvement. I would encourage you to read publications by Chuck Giancana and Barr McClellan concerning the Kennedy assassination report, the individuals mentioned in this screenplay.

I tend to be more skeptical of the government's official viewpoint since unfortunately no bureaucratic organization in America has ever existed that didn't have some political or social economic influence on their conduct.

In July 2013 a law, Smith-Mundt Act was repealed by Congress that previously prohibited our government from using propaganda against American Citizens or broadcast propaganda anywhere in America.

That law was put in place in the 1970s after revelations about World War 2 and later the McCarthy era when the public slowly became outraged at the amount of propaganda often used against American Citizens, which in some cases destroyed their lives or resulted in losing their jobs and livelihoods.

A good example is explained in the biography of Edward R. Murrow, it claims he had to fire William Shirer, the author of *Rise and Fall of the Third Reich*, because of the politics surrounding the RED scare of communism witch hunts and associated black ball techniques.

Even though after the Cold War, the Russians opened the KGB archives to 55 American researchers, and they did admit officially that Harry Hopkins, Alger Hiss, and Julius Roseburg were Soviet Spies. Many innocent lives were destroyed in the RED witch hunt of the 1950s.

The repeal of that *propaganda law by the Obama administration*, takes us back now to the 1950s. I do forecast future abuse.

So much for transparency.

I wanted to make a comment about abductees since I used them as part of the drama in the Screenplay.

I am not a skeptic about abductees. If an abductee reads this screenplay and it disturbs them by bringing back those horrible memories, I truly apologize. For those who might be skeptics, I would caution you not to discount things you have no experience with.

Here's a great question: Why would the story of an abductee be less accurate than an account of biblical passages which you never personally observed?

In such a case of the biblical passage you are operating on pure faith of the perceptions of another person.

I've studied Christianity, the Bhagavad Gita (Hindu) in its entirety, as well as the Tibetan Buddhist Pathway to Enlightenment, and could possibly make the case that those religions are all are correct.

But one should ask: how could they all be correct since they're different stories?

The most likelihood that all these religions including Islam is correct is because they were manifested in different time and dimensions that have merged on this planet in ways we don't understand due to our limited intellect.

The supernatural or paranormal aspects of these religions mentioned and those that were not, may be natural phenomena we do not have the mental faculties to fully analyze and vet.

And as such, I could see how abduction can occur where a person is physically here, but his spirit or *soul* if you will, is teleported to a different dimension, just like when you dream.

Did you ever notice how your dreams sometimes feel and appear so lifelike?

How do you really know you are not in that new domain for a brief period when your consciousness is taken to that moment and place?

Dreaming is a form of temporal space and time travel.

Hence abductions may manifest in physical events or mental events that mankind's extremely primitive knowledge and technology may be a million years away from achieving the faculties to understand it.

There are real persons, items, locations, and events scattered throughout the screenplay that can be researched for simple curiosity that will lead to vast amounts of information concerning those props used in the story.

For example: if one were to google "submarine UFO pictures," there are indeed numerous alleged pictures of UFOs taken from American Nuclear-Powered Submarines and articles written about events including the USS Trepang incident.

Having worked in aerospace and high technology for 49 years I've seen numerous magnificent designs and architectures of highly specialized equipment and its applications.

Much has been written about CIA's planes Lockheed built, U2, A-12, SR-71, F117A, F22, F35. Note Lockheed also builds the F16, but it was designed by General Dynamics. For a brief period, I worked on the F16 electronics.

Now one can find very interesting videos on YouTube even concerning the TR-3B which I think is the most fascinating exposure of advanced, possibly alien assisted aerospace developments.

Much of TR-3B remains shrouded from the public; hence, based on my own experience I know there isn't always disclosure which concerning Area 51, S-4, leads one to realize this screenplay provides information that is inspiring to future UFOlogists to research and if you do, you just might discover *there really is 51 reasons to think, it may be true.*

***

PROJECT ALPHA

Project Alpha was the secret space program that NASA, ESA, and RSA started as part of an International Space Defense to protect Earth. Project A had already put secret bases on the moon and Mars. The RSA Konstantin Tsiolkovsky (RSA-KT), which used nuclear powered hydrogen rockets made the Mars missions far more feasible and could do a round trip in slightly over 2 months.

The reactors onboard the RSA Konstantin Tsiolkovsky RSA-KT spacecraft super-heated hydrogen which created enormous thrust. The only problem was due to the shock waves created; the reactors were practically good for one mission only.

The RSA Konstantin Tsiolkovsky RSA-KT deployed into earth's orbit by chemical rocket boosters, the 2 stage rockets came in sections and were assembled in space. The second stage or rear engines produced the propulsion to get them to Mars and slowed down when the vehicle was rotated in flight to point the thrusters in the opposite direction for braking. The front section was the Martian Lander and the section behind it, the command capsule.

The lander touched down upright on the Martian surface with tripod supports deployed outwards to anchor it to the planet and to avoid tip over. 2 points as programmed touched down first with the full weight of the ship helping to drive 2 anchors into the sandy surface, then as the engines throttled back the craft tilted onto the third leg which was hydraulically adjustable to obtain a perfect level profile.

The astronauts then egressed out of the ship using a wench at first until they assembled a ladder prefabricated and easy to assemble and attach firmly to the bottom hull of the lander.

That section remained and was later utilized for storage and certain multiple use components used by later missions as spare parts if required. Finally, as the mission was ending the top half of the lander launched back into space and docked onto the command capsule orbiting Mars for the return trip.

The second stage was jettisoned, and the first stage took them home after accelerating to enormous speeds that allowed for only one month return trip, then braking and then entering an earth orbit.

The first stage remained in orbit and the modularized rocket motor unbolted and replaced since it was assumed would be damaged by shock waves while producing the tremendous thrust. Because of the sophistication of the modularization plug and play concepts mandated by this international secret project, nobody on earth knew except people in Area 51 and the ESA/RSA special operations directive located in Darmstadt, Germany; and Schepkina area of Moscow.

Lockheed and Russian Experimental Design Bureau-1 (OKB-1) built most of the spacecraft in joint projects including using contractors in Mexico and China to assemble certain components. China assured silence and future participation by being awarded the contracts.

Finding two large bodies of water on Mars simplified building the Alpha bases greatly. The liquids along with very powerful solar panels in turn helped create hydrogen which was used in hydrogen fuel cell power generators.

Underground cave structures discovered that once housed Martian life were utilized to protect the international space force from the elements. Engineers and architects were apprised of the presence of an abundance of Belite, Alite, Tricalcium aluminate, and Brownmillerite in the soil around the cave sites and with a little experimentation discovered only a minimal amount of chemicals and water was needed to create very high-quality cement.

In just a few short years of delivering steel rods, welding equipment, and building materials, vast, underground command and control for the new weapons silos were able to be constructed on Mars, and later the moon that was discovered containing a vast underground ocean, also allowed colonization and space defense facilities.

Part of the solar system now had a space defense, but unfortunately vast areas of exposure remained, and in those areas, as well as underground installations, 8 different alien races now had a presence, all deciding of the others' intentions and a possible land grab of their own.

DRAMATIS PERSONA

Note: I like Chinese language and Chinese people, so I used several Chinese terms in this screenplay. When you read those Chinese names and terms you will see they are spelled out in PINYIN.

PINYIN is the alphabetized written Chinese Mandarin language. Pinyin has tonal markers above each vowel. China developed pinyin to enhance learning Mandarin characters. A lot of street signs in China today have both Mandarin and Pinyin. Grade school children are taught Pinyin to accelerate their Chinese learning.

There are 5 tones in Chinese, a tonal language for each of the possible 35 vowels. Chinese dictionaries are laid out in tonal order. As you can see the last tone in the example below has no tonal marker.

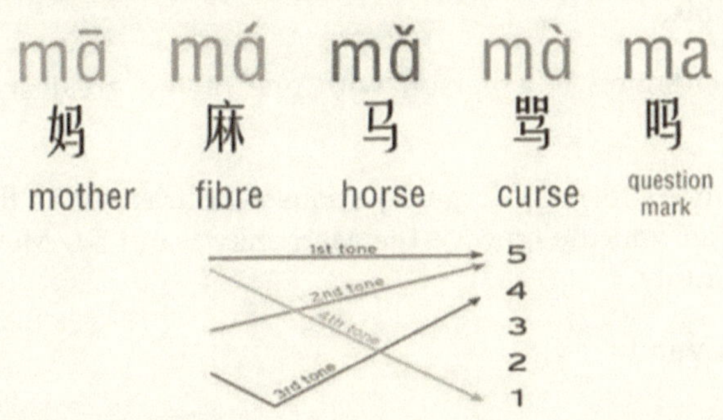

Throughout the screenplay are many examples of Pinyin and all are well exposed with appropriate information.

Vance, one of the main characters. This is the 4th Screenplay (Novel) where Vance has a major or leading role.

WÁNMĚI DE HUĀ SHÈNGDÀ DÁ QIÈ SĪ (pronounced: *Wan-may da Wa Shèngdà da Chia-sue*) [完美的花盛大达切斯] PERFECT FLOWER GRAND DUCHESS. Normally referred to as *Wánměi de Huā*. Vance's Alien lover. In part of the story when *Wánměi De Huā* is in Area 51 or about during their road trip and later at the Alamo Nevada Dude Ranch, her alias is Sandra.

Wánměi de Huā (a.k.a. Sandra) is the Měngjiàng Yún-Rén Empress.

Fierce Warriors Cloud People, (猛将云人 PINYIN: Měngjiàng Yún-Rén pronounced: Mung-jung yoon-ren).

Area 51 BASE COMMANDER, General Brazile.

Colonel Davy Jones, General Brazile's assistant.

Area 51 BASE SECURITY OFFICER, Major Barnes.

Grak, a Grey Alien, is the main antagonist in the story.

Struyograb, Tall White Alien, a protagonist in part of the story.

Anarchie and the Mergenky empires were part of the stories involving the Novels and Screenplays for Jeeapa II, Sasha Andromeda, and Black Ravik that Vance had a major role.

Drago, the Chamberlain for *Wánměi de Huā, a protagonist in the story.*

Boyd Bushman is a character who is a former Lockheed aircraft designer and UFOlogist. He meets Boris Potemkin FSB Russian Spy that sets off a series of tangential events.

Bob Lazar mentioned is a person with one of the greatest revelations to mankind.

Dr. Kara is Vance's former Mergenky spouse and traveled to the Andromeda Galaxy with her and the crew of the Mergenky Scout S1. Mentioned in this story for continuity.

CIA SPY: Gus Vandyke

CIA SPY: Beverly

CIA SPY: Roger

CIA SPY: Crystal

CIA SPY: Jeff

CIA SPY: Gary

CIA SPY Mark

CIA SPY Joe

Zorgjeck Wogar Grey Supreme Commander

Colony Class Planetary Conquest Vessel Ship's Captain (no name)

Clark Douglas Russian Mole in Area 51 and former acquaintance of Vance before Vance was abducted by the Mergenky fifteen years earlier.

Alex, security agent at Caesars Palace Hotel and Casino.

Carlos, Blackjack Dealer at Caesars Palace.

Mergenky Scout Class Commander Vickie from the original Jeeapa, is mentioned for continuity and to explain radical maneuvers *Wánměi De Huā* chose to do knowing Vicky's story during one of the pivotal space battles.

CIA SPY: Jack Pepperman.

Alexander Bortnikov high ranking FSB (KGB) official.

General Alexi Shoygu high ranking Soviet Air Force Officer with close ties with FSB.

Russian Pilot Dmitri Popov flying SU-27 ordered to shootdown Swiss Air Flight 1110.

Dudley Brown, Test Pilot flying C-130 cargo plane fitted with antigravity device. He is the target of Russian FSB espionage.

Ralph, Dudley Brown's CO-PILOT.

Rich, Russian Spy at the Alamo Nevada Dude Ranch involved with Dudley Brown.

Tanya, Boris Potemkin's girlfriend.

Phil, Bartender at Flamingo Hotel Casino Bar.

Měngjiàng Yún-Rén Security Chief (no name)

Měngjiàng Yún-Rén Science Officer. (no name)

Mr. Magic, bartender at Lawry's Restaurant.

Boris Potemkin (a.k.a MR. KEENEY, a.k.a. JACK) the main Russian Spy figure in the story.

Jimmy, FSB (KGB) SPY and watcher for Boris Potemkin (a.k.a. Jack).

Anastaysia Pushkin (a.k.a. Muriel) one of the leading female Russian Spies works directly for Alexander Bortnikov. Anastaysia was involved in the recruitment of Dudley Brown.

Susan Johnson, schoolteacher Gus meets at Caesars Palace Buffalo Bar.

Robert Simmons (a.k.a. Aleksandr Zubkov) FSB Spy based in Switzerland used to relay messages from spies in the field to FSB (KGB) Headquarters or send spies directives.

Communication Technician (no name) works for Alexander Bortnikov at Lubyanka building, Moscow, FSB (KGB) Headquarters. Receives messages from Robert Simmons and decodes them for Alexander Bortnikov.

Sheriff Travis involved in the Biker Incident on the Extra Terrestrial Hiway and other events.

Deputy Sheriff West works for Sheriff Travis.

Měngjiàng Yún-Rén Chief Interrogator (No Name).

Měngjiàng Yún-Rén Intelligence Officer (No Name).

Dietrich von Braun, a direct relative of the world-renowned missile designer.

General Sperberzing, Tall White Fleet Commander

Bud, Abductee Vance met on the Wogar Grey Command Ship.

Alexander Bortnikov's Receptionist (no name).

Colonel Babcock, Mars Base Commander.

Wogar Grey Tactical Officer (no name).

Wogar Grey Ship's Engineer (no name).

Leroy (actor) and Guadalupe (photographer) photographed Dudley in compromised positions for Anastaysia who planned to blackmail Dudley applying Gay sexpionage to obtain C-130 antigravity machine technical details and plans.

Mr. Durant provided the horses and gave horseback ride picnics with fishing to Dude Ranch guests.